JAMES JOYCE: THE CRITICAL HERITAGE
VOLUME 2, 1928–41

THE CRITICAL HERITAGE SERIES

General Editor: B. C. Southam

The Critical Heritage series collects together a large body of criticism on major figures in literature. Each volume presents the contemporary responses to a particular writer, enabling the student to follow the formation of critical attitudes to the writer's work and its place within a literary tradition.

The carefully selected sources range from landmark essays in the history of criticism to fragments of contemporary opinion and little published documentary material, such as letters and diaries.

Significant pieces of criticism from later periods are also included in order to demonstrate fluctuations in reputation following the writer's death.

JAMES JOYCE
VOLUME 2, 1928–41

THE CRITICAL HERITAGE

Edited by

ROBERT H. DEMING

London and New York

First published in 1970
Reprinted in 1997 by Routledge

2 Park Square, Milton Park,
Abingdon, Oxon, OX14 4RN
&
270 Madison Ave,
New York NY 10016

Transferred to Digital Printing 2009

British Library Cataloguing in Publication Data

ISBN 0-415-15920-2 (set)
ISBN10: 0-415-15919-9 (hbk)
ISBN10: 0-415-48751-X (pbk)

ISBN13: 978-0-415-15919-7 (hbk)
ISBN13: 978-0-415-48751-1 (pbk)

Publisher's Note
The publisher has gone to great lengths to ensure the quality
of this reprint but points out that some imperfections in the
original may be apparent.

Contents

v

CONTENTS

CONTENTS

vii

CONTENTS

CONTENTS

CONTENTS

176. Early reaction from Stanislaus Joyce

1924

Letter to his brother (7 August 1924), quoted in Ellmann, *James Joyce*, pp. 589–91, and in Ellmann, *Letters*, Volume III, 1966, pp. 102–6.

An extract from a long letter concerning *Ulysses* and *Work in Progress*.

. . . I have received one instalment of your yet unnamed novel in the *Transatlantic Review*. I don't know whether the drivelling rigmarole about half a tall hat [*Finnegans Wake*, p. 387] and ladies' modern toilet chambers [*Finnegans Wake*, p. 395] (practically the only things I understand in this nightmare production) is written with the deliberate intention of pulling the reader's leg or not. You began this fooling in the Holles Street episode [the 'Oxen of the Sun' episode] in *Ulysses* and I see that Wyndham Lewis . . . imitates it with heavy-hoofed capering in the columns of the *Daily Mail*. Or perhaps—a sadder supposition— it is the beginning of softening of the brain. The first instalment faintly suggests the *Book of the Four Masters* and a kind of Biddy in Blunderland and a satire on the supposed matriarchal system. It has certain characteristics of a beginning of something, is nebulous, chaotic but contains certain elements. That is absolutely all I can make of it. But! It is unspeakably wearisome. Gorman's book on you [*James Joyce, The First Forty Years*] practically proclaims your work as the last word in modern literature. It may be the last in another sense, the witless wandering of literature before its final extinction . . . I for one would not read more than a paragraph of it, if I did not know you.

What I say does not matter. I have no doubt that you have your plan, probably a big one again as in *Ulysses*. No doubt, too, many more

competent people around you speak to you in quite a different tone
. . . Why are you still intelligible and sincere in verse? If literature is
to develop along the lines of your latest work it will certainly become,
as Shakespeare hinted centuries ago, much ado about nothing. Ford in
an article you sent me suggests that the whole thing is to be taken as a
nonsense rhythm and that the reader should abandon himself to the
sway of it. I am sure, though the article seems to have your approval,
that he is talking through his half a tall hat. In any case I refuse to allow
myself to be whirled round in the mad dance by a literary dervish. . . .

177. Padraic Colum, 'Preface' for *Anna Livia Plurabelle*

1928

Extract from 'River Episode from James Joyce's Uncompleted
Work', *Dial*, lxxxiv (April 1928), 318–22; also appeared as the
'Preface' to Joyce's *Anna Livia Plurabelle* (1928), pp. vii–xix and in
Our Friend James Joyce (1958) by Mary and Padraic Colum, pp.
139–43.

Anna Livia Plurabelle is concerned with the flowing of a River. There
have gone into it the things that make a people's inheritance: landscape,
myth, and history; there have gone into it, too, what is characteristic
of a people: jests and fables. It is epical in its largeness of meaning and its
multiplicity of interest. And, to my mind, James Joyce's inventions and
discoveries as an innovator in literary form are more beautifully shown
in it than in any other part of his work.

But although it is epical it is an episode, a part and not a whole. It
makes the conclusion of the first part of a work that has not yet been
completed. . . .

. . . And so, like a river, it has gone on, and expanded, and gathered volume. . . . It is the same River that Stephen Dedalus of *The Portrait of an Artist as a Young Man* looked upon. . . .

[quotes from *A Portrait*, ch. IV, p. 167, and from p. 216]

So the later prose begins, and at once we are in the water as it bubbles and hurries at its source. The first passage gives us the sight of the River, the second gives us the River as it is seen and heard and felt. The whole of the episode gives us something besides the sight and sound and feeling of water. . . .

. . . It is this range we get in this episode: over and above the sight and sound and feeling of water there is in *Anna Livia Plurabelle* that range of images and thoughts, those free combinations of words and ideas, that might arise in us, if with a mind inordinately full and on a day singularly happy we watched a river and thought upon a river and travelled along a river from its source to its mouth.

But in this episode the mind's range has its boundary: the range is never beyond the river banks nor away from the city towards which the river is making its slow-moving, sometimes hurrying way. Dublin, the city once seventh in Christendom, Dublin that was founded by sea-rovers, Dublin with its worthies, its sojourners, its odd characters, not as they are known to the readers of history-books, but as they live in the minds of some dwellers by the Liffey, is in this episode; Dublin, the Ford of Hurdles, the entrance into the plain of Ireland, the city so easily taken, so uneasily held. And the River itself, less in magnitude than the tributary of a tributary of one of the important rivers, becomes enlarged until it includes hundreds of the world's rivers. How many rivers have their names woven into the tale of *Anna Livia Plurabelle*? More than five hundred, I believe. . . .

[quotes from p. 202]

There will be many interpretations of *Anna Livia Plurabelle*—as many as the ideas that might come to one who watched the flowing of the actual river . . .

[the critic adds his own recollections]

. . . I feel in this tale of *Anna Livia Plurabelle* the mystery of beginnings as it is felt through, as it combines with, a hundred stray, significant, trifling things.

Its author, the most daring of innovators, has decided to be as local as a hedge-poet. James Joyce writes as if it might be taken for granted that his readers know, not only the city he writes about, but its little shops and its little shows, the nick-names that have been given to its near-great, the cant-phrases that have been used on its side-streets. . . . This localness belongs to James Joyce's innovations: all his innovations are towards giving us what he writes about in its own atmosphere and with its own proper motion. And only those things which have been encountered day after day in some definite place can be given with their own atmosphere, their own motion.

Much should be said, and some time much will have to be said, about the de-formations and the re-formations of words in James Joyce's later work. Some of these de-formations and re-formations will not be questioned by readers who have an understanding of language: they will know that they succeed clearly in giving what the writer wants to give us. . . .

[quotes from pp. 215–16]

Everything that belongs to the dusk and the gathering of the clouds of evening is in this passage: the de-formations and the re-formations of the words give us the murk of the evening. There are other innovations in the language that are really difficult to explain. Or, rather, that would require the exposition of a theory to be properly explanatory. Let us say that words are always taking on new meanings, that they take on new meanings more quickly than we realize, and that, in the case of English, as the language becomes more and more wide-spread, the change is being accelerated. . . . James Joyce treats words as having shifting meanings: he lets us read a score of meanings into the words he sets down in his later work. . . .

178. Sean O'Faolain on the language of *ALP*

1928

'The Cruelty and Beauty of Words', *Virginia Quarterly Review*, iv, No. 2 (April 1928), 211, 222, 225 [208–25]. The same article appeared as 'Style and the Limitations of Speech', *Criterion*, viii, No. 30 (September 1928), 71, 83–4, 86–7 [67–87].

In a lengthy essay on current dissatisfaction with the language, Joyce is mentioned briefly in connection with the language of *Work in Progress*.

. . . One's mind naturally reverts to James Joyce who in his latest work 'in progress' has written many pages in this manner, and may do more in that manner before he publishes his work in book-form. . . .

[quotes from p. 16, then appearing in *transition*]

. . . We are not in the habit of hearing very much from this artist either about his meanings or his intentions but we can know at least that this is intended to be language and that these are presumably words; furthermore in writing thus Mr. Joyce has rejected valid English, and, one may conclude, for but one possible reason—that normal speech is insufficient for his needs. Nothing but necessity can bring language into being and nothing but necessity can justify its overthrow. . . .

As far as words are concerned style presents but one main problem to our consideration—that of the principle of selection. It is a query that naturally arises when we find ourselves sifting at the one time for words of quite various purpose and personality. Thus in Joyce whose maltreatment of language largely prompted this study I find at the same period, in the same volume a predeliction for lightsome and delicate words, homely words, and sonorous Miltonian words so that all these lie side by side—one might almost say—within the same covers: girdle, eucharistic, dawning, hymn, incense, crucifix, light, fragrance, unrest, dung, snot, bile, arrogant, lavishlimbed, all without the least discord but on the contrary as most people who have read the *Portrait of the Artist as a Young Man*, will agree with very beautiful results. . . .

Here lies the condemnation of such language as Joyce's. It is not merely ahistoric—not merely the shadow of an animal that never was, the outline of a tree that never grew, for even then we might trace it to some basic reality distorted and confused—but it comes from nowhere, goes nowhere, is not part of life at all. It has one reality only—the reality of the round and round of children's scrawls in their first copybooks, zany circles of nothing. It may be that Joyce wishes these meaningless scrawls to have a place in his design and if so nobody will grudge him his will of them. But we cannot be expected to understand them as language for they are as near nothing as anything can be on this earth.

Yet who cannot sympathize with this rebellion? It would seem that Joyce does not realize, however, that in language we are countering one of those primal impositions that give to life its inexorable character: he must see that in language there is an individuality which we must counter at every step, much as an actor must counter his own character to express ideas at variance with it. But a man who has had the great courage to accept so many of life's inexorable laws does unwisely to push a puppet in the actor's place; that offers us no release. It is a puppet without as much as the shape of a human being, and suggests the idea of a human organism for but one reason, that it has usurped the place of one. . . .

179. Gerald Gould, comment, *Observer*

9 December 1928, n.p.

. . . But a little language is a dangerous thing. When broadcast, it is apt to trickle exiguously. Mr. James Joyce says with commendable firmness: 'Icis on us! Seints of light! Zezere! Subdue your noise, you hamble creature! What is it but a blackburry growth or the dwyer-gray ass them four old codgers owns? Are you meanam Tarpey and Lyons and Gregory? I meyne now, thank all, the four of them, and the roar of them. . . .' But I don't know what he meynes, nor what he is meanam. It looks as if he had a spelling-bee in his bonnet, and had got confused by the buzz. Perhaps there were three bees, Tarpey and Lyons and Gregory, and the four of them made the roar of them. . . . Let us turn for advice to Mr. Padraic Colum, who tells us in a preface that '*Anna Livia Plurabelle* is concerned with the flowing of a River.' He adds that it is 'epical in its largeness of meaning and its multiplicity of interest.' And he praises, possibly to excess, 'James Joyce's inventions and discoveries as an innovator in literary form.' But I doubt whether it is really an invention to burble, since all babies do it: and it is no discovery that, if you make a noise like a carrot, there are creatures who will simply eat it. 'There will be many interpretations,' says Mr. Colum, 'of *Anna Livia Plurabelle*,' but I think he exaggerates. I think most people will get it in one. However, lest I do injustice, I will quote in full a remarkable passage which Mr. Colum himself selects as giving beautifully the flow of water: . . .

[quotes from p. 202]

. . . The objection to this sort of writing is its fundamental (and no doubt unconscious) aesthetic dishonesty. It shirks the difficulties, and pretends to have transcended them, as the tortoise pretended to have won the race for which he had never entered. It says: 'Young thin pale soft shy slim slip,' which is a mere accumulation of epithets, but perfectly clear; and then, dreading comparison with the genuine art which could get the same effect by the legitimate magic of phrase, it confuses the issue with rubbish. The result would gravel anybody; and 'she says herself she hardly knows whuon the annals her graveller was.' The only water it all suggests to me is water on the brain. I feel inclined to say to Mr. Joyce: 'Subdue your noise, you hamble creature!' For hamble is as hamble does. However, peats be with him! But isn't he a saucebox, to write '*lele*,' like Presto?. . . .

180. Unsigned review, *Times Literary Supplement*

20 December 1928, 1008

The dissatisfaction of the Irish with the English language and their efforts to change and revivify it make one of the most curious chapters in the history of English letters, but none has ever gone so far and made so many changes as Mr. Joyce. He is not content with an Irish dialect or with the simpler primitive tendencies of Irish writers, but he has attempted to change the whole face of the English language. *Anna Livia Plurabelle* is a fragment of a work on which he is now engaged, and here, as Mr. Colum explains in an appreciative preface, he is still writing about Dublin. But while his subject is akin to that of *The Dubliners* and of *Portrait of the Artist as a Young Man*, the treatment is altered out of all knowledge, though doubtless it is a development out of Mr. Joyce's intervening work. There is the same kind of poetry in prose, but it would seem that this has needed the stimulus of new language and new technical devices to prevent its exhaustion. *Anna Livia Plurabelle* is written in an outlandish dialect; the roots of English words can be recognized, sometimes after thought, but often the endings and the spelling are much changed. One is at times reminded of the devices of manufacturers in their trade names, when they spell words phonetically or change 'f' into 'ph.' Undoubtedly, though inexplicably, this has a value in advertising, but it needs great boldness to find in it something of value for poetry or for poetical prose. 'Frostivying tresses dasht with vireflies' is a good example of this device in Mr. Joyce's work. In addition to this there is every kind of euphuism, foreign words are used, and much alliteration and rhyme.

Certainly this is a new literary dialect, and it is possible to read it, though with more trouble than Chaucer demands; and one can see that if Mr. Joyce's real gifts of fantasy and poetry were in danger of exhaustion the invention of a new dialect is a conceivable means of restoring them. Mr. Joyce is, in fact, desperately and with remarkable courage trying to bring back the English language to a period like the Elizabethan, when each neologism was a happy discovery and the spout of words flowed freshly and with exuberance. At the same time he avoids the obvious and never satisfactory method of definite archaism; though

394

he does use at times archaic words, just as, lest any change should be neglected, he quite often uses the Irish poetical dialect of writers like Mr. Synge. It is an extraordinary attempt, perhaps to be matched with the attempt to revive the Irish language for a new Irish literature. It is probable enough that Mr. Joyce would be much happier with a language as triumphantly exuberant as that of the Elizabethan age, and that he could not excel in the polishing of Augustan lines when language (as perhaps now) needed the most scrupulous and careful handling. No one knows why a language should receive at moments a sudden stimulation and plunge into rapid growth, but it seems unlikely that this has ever happened as the result of a deliberate and conscious effort like that of Mr. Joyce. We may be fairly sure that such an effort will not change the literary language outside Mr. Joyce's books, but inside them there is little harm and great interest in the change. It cannot be denied that Mr. Joyce does at moments achieve an astonishingly vigorous diction, and there is sometimes beauty in his writing; though it is a beauty which can only be guessed at, like that of a poem in a language which we only half know. . . .

181. Æ, review, *Irish Statesman*

1928

Y.O. [George Russell, Æ], '*Anna Livia Plurabelle*', *Irish States-man*, xi (29 December 1928), 339.

This is a book for collectors. But I must hasten to warn the collector that the edition is limited and already over-subscribed. The collector must do the best he can to find one of the original purchasers and induce him to part with his treasure. For undoubtedly this is the kind of book which will go up in price even although it is but a fragment from a work in progress. The publication later of the complete work will never make the collector regard the complete work with the pleasure with which he regards a rare and limited edition signed by the author, and this book is the really extraordinary part of the work which is in progress and which is appearing in *transition*. As a technical feat, this strange slithery slipping, dreamy nightmarish prose is more astonishing than anything Joyce has yet written, and whatever else he may be, he is a virtuoso in the use of words. Padraic Colum writes a very interesting preface trying to explain this extraordinary dream prose where words run into each other, and are endowed with wild meanings arising out of arcane affinities with other words, the whole gurgling and slipping like water. There is not too much of it here to weary. It is a meditation on the Liffey, 'beside the rivering waters of, hither and thithering waters of, Night.' As a technical feat it is unique. A chapter excites us. The whole volume may prove a labour too great for many to peruse to its end. But this passage is certainly worth study, and perhaps if one could understand it the whole book could be understood. . . .

182. O'Faolain, reply to review in *Irish Statesman*

1929

'Correspondence: *Anna Livia Plurabelle*', *Irish Statesman*, xi (5 January 1929), 354–5; appeared as 'Almost Music', in *Hound and Horn*, ii (January–March 1929), 178–80.

A reply to the review which appeared in the 29 December 1928 issue (No. 181).

It is impossible to do adequate justice to such a book as this within the limits of a brief notice—it raises almost every possible kind of problem in the philosophy and psychology of æsthetics; . . . Then why not, Joyce says, can you not understand this?:

She was just a young thin pale soft shy slim slip of a thing then, sauntering by silvamoonlake and he was a heavy trudging lurching lieabroad of a Curraghman, making his hay for whose sun to shine on, as tough as the oaktree (peats be with them!) used to rustle that time down by the dykes of killing Kildare, for forstfellfoss with a plash across her.

Here, in the hope of escaping from the trammels of our imperfect speech to the greater freedom of a language that is at once virginal and ancient, Joyce has gambled on an intellectual theory and invented a technique where the controls are supposed to be more rigid, and, it follows, the power of the artist all the greater: but is it so? The extract given is one of the easiest in the little book. . . . The fact is that the more elusive his phrases are the more we find that our responses are liable to be a medley of sensuous images. Perhaps that is Joyce's wish, and if it is he has succeeded in what he set out to do, but if it is he can but blame himself if we inevitably ask ourselves—If this be literature, is literature worth while? . . . I cannot see that Joyce helps those who reply that art is frequently superior to reality. The sensuous responses of the mind to his new language are sometimes very delicate and pleasing, sometimes obscene, sometimes merely dull—well, so is reality— but most frequently, because this is language, and language has a biologically inexorable thirst for associations, they are empty of content. And that reality never is; and at that point, which is almost any point in this book—with a few delightful exceptions—Joyce's technique ceases to serve any useful purpose. That the mind should be in chaos is not at any time desirable.

Joyce's medium strikes at the inevitable basis of language, universal intelligibility, and though the sympathetic may burk at the word 'universal,' or the word 'intelligible,' it must be acknowledged that there is very little difference between issuing a tiny booklet of some nine thousand words in a limited edition at a prohibitive price and not issuing it at all.

Yet no genuine student of literature can dare be unfamiliar with it: it is one of the most interesting and pathetic literary adventures I know, pathetic chiefly because of its partial success: for even the most sympathetic and imaginative will have smiled wanly several times as they read and laughed in despair long before they end. It will undoubtedly have its influence on literature, and it deserves to; but it is not sane enough to be literature itself; it has taken a good idea to the extremity of foolishness. If Joyce had only written the entire book as he did the final paragraph, what a marvellous book it would be! If he had only accepted the inexorable truth that language is a very limited and imperfect medium—as he has with unparalleled courage accepted so many of the other inexorable facts of life! But he is here very much of his race, has his forebears in old Irish legend—is he not of the clan of Brendan who sailed for Ui Bhreasail, Bran who sailed for the Land of Heart's Desire, Ossian searching for the Land of the Ever Young, the Hag of Beare who had lived seven times over and still longed that her youthful flesh might return to her once again, and many others— Sweeney who lived on the tops of the trees that he might be like a bird, Cuirithir who would go in passion beyond Hell to Paradise, dreamers of the unattainable all. If there ever was an adventure which was a revolt against the despotism of fact this little book is one, and as such, if not as literature, it is priceless. . . .

183. Eugène Jolas, reply to Sean O'Faolain

1929

Extract from 'The New Vocabulary', *transition*, No. 15 (February 1929), 171–4. The same article, with suitable corrections, appeared as 'Style and the Limitations of Speech', *Irish Statesman* (26 January 1929), 414, 416.

This article and letter to the editor is a reply to Sean O'Faolain's review of *Anna Livia Plurabelle* in *Hound and Horn* (No. 182) and the article in the *Virginia Quarterly Review* (No. 178).

Mr. O'Faolain attempts to dispose of the Joycian onslought on traditional language by insisting on the 'immobility of speech', saying, in part: 'There are real limitations to the eloquence of words. These are mainly two—our vocabulary is not of our manufacture and it is limited; and meanwhile liberty to invent, and add to, and replace, is absolutely denied us—denied us, it would seem, for all time.' Basing his contentions on a high respect for historicism, he regards Mr. Joyce's new speech as 'a-historic', as failing to be 'a part of life', and chides him for running counter to the eternal laws of nature.

The most cursory glance at the evolution of English, or other languages, shows that speech is not static. It is in a constant state of becoming. Whether the organic evolution of speech is due to external conditions the people themselves bring about, or whether it is due to the forward-straining vision of a single mind, will always remain a moot question. . . . Should, therefore, James Joyce, whose love of words and whose mastery of them has conclusively been demonstrated, be denied the very right which the people themselves hold,—the right to create a vocabulary which is not only a deformation, but an amalgamation of numerous modern languages spoken in the world today? . . .

184. O'Faolain, reply to Eugène Jolas

1929

'Letter to the Editor', *Irish Statesman* (2 March 1929), 513–14. A reply to Eugène Jolas's earlier letter (No. 183).

I must assure M. Jolas that I have not attempted to dispose of Mr. Joyce's experiment in language by insisting on the 'immobility of speech.' On the contrary, the greater part of my original article was intended to prove that speech is a very mobile and fluctuating thing, and the major point was that the artist must seek for a point of suspension between the eternal coming-on and going-off of meaning. . . . M. Jolas will observe that I propose that precision is the cardinal virtue of good English prose, and I think it is evident that implication and suggestion—as vague and unprecise as possible, *just like music*—would become the cardinal virtue in good English prose according to Mr. Joyce's new manner. There we may agree to differ, and I doubt if there is any use in trying to argue the point further.

Yet the thing is too interesting to be dropped here. I am intensely
eager to know if Mr. Joyce, M. Jolas, and the other innovators he names
have really thought the matter out clearly, and have actually composed
an aesthetic which defends the confusion of the arts in this manner.
. . . There are passages of great beauty in *Anna Livia*, but their beauty
is the beauty of language. Will not M. Jolas tell us, if he knows, whether
Mr. Joyce really desires no more than a medley of sensuous images to be
the mind's response to speech? As I said in my former letter, if that be
his desire he has amply succeeded, but, as I also suggested there, he has
in that case raised the whole problem of the purposes of art and must
break on Pascal's gibe at those artists who add nothing to nature and
reality. The aesthetic or half-aesthetic behind *Anna Livia* denies that art
can add a jot to reality, and though Mr. Joyce is welcome to the joy of
that despair, from which no argument can raise him, I may be permitted
to ask M. Jolas if *he* realises this? . . .

. . . M. Jolas is at fault. The people do not create a vocabulary. They
accept it from the ages. Had he asked leave to adopt one word of Mr.
Joyce's invention there would be a great to-do about it, but to ask leave
to introduce a vocabulary! . . .

The truth is that Mr. Joyce is a Romantic of the first water, as his
latest adventure conclusively proves, and he is more—he is a Quixote
whose terrible earnestness is his downfall. He is not the only or the first
writer to attempt the impossible in this field, and nothing but his great
genius has saved him from utter failure. . . .

185. Cyril Connolly, review, *Life and Letters*

1929

Extract from 'The Position of Joyce', *Life and Letters*, ii, No. 11 (April 1929), 273–90. Also appeared in his *The Condemned Playground* (1946), pp. 1–15.

James Joyce has brought out a new book. It is a fragment of a longer one, and is called *Anna Livia Plurabelle*. We are used to the reputations of authors fluctuating from year to year, but Mr. Joyce's also fluctuates from place to place. He is resented in Ireland, neglected in England, admired by a set in America, and idolized by another in France. . . . Thus Joyce's only disciples in Ireland are the young realists of the post-rebellion period. In England the literary public is governed by good taste. . . . The general public is equally conservative, and the fate of a book like *Ulysses*, so hopelessly unpresentable when submitted to the Chelsea canon, is decided in advance. It is in America, where there is a large and less sophisticated general public, and in Paris, where there are a great many young writers anxious to experiment in literary form, that the 'Ulysses generation' has grown up. . . . Let us get a clear idea of *Ulysses* before we try to estimate the later work of its author. James Joyce is, by temperament, a mediaevalist. He has always been in revolt against his two greatest limitations, his Jesuit education and his Celtic romanticism. Each of his books reveals a growing fear of beauty; not because life is not beautiful, but because there is something essentially false and luxurious in the 'Celtic Twilight' approach to it. This tinsel element is very strong in Joyce's early poems, and is contrasted with an equally pronounced repulsion from it in *The Portrait of the Artist*. In *Ulysses* he has got it in hand, and is experimenting in other approaches to beauty, the pagan simplicity of Mrs. Bloom's reverie, the mathematical austerity of the catechism which precedes it. Only Stephen Dedalus, the Hamlet young man, thinks automatically in the diction of the Celtic Twilight; but in him the remorse, the guilty sense of loneliness which attacks brave but weak men who destroy the religious framework of their youth, has fused with his minor poet melancholy, and gives to his reverie the quality of a Greek chorus. . . . The central emotion of *Ulysses* is not indignation, but remorse; and remorse, though perhaps second-rate in life, is an emotion which entirely comes off in literature. Expiation and the sense of doom, which is the essence of Greek tragedy, are only a variation of this feeling; and though remorse seems so feebly static in real people, the very tranquillity and remoteness from acts lend it a glassy literary beauty. . . . Literary English has become very hackneyed, as a glance at any book of essays or a preface to an anthology at once will show, and Joyce in *Ulysses* set out to revive it by introducing the popular colloquial idiom of his own city, by forming new words in the Greek fashion of compound epithets, by telescoping grammar, by using the fresh vocabulary of science manuals, public-houses, or Elizabethan slang. . . .

Besides this he directed a stream of parody against all the whimsy and archaism latent in English prose style. . . .

The link between the new work of Joyce and *Ulysses* is chiefly one of language; though both are united by the same preoccupation with the aesthetic of cities, with the absurdity of our Jewish-American democracy, and with the capacity for being beautiful which this democracy yet retains. . . .

Here are two quotations, one showing the Hill of Howth treated again in a symbolic manner, the other the praise of Dublin, rhetorical as cities are—Earwicker (the Danish castle) is bragging to his wife, the Liffey, of all he has done for her. . . .

[quotes from *Haveth Childers Everywhere*, p. 535, and from p. 551]

The new book is full of fables, because the whole of the first part is really a *surréaliste* approach to the prehistory of Dublin, the myths and legends of its origin, Duke Humphrey and Anna Livia, the mountain and the river, from a black reach of which the city took its name. The first words 'riverrun brings us back to Howth Castle and Environs' suggest the melodies to follow. All the urban culture of Ireland is by origin Scandinavian; and, to emphasize this, Joyce has introduced the greatest possible amount of Norse words into his description of it. There are four parts to the new work of Joyce, . . .

[briefly summarizes the four parts]

The best way to read Joyce's new book, apart from this rare reprint of *Anna Livia,* is in a quarterly called *transition,* edited by Americans living in Paris. The contents are often as grotesque as the idea is enterprising. . . . Of course, it is not possible to pronounce a verdict on Joyce's work when it is so fragmentary. The best that this article can hope to prove is that the new work of Joyce is respect-worthy and readable. There is nothing insane in its conception nor bogus in its execution. Though to many a spinster fancy it probably will continue to lack the 'note for which we will be listening soon', to others, it promises amusement and a very interesting and strange approach to life and beauty. After all, it is an experiment; we are content to accord the wildest tolerance to the latest unintelligible—even uncommercial—pamphlet of Einstein—can we not admit a little of the same tolerance to something in writing we do not understand? It must be remembered that Joyce, besides being a lover of words, is an Irishman under no obligation whatever to rest content with the English language, and also that, while our Literature, unaware of a decline of the West or a defence of it, grows daily more bucolic and conservative, Continental Letters are nourished on an exhilarating sense of an uncertain future which makes the liberties of their volcano dwellers permissible—and which we are entirely without. Literature is in essence a series of new universes enforced on a tardy public by their creators. This one may be a fake, but it is not from a writer who has previously given us fakes; it may be a failure, but it is surely an absorbing one, and more important than any contemporary successes. I, personally, am biased as a critic by nationality, and by the same feeling for geography and Dublin, but still more by the enthusiasm which comes to everyone when they discover themselves through a book—a service which Joyce, Proust, and Gide have rendered generally to almost all our thinking generation; for me any criticism of *Ulysses* will be affected by a wet morning in Florence, when in the empty library of a villa with the smell of woodsmoke, the faint eavesdrip, I held the uncouth volume dazedly open in the big armchair—Narcissus with his pool before him. . . .

186. Arnold Bennett, comment,
London Evening Standard

19 September 1929, 7

The last of my rebels is James Joyce, a man who has done great stuff. I have referred before in these columns to his 'unfinished work,' and to the fragment of it entitled *Anna Livia Plurabelle*. This fragment has been published by Crosby Gaige, of New York, in a beautifully printed and produced volume as thin as a biscuit. Edition of 800 signed copies. A collector's morsel. A genuine curiosity. I am charmed to have it. But I cannot comprehend a page of it. For it is written in James Joyce's new language, invented by himself. Here are a few words from one page: limpopo, sar, icis, seints, zezere, hamble, blackburry, dwyergray, meanam, meyne, draves, pharphar, uyar. It ought to be published with a Joyce dictionary.

Someone (I read somewhere) said to Joyce: 'I don't understand it.' Joyce replied: 'But you will.' Joyce is an optimist. Human language cannot be successfully handled with such violence as he has here used to English. And *Anna Livia Plurabelle* will never be anything but the wild caprice of a wonderful creative artist who has lost his way.

187. Leon Edel on *Work in Progress*

1930

Leon Edel, 'New Writers', *Canadian Forum*, x (June 1930), 329–30.

James Joyce is the author of three books of prose fiction, two books of poems, one play, and a half-finished volume. It is a meagre production in these days of copiousness; but it has a profound influence on contemporary English literature. *Ulysses*, the story of a day in the lives of two Dubliners, and hence the story of one day in Dublin, and in turn of one day in the history of the world; the *Portrait of the Artist as a Young Man*, a study of the expanding consciousness of a young artist facing a conflict between religion and art: *Dubliners*, a book of short stories of Dublin life told with Flaubertian precision—these are the products of a brain sensitive to the beauty of language and to the individual meanings, the philological values latent in words; and at the same time a brain bearing the imprint of scholasticism, the Jesuit strain which Stephen Dedalus possesses—injected the wrong way, as he is told in *Ulysses*. 'To live, to err, to fall, to triumph, to recreate life out of life.' This is the cry that comes to the artist's lips in the *Portrait* in an outburst of profane joy. And this, I think, can be taken to be James Joyce's credo.

Mr. Joyce was recently persuaded to record a reading from his *Work in Progress*, which has been appearing at various intervals in *transition*, a journal of American expatriates and others, published in Paris. Listening to the record, in which Joyce's beautiful tenor voice has been reproduced with amazing clarity, the work for the first time took on, for me, a profound and poignant meaning: what had seemed before merely literary and linguistic virtuosity assumed form and shape and evoked a thousand suggestions.

Work in Progress is approximately half-completed: the remainder will not be written for a long time, if ever, since Mr. Joyce is suffering from serious eye-trouble, and since it is not a type of work that lends itself to dictation. Joyce, it is told, recently suggested to James Stephens (when the two, who happen to have been born on the same day and in the same year, celebrated their birthdays together in Paris) that he finish it; and it is interesting to reflect what the author of *The Crock of Gold* would have done with it had he taken Mr. Joyce's apparent jest seriously and added to the Joycean realism his land of philosophers and leprechauns. Fortunately we do not require the second half to arrive at some general estimate of what has been written. It has appeared thus far in periodicals: in the French journal *Le Navire d'Argent*, in *This Quarter*, in *transition*. . . . We have, obviously, adequate material to work upon.

But most valuable of all, it seems to me, as a study of how the work developed, is the original version of the Anna Livia section published in Adrienne Monnier's journal, *Le Navire d'Argent*, in September 1925, when *The Calendar* for which it was destined had refused to bring it out in England unless Joyce modified the text. This version was revised and expanded for *transition* of November 1927, and further revised and expanded when it was published by Crosby Gaige in New York in 1928 under the title *Anna Livia Plurabelle*. A careful comparison of the first and last versions throws interesting light upon Joyce's aims and particularly upon his method.

In its broad outlines the section known as *Anna Livia Plurabelle* is merely the conversation of two washerwomen by the river bank; it is growing dark; the air is filled with evening sounds; occasionally the flip-flap of the wet clothes on the wet stones breaks the talk; their backs bent and limbs stiff with the damp and the strain, the women work, and as they work their lively chatter becomes rapid, voluble. Night comes— night which is to be the domain of the whole work, even as *Ulysses* occupied itself principally with day: . . .

[quotes the end of *Anna Livia Plurabelle*]

. . . To hear Joyce read this passage is to hear the evening sounds fused, the movement of the water, the staccato phrases of the women . . . far from meaningless it takes on the beauty of poetry and in the deformed words there is considerable suggestive power.

The first difference which we notice between the original version and the final form is the comparative simplicity of the first and the definite complexity of the second. In the original version Joyce has written the conversation of the Irish washerwomen for the most part in current English; in the revised version he attempts to write the language as it is spoken. 'Safety pin' in the first, becomes 'seifty pin' in the second: 'tailor' becomes 'tyler': 'week' becomes 'wik'. It is another important change, however, which renders the new version complex, but which gives it a peculiar richness. Joyce begins to combine words, to deform them, and to utilize other languages. He does not introduce these haphazardly. Quite often foreign words are closely related to the English. 'I know by heart the places he likes to soil' remarks one of the washerwomen as she throws a garment into the water. In the second version this becomes 'I know by heart the places he likes to saale, duddurty devil!' The proximity of the deformed 'saale' to the English 'soil' and the French 'sale' is to be remarked. The same is true when Mr. Joyce expands this changing of the language from the simplicity of 'Wait till the rising of the moon' in the first, to 'Wait till the honeying of the lune, love!' Here he substitutes the French word for the English and gives the whole phrase an additional two-fold association, on the one hand with the English 'honeymoon' and on the other with the French equivalent *lune de miel*. He substitutes Italian quite as readily . . . 'poor little Petite MacFarlane' becomes 'poor Piccolina Petite MacFarlane': and in the same way the word 'mother' in the first version is changed to 'madre' in the second.

Notice, then, the change effected in these two passages and how the first is transmuted to the more intricate form:

chipping her and raising a bit of a jeer or cheer every time she'd neb in her culdee sack of rubbish she robbed and reach out her maundry merchandise

which becomes

chipping her and raising a bit of a chair or jary every dive she'd neb in her culdee sacco of wabash she raabed and reach out her maundy meerschaundize

And he changes 'She thought she'd sink under the ground with shame when he gave her the tigris eye!' to 'She thought she'd sankh neathe the ground with nymphant shame when he gave her the tigris eye!' In indicating that to emphasize his river motif Joyce used the names of more than five hundred rivers in this work Padraic Colum observes that in the latter sentence four rivers are mentioned, and the associations with 'nymph' and 'underground' are two more river references. More complex perhaps is the sentence inserted in the second version 'Reeve Gootch was right and Reeve Drughad was sinistrous,'—to the Parisian this comment on *rive gauche* and *rive droite* and the antithesis between 'right' and 'sinistrous' is of peculiar interest.

The work of necessity will lead to many interpretations. A whole book of criticism has already been compiled, and was recently published by Miss Sylvia Beach, in Paris. Mr. Joyce is giving us an important experiment; what will be its later value we cannot now estimate. But that it is worthy of consideration I am certain: on its evocative side, away from the particularized meaning, as Robert McAlmon has pointed out, it is of the greatest interest. 'To him,' Mr. McAlmon says of Joyce, 'language does not mean the English language, it means a medium capable of suggestion, implication, and evocation; a medium as free as any art medium should be.' And he adds 'It is unlikely that Joyce himself understands from a re-reading of his present writing all that he thought it has in the way of implication.' There is latent in this, perhaps, a confusion of the arts, a mélange of too many things: something akin to Father Castel's *clavecin des couleurs*. It is quite possible that Mr. Joyce is trying to do too much: that there is a limit to the suggestive power of literature. But this thing brings us to the realm of aesthetics. What concerns us at the moment is method in *Work in Progress*; there is sufficient in it, I feel, to warrant a close scrutiny rather than a careless dismissal. . . .

188. G. W. Stonier, review of *ALP* and *Haveth Childers Everywhere*

1930

Extract from 'Mr. James Joyce in Progress', *New Statesman*, xxxv, No. 896 (28 June 1930), 372, 374.

. . . *transition* has now ceased publication, but Mr. Joyce's work is still in progress; though what chance we shall have of seeing it, now that Mr. Joyce's one shop-window has gone, is uncertain. Mr. Joyce, apart from his achievement as a writer, demands not a little admiration, because he is one of the very few great writers of our time who have never cheapened or advertised themselves in any way. He has kept himself to himself, as the saying goes; and that alone, in an age of self-advertisers, entitles him to our respect. . . . *Ulysses* may sooner or later be available in England without the necessity of cheating the Customs, but I doubt if it will find as many readers as a book of its scope and imagination deserves. *Work in Progress* (to judge from extracts published from time to time) is even more withdrawn. . . . In *Work in Progress* Mr. Joyce seems to have set out to make his characters even more universal. The protagonists are Anna Livia (the River Liffey) and Everyman, who appears as Here Comes Everybody, Haveth Childers Everywhere and H.C.E. *ad infinitum*. Here you have Bloom and his cronies without their physical symbols—they are wind and air and stream, a cosmic muttering, still savouring strongly of the bodies which now are only ghosts. This tremendous disproportion between the mass of allusions to every typical phase or contemporary life and the thin disembodied chant into which they are poured is the most striking fact about *Work in Progress*. It is possible to regard this book as a proof that Mr. Joyce, recoiling further and further from the underworld of Mr. Bloom and Dublin, has at last really shut himself up in his own snail's-house, leaving for the exasperated reader only a track. It is an extraordinary fact that before Mr. Joyce's latest book has been published at all, or even completed by its author, a volume criticising it has already appeared in France. What a hurry Mr. Joyce's disciples are in! With what explanations and implications and examinations have they trumpeted the dawn—before even the first grey streak is visible!

Haveth Childers Everywhere and *Anna Livia Plurabelle* are the first bits of Mr. Joyce's new book to reach England: neither is more than forty pages long. The first is a collector's piece, beautifully printed and bound, but, to me at least, almost completely unintelligible. *Anna Livia Plurabelle* is sold very cheaply, and no doubt Mr. Joyce has chosen this particular section as one likely to attract a wider public or, at any rate, serve as sample of the book as a whole. I think that anyone reading it carefully for the first time should be able to follow most of the implications of Mr. Joyce's new speech. But it demands a little effort, and if our attitude is simply, 'Here is another good writer gone wrong,' we are not likely to get far. . . . With Mr. Joyce the cadences, the juxtaposition of words, the words themselves, are different. In reading him you begin reading again—or you leave off.

Work in Progress contains a very large number of invented words, of words spelt in unusual ways and compounded from almost every

European language. The idiom shifts from mediæval doggerel to negro slang in the same sentence, perhaps even in the same word. Mr. Joyce takes any liberty with language which will enrich the music or the sense of his prose. His preoccupation with words is shown in a passage from *Portrait of the Artist as a Young Man*, published in 1916: . . .

[quotes from ch. IV, p. 166, and uses that passage to explicate the method of *Anna Livia Plurabelle*]

Most of the failures in Mr. Joyce's new prose come from too much distortion and the introduction of patterns and allusions which merely bewilder the reader with irrelevant deftness. I cannot see that the introduction of 'catalogues'—a list of the names of rivers, for example, inlaid in the words of a passage like silver wire in wood—gives it any greater literary value than a poem written in the form of an acrostic. *Work in Progress* is said to contain the names of all the largest rivers in the world—the excuse being that the river Liffey is the chief character in the book and that these geographical allusions are all part of the ground-plan. This seems to me even more fantastic than the Homeric pattern of *Ulysses*. . . .

But it is advisable to approach this new book warily, as one would listen for the first time to a new and astonishing piece of music which at times jars on the ear. Whether language is capable of the musical extension to which Mr. Joyce attempts to push it (some of it is almost contrapuntal), I do not intend to discuss. We must have the whole of his book before it will be possible to venture judgment. Occasional passages in *Work in Progress* have amazed me by their beauty and complete originality; and these passages improve on being read a number of times. . . .

[illustrates this point and quotes approvingly pp. 215–16]

. . . Passages as finished and distinct as this are rare in *Work in Progress*. For the most part you are swept along in a gurgling stream of consciousness, in which Bloom and the Liffey and a Cro-Magnon chorus and the babble o'green fields seem all to be comically muttering together, and all to be one. Whether, after one glimpse into that green murky swirl, most readers will care to take the plunge is extremely doubtful. . . .

189. Unsigned review of *ALP* and *HCE*, *Times Literary Supplement*

17 July 1930, 588

In the light of recent research it is possible to demonstrate that the prodigious difficulties of Mr. Joyce's latest work, provisionally entitled *Work in Progress*, are at least the outcome of a logical and deliberate plan, even if it is impossible to follow with full understanding the details of its execution. As in *Ulysses*, the key to the new work may be found in a philosophical concept. Briefly, *Work in Progress* is an attempt to realize Vico's project of 'an ideal and timeless history': to create a composite image of human existence, regardless of time or space. Where language has seemed to Mr. Joyce insufficient for his purpose he has altered it. By deformation, punning and the interpolation of foreign languages he has given his English a suggestiveness, a capacity for multiple associations such as his theme demands. The narrative of *Work in Progress* is a simultaneous projection of many narratives. Externally it has to do with the history of Dublin, the myths and facts of its origin, but into the prose texture are woven strands taken from history and myths of all time. There is no sharp definition; it is part of Mr. Joyce's plan to keep his medium fluid and amorphous. His story is no more than the main current in a stream of associations.

But while a knowledge of what Mr. Joyce is trying to do, of the necessity for his curious technique, is valuable, if only to acquit him of the charge of writing nonsense, it must be admitted that, even with this knowledge, an understanding of his work asks more of our erudition and ingenuity than it is possible for us to give. At best our appreciation of *Work in Progress* must be a relative one, according to our lights, on a plane subsidiary to that of its conception. What we chiefly see in it is not so much an attempt to pack the universe between its covers as an attempt to give language a new vitality, to restore to words some of the energy and freshness of meaning which has been worn out of them. If we are to derive aesthetic satisfaction from the work as a whole, we must approach it with something of that free expectancy of mind with which we approach music. . . .

Anna Livia Plurabelle, ALP

Of the two fragments from *Work in Progress* before us *Anna Livia Plurabelle* is the likelier to yield this 'sensation of understanding' to the general reader, if he can approach it without prejudice and without asking 'too much explanation.'. . .

[briefly summarizes the 'plot']

. . . In the prose the flowing of the river and all its attributes are evoked simultaneously with the feminine qualities of the impersonation. Lack of an adequate scale of reference must mean that much of the inner significance of this fragment is lost to us. But there remains a delicate appeal to the senses which it needs no table of reference to appreciate. . .

[quotes from p. 204]

. . . The river has widened out, and the old women are so far apart that they cannot hear each other for the noise of the water: . . .

[quotes from p. 216]

. . . Myth envelops the gossipers, tellers of myths. One is changed to a tree, one to a stone—'Beside the rivering waters of, hitherandthithering water of. Night!'

The other fragment, *Haveth Childers Everywhere*, is more opaque generally. Ingenuity as well as an extensive knowledge of Dublin and its history are necessary to understand Earwicker's pompous recital of all that he has done for the city and for his Anna. Its implications are occasionally obvious, to Dubliners at least, as in the reference to street-names in

my nordsoud circulums, my eastmoreland and westlandmore, running boullo-wards and syddenly parading . . .

Read aloud, as Mr. Joyce's work should be, the prose of this fragment has a stateliness appropriate to its matter, in ponderous, masculine contrast to the streamlike melodies of *Anna Livia Plurabelle*.

190. O'Faolain, re-reading of *ALP*

1930

'Letter to the Editor', *Criterion* (October 1930), 147.

A re-reading of *Anna Livia Plurabelle*, with much more pleasure than at any previous reading, convinces me that in an article which you kindly published in the *Criterion* of September, 1928 [No. 178], I did not do complete justice to Mr. Joyce's new prose, and with your permission I should like to add a further word to what I said in that essay. I do not think that there is anything in that essay which I do not still believe, but it did not go far enough in its appreciation of the merits that do lie in Mr. Joyce's language. It becomes clear to me that a kind of distinction once properly made between prose and poetry is passing away. . . . This prose that conveys its 'meaning' vaguely and unprecisely, by its style rather than its words, has its delights, as music has its own particular delights proper to itself, and I have wished to say that for these half-conveyed, or not even half-conveyed suggestions of 'meaning' Mr. Joyce's prose can be tantalizingly delightful, a prose written by a poet who missed the tide, and which can be entirely charming if approached as prose from which an explicit or intellectual communication was never intended. In my article and elsewhere, I suggested that such prose is, as it were, morally deficient—being almost wholly sensuous—but that question I do not wish to re-open here. . . .

191. Philippe Soupault and the French translation of *ALP*

1931

Philippe Soupault, 'A propos de la traduction d'*Anna Livia Plurabelle*', *Nouvelle Revue Française*, xix (May 1931), 633–6.

This article accompanies a French translation of *Anna Livia Plurabelle* by Samuel Beckett, A. Peron, I. Goll, Eugène Jolas, Paul Léon, Adrienne Monnier, Soupault, and Joyce. At the beginning of the article, Soupault describes the way the translation was done so as to include the rhythm, the sense and the metamorphoses of words; a summary of the 'action' of the fragment, the place of the fragment in the whole work, and an avowal of accurate criticism precede the following comment.

There remains, however, a plan which ought to be brought to light with a little more force because it will more noticeably attract the reader's attention and because it is placed between the reader and the work itself. It concerns language.

In *Work in Progress*, Joyce takes us into, one by one, the questions which concern language itself. We already know through the reading of *Ulysses* that for James Joyce language was a living element of his work; I mean that he did not consider the words, syntax, or style as admitted facts. In his new work he definitely breaks the balance of the edifice, and, after the rupture, decides to remount to the sources. Throughout his life, James Joyce has listened with attention, with complaisance to those he considers the true creators of language, the people, and he has followed with a patience which characterizes his 'genius' the steps of the verbal instinct.

Having pondered over the examples, he makes an appeal to the spontaneous creations in appearance of vocabulary, and to the metamorphoses which it undergoes. [an example] . . . For each episode and for each part of his *Work in Progress*, James Joyce adopts a category of names which ought to give to that episode and to that part a tone, in the musical sense of the term. For *Anna Livia Plurabelle*, these are the names of rivers. In almost all the sentences a word carries with it the name of a stream or of a river. These words charged with a double sense will be again like their neighbors enriched with meanings, allusions, recollections or new indications . . . They are in some way cut in facets.

The great difficulty is to leave to these words a 'human' sonority and a 'human' aspect. It is there that the prodigious sense of the language which Joyce possesses intervenes. I have been able to see him create under my eyes these new words and scarcely were they born but they lost their appearance of newness. They are immediately a part of the vocabulary . . .

. . . James Joyce does not travel in a little space. His design in this new work is to create new myths. The time has not yet come to comment on a work whose importance still escapes us.

192. French comment on *Work in Progress*

1931

An unsigned notice, 'James Joyce et le Snobisme', *Le Monde* (2 May 1931), 4.

It is sufficient for a writer who knows English well to translate Shakespeare. Two embellishers, a critic, an American poet, a German poet, an editor, a French writer and the author himself are not too many to translate James Joyce. Poor Shakespeare!

[refers to Philippe Soupault's comments on the difficulties of translating *Anna Livia Plurabelle* in the *Nouvelle Revue Française*, see No. 191]

Soupault affirms that 'the time has not yet come to comment on a work the importance of which still escapes us.' At the risk of passing for an imbecile, we prefer not to wait and to declare immediately that such a labor does not surpass the importance of certain 'parlor games' (*jeux de salons*). The pastime of intellectuals juggling with words, syllables, sounds, allusions and correspondences, this is not a new way leading toward regions still unknown; it is the manifestation of a dilettantism and of extreme estheticism.

It was necessary, finally, to replace Proust which overworked *snobisme* today abandons. Joyce who was a talented writer no longer aspires to another destiny.

193. Max Eastman, interview with Joyce about *ALP*

1931

Extract from 'Poets Talking to Themselves', *Harper's Magazine*, No. 977 (October 1931), 563–74. Also appeared in Max Eastman's *The Literary Mind* (1931), pp. 97–102.

I had the pleasure not long ago of hearing James Joyce read—or rather recite, for he can no longer see the letters—a few pages from his *Anna Livia Plurabelle*, and discussing with him its unintelligibility. I wonder if he will object if I employ the memory of that conversation in order to prove by the example of a brilliant genius that literature is not of necessity a communicative art. . . .

Some other words of his in that conversation I saved [Joyce had referred to Eastman's essay 'The Cult of Unintelligibility' (see No. 223) as 'sound celticism'], because they led me to this step beyond the position taken in that essay—they led me to think it is erroneous in the first place to *define* literature as communication. . . . He told me how glad he was that, even though I found so much of him unintelligible, I had at least enjoyed his humor. . .

And then he told me that into the prose of the little book in question —*Anna Livia Plurabelle*—he had woven the names of five hundred rivers. The book in a certain sense is, or is about, a river. Indeed, I now remember that Joyce told me before reciting a passage from it that either two people, or a rock and a tree, or the principles of organic and inorganic nature, are talking to each other across a river. One of his learned commentators has since issued a paper to the effect that it is the two sexes, male and female, which are talking across this river; another maintains that it is two washerwomen—but I believe only what Joyce told me. . . .

Joyce was reciting his lines for me, to 'give pleasure' to me, lines on which he had worked six hundred hours and woven into them the names of five hundred rivers, and yet I did not hear one river. I have examined them patiently since and have not yet found more than three and a half rivers. Moreover, having had something to do with inductive and deductive logic, I know that if it took six hundred hours to weave those rivers into that prose, it will take something like six thousand hours to weave them out. I cannot help asking myself how many people will do this work, and how much fun they will have doing it. If Joyce's artistic motive really is to give pleasure to others, it seems fair to say that he has wasted about five hundred of those six hundred hours burying the names of those rivers where people who might happen to want them would not be able to find them.

Of course Joyce is deceiving himself when he says that his principal motive is to give pleasure to others. . . .

'The demand that I make of my reader is that he should devote his whole life to reading my works.' He smiled as he said that—smiled, and then repeated it.

And my answer was, 'You absolutely insist on giving them all that pleasure!'. . .

Joyce believes he is writing his present extremely unintelligible prose because, whereas *Ulysses* gave us a day in the life of a man, his present work gives us the night. 'In writing of the night,' he said to me, 'I really could not, I felt I could not, use words in their ordinary connections. Used that way they do not express how things are in the night, in the different stages—conscious, then semi-conscious, then unconscious. I found that it could not be done with words in their ordinary relations and connections. When morning comes, of course everything will be clear again. I'll give them back their language. They really needn't worry and scold so much. I'll give them back their English language. I'm not destroying it for good!' . . .

. . . At any rate I do not for one moment believe that the idea of writing about the night is anything more than an interior pretext upon Joyce's part for amusing himself with words in the way he chooses. The tendency appears often enough—and with no such pat reason—in *Ulysses*. . . .

Joyce may be trying utterly and absolutely to give *himself* to a series of experiences which he connects in some way with the process of falling asleep—to give himself to them and to the words which revive and enrich them for him; although of that, too, I am skeptical. But he is not devoting a moment's attention to the very complex and delicate problem of the strategy by which he might possibly contrive to communicate *some* of those experiences to somebody else. His character as a stylist in this recent work does not lie in any loose semblance to the operations of a drowsing mind, nor yet in the scope of his linguistic researches. It lies in the fact that he is doing an intellectual and imaginative labor gigantic in its proportions, obdurate in its persistence, with no practical end in view whatever, not even that of communicating his experience, but solely to perfect himself in the art of playing by himself in public. . . .

These professional critics are all eclipsed, however, by C. K. Ogden, who tells us, in his preface to Joyce's latest installment, *Tales of Shem and Shaun*, that in order to adjust our minds to the values of this new kind of literature, what we have to do is learn to talk Eskimo. Joyce, it seems, does not know Eskimo—and neither, I infer, does C. K. Ogden —but Joyce has conscious 'affiliations with his Norse ancestors,' and Ogden seems to think that the only way to outwit his unintelligibility is to go 'still farther north' and learn a still more difficult language. This geographical approach to literature will become easier, of course, for warm-blooded natures after Mr. Wilkins has opened a route under the ice. . . .

. . . In view of these facts, Ogden concludes: 'At least a decade may be necessary before Mr. Joyce's "word-ballet" yields its secret even to an adjusted mind.'

To this it might seem reasonable to add that, inasmuch as Joyce himself does not understand Eskimo or use any of the words out of this language, and the reader has spent this first decade merely in order to get into a proper geographical position and overcome his nervousness in the presence of 'infixes'—it might seem reasonable to grant him a couple more decades to devote to the study of the actual Joyce. Indeed, I, for my part, think that after going way up north and talking Eskimo for ten years in order to get into the right longitude and lexitude for approaching 'Mr. Joyce's symbolic condensation,' it would show unseemly and unscholarly haste to dash right down to the Tropic of Cancer and plunge into Joyce himself, as though there were no degrees of latitude or stages in the concentration of a symbol. Surely a mind properly consecrated to the process of adjustment would not ignore those 'Norse ancestors' from whom Joyce really did borrow some words. I would suggest a very gradual southerly movement, about ten degrees to the decade. That would bring you to Paris in time to be buried with an uncut first edition of *Work in Progress* on your chest and the proud joy in your bones that you died with an adjusted mind.

Just how much, and at what, my canny and learned friend Ogden is smiling in his preface to *Tales of Shem and Shaun*, I will not try to determine. Suffice it to say that he locates the values of unintelligible literature somewhere up in the Artic Circle beyond the reach of the non-Eskimo reader. . . .

194. F. Scott Fitzgerald and Joyce

1928

John Kuehl, 'A la Joyce: The Sisters Fitzgerald's Absolution', *James Joyce Quarterly*, ii, No. 1 (Fall 1964), 2 [2–6].

By now it is common knowledge that when Scott Fitzgerald met James Joyce at a Sylvia Beach dinner party during July of 1928 he threatened to jump out of the window in honor of Joyce's genius and drew a picture in Miss Beach's copy of *The Great Gatsby* showing himself kneeling beside the master who has a halo on and whom Miss Beach asserts Fitzgerald 'worshipped.' What is not so well known, however is the extent to which the idolater read and used the works of his idol.

Fitzgerald possessed copies of *Dubliners* (The Egoist Press, 1922 edition), *Chamber Music*, *Pomes Penyeach*, *Ulysses* (in which there is a card from Joyce dated 11.7.928), and *A Portrait of the Artist as a Young Man* (in which Joyce has inscribed on the front flyleaf: "To Scott Fitzgerald/James Joyce/Paris/11.7.928). On June 25, 1922, he said of *Ulysses*: 'I wish it was layed (*sic*) in America—there is something about middle-class Ireland that depresses me inordinately—I mean it gives me a sort of hollow, cheerless pain. Half of my ancestors came from just such an Irish strata or perhaps a lower one. The book makes me feel appallingly naked.' He borrowed the term he employed to describe Dick Diver of *Tender is the Night*—'a spoiled priest'—from it and jotted in the 'Literary' section of his notebooks: 'Must listen for conversation style à la Joyce. . . .'

195. Ellen Glasgow on the novel

1928

Extract from 'Impressions of the Novel', *New York Herald Tribune* (20 May 1928), 1, 5.

The critic surveys the modern novel—Proust, Joyce, Lawrence, Tolstoy, Dostoievsky and Tchekov.

Much has been made in recent criticism of the bold modern plunge into subjective experience. In reading some of these eulogies of the new psychology one is almost persuaded that introspection is as modern as aviation and that reality was first discovered by Mr. James Joyce while he was looking over the shoulder of Mr. Leopold Bloom. But is the matter so simple as this? Compared with the mental involutions of Mr. Joyce or Mr. Lawrence, the great English novelists may appear a simple-minded assemblage, interested, not in pathological symptoms, but in this, too, too solid flesh and other tangible substances. . . . After all, no invention was ever bold enough to startle to-morrow. The sunflower of Oscar Wilde looks to us as faded and as brittle as a pressed leaf in a book; and the mud of *Ulysses* will harden probably into clay before the stream of consciousness has run dry in the novel. . . .

196. Denis Marion on Joyce

1928

'James Joyce', *transition*, No. 14 (Fall 1928), 278–9. First appeared in *Variétés* (Brussels), Iᵉʳ Année, No. 3 (15 July 1928), 156–7.

. . . And since unanimity is unobtainable on any one subject, at least James Joyce has the rare merit of leaving no one indifferent. He is insulted or admired. G. B. Shaw termed him: a dirty little rascal, and H. G. Wells and Arnold Bennett have publicly hailed him as a very great writer. . . . There are other surprises for the curious who, with the help of translations or a relative familiarity with English have arrived at a certain knowledge of *Chamber Music, Dubliners, Portrait of the Artist, Exiles, Ulysses,* or even *Work in Progress,* which is at present appearing in *Transition.* They discover a man of the Rennaissance with a limitless curiosity, in love with life, with all of life, even to its most despised manifestations: a pupil of the Jesuits who combats his teachers with their own weapons, implacable knowledge, cold substantial reasoning, an abundant, generous casuistry; the real creator of the interior monologue as a literary genre (because, if you want my opinion, *Les Lauriers sont Coupés* is pretty bad); a writer who is taken up with a living philology, utilising, as it has never been done, the slang, the dialect of Dublin, the obscene words which are so numerous in English, and going so far now as to truffle his tales with foreign words: in short, to end on the most banal of eulogies, but also the truest, the epic poet of the modern odyssey which takes a man from midnight to midnight, through events of the least possible importance, that is to say, of the greatest interest, since they suffice for the provisioning of eight hundred pages of prose. . . .

197. Sisley Huddleston on Joyce and Sylvia Beach

1928

Extract from *Paris Salons, Cafés, Studios* (1928), 208–20.

Chapter 15, 'Shakespeare and Company', is an account of Joyce's associations with Sylvia Beach, publisher of *Ulysses*.

. . . 'It is impossible,' said Joyce. 'You will lose money.' 'Nothing is impossible,' replied Sylvia Beach with American determination.

'It [*Ulysses*] will not interest the public,' returned Joyce.

'It is a masterpiece,' declared Miss Beach, 'and come what may it must appear.'. . .

. . . For years in Italy and in Switzerland this Irish exile had . . . set down, without respite, without hope, impelled only by his artistic conscience, the pages that were to make up *Ulysses*. All that had gone before—his *Dubliners*, (short realistic stories) his poems (delicate notations), his *Portrait of the Artist as a Young Man* (in which is foreshadowed his subsequent style)—were merely preparatory exercises for the greater work. . . . Its most characteristic feature, apart from its unexampled frankness, was its use of the monologue intérieur. Joyce does not claim to have invented the monologue intérieur. . . . Yet in *Ulysses* Joyce made the monologue intérieur his chief method. When you read a passage of *Ulysses* you can scarcely distinguish between what is passing externally and what is passing internally. . . .

[publishing history of *Ulysses*]

. . . For my part, though I could not approve of a great many passages —and still deplore them—I was unable to resist the conviction that

Ulysses was a production of genius. I wrote to Mr. J. L. Garvin, Editor of the London *Observer*, telling him of my conviction, but also telling him of passages which would certainly call forth rebukes and cause the book to be banned. . . .

[see Huddleston's review, No. 104]

It is, of course, absurd to suggest that Joyce had pornographic intentions. I have come into closer relations with Joyce than with any other man in Paris, and it is almost ludicrous to be obliged to protest that he is sincere. We must take his work for what it is. Those who read it for its unpleasant passages will quickly grow weary. It requires high culture to appreciate its comic and sublime contrasts, its exposure of the irrelevance and the irreverance of mankind before the great facts. Gross animality and subtle spirituality intermingle. Blasphemy and beauty, poetry and piggishness, jostle each other. But, as I said in my review, one becomes tired of beastliness always breaking in. I asserted that the vulgarity of life was exaggerated, and that Joyce had magnified the mysterious materiality of the universe. . . .

[quotes from a review in the London *Evening Standard*, 'A Monstrous Book']

Ulysses is the talk of all the places where men congregate who are interested in writing, and this talk has been going on for a month or two. But not till Mr. Sisley Huddleston sent a column about it to London have the references been freely and openly made . . . After the *Observer* published his review people said: "Ah, not pornography but a work of art, which may mean something." Word of *Ulysses* spread. Subsequently came Mr. Middleton Murry with a *Ulysses* page in the *Nation and Athenaeum* [see No. 98], Mr. Arnold Bennett following with a page and a half in the *Outlook* [see No. 106]. . . .

'Bound in blue paper and having the external appearance of a British Blue Book, *Ulysses* is monstrous in size as well as character. Its pages are about a foot square, and it weighs some pounds avoirdupois.

'Those hearing of it for the first time will ask, What is it all about? . . . Consequently, *Ulysses* is copiously peppered with words that are heard only where social restraint is disregarded or unknown.

'Frequently the terminology of Mr. James Joyce—hope of the Newest Movement in Letters—is identical with that which rules in the back streets of Port Said or Marseilles. . . .'

Joyce's methods, as he described them to me, are interesting. He does not start at the beginning and work to the end. He works over this or that passage, marks it with this or that colour, pigeonholes it on a sort of card index system, and gradually pieces the many passages together.

That he is laborious may be judged from the fact that he spent no fewer than 1,200 hours over a single chapter of a later book which appeared in one of the little magazines of the quarter edited by Eugène Jolas and Elliot Paul—*transition*. . . .

'Critics who were most appreciative of *Ulysses*,' he told me as we talked together one afternoon in his cool quiet study by the Champ de Mars, 'are complaining about my new work. They cannot understand it. Therefore they say it is meaningless. Now if it were meaningless it could be written quickly, without thought, without pains, without erudition; but I assure you that these twenty pages now before us cost me twelve hundred hours and an enormous expense of spirit.' . . .

The idea of Joyce, as it developed, was that words as we know them are worn out. They are like pieces of money that have become thin and on which the effigy is effaced. So he invented what is virtually a new language. He telescopes existing words, or gives them a fresh and often humorous twist, and he takes his expressions from every human tongue. Always is he careful of the rhythm. Yet it is not mere sound that he seeks: he packs his phrases full of sense. He declares that the sense is simple, but certainly everybody does not find the score of implications which Joyce tries to put into a single sentence.

I frankly presented the critic's point of view. 'If indeed you have a dozen meanings in two words, the result is meaningless to the reader. How can he be expected to know what is in your mind? Thus excess of meaning becomes the same as lack of meaning.'

If the later writing of Joyce is read aloud it greatly gains. One realises the sense of strange words. Joyce has an extraordinarily good reading voice, and on the afternoon of which I am speaking he read to me a short passage and then commented upon it. His commentary was illuminating. I have no desire to misrepresent him, but as I remember he would take a phrase such as: 'Phœnix culpa,' and would then explain. 'Now here you have a suggestion of felix culpa—the blessed sin of the early Church fathers—that is to say the downfall of Adam and Eve which brought Christ into the world; and you have the suggestion, not only of the Garden of Eden, but of Phoenix Park in Dublin, and of Irish history with its wrongs and crimes, and you have the eternal way of a man with a maid, and you . . .' *Tout cela!* as Dr. Mardrus, the French translator of *The Thousand and One Nights*, constantly exclaims!

All this is excessive, but one was almost convinced when one heard Joyce read in his thin clear voice, with perfect articulation, with musical intonation, with ever-changing mimicry, a passage alternately humorous and poetical. . . .

[quotes from a conversation with Padraic Colum]

'The big new thing in literature is contained in Joyce's work, which shows there is more in writing than telling a story. Joyce is an honest and sincere man, and readers should be patient and wait to see what he does. . . .'

[quotes a comment by Valéry Larbaud]

'My admiration for Joyce is such that I do not hesitate to affirm that if one writer among our contemporaries will pass to posterity, that writer will be Joyce.'

It is an opinion that, whatever reservations I make about certain phases of his work, I cannot but endorse. It is possible that he has gone to extremes; that his epoch-making volume represents an end rather than a beginning; that imitations, which are numerous, are generally poor; and that the influence which Joyce has on the French and American writers has often produced undesirable fruits; but he has strongly impressed his own generation, and future generations will read him if only in a spirit of curiosity. . . .

198. A French comment on Joyce the Romancier

1928

Marcel Brion, 'Les grandes figures Européennes: James Joyce, Romancier', *La Gazette des Nations*, No. 8 (3 March 1928), 4.

It seems premature today to trace a portrait of James Joyce. He has had so many metamorphoses at which to assist that they prevent us from yet closing him into a fixed form. The evolution of his work has been so rapid, so extraordinary, from *Dubliners* and *A Portrait of the Artist as a Young Man* to *Ulysses*, and a great difference exists even between this last book and 'Work in Progress' which is appearing in *transition* . . . that we can only give a provisional value really to every judgment about Joyce, susceptible to every revision and modification.

We can, however, say even now that the work of James Joyce is one of the most important literary events of our epoch, and I don't know to what date it would be necessary to go back to find something comparable to it. I will not attempt here to analyze this work, the extent and complexity of which would· require a volume, but only to outline some traits which express the physiognomy of the man and of his contribution.

We have already named two books by Joyce, *Dubliners* (*Gens de Dublin*) and *A Portrait of the Artist as a Young Man* (*Dedalus*). *Dubliners* is a collection of short stories, which present certain aspects of Irish life. *A Portrait* is clearly autobiographical.

Joyce intended to compose a short story which would have described a day in the life of any man, to whom nothing happened except the most ordinary events of existence. But this singular alchemy, which presides at the birth of great works, took this subject which ought to have furnished in the plans of the author only a story of some pages and made a book of it, enormous in its bulk, immense in its significance and in the date which it marks in the literature of today and tomorrow, this obscure and marvelous book forbidden in England and in the United States and which numbers a crowd of enthusiastic readers, *Ulysses*.

Eighteen hours in the life of this everyman, Leopold Bloom, constitutes the matter of this extraordinary work. Composed as the title indicates on the plan of the *Odyssey*, bound by subtle allusions to the Homeric poem, which it follows, chapter by chapter, like a sort of bizarre projection, *Ulysses* is, I do not fear affirming, the most prodigious book of our times. Not only for its intrinsic value and Joyce's own genius, but especially for its impetus which will give birth to a whole new literature. In this regard, I could only compare it to a work with an equal power of suggestion and influence, that of Marcel Proust.

One does not define *Ulysses*; one must loose and find himself several times in the labyrinth, full of darkness and light, to understand the substance, the import. There is something medieval in this book which has the allure of a 'summa' and as with medieval works one would wish that it were accompanied by indispensable glossaries and commentaries. The anecdote is insignificant, but each event of this day of Bloom, a burial, a walk on the sea-shore, conversations in an office, in a bar, in a hospital, create a host of ideas, comparisons, remembrances.

The art of Joyce is of a certain 'textile' material. The themes cross and are sometimes composed like the design of cloth, with an apparent disorder which obeys, in reality, the most rigorous logic and of which we are only aware by frequently regarding the reverse side of the cloth. He projects all the volumes on two dimensions of this moving and many-hued square; he poses here and there landmarks, often well hidden, without which we risk being misled and tripping in the tangles.

There is in this book both the imagination and the verse of Ireland, and a decorative, asiatic sense. We are not, then, surprised that *Ulysses* has encountered a great number of fervent readers in China, many of whom get together to read it and comment upon it.

Joyce's work *Ulysses*, and even more *Work in Progress*, gives us the impression of assisting at the birth of the world, because we perceive in the aspect of chaos, a creative will, constructive, architectural, which has spilled around it the traditional dimensions, concepts and vocabulary, to find in these scattered materials the elements of the edifice. Joyce has created his language, by writing words as they are pronounced—and you can imagine how that disfigures English!—by introducing foreign words or dialectical forms, and by making up all pieces which do not exist and which he needs. And he does it with an unheard of creative power, an inventive imagination, unique perhaps, but which relies on an unbelievably vast culture. The verbal richness of Joyce greatly surpasses that which seemed unequalable, that of Rabelais, but then which in him obeyed an amused fantasy; Joyce puts it in the service of a philosopher. *Work in Progress* appears built in large part on the theory of history of Vico, of a true recreation of the world, of ideas and of forms.

Because, contrary to appearances, the genius of Joyce is essentially as a director, a constructor, he orders and he constructs according to his own laws and without bothering about traditions or customs. And this is the prodigiously innovating impetus of the genius which offers us the dazzling spectacle of a Genesis.

199. Rebecca West on Joyce

1928

Extract from 'The Strange Case of James Joyce', *Bookman* (New York), lxviii (September 1928), 9–23; later appeared in *The Strange Necessity* (1928), pp. 1–67 [1–215].

See the reply by William Carlos Williams, 'A Point for American Criticism', in *Our Exagmination* (1929, Paris; 1962, New York), pp. 171–85, and Miss West's reply, 'Letter from Europe', *Bookman*, lxx (September 1929), 664–8.

[The article begins with Joyce's poem 'Alone' from *Pomes Penyeach*, which Miss West has just purchased.]

. . . It is, as one might say, by Mr. James Joyce. It is one of the poems, and not noticeably the worst, included in the collection he has called *Pomes Penyeach*. And because he had written it I was pleased, though not at all as the mean are when they find that the mighty have fallen, for had he written three hundred poems as bad as this his prose works would still prove him beyond argument a writer of majestic genius. Indeed, the pleasure I was feeling was not at all dependent on what my conception of Mr. James Joyce is: it was derived from the fact that, very much more definitely than five minutes before, I had a conception of Mr. James Joyce. Suspicions had been confirmed. What was cloudy was now solid. In those eight lines he had ceased to belong to that vast army of our enemies, the facts we do not comprehend; he had passed over and become one of our friends, one of those who have yielded up an account of their nature, who do not keep back a secret which one day may act like a bomb on each theory of the universe that we have built for our defense.

For really, I reflected . . . this makes it quite plain that Mr. James Joyce is a great man who is entirely without taste. So much is proved by the preservation of this poem against considerable odds; for it was written at Zürich in 1916, and there was the removal to Paris, there were eleven years, there was space and there was time, in which to lose it. And lack of taste, when one comes to turn over the handicap he has laid on his genius, is the source of nearly all of them. It explains, for example, the gross sentimentality which is his most fundamental error. What do I mean by sentimentality? I had to think. . . .

Now one hears that *shock* very often in modern literature, in the writings of persons who have practised some revolutionary austerity regarding the superficialities of writing, and feeling, therefore,—having a streak of Puritan optimism in them—that they must thereby have bought salvation by it. . . . *Shock*. One hears the sound again and again in *Ulysses*. Seduced by his use of a heterodox technique into believing himself to be a wholly emancipated writer, James Joyce is not at all ahead of his times in his enslavement to the sentimental. That is manifest in isolated incidents. For example, the volitional character of Miss Brill is nothing as compared to that of Gerty MacDowell, the girl who sat on the beach to the detriment of Mr. Bloom's chastity. Her erotic reverie is built up with as much noisy sense of meeting a special occasion as a grand-stand for a royal procession, in order that we may be confounded by the fact of her lameness. *Shock*. But, more important, his sentimentality deforms the conception of one of the two protagonists, and that the one which should have been presented with the most careful sincerity and grace: the young Stephen Dedalus, whose quarrel with the grossness of man's theory of living (as symbolized by the Roman Catholic Church) and the grossness of man's living (as symbolized by Leopold Bloom) is meaningless unless they are destroying in him a sincere and graceful spirit. But the young man is transparently a hero. His creator has given him eyelashes an inch long. And how he comports himself! He rolls his eyes, he wobbles on his base with suffering, like a Guido Reni. This is partly, of course, a consequence of Mr. Joyce's habit of using his writing as a means of gratifying certain compulsions under which he labors without making the first effort towards lifting them over the threshold that divides life from art. An obvious example of this is his use of obscene words. This might be a perfectly justifiable artistic device. I would hesitate to say that some artist may not at some time find it necessary to use these Anglo-Saxon monosyllables, which are in a sense so little used and in a sense so much, for the completion of some artistic pattern. But that Mr. Joyce is not that artist, that his use of obscene words is altogether outside the esthetic process is proven by that spurt of satisfaction, more actual but also more feeble than authentic artistic emotion which marks the pages whenever he uses them. Simply he is gratifying in his maturity the desire to protest against the adult order of things by the closest possible verbal substitutes for the practical actions, originating in the zone against which adults seemed to have such a repressive prejudice, by which he could register such feelings in his infancy. . . . There is working here a narcissism, a compulsion to make a self-image and to make it with an eye to the approval of others, which turns Stephen Dedalus into a figure oddly familiar for the protagonist of a book supposed to be revolutionary and unique. In his monologues on esthetics, in his unfolding of his theory concerning Shakespeare, he enjoys the unnatural immunity from interruption that one might encounter not in life but in a typical Freudian wish-fulfilment dream. . . .

Now if a writer can juxtapose sentimental material like this alongside material to which his imaginative experience of it has given absolutely just values—like the exquisitely pathetic picture of the visions of a sweet and ordered life that sometimes come to the squalid Dublin Jew, Leopold Bloom, evoked in the question-and-answer part of the book simply by cataloguing the specifications of the little country place of which the creature often dreams—he has really remarkably little taste. . . .

And James Joyce does go wrong. This is not to say that he does not write beautiful prose. . . .

[illustrates this point with several passages]

But that does not alter the fact that James Joyce is safe only when he stays within tradition: or one might say rather within a tradition, for the times when he is best able to give perfect form to his genius are when he is not trying to escape from the influence of his classical training. There are two stories in *Dubliners* which are among the most beautiful short stories that have been written in our time; and both of them guide their exquisite spirits to deliverance along a path prepared by Latin poetry. One of them is called 'A Sad Case':

[summarizes the plot of the story]

Through these pages, in which the suffering of the man and woman stand up in the night like vast columns of a ruined temple, exquisite and desolate integers of a final and irremediable incompleteness, there sound precisely those accents which in one's schooldays one groped for and could not find when one tried to translate the passages in the Aeneid where people grieve, where they say, '*manibus date lilia plenis*' . . .

The sentences are austere in color, they drive straight down, they bring the earth something not soothing yet a benefit, like the gray spears of rain, like the lines of Virgil.

And in the other and still more marvellous story, 'The Dead', which is one of the few masterpieces of mysticism, it is Lucretius who is recalled.

[summarizes the plot of the story]

These two stories by themselves should explain why we rank James Joyce as a major writer. But the uncertainty of his power over his medium is manifest when he makes use of the same tradition with equal vigor and the most fatuous results. There are two colossal finger-prints left by literary incompetence on *Ulysses* which show that a pedantic accuracy about the letter and an insensitivity about the spirit can lead him wildly astray even while he is still loyal to the classicism. It was M. Valéry Larbaud who first detected that the title of that great work was not just put in to make it more difficult, but that there exists a close parallelism between the incidents of the *Odyssey* and *Ulysses*: that Leopold Bloom is Ulysses, Stephen Dedalus is Telemachus, Marion Bloom is Penelope, the newspaper office is the Cave of the Winds, the brothel the Place of the Dead, and so on. This recognition plunges Mr. Joyce's devotees into profound ecstasies from which they never recover sufficiently to ask what the devil is the purpose that is served by these analogies. The theme of *Ulysses* is essentially Mani-chæan: Leopold and Stephen are Ormuz and Ahriman, the dark force of matter that rots as well as blossoms and the spirit of light that emerges from it and contents with it. But surely there was nothing in the philosophical world more alien from the Greek genius that Manich-æanism, since the motive force which inspired it was its need to prove that there was no conflict between nature and beauty, and that whoso accepted the one begot the other by the act of acceptance.

The other finger-print he has left on his own masterpiece springs from not so fundamental a confusion, but it is as ominous in its bearing on his fitness to invent a valid new method. His devotees never weary of pointing out as evidence of his scholarship that the scene in the Lying-In Hospital consists of a series of parodies of a large number of great writers ranging from the Early English to the Victorians: the theory being that the mind of Stephen Dedalus picks up the bawdy conversation of Bloom and the medical students and translates it into terms of the literature in which he had been saturating himself. What they never pause to notice is that even as parodies—and perhaps the parody is the art-form which produces the largest percentage of execrable specimens—these are noticeably bad. The imitations of Bunyan and Sterne, even allowing for the increasing cloudiness of drunkenness, completely disprove all that is alleged concerning the quality of Stephen's mind. . . . The problem of art is to communicate to the beholder an emotion caused in the artist by a certain object; and though it is possible that every attribute of that object, all its relations in time and space, are relevant to that emotion, it is not very probable. . . . So far from being a way of handling the literary medium, inclusiveness is a condition which may or may not legitimately exist in a work of art owing to factors quite outside the conscious control of the artist; and which does not legitimately exist in *Ulysses*, since many of the excrementitious and sexual passages have a non-esthetic gusto about them which implies that, in order to write of them at all Mr. Joyce has had to step out of his artistic process, even to the extent of losing touch with his characters. For every now and then Leopold Bloom, in whom there is no reticence, in whom there cannot be reticence since it is among the restrictions of life which he has foregone because he suspects them of being purposive, adopts toward sexual matters a coy titillating hesitancy. . . . Inclusiveness is therefore in these instances esthetically fatal to Mr. Joyce.

Incoherence, that is to say the presentation of words in other than the order appointed by any logic of words not in sentence formation, is at least a real device and not just a condition, and while it also is suitable for the handling only of a special case, that special case is certainly contained in *Ulysses*. But unfortunately Mr. Joyce applies it to many things in *Ulysses* as well as that special case. To begin with, he writes down these strings of words as if they corresponded to the stream of one's consciousness; as if, should one resolve to describe one's impressions as they came, one would produce isolated words and phrases which would not cohere into sentences. . . . But of serious representation of the court jester there was nothing. That is why there is such tremendous force behind *Ulysses*; it is the liberation of a suppressed human tendency. And that is why James Joyce is treated by this age with a respect which is more than the due of his competence; why *Pomes Penyeach* had been sold to me in Sylvia Beach's bookshop as if it had been a saint's medal on the porch of Westminster Cathedral. . . .

Every thought of that long day in which Leopold Bloom is exhibited, every action, has that peculiar squatting baseness which comes of a deliberate regression; for though he is entirely absorbed in the dingiest phases of his environment this is by a deliberate though unconscious choice, for he has ability above the average. . . .

I do most solemnly maintain that Leopold Bloom is one of the greatest creations of all time: that in him something true is said about man. Nothing happens to him at the end of *Ulysses*. Nothing is suggested in the course of the book which would reconcile him to the nobility of life. Simply he stands before us, convincing us that man wishes to fall back from humanity into the earth, and that in that wish is power, as the façade of Notre Dame stands above us, convincing us that man wishes to rise from humanity into the sky, and that in that wish is power. But it is when one considers the rest of the work in both these expressions of man's desires that one is overcome by fury at Mr. James Joyce's extraordinary incompetence. . . . There are, as a matter of fact, some pretty bad holes in Mr. Joyce's façade, for again and again Leopold Bloom is represented as receiving impressions directly in the form of gibberish, without any translatory efforts on his part.

But worse still, two other characters in the book are made to use gibberish, though that is so much outside their characters that it renders the book pointless. In *Ulysses* the figure of the Son is divided into two persons—Stephen Dedalus, who is alive, and Rudy Bloom, who is dead —in order to convey that the Son is perpetually alive and perpetually dead, that he is always being born and being killed, and that though it is the Father who kills him he mourns him after his death. . . .

But Stephen talks and thinks gibberish nearly as much as Leopold Bloom. The very characteristic which is most expressive of Leopold's difference from Stephen and the need to destroy him is constantly manifested by Stephen himself. This robs the book of much of its effect, and it is only to be explained by supposing that Mr. James Joyce, when he found himself attaching gibberish to the person of Leopold Bloom, simply did not understand what he was doing, and imagined, as many of his followers have since done, that he had discovered a new method of universal applicability. . . .

Mr. Joyce's incompetence in his treatment of the Mother interferes a little with the function she plays in the book, but not seriously, because she is conceived and executed with a magnificent integrity of feeling. She is divided into two persons, into May Dedalus and Marion Bloom, for the same reason that the Father was bisected; since the Mother is seen in relation to the Son, Stephen Dedalus, it is necessary that all the sexual aspects of her which he could not bear to contemplate in his own mother should be isolated in some other woman. That is Marion Bloom. . . .

All these attitudes, arising out of reproduction, that have ringed history and the globe are to be found in this dingy little room in Dublin, in the innocent and depraved, the tender and callous, musing of Marion Bloom. They move, these creations of her need to be fertile; this one serves her youth and goes, that one serves her maturity and goes, even she throws the noose of desire round Stephen Dedalus and draws him near to her. The Mother is going to draw the Son back into her body; by his consent he will become the Father, who will beget a son. By observing the rhythm of Marion Bloom we have been given knowledge, not otherwise stated, of the rhythms of Leopold Bloom and Stephen Dedalus. Surely it might be said that 'all enter the mind at once, and extend one another into a common entity'. It is not the philosophy which gives the book beauty. That eternally Leopold Bloom and Simon Dedalus will kill Rudy Bloom and Stephen Dedalus, but that that will be no victory, since eternally Marion Bloom and May Dedalus will raise up their enemies against them, is not a happy ending on the facts. Personally I would prefer man to draw a better design, even if it was drawn but once and was not repeated like the pattern on a wall-paper. But I claim that the interweaving rhythms of Leopold Bloom and Stephen Dedalus and Marion Bloom make beauty, beauty of the sort whose recognition is an experience as real as the most intense personal experiences we can have, which gives a sense of reassurance, of exultant confidence in the universe, which no personal experience can give.

200. Carola Giedion-Welcker on *Ulysses*

1928

'On Ulysses by James Joyce', *Neue Schweizer Rundschau*, xxi (1928), 18–32.

It has been necessary to extract rather severely this very long and very comprehensive article; each episode is examined in great detail.

Present: The present streams as a conscious and determinant main-experience from this book. What is the subject? We. Our daily existence, our inner and outer reality, as entirety or detail. As in the exact sciences, it is excavated, stated, disenchanted; it is not, in the traditional sense of poetry, made music from a higher level. Why this title? To discover the metamorphoses of the same, always returning primary elements of life, through the centuries, through time: wandering, fighting, birth, friendship, love, death. A huge transformation from Homer to us. In penetration, it grows out of a tenable outer parallelism to the *Odyssey*, the 'today' in harsh discrepancy and distance. Like the Oihopa ponton become the snot-green ocean, the pathetic helmets and swords changed to banal felt-hats and Chaplin-canes. The gracious Nausikaa corresponds to a kitschy teenager with jammed erotics, the cyclops who throws boulders corresponds to an irascible, nationalistic, middle-class man, who cuts up rough with empty cans . . . and so on, ad infinitum.

Wandering: Wandering has always been the motif for epos and novel. Odysseus, Siegfried, Pantagruel, Simplizissimus, Wilhelm Meister, the Grüne Heinrich, they all wander; that means that they pass through space in time; they walk through the world and through themselves. Mr. Bloom, the main character of the novel, walks through one day, one night in Dublin. The extensive time of the traditional novel shrinks to the intensive time of nineteen hours. Here, it is even a certain day: June 16, 1904. We experience this man, who does not possess anything extraordinary in his inner or outer being, up to the last. In

437

literature, did one ever learn so much about one person? Scarcely. Mr. Bloom—he is an advertisement-acquisitioner at a Dublin newspaper—is not only X-rayed in a physical-psychical manner, that all important past experiences of his 'I' are drawn into present experiences of this day by experience-associations, but Mr. Bloom also does everything in front of the reader's eye, that in our decent world is usually done behind locked doors. That means this: Mr. Bloom walks around without a façade. Since the sensual is this man's main sphere, it also takes the main place. He is introduced with the statement of his love for inner-organs of animals, especially the ones of mutton. From there on, he trods transparently through his banal, Irish day. Through his kitchen, through the bedroom-smells of his Spanish, primadonna wife, through the streets shopping, to the Poste restante, into a Catholic church, taking a bath, even to his comfortably carried-out digestive functions. . . .

[here follows a discussion of the funeral]

Newspaper: The time-thread runs on. Bloom, in his professional sphere, in the editor's office of a large, influential Dublin newspaper. A multi-colored, literarily glued picture: headlines, advertisements, catchwords from the editors' conversations, fragmentary telephone conversations, rattling machines, compositors, screaming newspaper-boys. Beside this, excerpts from reports about politics, technique, sports, weddings, births, society, history, landscape, pathos are mixed to a dough, penetrate each other, rotate as a multi-colored mass. We look into the intestines of a giant apparatus of today. That which comes out is the daily fodder of our brains. . . .

[here follows a discussion of the 'City at Noon', 'Bar', 'Battle', 'Eros', 'Birth', pp. 20–3]

Stephen Dedalus: The same as Bloom, Stephen is not comprehensible. He is in opposition to the standardized city-type, a single, rare original. A twenty-two year old mind, instructed early in the scholastic discipline of thinking; a mind which always looks inside, and is constantly on a pilgrimage through itself. The sharp brightness of his intellect and the fantastic half-darkness of his Irish soul produce the tragic conflicts of his being. A tenuous relationship to life and a certain strangeness keep him apart from the robust and sly life-heroes of his next acquaintances, from Buck Mulligan, the Irish medicine-man, and Haines, the English literary man. This middle-class existence—he is a supply teacher—one learns through a fragmentary class-period, in

438

which his spiritual figure becomes solid. Penetration of present and past. Remembrances, torturing complexes, his own youth, Jesuit school, conduct at his mother's deathbed. Then Stephen, wandering by the sea, full of Thomian thoughts about hyle, form, space, and time. Abstract reflection is mixed with momentary perception: the landscape is mystically Irish-pantheistically covered, in between is caustically surrealistic garbage-can smell. Not only the rhythm of the waves, horizon, distance, rocks, but also washed ashore fragmentarian, stranded goods, cork, wood, shivers, animal and human carcasses belong to this seacoast experience. Again and again, beside the bright splendorous side is the crumbling reverse side of things. Stephen submerges for awhile, emerges shortly, and finally he is in fullest spiritual brilliance and at the same time in fullest bizarreness at the convention with the young, Dublin, literary men and artists in the bookstore.

Conversation about art and genius: Here, Stephen discloses with the great example, Shakespeare, Joyce's basic attitude toward esthetic and ethic questions. Ideas which are scattered and brood in *Portrait* are compressed here with final clarity and precision. Fundament of every art? Deepest life, experience. Its goal? Revelation. 'Art has to reveal to us ideas, formless spiritual essences.' As art originates from life, so it reacts to life; 'The movements which work revolutions in this world, are born out of the dreams and visions in a peasant's heart on the hillside.' What is genius? Heightened spiritual pluralism, genius is 'myriad-minded.' Shakespeare is in all his creations: he is Hamlet, father and son, Iago and the Moor at the same time. 'He is in all. He acts and is acted on.' Genius is, in itself, a norm for experience, matter, moral. Only that which has been latent inside becomes externally immediate. 'Every life is many days, day after day. We walk through ourselves, meeting robbers, ghosts, giants, old-men, young-men, wives, widows, brothers-in-love. But always meeting ourselves.' Subjective and objective worlds flow into one another. The prototheme of wandering and expulsion is also a main motif for Shakespeare. 'Banishment from the heart, banishment from the home.' Instead of the light, Homerian counterchord, Penelope (waiting, faithful love), here the always weighing, dark minor chord of adultery and treason. The type Shakespeare and the type Bloom are, in this sense—with all consciousness about their quality-distances—members of the same chain. That means: penetration of microcosm even in the psychic. Horoscope-connections between both, which Bloom remembers later when he looks at the night-sky, indicate the same thing, with a humorous coloring. A second relation, which like a leitmotif goes through the novel, is discussed at this place: the relation between father and son. Hamlet *père et fils*. Odysseus—Telemachus, Bloom—Stephen.

Father-son problem: It says in the theologically educated mind of the Jesuit pupil: consubstantially between godfather and son. Fatherhood as apostolic consequence only in the mystical, not in the real sense. 'A real father is a necessary evil.' The European church finds basis in this mystery, not in the especially Italian madonna-cult. 'On that mystery, the church is founded, like the world, macro- and microcosm, upon the void. Upon incertitude, upon unlikelihood. *Amor matris* may be the only true thing in life. Paternity may be legal fiction.'

[here follows a discussion of 'Walpurgisnight', 'Coachman pub', 'Relation', pp. 25–7]

. . . The basic question: Does an inner-relationship exist between these two? Yes. An analogy of structure is ascertained. The differences, however, are crucial because spiritual expansion and attitude toward the world prove to be diametral. Bloom, from the wide basis of the receptive, liberal bourgeois emphasizes the importance of general education and a physically cultured existence, whereas Stephen, from his exceptional, mental summit-point, derives the basic powers of life from the special dynamics of the genius. These are the original contrasts of the culture-idealism, seen from the perspective of the cultural producer and the civilization, grown out of the sphere of the cultural consumer. There, the sharpened point of view of only the individualistic, here the broad niveau of the regularly normal. The same as Stephen and Bloom live in different 'spiritual rooms,' also the time-levels on which they stand are different. That means separation of generations. Joyce expresses the situation in this way: 'What was Stephen's auditive sensation? He heard in a profound, ancient, male, unfamiliar melody (Bloom sings a Hebrew text), the accumulation of the past. What was Bloom's visual sensation? He saw in a quick, young, male, unfamiliar form, the predestination of a future.' Final result: Stephen and Bloom part. . . . .

[here follows a discussion of Marion Bloom, pp. 28–9]

Fragment: The baroque abundance of the material which Joyce spreads out in front of us on these 732 pages of his novel, is the smallest part of reality, seen through a magnifying glass. The time is very short; one day, a part of a night, a certain date, June 16, 1904. The place: Dublin, that means the big city as a focus of collective activity. A point on the terrestrial globe, which is also a point in space. This is the stressed, relativistic attitude. Through this limited space, in this limited time, people from all sorts of individual and social levels move—this is in opposition to Proust, who gets his characters almost entirely from the mobility itself. They move internally and externally, rhythmized through the times of day, professions, functions of the body, events.

Typification: Even the great, permeating events of the novel are not made into interesting, special cases, but are brought before us as generally human, collective cases. Likewise, out of the main character, Bloom, the representative of the human average, spiritually standard material has been produced. That which is left of the individual type of humanity is very little: an aroma, impregnated with the genes of an old race. Clichés, automatic brain-rattling, parakeet chattering dominate. His wandering is the daily trot of an inhabitant of a small town. Exceptional things only crystallize in the abstract mind, in the genius; that means in Stephen Dedalus' brain. In reality, a lonesome, sensually detached poet philosopher, who has been cheated by the real life.

Psychology: This generality and speciality within the psychic receives a strange transparency from Joyce. Not the façade-culture with elaborated artistic handicrafts is important, but rather to make the human interior rooms, their abundance, tensions, dreariness visible. Man has a multi-split 'I', the composition of which, out of tribal-historical taint, characterological quality, superindividual, worldly will, is examined psychologically, deeply. It is streaming out of him, he is reflected in others, he is only a fragment of a great mass of people. Rounded-off being, harmony, synthesis are sham greatnesses, which we still today steal from past times, for ornaments.

Space and Time: The two great containers of reality, space and time, envelop and bear the entire mass of the novel. According to Bergson, the living-spiritual and intuitive world is placed above the mathematical-physical world of matter, of space; one can comprehend this through analysis. Above the scientific method stands the metaphysical, which points to everything living-dynamic. The work of the reconstruction of the space-time problem is a phenomenon within modern sciences and art. Within the literary, Bontempelli, the founder of the Italio-European *Novecento*, thinks it is 'the task of the twentieth century to build anew on these basic foundations.' George Antheil, the inaugurator of mechanical music, believes that the most important aim of the music of the future is the conscious penetration of the music-space with time; the 'abstraction in the time-space, the new and true dimension of music.' Programmatically, for the pictorial art, it says in 1920, in the realistic manifest of Gabo, 'To realize our world-experience in the form of space and time, this is the only goal of our creative art.'

Movement: The world which Joyce unfolds finds itself in a false static, and therefore it is only relatively graspable with a scientic matrix of coordinates of the space-temporary. The external strokes of a clock, which scan the novel, are present, but they are only to be valued as a measuring, helping means. Everything really living is temporal, moves, changeable, and cannot be banished with scientific methodology.

Futurism: Out of this philosophy of life, strong points of contact with the futurists develop. Their magic vibration seized the Joyce novel. Since life is movement, the cinematic-technical transmission—which has been previously mentioned—is understandable from the inside. The principle of penetration, which all modern optics, art, and movies are infused with, receives here poetic formation. Sensual and cerebral, somatic and psychic, environmental and internal worlds grow into each other. Events and thoughts are never isolated, but are always penetrated by thousands of minor sounds. Into the *one* collecting container of consciousness flow together even temporarily divided things: the simultaneity.

Also, the classical, static word usage begins to waver. In accordance with the dadaists, Joyce displaces and bastardizes words, parts of words, shakes them like a fool together, to extract new life from worn-out and misused cliché-forms. Thoughts are in the *statu nascendi* as a fermenting mass of dough, disclosed and not served as a fully baked article. That is why they are often incoherent, torn-off, fragmentary. The style is always changing; there is no general, poetic idiom. Each matter of the book sounds different; each has its own atmosphere. A material-justice in the higher sense. Parody of historically frozen characterization of social, psychic, intellectual forms of existence result in different linguistic expressions: old chronical-style, newspaper-style, magazine trimmings, classical prose, alley and college slang. The poet, Joyce, does not stand as a conductor in the foreground, as a visible mediator, but as a magician behind the scenes to light and awaken them. Therefore, little description, usually direct contact between the reader and the matter, through the inner-monologue or dialogue. Through this exceptional technique, an unfulfilled vividness and directness of existence, soul, and event is achieved. It streams forth from the basic substances of our discordant existence. Beside shining elementaries there is dullness, moldiness, stereotyped rigidity, reflectorizing automatism.

Beside grand pantheistic empathy in everything living or dead (Joyce does not merely *happen* to be an Irishman), there is searing, anarchic pessimism, by which the world is vulgar, sick, and mendacious, and challenges to biting criticism. *Ulysses* cannot be categorized with the catchwords 'futurism' and 'verism'; in this work, tendencies of periods of all directions are broken. The psycho-analytical, basic attitude, which is already visible in *Portrait*, the flowing transition from bodily to spiritual, the 'expression pure' of the unconsciousness, the higher reality of coincidence, illusion, fantasy, and dream meet undesirably with the surrealistic party-program. But even with this, the last saving formula for Joyce has not been found; while the irrational world of fantasy is dominating, Joyce interfuses his poetic work with an exact, technically mathematical framework, and X-rays his world with a scientific coldness and sharpness. A synthesis of art and technique. The material is analyzed up to the last. A pondering and relating of all contents of the novel, forward and backward, from part to part, up to the technique of sentence structure, where, through refrain-like repetition and correspondence, the inner-relations are revealed. To transfer this to the musical: a mirror-fugue, through which one can go from the front to the back and from the back to the front. The arguments between man and world, the spiritual core of all great novels, becomes in Joyce, a great poetic-philosophical revelation about the inner and outer world, about subject and object, about matter, space, and time. They are the problems of the present philosophical and physical theories. Behind all this stands a deeply pessimistic anarchism, which crystallizes in Stephen's exclamation, 'Lord, help my unbelief.'

We stand in front of a similar picture of the world, as T. S. Eliot, the English contemporary of Joyce, forms in his *Wasteland*: tragic discrepancy of a transition-time, which, claimed by the past and by the future, ripens to a new synthesis under the pressure of historical burden.

201. Stefan Zweig on *Ulysses*

1928

'Anmerkung zum *Ulysses* [Observations Concerning (*Ulysses*)]', *Die Neue Rundschau*, xxxix (1928), 476–9; reprinted in *Der goldene Schnitt: Grosse Essayisten der Neuen Rundschau, 1890–1960* (1960), ed. Christoph Schwerin, pp. 283–6.

Directions for use: One should first seek a solid support so as not to have to hold the book in his hand forever; this volume is almost 1500 pages long and makes one weak in the knees. First, one takes the accompanying prospectus of 'the greatest prosework of the century' and the 'Homer of our times' carefully between the second and third fingers, tears up these loudly rebuking, exaggerated notes of complaint and throws them into the waste-paper basket in order not to be enticed by the fantastic expectation or the wild claims. Then sit yourself down in an armchair (because it will last a long time) and restrain all patience and judgment (because it will also make you angry) and begin.

Kind or species: A novel? No, certainly not: a witches' Sabbath of the spirit, a gigantic 'Capriccio,' a phenomenal cerebral *Walpurgisnacht*. A film of psychic situations, buzzing and flitting in 'Expresstempo,' in which enormous landscapes of the soul, full of ingenious and the most highly gifted details, go reeling by, a double thought, a triple thought, one after another, through one another, beside one another, sensation of all sensations, an orgy of psychology, with a new technical slow moving camera, which analyses each movement and emotion down to their atoms. A tarantella of unconsciousness, a frantic, rushing flight of ideas which whirlingly float indiscriminately with themselves with the greatest subtlety and banality, fantastic and Freudian, theology and pornography, the quality of a lyric and as coarse and vulgar as a coachman—a chaos, therefore, not stupidly imagined by a drunken brain overcome with alcohol and wrapped in demonic gloom, but instead imagined by a cutting, intellectual, ironically cynical and bright intellect. One strides with rapture, one fumes with exasperation, one wears out and senses himself being whipped, and finally one becomes dizzy as if he had ridden for ten hours on a merry-go-round or had listened to incessant music, each dazzling, clear as a flute, then again coarsely and vulgarly as a drum beat and wild as a jazz-band, always to the consciously modern word—the music of James Joyce—which gives itself to the most refined orgy of language which was ever undertaken in all of language. There is something heroic in this book and at the same time something which lyrically parodies the art; therefore, it is authentically and rightly a witches' Sabbath, a black mass, in which the devil apes and mimics the Holy Spirit in the most audacious and most provoking manner, but also a solitary thing, an unrepeatable thing, a new thing.

Source: Something evil is its root. A hate, or an early emotional state of a wound in the soul dating back to his youth, is stuck in James Joyce. In Dublin, his home city, he must have been hurt by the citizens whom he hates, for everything that this ingenious man writes is revenge on Dublin: his early book, the wonderful uninhibited autobiography of Stephen Dedalus and now this fierce analytical journey of the soul. Not in ten pages out of the 1500 does one find cordiality, devotion, friendliness; all are cynical and sneering and of an organic power of rebellion, all explosive, of inflamed nerves flung in a racing tempo which at the same time intoxicates and bewilders. Here a man explodes not only in cry, not only in scornful word and in grimaces, but also out of all his intestines, he empties his resentments, he vomits his overdue feelings with a force and a vehemence which makes one sincerely shudder. The most ingenious bluff cannot hide the enormous emotional feeling, this shivering, this vibrating, this frothing and almost epileptical temperament with which a man here forces his book into the world. . . .

Art: It reveals itself not in the construction but instead in the words. Here Joyce is absolute master, a Mezzofanti of language. I believe he speaks ten or twelve foreign languages and brings out of them his own entirely new syntax and a turgid, exuberant vocabulary. He masters the entire key-board of the most subtle and metaphysical expression down to the sewer nonsense of a drunken hussy. He rattles down entire pages of lexicography. The region of ideas and concepts is overstrewn with machine-gun fire of attributes; he performs with a stupendous bravura upon all trapezes of sentence construction and writes quite well in the last chapter, which I believe reaches over sixty pages. . . . In his orchestra the vowel and consonant instruments of all languages are mingled, all technical terms of all sciences, all jargons and dialects; out of English Joyce derives a pan-European Esperanto. From peaks to valleys, this ingenious acrobat swings like lightning; he dances between clashing swords and swings over all chasms of deformity and shapelessness (and one must show all kinds of reverence for his translator, Dr. Goyert . . .). The achievement in language alone attests to the genius of this man. In the story of more recent English prose, a particular chapter begins with James Joyce of which he himself is the beginning and the end.

Summary: The book is a moon-stone, overhead in our literature, a grandeur, a fantastic one of its kind, an heroic experiment of an arch-individualist, of an eccentric genius. There is nothing of Homer in it, whose art moves in the parity of the line; meanwhile this glittering canvas of the spiritual underworld even through its noise and racing along fascinates the soul. Nor is there any Dostoyevski, although it is nearer to him through fantasy of vision and the exceeding overabundance. In reality, every comparison for this solitary experiment goes completely amiss. The inner isolation of James Joyce bears no connection to anything previous. It does not match anything and will therein have no successor. A meteor of a man, full of dark original force, a meteor of a work of 'paralyzing' art, like that medieval magic writing in a more modern way. . . . However, for all that, it is an immovable, fixed achievement: this book, an ingenious curio, will remain like an erratic block, unconnected with the productively effective world around us. And if time has preserved it, it will perhaps become revered like all Sybilline voices of humanity. In any case, what about the attitude today: there is respect for this self-willed, vehement, and ambitious achievement. Respect, respect for James Joyce.

202. Gerhardt Hauptmann on *Ulysses*

1928

Ezra Pound in a letter to Joyce (23 December 1928), in *The Letters of Ezra Pound* (1950), ed. D. D. Paige, p. 221.

. . . The Noble Gerhardt [Hauptmann] is struggling both with *Ulysses* (im Deutsch) and with the germanly traduced works Wm. He sez *Ulysses* in choimun is like looking at a coin through his microscope, can't see it cause its aggrandized to such etc. . . .

203. Ernst R. Curtius on Joyce's works

1928

Extract from 'James Joyce', *Literatur*, xxxi (December 1928), 121–8.

Ulysses by James Joyce is now available to German readers. This huge and monstrous work should be understood and appreciated. The time is not yet ripe for a final judgment; only after decades will we be able to measure what Joyce means for our own era—the beginning of a new literature, or a distant grand monstrosity. It is already certain that we are dealing with a work of exceptional greatness and significance.

But this work is bewildering and difficult as no other in modern literature. The author has intentionally avoided everything which could illuminate the reader's understanding, and, therefore it is not surprising when many (and even some critics) turn away disappointed and unsatisfied from this creation which was recommended to them as genial and which they then perceive as a gigantic and senseless arbitrariness.

But he who strives to understand *Ulysses* find himself enriched by fantastic mental experiences. One can understand *Ulysses*, or at least learn to understand it. Because the work is not, like certain products of Dadaism, an intended orgy of the irrational, an explosion of meaningless automatics, but rather a complicated construction of the highest consciousness, it is therefore accessible to intellectual analysis. But a concentration of attention is necessary which one normally is not accustomed to giving when reading a novel. One has to work through the 1600 pages of the German text . . . with the same mental attention with which one reads a difficult philosophical text. And even that is not enough. *Ulysses* cannot be understood within itself, but only through the complete works of its creator.

[here follows a lengthy biographical account and a literary history of Joyce's works]

He used the lyrical, the epical, and the dramatic forms, and in each he proved to be a master. But he started—and this seems to me very significant—as a critic. . . . In this essay ['On Ibsen', *Fortnightly Review* (April 1900)] we find a sentence which we today can literally apply to Joyce himself: 'This work is ruled by the highest order, by a clock-like routine, which one seldom finds in a genius.' Joyce's production, too, shows a strictly necessary concatenation, a conformity with the inner coherence, which in itself is an aesthetic enjoyment.

[here follows a brief summary of the solitary artist figures in the earlier works]

The *Portrait* gives us the self-description and self-analysis of the artist whose name is James Joyce. It shows the forces which influenced him: the Irish fate, i.e., political, cultural, religious opposition as life-atmosphere; education in the Jesuit boarding-school; his home, poisoned by the economical ruin with all its degrading results. In this milieu the spiritual drama of the young Stephen Dedalus happens.

[A lengthy summary of the plot follows here.]

But the way to *Ulysses* passes over *Dubliners* and *Exiles*; it is the way from the lyrical to the epic and dramatic expression. In the *Portrait*, this gradual progress of the artistic means of expression is represented as a necessary progress of a psychological nature. . . . It is the way from the completely personal emotion to a description which is nourished from the personality, and from there to an autonomous, depersonalized creation. . . .

. . . But at the same time the book is the preparatory work and a masterly exercise for *Ulysses*, not only in the sense that many people whom we will meet again in *Ulysses* appear there for the first time. But also, through *Dubliners* Joyce became capable of using Dublin in his later great work as a symbolic scene of his human tragi-comedy. In *Ulysses* Dublin is the connection of all human and cosmic relations. To be able to make Dublin serve his purpose, Joyce first had to take it up demographically, as he did in *Dubliners*. . . .

Exiles also forms an important member of the history of the origins of *Ulysses*. Motives from the *Portrait* emerge again: the break of the disbelieving son with the pious mother; the expatriation; the Irish cultural problem. But the ethic problem of the play is this: are deeply connected people able to live together on the basis of complete righteousness? . . . Two psychological components act together in this drama: a constrained urge to be righteous, which almost borders on exhibitionism, and the knowledge of unbridgeable loneliness of each soul, which borders on desperation . . . The strongest guiding principle for the composition of *Ulysses* seems to me to have been the analogical urge for self-revelation or—what means the same—the revelation of the nature of all mankind. The shock-like effect of *Ulysses* results from the fact that in this book all repressions are broken through. And what is more —and this is new—methodically. . . .

. . . In *Ulysses* all this [sexuality objectively viewed] is opened up, and this makes the book a museum of sexual psychology and scatology. [Valéry] Larbaud indicates [No. 118] that we do not have to look to the French naturalists for the models of this objective treatment of these proscribed areas, but rather at the Jesuitical moral-theologians. He is probably right. But the influence of Jesuit methods is much greater. To demarcate this influence more specifically would be an enticing task for an expert. . . .The outsider can hardly tell what is specifically Jesuit, scholastic, or Catholic in Joyce. But the stamp of these spiritual powers clings to Joyce like the character *indelebilis* to the priest. Stephen—in *Ulysses* also—thinks according to the scholastic method. Entities, entelechies, forms and modalities occupy his mind. He raises Aristotle above Plato. Dogmatic formulas, like consubstantiality, serve him in phrasing his personal problems in life. Liturgical texts always emerge associatively in Stephen's consciousness. He lost his belief but he does not long for it. . . .

. . . The critics have argued about the worth and significance of this chapter [15]. I think one can only understand it out of the depth of the Catholic consciousness. I do not see grotesque humor in it, not the superiority of a new artistic experiment, or of an icy-cold nihilism, but rather the choking desperation of the fallen creature. It seems to me to occupy the same place in the plan of *Ulysses* as the description of hell in the *Portrait*. It is hell: sin only knows about itself, no longer about God.

. . . These are the hints [of negative Catholicism] out of which we have to understand the spiritual changes which lie between the Stephen of the *Portrait* and the one of *Ulysses*. Do they signify a 'defeat' after the triumphant victory song with which the *Portrait* ends? Perhaps. But let us not forget that the ugly meanness of life is already present in *Dubliners*, that the binding of the soul to the animalism is already present in the *Portrait* as a principal experience. Certainly Stephen's soul has received since then a new wound caused by the death of his mother and by the repentance which is connected with it. Perhaps in this way the 'defeat', the bitterness of *Ulysses*, is explainable; the beauty-dream of the poet had to make room for the hostile, destructive powers of analysis, of mockery, of parody and of blasphemy. . . .

. . . One has to understand Stephen's inner and outer biography (which is mostly congruent with Joyce's) to understand *Ulysses*. But one is not allowed to forget that Stephen is not the main character in *Ulysses*. The main character is Leopold Bloom. But not as an individual, but as a type. Bloom grows above his milieu, race, and time-conditionality (which are exhaustively treated) into a universally true incarnation of human nature. . . .

With this we come to the problem of symbolism in Joyce. The symbolism of *Ulysses* is twofold . . . a complex symbolical relationship underlies the entire work: each episode corresponds to a special science, an art, an organ of the human body, a color, a technique. Larbaud takes chapter four as an example:

[summarizes Larbaud's analysis]

. . . But there is a second type of symbolism in *Ulysses*: form, action, and characters of the work form an analogy to the *Odyssey*.

[a brief explanation of this second type of symbolism]

. . . But we do not have the key for the first symbolism, an exactly worked out system of corespondences. It exists, but only in the possession of the author and a few initiated friends. The critics have not worked with this system yet.

[here follows a long analysis of the form-consciousness and the theological antecedents of the Homeric parallels]

Which means—this I would like to emphasize—that the Odysseus (and the Father-Son-Daedalus) symbolism is no literary game, but a meaningful expression of the relativation of the personality. The relativation of the person is Joyce's main problem; it is in conjunction with the relativation of time, a main theme of *Ulysses*.

The contents and meanings of *Ulysses* are not at all exhausted by these remarks. These remarks serve only to facilitate the access to the understanding of a work which is one of the most important spiritual events of our time.

[the essay closes with a note about the German translation]

204. William Carlos Williams on *Ulysses*

1928

'It was fine to hear from you', *Mercure de France*, cccxlvii (August–September 1963), [114–16], 115.

From a letter written to Sylvia Beach (24 June 1928).

Yes, by all means use the pages I contributed toward the appreciation of Joyce's new work. And send me a copy of your publication when it is ready . . .

[refers to Williams' contribution to *Our Exagmination*]

. . . Joyce is too near me for me to want to do less than he did in *Ulysses*, in looseness of spirit, and honesty of heart—at least.

1928: *Ulysses*

I have something more to say of Joyce's new work which I'll get out of my system some day soon. In short it is this: that valuable as it is, it is a development of but one theme which was touched on in *Ulysses* —one manipulative theme, that is. But it leaves too much that was magnificent in *Ulysses* undeveloped and he must now write the other theme out in another book after this (new) one. I require a very explicit, limpid, flaringly truthful development of the meaning as contrasted with the all important words—from Joyce now. For which he may tell me to go to hell if he wants to—or do nothing about it, naturally. Oh well—. . . .

205. Jack Lindsay on the modern consciousness

1928

Extract from 'The Modern Consciousness', *London Aphrodite*, No. 1 (August 1928), 17–18.

One man of at least far bulkier stature buttresses this dull synthesis of despair: James Joyce—though an occasional vividly precise phrase redeems him from the dullness of the pure Intellectualists. A depressed Irishman, a very fine realist of minutiæ—in one vast neurotic upheaval he vomited up all the spattering material of an existence on earth. Not that the plentiful lavatory epigraphs thrown up define a condition of frank self-revelation. . . .

He is therefore the utter antithesis to Rabelais, who binds together all the excreta of experience in one tremendous rhythm of overpowering laughter. Joyce, intellectually revolted by the necessities of life, pours out every little contact of horror, pain, and filth, as if he hopes to empty his life that way, to scrape the last touch of flesh from his contaminated mind.

Having thus discarded all the larger unifying factors of experience and delved into the slushy material of his subconscious memory, all that is left for him is pure sport with the formal elements of the word; and he is now playing a ponderous game with the dictionary, laboriously chopping up the language, getting amusement out of tiny interrelations and divisions of the rudderless consciousness. . . .

[quotes from *Anna Livia Plurabelle*, p. 199]

206. Robert McAlmon on Joyce, *transition* and *ALP*

1928

Extracts from *Being Geniuses Together: An Autobiography* (1938), pp. 179, 247–8, 250, 251, 268, 282–4, 286–7, 293.

Dos Passos, Jules Romain and others have broken with that 'classic' formula, as indeed had Cervantes long ago. Joyce did retain a precious and literary nostalgia for the Greek poetizing, word-prettifying qualities dear to Pound's heart, *melopoeia, logopoeia, phanopoeia*. That is, an interest in words as words for their evocative and suggestive qualities to the extent of being indifferent to the larger qualities of material, content-concept and the whole compositional realization of relationships rooted in a social order. . . . [p. 179]

Nevertheless, *transition* had its place. Bright people learned what some had thought years back, that Joyce, great genius that he was, was the end of a method and of an epoch rather than the beginning. He had carried words as words to a literary end as far as they could be carried; and younger writers were released to explore new materials and newer phases of social and psychological and circumstantial quantities and qualities. So far from having said all about life, Joyce's genius was a provincial and limited one intellectually and as regards types and phases of life. Because of this it had tremendous intensity, often too mainly introspective. His father, Dedalus, Buck Mulligan, Molly Bloom, and the newspaper and library scenes in *Ulysses*, saved that book from excessive-introversion in these passages, but his later *Work in Progress* went beyond the beyond. It was nice to hear him read it in that soothing 'Irish-tenor,' but to read pages of that punning, sentimental-remembering, meandering-wondering about life–death–birth, naughty jokings and flippant obscenities, was quite beyond my capacity and that of most people who knew Joyce and who 'understood' him. Bill Bird, I, and others would glance at any new extract and chuckle at an allusion or a pun or a witticism here and there, but it would not carry the interest on through several pages of a book. . . . [pp. 247–8]

Unlike as Stein and Joyce are as regards personality, mind, outlook, and writing methods, people will group them. They are as unlike as the north pole is from the equator. Joyce knows words, their rhythms, colour, assonances, capacity to evoke, their histories, and their emotional significations. Stein fumbles and mauls them and gradually something emerges as so much mud emerges into some sort of form in the hands of a maladroit child. Stein's wit is sluggish; Joyce's is almost too quick, constant, and around a limited range of experience, variable. They have in common only a tendency to withdraw themselves from the horde, to make themselves precious, but that tendency is light indeed with Joyce, and would not be in him at all if it were not that his eyes do not allow him to be as gregariously free and easy as he would like to be. He is not afraid of being unmasked for he is sure of himself, and I have never known him to boast without immediately withdrawing the boast in a 'what do we all know about it' manner. That cannot be said of poor Gertrude. She boasts and is hurt if her listener does not boost her boast. . . . [p. 250]

Joyce on the other hand quite healthily admits doubts. 'Do you think I may be on the wrong track with my *Work in Progress*? Miss Weaver says she finds me a mad man. Tell me frankly, McAlmon. No man can say for himself.' That day, one of my more earnest and kindly days, I assured the gentleman that of course he was not mad, as yet, just touched enough for genius in the James Jesus Joyce manner. . . .

When the Quinn collection of manuscripts were sold the one of *Ulysses* brought a surprisingly low price, but Joyce said resignedly, 'Probably they are right. Who can say what the next generation will think of me? What do we think of the great men of the past generation?'

Now he declares that he is tired of hearing about *Ulysses*. There has been too much said about the book. When I suggest that perhaps in *Dubliners* there is writing of his much more apt to last he does not disagree and wonders also if he might not have developed that style of writing rather than going into words too entirely. It was his eyesight, his inability to keep on reading freely, his incapacity to drink much without paying too great a price as regards his health, and his poverty, and the war, that decided many things which relate to his style and approach to writing. Nevertheless, his infatuation with words was born within him. . . . [p. 251]

At one tea gathering he gave a reading of his *Anna Livia Plurabelle*. Mary and Padraic Colum, Hemingway, Bill and Sally Bird, Sylvia Beach, Stuart Gilbert, Thomas McGreevy—in all some twenty people —were seated about the room, grave as owls. I didn't know the Colums. The others I knew or at least knew by sight.

Joyce began reading. The passage is effective, read in that 'Irish tenor' voice of his. In the passage, he told me, was the word Peace in some twenty-nine languages, the names of hundreds of rivers on earth and a few in heaven, hell and hades, and the passage was melopoetic, to suggest night and the flowing of the river, the Liffey. Strangely these facts don't and didn't impress me any more than the pattern of *Ulysses* as taken from Homer's Odyssey impresses me. It is the motional and sensitive writing which gives it what greatness it possesses. It could be dull, inanimate and pretentious if it were not that Joyce is full of sentiment, sentimentality and Irish twilight, even when he is most cruelly ironic. Certainly he read the passage to give it full emotional value. It was night, night, night, life haunting me and wonder and despair and the mystery of birth and life and death and twilight and the dark river ever flowing and Joyce-Hamlet delving into the mystic and eternal chaos questing-Stephan Dedalus a little less precious, a little less the esthete, intent upon the incarnate spirit—

But I listening, saw those grimly determined faces which would look intense and intent. Mary Colum now and then forced herself to see a comic touch and smile, but Mary's position as an intellectual critic forced her to 'understand.' The others looked at space or at Joyce and nodded their heads and Joyce's melodious voice continued . . . Holy, holy, holy—and not a one of them got more out of that reading than I did, and I had read the passage, indeed Joyce had read it to me himself. Hemingway commented afterwards that the passage did actually give one the feeling of night and of the flowing river. . . .

The passage is moving, does evoke thoughts of night and the deep, dark, flowing river. I would never read that passage in bed when a night *crise*, of despair about the value of life is assailing me. But Joyce is too good a writer to need sacred-cow hero-worshipping and blind adulation. He has had a great deal of that from various women, who have too much religion or art or 'faith' to feel anything but reverence for all that he writes. . . . [pp. 282-4]

At the time Joyce told me he was studying a new foreign language, Lapland, or Eskimaux, to develop his style and his word-genius—out of which study he learned the word for peace in so many languages. I recalled a remark of Anatole France. A man commented upon his wonderful erudition and France smiled, saying, 'yes, Le Petit Larousse.' Joyce smiled acknowledgingly and liked the story and the insinuation. Would, one wonders, T. S. Eliot? Of course Joyce has this advantage. He does actually possess a tremendous erudition and a marvellous memory. Joyce contributed the comment that Huysmans also had his little methods of appearing to be startlingly erudite. . . . [pp. 286–7]

207. H. G. Wells deserts the standard

1928

Letter to Joyce (23 November 1928), quoted in Stuart Gilbert, ed., *The Letters of James Joyce*, Volume I (1957), pp. 274–5, and in Richard Ellmann, *James Joyce*, pp. 620–1.

I've been studying you and thinking over you a lot. The outcome is that I don't think I can do anything for the propaganda of your work ['*Work in Progress*]. I've an enormous respect for your genius dating from your earliest books and I feel now a great personal liking for you but you and I are set upon absolutely different courses. Your training has been Catholic, Irish, revolutionary; mine, such as it was, was scientific, constructive and, I suppose, English. . . .

Now with regard to this literary experiment of yours. It's a considerable thing because you are a very considerable man and you have in your composition a mighty genius for expression which has escaped discipline. But I don't think it gets anywhere. You have turned your back on common men, on their elementary needs and their restricted time and intelligence and you have elaborated. What is the result? Vast riddles. Your last two works have been more amusing and exciting to write than they will ever be to read. Take me as a typical male. Do I get much pleasure from the work? No. Do I feel I am getting something new and illuminating as I do when I read ——'s dreadful translation of Pavlov's badly written book on *Conditioned Reflexes*? No. So I ask: Who the hell is this Joyce who demands so many waking hours of the few thousands I have still to live for a proper appreciation of his quirks and fancies and flashes of rendering?

All this from my point of view. Perhaps you are right and I am wrong. Your work is an extraordinary experiment and I will go out of my way to save it from destruction or restrictive interruption. It has its believers and its following. Let them rejoice in it. To me it is a dead end.

My warmest wishes to you, Joyce. I can't follow your banner any more than you can follow mine. But the world is wide and there is room for both of us to be wrong.

208. John Eglinton on Joyce's emancipation

1929

Extract from John Eglinton (W. K. Magee), 'Irish Letter', *Dial*, lxxxvi (May 1929), 417–20.

. . . Joyce is, I should think, the idol of a good many of the young men of the new Ireland. Is Joyce then what my ethnological friend would have called a 'key-personality'? I am inclined to think that he may so one day be considered, and so to a certain extent even accounted for. He has, apparently, abjured Ireland; the subjects of all his ridicule are Irish; moreover, it is improbable that when the new censorship begins to operate, the mind of the youth will have any but furtive opportunities to form itself upon Joyce's writings. Joyce is, none the less, in several respects a champion spirit in the new national situation. In him, for the first time, the mind of Catholic Ireland triumphs over the Anglicism of the English language, and expatiates freely in the element of a universal language: an important achievement, for what has driven Catholic Ireland back upon the Irish language is the ascendancy in the English language of English literature, which, as a Catholic clergyman once truly asserted, is 'saturated with Protestantism.' In Joyce, perhaps for the first time in an Irish writer, there is no faintest trace of Protestantism: that is, of the English spirit. . . . we are obliged to admit that in Joyce literature has reached for the first time in Ireland a complete emancipation from Anglo-Saxon ideals.

There is another point of view from which Joyce appears to belong to the present moment in Ireland—in his almost pedantic preoccupation with language. In the understanding of Joyce's attitude to language, a foreign critic is at a disadvantage compared with one who is acquainted with Joyce's race and upbringing. . . .

Critics of Joyce appear to me to ignore too much his peculiar origins, and it would be advantageous for the critical comprehension of Joyce generally and for Joyce himself—as it is for every important writer— that a country should be found for him. . . .

209. Jack Kahane comment on *Ulysses*

1929

Extract from *Memoirs of a Booklegger* (1939), pp. 218, 238.

. . . Is, or is not, *Ulysses* one of the great books of all time? Perhaps we are still too near to it to decide. A masterpiece of technique, yes; brimful of erudition, of humour, of a whirl of west-windy exuberance, the west-wind that blows from Ireland. What is its permanent value? I don't know, and nobody knows, but I do not think it is one of the great works of all time, in the sense that the *Odyssey* is, or *Faust*, or *Hamlet*; for I seem to detect a certain poverty of imagination lurking behind the brilliance and the extraordinariness.

These reflections are, perhaps, irrelevant. At that time my admiration for *Ulysses* was ardent and unadulterated, and, as a budding publisher, my dearest ambition was to publish something, anything, by THE GREATEST EXPATRIATE. . . . James Joyce himself, great artist as he is, has never had but one thing to say, and so has been forced into experimentalism by the inner necessity to say it again and again, but in different ways. But how well worth saying it is and what a vast and poluphloisboisterous writer is Joyce ! . . .

210. Wyndham Lewis to A. Symons on *Ulysses*

1929

Letter to A. J. A. Symons. From *The Letters of Wyndham Lewis* (1963), ed. W. K. Rose, p. 188.

Symons had written (p. 188, note 1): '*Tarr* seems to me really to be what *Ulysses* is given the credit for being—the novel of the last 20 years; and it seems to me to hold more of novelty and instructiveness (technically) than any compound of unpunctuated slang' (27 September 1929).

. . .—Meantime it is not the 'unpunctuated' picture of *Ulysses* that I had in mind when we discussed it the other evening—that is merely a device (employed by Schnitzler a very long time ago in a story of his [ed. note: either *Leutnant Gustl* (1901) or *Frau Berta Garlan* (1901)]) for presenting the disordered spouting of the imbecile low-average mind—it has no other justification (and, I agree, it is a pity Joyce has adopted that gibbering as a vehicle for the expression of *everything*, as at present). . . .

211. Adrienne Monnier on *Ulysses* and French public

1929

Extract from 'l'*Ulysse* de Joyce et le public français', *La Gazette des Amis des Livres*, iii, No. 10 (May 1940), 50–64. Translated by Sylvia Beach in *Kenyon Review*, viii (Summer 1946), 430–44 (from which this text is taken), and later appeared in *Kenyon Critics*, edited by John Crowe Ransom (1951), pp. 75–88.

Mlle. Monnier summarizes a few French critics and adds her personal view on the book she helped to translate.

. . . In the first place, I must admit that we had a good appetite for the big book that was set before us. . . . But I must confess that if we read the book all the way through, it was not without a frequent temptation to abandon it on the way. . . .

The first chapter we liked very much—in fact we had read it before as it had appeared in *Commerce*. It is a lively tale told with excellent realism and its poetic passages are surprisingly vivacious. One or two lines about the sea or the old milkwoman strike a new note and enchant us.

Second chapter: it begins to go uphill. Stephen has been our hero, so far; now he resolutely turns his back on us. The tone is no longer that of the narrative, there is not a path, sentences are more and more chopped-up, with references to a lot of things about which we know little or nothing, such as: the history of Ireland; ancient history; philosophy; scholastic theology; early English poetry.

Third chapter: we are completely lost. It is the part that appeared in the *N.R.F.* under the title '*Protée.*' The references are getting more and more obscure—insupportable. And now, Stephen not only turns his back on us, but he murmurs unintelligibly to himself, and we feel we are intruding. The book falls from our hands for the first time. . . . Reading on, we can find no connection whatsoever with the *Odyssey;*

on the other hand, here scrupulously noted are the thoughts and acts of a man. The little choppy sentences with their exaggerated use of allusions—it is the famous 'interior monologue'—still exasperate us a good deal, but we are beginning to get accustomed to this manner now, and at least the main character is no longer bookish, smug Stephen. . . .

Thus we follow this excellent Mr. Bloom in his many comings and goings, as he walks in the streets of Dublin, goes to the bath establishment, a funeral, drops in at a newspaper office—and this continues for five chapters which we find to a certain extent very satisfactory. It is curious, indeed, what pleasure the picturing of familiar things gives us—that ever-known country which we know so well. It is quite lifelike, we say, meaning that we have attempted to recreate and to restore to the Gods their gift to us: Art: the give-and-take with the powers above; admission to the Immortals. . . .

Now we come to an episode that is no less arduous than that of the Cyclops, and if we are going to understand it, we shall need to know something of what the author meant. The 'Oxen of the Sun' takes place in a maternity hospital. Mr. Bloom has come to inquire about Mrs. Purefoy, and finds himself among a number of his friends including Stephen Dedalus.

This episode is composed of a series of parodies of prose from the Anglo-Saxon, down through the 15th, 16th, 17th, 18th, and 19th Centuries to the present day and the latest American slang. The method adopted here is an attempt to represent the development of the embryo by the development of English prose. The following, according to Joyce's own hints, are the writers whose style he has imitated each in turn: Mandeville, Malory, Bunyan, DeFoe, Swift, Sterne, Addison, Goldsmith, Junius, Gibbon, Walpole, Lamb, DeQuincey, Landor, Macaulay, scientific reviews of the first half of the 19th Century, Dickens, Thackeray, Carlyle. This means, as we see, a terrifying virtuosity. If the episode were not, in some places, exceedingly licentious, it would make an excellent school exercise.

The chapters which follow, though they are the most admirable, I think are not really difficult, and one doesn't have to be initiated to enjoy their beauty. The long episode in dramatic form, that takes place in the brothel quarter, and terminates the second part of the work, is, in itself, an undoubted masterpiece. . . .

On reflection, we conclude: that *Ulysses* is a notable literary enterprise. It has many a time been described as a *Summa*, an encyclopedia. All science, every manner and method are here; none of the resources of expression is neglected in the conquest of every possible object of expression. And now, the first criticism that we, as Frenchmen, would be expected to make: does its encyclopedic breath radically affect its artistic value? Rather than a masterpiece, have we not a pile of works that evokes Babel and might suffer the same fate? Certainly we are in the presence of a monster, 'distended, deformed in every direction by a vain emulation of the universe's immensity,' as Jules Romains would say. Adding, 'we forget too often that if life is the material of art, the work of art is in itself a living body. The miracle in art is not so much the absorption as the organization of matter.'

Does the famous 'interior monologue,' for example, constitute an appreciable literary gain? No, on reflection, for if it registers completely the cerebral mechanism, its value is purely a scientific one; if it means a new convention, there is no reason why it should be preferred to ordinary analytic methods. Besides, as M. Auguste Bailly justly observed, the integral psychic unfolding, with its layers of planes, cannot be reduced to the linear transposition to which handwriting obliges us. The interior monologue, as used by Joyce, cannot avoid the arbitrary, and analysis, in freeing the currents that are essential to consciousness, exposes the springs of an act or a feeling still more adequately.

And now another criticism: why the devil have there been established so many useless and haphazard parallels with the *Odyssey*? And why, if the author must have these parallels, has he given us his book with no titles to the chapters, nor preface, nor anything that might serve as a guide? Nobody, to tell the truth, is capable of finding out the meaning with which his book is stuffed: the best works that have been done on the subject are, it must be confessed, almost entirely based on his own suggestions; initiation always comes from himself. We admit the fact that obscurity may be the result, as Valéry says, of 'an accumulation of work,' but not of the deliberate intention to be obscure.

The composition of *Ulysses*, if one thinks it over, seems a maniacal, senseless, teasing thing. It constantly requires, on the part of the reader, an immense effort that is not always rewarded. One gets nothing but riddles, obstacle-jumping, mortification. Life does not treat us otherwise, it is true, but art is opposed to brute nature, according to its own definition, is it not? It belongs to nature, but represents essentially the elements in their order and hierarchy, dispensing harmony and contemplation. . . .

Well, there you are; *Ulysses* is not a work of art, neither is it a success as a novel, nor is it an elevated production. It is not beautiful, clever nor sublime at all. And yet, when this is said, we are uneasy, we feel that we have not rendered a judgment and that this book towers over us and is our judge. . . .

I do not agree with Curtius [No. 212] that Joyce's work is born of the spirit's revolt, but would say that it was born of submission of the spirit. Yes, submission of the spirit to nature, to matter; matter in its philosophical definition as *all physical or mental given facts ready made and worked out subsequently.* . . .

It is also through submission of the spirit to reality, to all physical or mental facts, that he possesses and utilizes so much book learning. With him, the importance lies, not in formulating a personal interpretation of Ideas, of God, which seem to him, perhaps, to defy all reasonable interpretation, but to know what has been expressed about them, what, drawn from their eternal essence, has become incorporated with an act, a doctrine, a tradition or a book, what has become material for observation, experiment, what has begotten the present. He is not concerned with the possibility of truth in a belief, but with the power it may have gained by twenty centuries of accumulated authority. That is a part of the inventory, of the potential evaluation of the resources and reserves of this world. With him, there is a kind of 'unanism' in time, as may be seen even in the plan of *Ulysses.* It is not indeed from Joyce that we are to expect a criticism of systems in force, a shaking of established customs. The purely passive resistance with which he confronts them at times, serves rather as a flying buttress to consolidate them. His mockery, seldom manifested, he reserves for the pretensions of the passing moment,

Yes, contrary to what it seems, he does not seek to reform nor to satirize. He never places himself above what he describes, he doesn't draw up a report showing an unfavorable balance of effort and result, he doesn't 'pile it on,' never blames at all, nor uplifts anything. He is only true, terribly true, and that is indeed the reason why he offends us. . . .

212. Ernst R. Curtius on *Ulysses*

1929

'Technique and Thematic Development of James Joyce', *Neue Schweizer Rundschau*, (January 1929), translated by Eugène Jolas in *transition*, No. 16–17 (June 1929), 310–25 (from which the present text is taken); appeared as *James Joyce und sein Ulysses* (1929).

A lengthy analysis of the technical and thematic development leading through all of Joyce's works to *Ulysses*.

Joyce wants to present an integral reproduction of human experience (external and inner experience). He reproduces the stream of consciousness, without filtrating it logically or ethically.

Here association in its various forms plays a principal role. For the most part Joyce omits to explain the genesis of an association. This is one of the reasons for the difficult comprehensibility of his work. Let us take a significant example. After midnight Bloom and Stephen stop in a cabman's shelter. A knife is lying on the table. Stephen begs Bloom to take it away: '. . . oblige me by taking away that knife. I can't look at the point of it. It reminds me of history.—Mr. Bloom promptly did as suggested and removed the incriminated article, a blunt, horn-handled ordinary knife with nothing particularly Roman or antique about it to the lay eye, observing that the point was the least conspicuous point about it.' This may be found on page 590 of *Ulysses*. Like Bloom, the reader will not be able to understand how the knife could remind Stephen of Roman history. Nor does the author solve this question.

But if we read *Ulysses* over again, we find the key on page 25. Stephen is holding class. Pyrrhus. His death. 'Had Pyrrhus not fallen by a bedlam's hand in Argos or Julius Caesar not been knifed to death.' Here we have the explanation for the genesis of the association 'knife —Roman history.'

Such processes of consciousness in *Ulysses* are simply noted down, taken down in short-hand, whereas in the *Portrait of the Artist as a Young Man* they are still explained. Example: Stephen is talking about philosophy with a priest, who meanwhile is making a fire with candle butts.

[quotes from ch. 5 and explains the chain of associations in this passage and others from *A Portrait*]

These examples might illustrate how a motif, offered conjointly with the reality of external events and mirrored in poetic form (Milton, Shakespeare) is enlarged in the case of Stephen to a symbol of his problems of life: death, misery, sorrow, repentance. For in the last quotation the seadeath-theme is fused with that of repentance: Agenbite of inwit.

Repentance, or rather the torture of conscience, the bit (re-mords, agenbite) of conscience, (inwit) is indeed one of the factors which dominate Stephen's inner life. And Stephen-Joyce calls it by the name of the Chaucerian work of devotion written by Dan Michel of Northgate: *Againbite of Inwit*. Like a musical motif this name emerges again and again, weighty with importance, in *Ulysses*. . . .

We see then that the associative thought formation of Stephen, the pupil of the Jesuits, shows a continual tendency to philosophical-theological speculation. . . . Joyce delineates his characters by presenting the individually differentiated kinds of association processes.

[illustrates this point with Leopold Bloom and Molly Bloom]

[after quoting a passage from p. 364]

This passage is a good example of the fusion of various series of associations; and also the difficulties of Joyce's text. But those difficulties can be solved. The reader must be patient, read the book carefully, until he knows all the psychological key-words. This is not very easy considering the bulk of *Ulysses*. But only those will do justice to the art of Joyce who analyze the complexity of the almost incalculable number of motifs in this work. *Ulysses* is an intellectual puzzle. At first we see only a chaos of irregularly shaped construction stones. But if the reader is patient, he will succeed in putting them together so that they make a magnificent picture. And he will be astonished again and again at the wellnigh infinite multiplicity of the relations and possible combinations.

I have so far spoken only of the reproduction of the stream of consciousness. But just as with the associations, it is also necessary to grasp the events and characters through a synoptic process.

1929: *Ulysses*

[analyses one element, the 'bee-sting' of p. 155 throughout the novel]

We have found already in the analysis of the omphalos complex that birth is a central theme in *Ulysses*. This is true of Stephen as well as Bloom. . . .

We might call the birth-theme the geometric point at which all the ground motives of *Ulysses*, nay, of Joyce's entire intellectual world, intersect.

The complex of the father-son problem proceeds from this point. But also the problem of sexual polarity—the relation between the male and female principle—is in many ways connected with it.

[analyses this latter theme in Molly and Leopold Bloom—Stephen]

The icy coolness of the pure spirit surrounds Stephen like an impenetrable aura. His thinking transcends earth-bound reality in every direction. He would like to shake off history like a nightmare. . . . He broods over the metaphysics of the possible which did not become real (pp. 26, 186, 372, 402). He meditates about the collapse of time and space (pp. 24, 542), and about the mutual relations of these two systems of order (pp. 37, 209).

The relativation of all organized orders is perhaps the most comprehensive intellectual perspective in which we might consider Joyce's work. Relativity of time and space, of the actual and the potential, personality, sexuality, life and death. It is only from out of this ideology that Joyce could compose the Walpurgis-night of the 15th chapter, in which inorganic things speak, in there appear dead men or absent persons, in which animal and human forms, male and female figures are metamorphosed. But also the symbolism and the parodies, in fact really the entire composition of *Ulysses*, rests upon an esthetic relativism.

In order to illustrate this, I should like to analyze the technique of two chapters in *Ulysses*.

[here follows an analysis of the esthetic relativism of chapters 11 and 12]

But each of the eighteen chapters has its own technique, and would therefore require a special analysis. All the chapters, however, have one thing in common—and we have proved it in our analyses—: each passage, each sentence, each fragment of a sentence, is comprehensible only in relation to another one. In this, too, we find the relationship of Joyce's creation with music. We must read *Ulysses* like a score and it

468

could be printed like a score. In order to really understand *Ulysses*, we would have to be conscious of every sentence in the work—a task which is almost impossible. But what is this when measured with the energy of intellectual tensity which the author disposed of in the conception and execution of its totality in order to survey and rivet together the thousand relationships of his steel-girded work. If we look at it from that standpoint alone, *Ulysses* must seem a practically incomparable, gigantic achievement. . . . To which genre shall we ascribe *Ulysses*? The book is a chronicle . . .—novel—drama—epos—satire—parody—summa. It is a new inferno . . . and a new Comédie Humaine . . . Symbolism and scholasticism bring it near to the middle ages. It is the universal and yet particular, the magnificent, cruel, exalting and depressing work of a solitary man, of a proud man—of a genius.

A genius? I put the word down and already it seems to me questionable. . . .

The highest intensity of the mind, the highest degree of inventive and presentational power, do not as yet constitute genius, if the work lacks this enlightening and fructifying power.

Joyce's work comes from the revolt of the spirit and leads to the destruction of the world. With an inexorable logic there appears in Joyce's Walpurgis-night, amid larvae and lemures, the vision of the end of the world. A metaphysical nihilism is the substance of Joyce's work. The world—'macro- and microcosmos'—is founded 'upon the void.'

Joyce's intellectual energy has an intensity of which we can speak only with the highest admiration. His artistic expression dominates all linguistic and compositional forms with a free mastery. In the comic story, the satire, characterisation, invention, he is the peer of all the masters of the literature of the world. His work has the unmistakable sign of the great: inexhaustibility.

And yet, in the final analysis, it remains sterile. This entire wealth of philosophical and theological knowledge, this power of psychological and esthetic analysis, this culture of the mind educated in all the literatures of the world, this ratiocination which is so far above all positivistic platitudes—all this is finally nullified, refutes itself in a world conflagration, in a sprinkling of metallically irridescent flames. What remains? Odor of ashes, horror of death, apostate melancholy, tortures of conscience—Againbite of Inwit.

And yet we should not conclude with this. The complete negation of meaning and being is a catharsis. Only he who has seen the abyss, can hope to arise once more into the spirit's empire of light. The inferno of *Ulysses* is, considered in this way, itself a purgatory. . . . He knows that the ultimate intellectual decisions are metaphysical and religious. His Lucifernian book confronts us with this decision. It is a work of the anti-Christ. It deforms man and the world. The answer to this can be given only by a voice which, like Dante, might set forth the mystery of transfiguration and of the Vita Nova.

213. Jean Cassou, review of French *Ulysses*

1929

'James Joyce, Poète Épique', *Les Nouvelles littéraires* (9 March 1929), n.p.

A review of the French translation of *Ulysses* by Auguste Morel and Stuart Gilbert.

An unparalleled monster has just been born: the French translation of James Joyce's *Ulysses* has appeared . . . One is finally going to be able to approach this work which, like all the decisive events of literary history, is presented under the abrupt aspect of scandal and seems to draw all the technical and moral and seems to put a final point to the secular under-standing which is called poetry. It is the fate, in fact, of works of this type to obstruct all the issues and to appear at first as the sum as well as the failure of all literary exercises and of all literature. To attempt to write and to invent seems in vain after a virtuoso as universal as Joyce has demonstrated the vanity of all styles and all methods. A certain time is needed for the phenomenon to become tame and to be polished and for the categories into which it can be classified to be discovered. . . .

What will be the public reaction to this block of 870 enormous pages in which resound the tumult of all the discordant voices of the conscious and in which the order which presided over their conception only presses very slowly and very far away? Never has art approached nature so closely, or produced a work which resembled it so closely. One advances across its formidable noise as one would do across a world, across the world. And if there is in it something regular and providential, this something is found in the forefront of the work in the same rapport as the law of universal gravitation is found in the fore-front of the universe we inhabit. It is well known that Joyce has sustained his book with the structure of an entire, vast and intelligent symbolism, and even the title of *Ulysses*, the correspondence of certain passages to the *Odyssey*, that also, indicated in one of the last chapters, of certain mysterious and of certain sacrifices of the Old Testament—all these give us some precious keys. But these points in the landscape, and these more or less explicit meanings, do not clarify the work any more than the great sonorous hypotheses to which man attempts to submit the movement of the universe. Nothing is more abstract than Joyce's book. It is a concrete thing, organic, living with its own life and through which one proceeds as among the elements which are still unnamed and which await a name. Its proportions wait to be measured, its principles to be discovered or explained. . . .

Did Joyce compose his work with fragments of living flesh. The abstraction extends, as far as possible, to all submerged by this flood of palpitating nature, this time, this rhythm and this space equal to the time, to the rhythm and to the space which we know in reality. Here nothing is transposed. Our life, our desires, our digestions, our secrets, our boredoms, are found in these pages which live, desire, eat and digest, close and undress, open and give up, are bored and lost as long as the boredom. Words are transformed into things, into animated things: those which the abstract and the ideal contain die smothered under I don't know what biological protuberances, what irresistible vegetable urges which obscure their conventional meaning and bring us into singular physical, tellurian operations. Finally, one embraces rather than understands what Nietzsche understood perhaps by the sense of the earth.

How to retell *Ulysses* after a first reading? How to retell this Dublin day more vast than all the centuries of history, to describe the stellar movements which separate Stephen Dedalus and Leopold Bloom and connect them one to the other? How to retrace the routes through which one crosses the underbrush of all languages, slangs, Middle Ages vocabulary, vocabulary of journalism, spoken style, academic dialogues, unbridled and entirely pure poetry, in order to finally approach the extraordinary interior monologue of Penelope? The most astonishing part of the book, that part in any case which will provoke the greatest number of commentaries is without doubt that of the house of prostitution (Circe); this nocturnal pandemonium where all is phantasmagoria, where the least form scarcely born is soon transformed, where the mind, breathless and dazzled, is drained into a real orgiastic delirium.

The opposition between the plays of style and of the expression of the author and the tempestuous dynamism which carries the work and swells and penetrates all its elements is not one of the less comical effects of Joyce. This buffoonery is of an incalculable grandiosity. There is likewise a singular comic effect in the pedantry of Joyce, pedantry particularly represented through the character of Stephen Dedalus, brought up by the Jesuits, and which extends up until the form of the next to the last chapter (Ithaca), conceived in questions and answers of an invaluable drollery. This pedantry has a precisely scholastic character . . . It is a generous pedantry, entirely different from the pedantries in use today and which, by way of difference from these, drains its object and, consequently, assimilates it to the universal. Thus one feels perpetually brought into contact with something vaster than the small passing preoccupation of the narrative. . . .

And there is also the obscenity spread out through the book and which is indeed the strongest which has ever been dared, taking on a strange grandeur. The author displays it with a particular complaisance in the final chant, the reveries of Bloom's wife, with her husband lying beside her. It is reverie of a baseness, of a coarseness, of a frightening vulgarity, but marked with a sort of comic necessity, so well done that she finishes by carrying the sacred mark of that which could be the discourse of a star. Through a miracle of poetry, *Ulysses* is achieved on pages of the most brutal salacity which produces the highest impression of the sublime.

[a paragraph's discussion of Joyce's 'implacable justice']

. . . One knows that an observer of the heart of the man and of life in society could have placed here the cruel and the bitter. But never, never would he have attained the frightening naturalness of Joyce's narrative and the impression that is left in the Ormond Bar, among these men, of the absence of Bloom. Absences, presences, sentiments of beings, their strengths, their appetites, their indifferent words, their lightness and their obscurity—all is treated as one imagines it would be by Saturn, father of the gods. All returns to its origin, holds there, is silent, then lives its microscopic and infinite life there, vibrates, and is destroyed there.

[article concludes with a word of thanks to the translators]

214. Arnold Bennett on the influence of *Ulysses*

1929

Extract from 'The Progress of the Novel', *The Realist*, No. 1 (April 1929), 9, [3–11].

. . . I think that James Joyce has both invented a new method and enlarged the field of psychology. Joyce is a genuine innovator; the influence of *Ulysses* has already been, and doubtless will in the future be, considerable. But he too is a wall-builder. Also he lacks discipline and decency. I would call him the noble savage of the novel. . . .

215. Marcel Brion, review of *Ulysses*

1929

'*Ulysse*', *La Revue hebdomadaire*, iv (20 April 1929), 365–7.

A review of the French translation of *Ulysses* by Auguste Morel and Stuart Gilbert.

The French translation of the extraordinary work of James Joyce, this *Ulysses* which is one of the most considerable and prodigious monu-ments of modern literature, has been awaited for a long time as a literary event of great importance. This text, whose reading is difficult even for those learned in current English, has disappointed and rebuffed numerous good wills. The language of Joyce is, in effect, an absolutely original creation, with principles one must familiarize himself with, if he wishes to understand this work. I would even say that the linguistic phenomenon is more curious, more new in this Irish writer, because it is affirmed in an ever more complete manner in his recent work which we believe he has not yet completed [*Work in Progress*].

The language of Joyce, then, can be considered both as a key and as an obstacle, according to how one analyzes the methods of composition, or how one collides with it, stopped by the strangely uncommon aspect of the sentences and words.

The subject of *Ulysses* is well known. The scope of this voluminous work . . . is reduced to the minimum, and extends through the duration of eighteen hours.

[a brief paragraph of summary]

I will not develop here the parallel evolution of *Ulysses* and the *Odyssey*, nor the analogies which associate the characters of this book with the heroes of the Homeric epic. These are often extremely subtle and far-fetched, and it is well to leave to the reader the bother of dis-covering them. This task will be for the erudites a sort of refined game, that of finding, for example, in the chapter of the composition of the journal the traits of the Cave of Aeolus, or in the audacious interview of Bloom and the young girls on the beach, an echo of the Nausicaa episode.

If it were necessary to define *Ulysses*, to place it in a literary genre, it could only be said that properly speaking it is a novel. The chapters are linked in a rather arbitrary manner and there truly is an intrigue. I would be more inclined . . . to see in it a sort of immense epic poem, similar not to those of antiquity but of the Middle Ages. There is everything in *Ulysses*: long digressions on the siege of Troy, on the Shakespearean problem, on gynecological medicine, etc. A crowd of characters appear and disappear, reappear elsewhere under different forms or with different tonalities. . . .

In that respect, the analysis of *Ulysses* leads us to see in its construction an order of composition, in all points similar to the musical composition. The development and the interlacing of themes, in particular, evoking irresistibly a sort of immense and complex symphony. It is no longer a question of *Chamber Music*—the title of a volume of poems of Joyce— but of an orchestration extremely powerful and refined. To infer from the musical formation of Joyce and from the influence which the music has over the subjects of *Dubliners*, on the composition of *Ulysses* and the numerous allusions which are made there, the characters of his linguistic invention is very seducing. One speaks frequently of the 'architecture' of *Ulysses*, and the closeness is exact, but it would be more accurate to speak of the 'music.' [Ormond bar episode analysed, briefly, in musical terms.] The result is that the only efficacious way of approaching the first reading of *Ulysses*, the excavatory reading, would be to 'decipher' it, as I have, as a sonata or a fugue.

Because, it is necessary to repeat—whatever dread that may hold for the lazy reader—, it is necessary to reread several times (the number of times varying according to the degree of emotional involvement or of tenacity or of instruction of the reader), this book which cannot ever be entirely exhausted. It would be in vain, then, here to enumerate its contents. Nor would it be wise to speak of the commentaries that the book has called forth: these at the present time would almost fill a library.

[the article concludes with praise for the translators and publisher]

216. Marc Chadourne, comment on *Ulysses*

1929

Extract from 'Un Evénement: *Ulysse*', *La Revue Européene*, No. 5 (May 1929), 1818–33.

This article is a lengthy and comprehensive account of the general outlines of the 'plot' of *Ulysses*, an analysis of each of its episodes, and a comment on its structural, homeric and symbolic features. What is reprinted here is only the general 'placing' of the novel (pp. 1819–20).

. . . *Ulysses* has already appeared to some (as the first witnesses of international criticism have assured us) as a book of the same weight [as *Gargantua et Pentagruel*, *Faust*, etc.], called to mark in literary history a date as decisive, an event as considerable as the Rabelaisian novel marked at the threshold of the Renaissance, which is, in short, the work which it most resembles and which it seems to have had the mission to reproduce with a more intelligible sense, more tragic also, for the new times. Incontestably, *Ulysses* is one of those great books which are gorged with the mass of accumulated knowledge of an epoch, and all blown up with its currents, overflowing genres, categories and normal proportions, expressing and summarizing in its totality the most deaf, the most tellurious effort of the human toward the understanding and the exteriorization of the human. . . .

217. Paul Souday, opinion of *Ulysses*

1929

B. J. Kospoth, 'All Joyce Says Has Been Said Many Times in French, Declares M. Souday . . .', *Chicago Tribune* (European edition) (5 May 1929), 2.

French literary criticism, as represented by M. Paul Souday, famous Parisian arbiter of letters, is not inclined to wax enthusiastic over the ambition of James Joyce and other contemporary writers to create a new language.

'To contend that it is necessary to invent a new vocabulary and a new syntax in order to express new thoughts and sensations, amounts to saying that one cannot play Debussy on the piano because it is an old instrument which was invented long before his time,' M. Souday declared, when interviewed by *The Tribune* yesterday in his home opposite the Institut de France, in the midst of the Left Bank's world of books.

M. Souday enjoys the reputation of being the foremost literary critic in France today; he has known most of the great French writers of the immediate past and his word, as printed in the columns of *Le Temps*, is feared and respected by his contemporaries, however celebrated or successful.

'I have not yet read *Ulysses*,' M. Souday confessed. 'I am told that the French translation, which I have just received, is an excellent piece of work, and I am inclined to believe it, as it has been done by M. Valéry Larbaud, who is a fine writer. Joyce's earlier works, I must confess, did not greatly impress me. It seemed to me as if all he had to say had been said before in France many times.

'As for all this talk about forging a "new language," I can't help thinking it is all what we Frenchmen call a *blague*. However new or revolutionary a writer's ideas may be, he should be able to express them in a clear, classical style. It suffices to express anything, if but wielded aright. . . .'

218. Marcel Thiebaut, review of *Ulysses*

1929

Extract from 'Ulysse et James Joyce', *Revue de Paris*, iii (15 June 1929), 944–58.

This very long article contains a biographical sketch, a summary of the 'plot', a chapter-by-chapter analysis of the Homeric parallels, correspondences, dominant symbols and style; it concludes with this comment (pp. 957–8).

We apologize for having insisted at such length on the analysis of these chapters, but perhaps this work is not absolutely useless if one wants to give an idea of an extraordinarily complex work which has aroused the intense curiosity and has provoked the most lively polemics in every country and in the world of letters.

If, however, this exposé has appeared long, it is certainly far from being complete. Like a cathedral, this neo-medieval work contains an infinite quantity of motifs and symbols, all subtly worked. It is the work of a great lettered man who does not preoccupy himself enough perhaps with the public (all the correspondences which we have indicated one can only discover one by one, after patient research). It dazzles by the luxuriance of the gifts which are deployed there, irritates and enchants in turn. One finds a hundred reasons for pronouncing the word genius and sometimes one has on one's lips the words childishness and mystification. However, the power and the originality of this work, the magnificence and monstrousness are unquestionable. The reading of it is not easy but as soon as it is finished, one feels with some certainty that he will come back to it often, that he will reread it and that he will love it more. When this burlesque and infernal cycle is traversed, most of the novels of today appear pale and cold: that is because there is in Bloom, in Stephen, and all their acolytes a marvelous power of life. And then this singular descent toward the Middle Ages and its symbols is finished by attracting and seducing. One is caught as in an art and a game.

Mr. Joyce today is writing a new work, *Work in Progress*, in a style so difficult that, if one can judge by the extracts published in the reviews, the most cultivated Englishmen themselves will have trouble understanding it. Take care Mr. Joyce. It is not necessary that you write only for yourself. *Ulysses* reveals that there is some tendency in that direction; it is not necessary that one day, separated forever from the crowd, such a sibylline and solitary prophet, he may become the prey only of commentators, who against all the rules of physiology, will succeed in fattening themselves on a rare and wise food which they will not have digested.

219. Brian Penton, comment on the form of the novel

1929

'Note on the Form of the Novel', *London Aphrodite*, No. 6 (July 1929), 435–7 [434–44].

. . . Of course Dreiser does not exhaust the Realistic Novel. Joyce has found and developed possibilities in it and he has tried to vitalise its abstractions by relating every statement directly to the blood of his characters and giving the dimensions a valid existence in the form of the novel. But for all that I cannot help coupling him with Firbank in some discerning subconscious association of their characteristics. What a monstrous fantasy the Dublin of Bloom and Daedalus is. Having recovered from the weariness of climbing the dunghills of Joyce's diarrhœtic irrelevance I look back on Bloom's day and see a rushing nightmare of more than Scheherazadian lunacies. It is an opulent dream. Anything might happen there without surprising me. He conquers the intractable dimensions by lifting Dublin to a new point of relativity where all local values cease to exist. . . .

Joyce tried to be a realist but, such is the inconsequentiality of matter, reality collapsed under his fingers into a million mad distortions beyond the power of Merodack-Jeanneau to conceive. He did, however, create a convincing world; not an abstract of a world but, according to my definition of reality as sensation in the blood, a world I can feel and smell. He creates all the dimensions of a convincing world but, regrettable lack, puts nothing in them. . . . Joyce made a mistake in believing that there was a difference, a distinctive difference, between the mass of sensations that flow through the semiconscious of a bus conductor and those that are the only content of a bishop's mind. To create character, or rather to convey character, he would have to do more than merely set these down in their diffuse incoherence. Selected they might faintly unentertainingly etch the outlines of an individuality, but Joyce scorns artificial selection. Character is vividly developed, however, only by showing the individual's peculiar conscious or semi-conscious effort to justify or ennoble or escape or realise in self-consciousness the processes in the back of the mind.

Joyce has made one definite contribution: he has conclusively reduced all the pretensions of the realistic novel to absurdity. If he had written a parody on it he couldn't have done better than *Ulysses*. He has finally destroyed too any surviving hope in the Zola-Dreiser-Moore-Hardy-Flaubert convention, for at least he was a serious artist trying to make a serious artform of the novel and to say what he had to say with devices not too shockingly artificial. He deserves nearly all the respect we can spare. Instead of borrowing the old matrices Flaubert had left for moulding the fluid material of life into a neat ingot, rounded, smoothed, stamped, and weighed to neat proportions he did try to define a form in which he could show life sprawling in every direction, ceaselessly interlocking, entangling, changing its centre, its balance, scattering, coming together again—eternally blindly yet interactively restless. He did not drive a channel into this turbulence and in tidy but artificial isolation examine life damned momentarily for observation around a central theme and character. He understood the relativity of minds caught in the reverberating consequences of action but impotently divorced on oblique axes of personal equation, and when I revive from the boredom of following Bloom's mind through the minute trivialities of his unexceptional movement I do feel that life has been roaring in my ears. But it is all so vague while I read and doughy.

What I protest against is the consuming dullness of the book, a result immediately of its interminable vomit of irrelevant sensation associations and further back, fundamentally, of Joyce's failure to centralise his material. I applauded him a moment ago for having avoided the convention of centralisation; now I reprove him for the worse fault of having not enough will to bind the material in a dynamic unity without the aid of the convention he discarded. He is helpless. He loses control of the material which washes everywhere about his impotent hands that promised to canute control the sea and rescue the landscape from the abomination of dykes. The cliffs of his formidable pretensions crumble till at last no form remains, only a froth of waters bewildering to look upon. Joyce is the weak man who tried to do a big job. In his heroic debris he deserves applause. . . .

220. S. Foster Damon on *Ulysses* and Dublin

1929

Extracts from 'The Odyssey in Dublin', *Hound and Horn*, iii
(October–December 1929), 7–44. Also appeared, with 'Postscript,
1947', in *James Joyce: Two Decades of Criticism* (1948, 1963), ed.
Seon Givens, pp. 203–42 (from which the present text is extracted).

This book [*Ulysses*] is perhaps the most thoroughgoing literary
attempt to analyze the ancient problem of evil since Goethe's *Faust*.
Joyce is well aware that he risks comparison with Dante and Milton,
among others; he provokes and challenges such comparisons. As one
might guess from the title, his book is a deliberate contrast throughout
with the *Odyssey*. Moreover, George Russell has stated that it is the
Inferno of an unfinished trilogy; so Dante is involved. In the text, the
father-son problem of Hamlet is discussed, and has influenced the plot
radically. To the names of Homer, Dante, and Shakespeare, we must
add that of Blake, for all the modern Irishmen have read him. Probably
Milton suggested the first part, and Goethe's denying spirit, Mephistopheles, may have influenced the conception of Malachi Mulligan.
. . . [pp. 203–4]
　The influence of Dante's *Divine Comedy* is not so obvious, yet I
think that it is perfectly demonstrable. . . . Thus there are three levels
in Dante's scheme of things: the Hell of the exterior world, the Purgatory of his own consciousness, and the Paradise of the supersensuous.
　Joyce uses these three levels, and without some recognition of them
we cannot understand his book. But he does not treat them as spatially
or temporally separate: they are co-existent and interpenetrative. Most
of the characters in the book appear to live wholly in the first plane: the
Hell of this world, where they seem to be very much at home. Those
persons, however, whose minds Joyce lays open for us (as Dante laid
open his own mind to himself), live in Purgatory. They are constantly
suffering for and expiating their sins. Though they do not suspect the

existence of a Paradise, a Paradise exists—the ideal within is the very thing that makes them suffer. But its existence shines clear only for a few brief flashes, which we must discuss later.

Shakespeare could not give Joyce any solution for the problem of evil, for he had no solution. . . .

Ulysses, then is composed of these three elements: the symbolic narrative of the *Odyssey*, the spiritual planes of the *Divine Comedy*, and the psychological problem of *Hamlet*. Homer furnishes the plot, Dante the setting, and Shakespeare the motivation.

But all these things are concentrated into the chance doings of a few people on a particular day in Dublin. . . . [pp. 205–6]

Just as Stravinsky built *Petroushka* out of hand-organ tunes, accordions, dancing gypsies, and cheap waltzes, so Joyce weaves the texture of his book out of vulgar talk and vulgar literature; and he does this with a gusto which beats Cummings and Sandburg, and, indeed, has been generally forgotten since the days of Smollett. Yet there is singularly little fun in all the gusto. We overhear smutty jokes, but they are not addressed to us, as audience. An atrabilious sardonic light lies over the whole city and gives it something of the aspect of a city in a nightmare. Terror, pity, and above all, disgust, assail us on all sides. It seldom occurs to us to laugh.

What particularly depresses us at first is the frankness of the text. Most people manage to scramble through *Ulysses* for the first time by leaping from obscenity to obscenity, like Eliza crossing the ice. One's attention is turned violently upon the very things it normally avoids. We feel as though we were forced, while brushing our teeth, to study the washbowl. But, on second reading, all these things fall into their places. Though Dublin, in 1904, evidently did not have a decent system of American plumbing, we know that these disagreeable facts exist; we remember also that anyone who lives in a big city hears daily all these hitherto unprinted words; and now they fall as flatly upon the eye as they did upon the ear. . . . [p. 208]

But though this is about all that the two main characters in the book do, such peregrinations in squalor are only outward and accidental. They tell almost nothing of the real plot. That lies in those thoughts which choke even mental utterance as they emerge in the mind; here Purgatory begins. On this plane—the consciousness and its borderland—we expiate our sins and work out our salvations.

Here Space and Time themselves are affected by the demands of the profounder world. Simultaneousness of action (notably in the section

'Wandering Rocks') demands disintegration of space: sentences from events elsewhere break through the scene before us; the tap of a blind man's cane punctuates a discourse that is unaware of it; the bell at an auction room starts a bicycle race in another part of the city. Time, however, does not disintegrate; instead, it expands and contracts like an accordian, especially when its inhabitants have been drinking. Enormous reveries of apotheosis and martyrdom intervene between question and answer; and, again, important events take place without being noticed.

In short, Joyce, having recorded a 'slice of life' far more detailed than anything Turgenev or Maupassant ever achieved, and having reached the limit of all 'realism' whatsoever, bends his gaze upon his subject so intensely that the gates of the mental world swing open. The magical eye pierces the object. Realism is transcended. The veil of matter is rent and drawn aside, and the psychological realm—the stage of the true drama—is revealed. . . . [pp. 215–16]

Yet the plot, once unraveled, is simple. It is a study in loneliness. Two carefully contrasted characters (Stephen and Bloom), both desperately unhappy and thoroughly aware of the Hell in which they live, meet at last; but any friendship between them is impossible, because they have nothing in common; and they part again. . . . [p. 221]

Thus Bloom is Ulysses, the wanderer, in search of his home, his wife, his son. But the keynote to his character is not to be found in Homer. For Bloom is the opposite of Stephen; and the opposite of Satan is the Christ—the Christ who constantly sacrifices the selfhood and approaches everything with love and humility, only to be rejected and crucified.

The contrasts between Stephen and Bloom extend to such small details as that Stephen won't bathe, while Bloom's bath is emphasised. Stephen drinks but scarcely eats throughout the book; Bloom eats but takes only two drinks at the disastrous party. Stephen is haunted by his mother's ghost, Bloom by his father's. . . . [pp. 230–1]

There is not much to choose between them, after all, though we may say that Stephen is the more enviable and Bloom the more likeable. But we feel very little envy or liking; instead, we are overwhelmed with a profound pity—a pity that is only heightened when we realize that outside a book they would be unendurable. Joyce has held the scales even between Christ and Satan; he has discovered that neither is the God of This World.

But have Satan and Christ nothing to say to each other when they meet in Hell? Cannot one despair cry to another?

The nighttown scene is the dramatic climax of the book, but the heart of the tragedy lies in the conversation of Stephen and Bloom afterward. . . . [p. 234]

The reveries of Mrs. Bloom, as she also drops off, conclude the book.

These reveries are the climax of nastiness in the book and stamp Marion Bloom as one of the most unpleasant characters in all literature. Her cheap tastes and her illicit loves are paraded at full length. As she unravels the web of that day's weaving, her thoughts wing their ignoble flight through her brain, unchecked by any 'censorship,' naked of any fantasy, with a frankness which outdoes Swift's *Lady's Dressing Room*.

This section of the book forms, however, the epilogue necessary to complete the study of Hell. Stephen and Bloom have both striven to escape; and one might conclude from their ill success that the best way to live is not to struggle but to sink back into the mud and take things as they come. For Marion Bloom is the Woman who Does, with apparently none of the inhibitions that torture her husband and Stephen. A miserable vulgarian, she tastes life at the full. She represents all the immodesty of nature, uncurbed by discipline of love or pain. . . . [pp. 235–6]

And this 'Yes,' with which the book ends, is the affirmation of eternal Paradise of Dream against the 'No' of the temporal Hell which is this world. . . .

After this article was published in the *Hound and Horn* for October–December, 1929, I learned that Joyce's complete list of parallels with the *Odyssey* was secretly being circulated, under the strict stipulation that it should never be used *in toto*. I had not then, nor have I since [i.e. 1947], seen this list. Mr. Edmund Wilson, my informant, indicated several errors I had made; I have corrected these, with a few more of my own discovery, and have omitted an entire paragraph of now useless conjectures. Otherwise, the article is reprinted as it originally appeared.

I am surprised that no critic has followed up the implications of my identification of Bloom and Dedalus with Christ and Satan; indeed, virtually every critic has ignored this identification completely. Yet it is the great clue to the fundamental structure of the book. The surface realism represents the Body; the parallels with Homer, the Mind; and the parallels with sacred history, the Spirit. For beneath the Greek parallels lies another set, which bases the book on Catholic philosophy. . . . [pp. 239–40]

221. Edmond Jaloux on the English novel

1929

Extract from 'Notes sur le roman anglais', *Échanges*, No. 1 (December 1929), 148 [143–8].

In a survey of the English novel, Joyce is the subject of the last paragraph.

With Joyce an entirely new novel is born. Up until now, even in Marcel Proust, the novel was situated almost outside of man in his effort of projection on the world. In Joyce it is entirely in man's head; he has almost no issue with the universe. Such a phenomenon happens for the first time in the history of literature; it is full of incalculable consequences. A single individual in the infinite labyrinth of his little life conducts a formidable epic which resounds uniquely between the walls of his skull. This is the logical outcome, the supreme flower, of this secret anarchy of the solitary which I spoke of earlier. Morally, *Ulysses* is Robinson Crusoe, but Robinson Crusoe dedicated to his deserted island in the midst of the crowd and becoming intoxicated with his abandonment.

222. Padraic Colum assisting with
Work in Progress

1929

'Working with Joyce', *Irish Times* (5 October 1956), 5; (6 October 1956), 7; later included in *Our Friend James Joyce* (1958), by Mary and Padraic Colum, pp. 156–61.

Memoirs of an evening in 1929 when Colum assisted in the typing of *Work in Progress.*

. . . One of the things we conferred about, on the evening when my abstinence was broken down, was the proper person to write an introduction to it (actually *Haveth Childers Everywhere* was published without an introduction) . . . This introduction was a job for an architect, or a mayor, or a building contractor, as it dealt with the building of the city.

It was curious, but it was also characteristic of Joyce, that he believed that anybody so externally-minded as a builder or an administrator would be competent to write an introduction to *Haveth Childers Everywhere.* Joyce actually thought that, on one level anyway, his later work had a public appeal. 'My brandold Dublin lindub, the free, the froh, the frothy freshener'—that is really a good slogan for the Dublin brew, and Joyce was disappointed that the Guinness's did not use it instead of the commonplace 'Guinness is good for you'. . . .

What did my contribution to this production amount to? I typed pages. From time to time I was asked to suggest a word that would be more obscure than the word already there. Joyce would consider my offer, his eyes with their enlarged pupils behind glasses expectant, his face intent, his figure upstanding. 'I can't use it,' was what he would say five times out of six. . . .

I have suggested that in *Finnegans Wake* Joyce's art is akin to the caricaturist's. It presents the human being as an oddity. But its real intention is to be wittily revealing by exaggerating some feature or some tendency. In this connection there comes into my mind the cartoon of the German army marching into the Balkans along the great nose of Ferdinand of Bulgaria. The revelation that was in this caricature depended on the public knowledge of that outsized royal nose. In *Finnegans Wake* a public knowledge of this kind is not available. . . .

For the writing of *Finnegans Wake* Joyce had to have much information. The state of his eyes prevented continuous reading. Now, anyone who has read *Portrait of the Artist* or *Ulysses* knows that he had read immensely: he had a retentive memory besides. However, as he was entering new areas he would have to have new prototypes, and these would have to be supplied with idioms and idiosyncrasies. This meant a mass of reading, and the reading had to be farmed out among his friends.

What they were to read for could not be defined. He did not want any of us to brief him, say, on astronomy or finance. But the name of a star or a term in finance—'sterling' say—would give him something that he needed. At a time later than the time I am speaking of here, he asked me to read *Hudibras*. Evidently this reading was planned, for he had the volumes already—two old-fashioned volumes, I remember. He did not want me to give him incidents or quotations from Butler's poem; for him its interest was in the fact that, like *Don Quixote*, it had two associated and contrasting characters. How was the association and the contrast made? As we went for walks along the streets I would tell him about the doings of the pair. What use he made of the information I never found out.

Because *Finnegans Wake* dealt with night-life, he wanted to know about other books that proceeded from night-life: the *Arabian Nights*, the *Thousand and One Nights*. Of course, he knew that practically all the stories in the collection so named are as much of the daylight as any other collection of stories. Still, the frame-story has to do with nights, and, we are told, part of the collection originated in 'night-walkers' stories'. . . .

488

223. Max Eastman on unintelligibility

1929

'The Cult of Unintelligibility', *Harper's Magazine*, clviii (April 1929), 632, 635 [632–9].

Two tendencies are confused in the literary movement called modernist which ought to be distinguished. They are clearly distinguished for me, because I like one of them and the other I regard as an affliction. But many people see only one tendency here and are puzzled to define it. The tendency that I like might be called the cultivation of pure poetry. The tendency that I do not like I call the cult of unintelligibility.

If you pick up a book by Hart Crane, E. E. Cummings, James Joyce, Gertrude Stein, Edith Sitwell, or any of the 'modernists,' and read a page innocently, I think the first feeling you will have is that the author isn't telling you anything. It may seem that he isn't telling you anything because he doesn't know anything. Or it may seem that he knows something, but he won't tell. In any case he is uncommunicative. He is unfriendly. He seems to be playing by himself, and offering you somewhat incidentally the opportunity to look on. . . .

James Joyce not only polishes the words that he sets in a row, but molds them and fires them in his own oven. From free grammar he has taken a farther step to free etymology. . . . Joyce, in his recent writing, makes up words to suit the whim-chances of a process going on only in his own brain. . . .

[quotes from *Work in Progress, Finnegans Wake*, p. 116]

This literary form also finds its involuntary parallel in the madhouse. There too the inevitable step is taken from free grammar to free etymology. . . . Indeed anyone can imitate both these symptoms by compelling himself to talk faster than he can think or feel. But he cannot imitate them with the rare and various genius of James Joyce. Joyce is equipped for creative etymology as few men ever were. He has a curious and wide learning in languages and their ways; he has a prodigiously

489

fine ear. You feel that he lives in a world of spoken sounds, through which he goes hearing as acutely as a dog goes smelling, that all the riches of his mind are but an ingenious complication of the neural paths from ear to tongue. The goal toward which he seems to be traveling with all this equipment of genius is the creation of a language of his own—a language which might be superior poetically, as Esperanto is practically, to any of the known tongues. It might be immortal—as immortal as the steel shelves of the libraries in which it would rest. But how little it would communicate, and to how few. When it is not a humorous emotion—as praise God it often is—that we enjoy with Joyce in his extreme etymological adventures, what is there that we experience in common with him? A kind of elementary tongue dance, a feeling of the willingness to perform it. This may be enriched a little among the devoted by prolonged hard work with a pile of dictionaries, but in the main the richer values—except the mere value of devotion— will be supplied by the reader's own mind and imagination. They will be accidental and his own. . . .

224. Harry Crosby answers Max Eastman

1929

'Observation Post', *transition*, No. 16–17 (June 1929), 197–204.

An answer to Max Eastman's 'The Cult of Unintelligibility', No. 223.

. . . ∴ Mr. Eastman=Public Opinion. And as Public Opinion despairs, so Mr. Eastman despairs because he finds Crane and Cummings and Joyce unfriendly. He feels they are uncommunicative. He begrudges the fact that they only incidentally allow one to look on not realizing the privilege of being allowed to look on with Crane or Cummings or Joyce. . . .

Let us now pour Irish Whiskey into our glasses and begin by agree-
ing with Mr. Eastman about James Joyce: that Joyce not only polishes
the words which he sets in a row but moulds them and fires them in his
own oven; that from free grammar Joyce, who is equipped for creative
etymology as few men ever were, has taken a further step to free
etymology; that Joyce has a prodigiously fine ear and a fine sense of
humor. But when Mr. Eastman contends that Joyce speaks a private
language whose meaning cannot be conveyed to the reader, when he
contends that the literary form of Joyce's *Work in Progress* finds its
parallel in the madhouse, and when he contends that the only thing the
reader can experience with Joyce is a kind of elementary tongue dance,
I cry NO. The fact that a Stuart Gilbert, a Rodker, a McAlmon, a
MacLeish, a Jolas can follow with intense pleasure the footprints of
Joyce's brain along the path of the ecliptic through the thunderclap,
beyond the marriage according to auspices, beyond the burial of the
dead, into a divine providence (I refer to the four cardinal points of the
book) is sufficient justification, if a justification were necessary, of this
Work and of its Sanity. Are there as many men can follow Einstein?
But because only a handful can follow him should this detract one iota
from his achievement? Ask not the Eagle to descend to the crow but let
us train ourselves to become eagles. Let us spread new wings as if for
flight. . . .

Joyce is the Great Alchemist of the Word, the Paracelsus of Prose,
the Transmuter of metal words into words of gold.

[illustrates this point:]

. . . he removes the letter 'g' from the word 'strength' when he wishes
to show the dying out of desire like the dying out of the colors of a
rainbow; he refers to the days of the week as moanday, tearsday, wails-
day, thumpsetay, frightday, shatterday, Sear of the Law; he speaks of
faith hope and charity as fakes hoax and carrotty; . . . he compares the
smoking of a domestic cocoa-pot to Popocatapetl; when he uses the
word 'kicksheets' he is thinking of Shakespeare's Doll Tearsheets; he
writes ichabod, habakuk, opanoff, uggamyg, hapaxle, gomenon,
ppppfff to describe the gutteral and inarticulate sounds of peasants
engaged in amatory struggles in the dark. . . .

[and quotes extensively from 'The Mookse and the Gripes']

Is this the cult of the unintelligible? Is this a literature of the madhouse? I think that Mr. Eastman will agree with me that it is not and that

this is as pure poetry as man has ever been privileged to read. But whatever he or the public agree or do not agree upon is of small consequence to those who believe as I do that Joyce is the Central Luminary of Modern Literature around which revolve the Fiery Comets of the True Dawn. . . .

225. C. K. Ogden on linguistic experiment

1929

'Extract from 'Literary Experiments', *Psyche*, No. 37 (July 1929), 85–7.

Elsewhere in this issue reference is made to current literary experiments in the creation of neologisms, and the publication of the latest work of the author of *Ulysses* will focus attention on the subject in circulation.

Readers, however, who are unsympathetic to linguistic adventure, and unfamiliar with the milieu from which these particular innovations have emerged, will find themselves at a disadvantage. That such may be encouraged to pause for a few moments before allowing their impatience a free rein, a few suggestions from a standpoint which is primarily orthological may not be out of place. . . . There is the mental factor—the ideology of half a lifetime; the environmental—for James Joyce, though he can write standard English and lives in Paris, is neither an Englishman nor a Parisian; and the experimental—the factor of symbolic innovation. Each may be noticed in turn.

The mental factor in the case of Mr. Joyce is not more of an obstacle than has been surmounted by readers of many of his contemporaries. . . .

Then there is Dublin. Some of us failed to be born and bred on the banks of the Liffey, and to that extent we are at a disadvantage in interpreting some of Mr. Joyce's basic symbols. . . . His *pietas* is so transparent that the effort required to shoulder this load need not be greater than we made in our childhood in the interests of old Anchises.

When, however, we turn from the environmental to the experimental, there yawns a greater gulf. Many who find themselves bored by local lore are overcome by absolute inertia when urged to the acquisition of new linguistic tricks after the age of twenty-one. . . .

If we separate the functions of language into four main divisions—Sense, Feeling, Tone and Intention—it is clear that Mr. Joyce's neologisms chiefly provide blends of the three last. He is not concerned, as is the scientist, with the creation of new names, so much as with the development of fresh emotive and invective gestures. . . .

Mr. Joyce's symbolic condensation, in fact, corresponds closely enough with his theory of Time—a theory, incidentally, responsible for the rattle of Lewis-guns which still resounds through 'The Mookse and the Gripes'. The intensive, compressive, reverberative infixation; the sly, meaty, oneiric logorrhoea, polymathic, polyperverse; even the clangorous calembour, irresponsible and irrepressible, all conjure us to penetrate the night mind of man, that kaleidoscopic recamera of an hypothecated Unconscious, jolted by some logophilous Birth-trauma into chronic serial extension. . . .

226. Arnold Bennett on the oddest novel

1929

'Books and Persons: The Oddest Novel Ever Written', *Evening Standard* (8 August 1929), 7.

On the Continent, the most *discussed* English author is James Joyce. And perhaps rightly so. *The Dubliners* and *Portrait of the Artist as a Young Man* both show genius. *Ulysses* contains the grossest obscenity. It may not be a great whole. But it is a work distinguished by much greatness and still more originality. It has pages which no novelist in any country has ever surpassed. Its influence has been and is enormous.

And now after five years of hard labour, it has been integrally translated in French by Auguste Morel and Stuart Gilbert. That the translation has been revised from start to finish by Valéry Larbaud is a sufficient guarantee, not merely of the excellence of the translation but of the artistic value of the work. . . .

Miss Beach has just published in English, a book by a dozen more or less young authors about Joyce's new and still unfinished novel at present provisionally called *Work in Progress* The title of the explanatory volume is too absurd to be quoted [i.e. *Our Exagmination* by Samuel Beckett and others]. And some of the contents are absurd. On the other hand some of the contents are not. Mr. Stuart Gilbert and Mr. John Rodker write well enough about it to compel respect for it.

Work in Progress is understood to be a novel about heroes. It may be. I read (I should say, I examined) various excerpts from it when portions of the book appeared serially in *Transition*, and I must say that I haven't the least idea what the story is about.

For this work James Joyce has invented, concocted, and conjured up a sort of superportmanteau language of his own. He has obviously had a vision of the possible evolution of the English tongue. None but a man of very remarkable gifts of imagination and pure brain could have had such a vision. It does immense credit to his brain and his imagination. But little to his commonsense.

The more you study his language (by the light of Stuart Gilbert's essay) the more you are impressed by the man's learning, ingenuity, and astounding capacity for multiple allusiveness.

Anyone who is prepared to make the reading of James Joyce's new, incomplete book a life's career, and who has the lexicographical skill to construct a James Joyce encyclopædic dictionary might conceivably derive emotional benefit from *Work in Progress*, and might procure the same benefit for at most a dozen other bizarre human beings. Apart from such thirteen human beings, *Work in Progress* will not be read, because it cannot be read by any individual normally constituted. *Ulysses* has had many respectable imitators.

Work in Progress will never be respectably imitated. I think it ought to rank as the oddest novel written. It will probably be unique.

If James Joyce is content with a possible thirteen readers, that is his affair and his alone. But to me the entire business is queer in a high degree. Indeed I do not hesitate to give my opinion that James Joyce has been culpably wasting his time (and other people's), and his genius. Also I regard it as a bad sign that an unfinished work should be the subject of an exegetical volume (200 pages) by twelve ardent disciples. Of ardent disciples the sane person should always beware. I recommend the discipular book solely to those with a passion for the curiosities of literature. . . .

227. C. Giedion-Welcker on Joyce's experiment

1929

'Ein Sprachliches Experiment von James Joyce', *Neue Schweizer Rundschau*, xxii, Heft 9 (September 1929), 660–71. Translated by Eugène Jolas in *transition*, No. 19–20 (June 1930), 174–83. Later appeared in *In Memoriam James Joyce* (1941), ed. Carola Giedion-Welcker, pp. 37–49 (from which the present text is taken).

The latest Joyce who for the time being has appeared only in fragments in the American magazine *Transition* (Paris) under the deeply significant title of *Work in Progress* makes upon the preparedness and cooperation of the reader much greater demands than did *Ulysses* in 1922.

In *Ulysses* the problem was to penetrate a complicated intellectual structure and above all to illuminate it mentally. Here the entrance to the intellectual content seems first of all deformed by a new and difficult composition and linguistic frame. Form and contents, more-over, interpenetrate each other much more intensely, are transposed onto a remote abstract plane. . . . Poetry is for Joyce the linguistic-sound expression of mental extracts distilled to their utmost. This does not mean, as generally in modern contemporary literature, discovering a new nuance of an established colloquial language: Joyce creates on principle an entirely changed linguistic medium. Language is to him a means for composition, association and symbolisation. By emphasizing the acoustic phenomenon (the book, therefore, can only be understood by reading it aloud) we are led into a completely new world of sound associations that do not stop within the English language, but have their effect internationally.

To be able to penetrate these problems in composition we require a knowledge of the substance. The theme? Not a special one. The characters? None specially established and delimited. A great intellectual scaffolding in which the details, characters and events, are interchangeable.

The intellectual programme of Giambattista Vico, with whose ideology Joyce has intensely occupied himself in the last few years 'to write an eternal, ideal history, in accordance with which the history of all peoples runs'—one would like to place as a motto over the whole work. The Joycian history of humanity does not, of course, develop at one time, in a chronological sequence, but is composed of many motley-colored mosaics and projected onto an ideal plane where only intellectual and linguistic relations are valid. The enchainment occurs ideologically, not chronologically. Just as humanity is not formed by closed unities; but is embodied by a great human ensemble picture. Joyce is interested as little in a precise situation of generations as in the limitations of human or geographical speciality. This means: Temporal strata and spatial frontiers are eliminated: Neither beginning nor end. A great circular course. . . .

To uncover the essential identity of everything human under the variety of external phenomena is the basic point. Primitive questions are asked of mankind; Vico calls them 'the true motives which have been handed down through the long course of time and the change of languages and morals hidden under poetry'. What does Joyce do? He delves into the great vessel of history, saga, poetry, and finds there, in spite of different time and space illumination, basic characteristics of human existence.

In the final analysis everything circles around the great primitive instincts of power, procreation and nutrition. Personified in giant mountain-men who lie on flowery meadows, who sleep, love, eat; who whisper in echo many things of deep meaning. The description of their bodily get-ups approaches the phantastic.

Historic, legendary, biblical situation surge up. Continuous leitmotives: power, fall, love, death, sleep, nutrition, fight and quiet are not, as in *Ulysses*, compressed into a closed frame: a day in Dublin; so and so many persons acting on that day, with their associative circles backward and forward; thus after all a basis, a time-space development. But here: ever recurring ideas dipped into eternally changing, changeable husks, and projected into an absolutely unreal sphere. An all-time, an all-space, a logical *unanimism*. With giant boots Joyce strides through countries, through centuries, through intellectual dimensions. . . .

Man represents in the world the principle of power. Mythos and history furnish the material. Strength (as their basis eating, drinking, sleeping) and sexuality are the primitive forms of his existence. His cosmic symbol is the mountain. Beside poetic inventions Shem, Shaun, Jaun (Juan), Yawn, etc. there are historic characters: Napoleon, Wellington, Gladstone; also legendary ones: Finn Macool; also biblical ones: Adam, Noah; Michael, Lucifer. As pan-heroic vessel: Humphry Chimpden Earwicker, H. C. E. 'Here comes everybody. Homo capite erectus. Hear, calls, everywhair'. As a chemical joke: H_2CE_3. The physical description of this 'clean-minded giant' who is considered a white caterpillar by his calumniators, goes into the grotesque-pre-historic: 'Bulldog boots, walrus moustaches' etc. . . .

As complementary color to the massive-heroic type of virility (deep blue) a feminine fluid serpentines under numberless names and shades through the book. This many-headed complete phenomenon composes itself out of movement, vivacity, playfulness, garrulity, eroticism, maternity, love of clothes, fantasy, caprice, irrationality. As cosmic symbol: The River. Many river and feminine names, invented ones and those that existed and exist, symbolize this. Eva, Esther, Astarte, Isolde, Venus temptatrix, Pipette, Nuvoletta, Stella etc. As her great collective name: Anna Livia Plurabelle. 'Anna was. Livia is, Plurabell's to be'. . . .

Behind a thousand-fold variety of nuances there gleam forth always the same basic substances. This image: woman, child, hetera (in this sense she is also circumscribed: Pluhurabelle), mother, the stream is con-centrated in a chapter published by Crosby Gaige in a special edition in New York: *Anna Livia Plurabelle*. It is certainly the most transparent and artistically the most concentrated of all the fragments published so far. . . .

[an account of the *Anna Livia Plurabelle* section (pp. 196–216) follows here]

What Joyce puts here is a great interpenetration of the unique and the general, of low banality and ultimate symbol. Mythos? Meta-morphosis? At any rate: Out of the transitory gossip of the washer-women there grows a poetic vision which is grasped with final formal intensity and sensitivity.

For that which Joyce does now lies—as we said in the beginning—above all in a linguistic revitalisation. That is attempted from the rational and intuitive side. Once through an international and social process of

interpenetration, then through resuscitation and bringing into relationships of the subconscious and associative life which is hidden in the
linguistic. . . . In order to compress all human matter in its every
aspect into the word, the whole world must linguistically yield all its
saps. Joyce acts as an international word-mixer.

Thus *Work in Progress* becomes a fantastic, individually formed
esperanto. With that, of course, also (because subjectively) a cryto-
graphy comprehensible for many only with difficulty. Therein lies a
question as to its justification for existence which one has to ask of a bold
literary experiment of genius in this respect.

What in fact happens to the word as used by Joyce? . . .

The problems which Joyce posits thus in a literary sense stand, in
spite of personal and temporal coloring, generally in mental contact
with the past. . . .

Joyce proceeds from the word-sound. Therefore his english is
written mostly as it is spoken. Hearing is a primary thing for the
language; not the sight of the letters. The meaning of the text is also
comprehensible only through reading aloud. The meaning is always
multi-colored. Just as the word is the acoustic result of a thought, so the
sound-associations resolve again new ideas and word pictures. . . .

The glittering multi-significance of a sound, its mental complication
and flux is crystallized by Joyce sometimes in a one-letter amalgamation.
If he says about Shaun's speeches: 'How mielodorous is thy bel chant'
we find that in the place of the word melodious this deformed word is
chosen because still new associations are brought into it: miel (honey)
odorous; thus olfactory and odorous nerves are brought into play. The
basic word floats of course still in the neologism. In the fable of the
Ondt and Gracehoper he does not write conventionally 'grasshopper'. For
the description of the grasshopper's character Joyce uses this change. . . .

The key-note of the whole is humorous, jocular mocking. The
reader should smile and laugh. A playful 'tomfoolery' rich in allusions
behind the external nonsense of which there lies hidden a deeper meaning. The Irish race has not produced in Joyce the only present and
historic representative of this attitude. For between Swift's *Gulliver* and
Work in Progress there exists a mental and climatic relationship. Puns,
deformations of proverbs, witty, timely allusions, utopian prophesies,
the giving up of all normal measures and especially the delving into an
unreal dream-and-fable-land is common to both.

The entire atmosphere of *Work in Progress* is *nocturnal* and dreamlike.
It wells out of the sphere of the subconscious. Its laws play in subterra-

nean zones. 'Roll away the reel world', (reel means optic: jigging, and phonetic: real). Nor have we here the feeling that an individual man is speaking, but as if a sound came from some giant mental vessel. . . .

That which Joyce—judging from the fragments published up to now—presents, is still today a product of the laboratory. That is, the transformation into small coin, its expansion to the broad public cannot be gauged as yet. Joyce himself expresses the situation jocularly like this: 'For that is what papyr is meed of, made of, hides and hints and misses in print. Till we finally (though not yet endlike) meet with Mister Typus.' Generally artistically we stand perhaps at a period, when an all-embracing synthesis is still premature, which calls above all for an offensive in detail, for new roads of recognition which some day will be united organically into a whole.

In this way Joyce interests us especially as an experimentor of linguistic possibilities of expression. *Work in Progress* is—as the title indicates—not a closed solution, but an evolutionary process. But here positively tangible: the productive controversy with the basic elements of the poetic material: language, today still a petrified and exhausted form. Through the free association of word and thought, Joyce changes it from a carrier of mental content, become more or less passive, into an actively functioning mediator of the ideological. . . . Joyce sometimes, with his manifold associations, presses whole pages into a sentence or into a word, while others would need these same pages for the description of their material. But the time gained by it is likely to be a fictitious one, for the reading of these cablegrams requires from the patient reader probably more work-hours than any other contemporary european literature.

Whether the burden in this is an absolute or a relative one only time can tell. . . .

But after all we have said so far, we are probably justified in placing Joyce in a central radio station rather than in an isolated tower of ivory.

Let us also recall here the realisation of futuristic attempts through technique. When Marinetti in 1911, for the first time, presented to our retina made weary by static optics his new dynamic system, it seemed to us a purely esoteric affair. Today almost every cinema of the suburbs realizes those 'optic' utopias.

Thus 'Utopia' becomes a standard, as soon as basic elements are contained in it which have a survival value. Joyce seems to stand in universal connection with the vitality of present and past. For this reason a good deal of the future will probably belong to him. . . .

228. Michael Stuart on *Work in Progress*

1929

'Joyce after *Ulysses*', *This Quarter*, ii (October–December 1929),
242–5.

Commentators on *Work in Progress* have sometimes spoken as if the
principal characteristic of the 'polyhedron script' were philosophical or
linguistic, tending, as systems of thought or classifications always do, to
what is abstract and finite. A certain philosophy, something of the
essence, the *quidditas*, of Vico, Bruno and Scholasticism is, indeed, an
element in the latest creation of Joyce:— that the work shall lead from
preoccupations of the moment to generalizations is important. That it
shall delight and amuse us is of greater importance: and a broad, vigorous
humour, touching the homely aspects of life it must be too—the
laughter of a curiously familiar Dublin race inhabiting a dream-city of
Dublin. . . . Nor can the more than Rabelaisian ribaldry suggested or
expressed on nearly every page of the work with the pagan frankness of
a soul that has rediscovered for itself the delights of 'nature at her
naturalest' do any other than sustain the general humorous effect of
puns, spoonerisms, calembours, polyglotal word-compounds, and all
the variety of verbal inventions calculated to evoke laughter. . . .
Joyce, limited by the exigencies of the dream world where neither
deliberate logic nor memory of the past dream-actions exists must have
his recourse to the word, the multi-colored, age-wise, perennially
youthful interpreter of the spirit, the strangest of creatures, the word,
'as cunningly hidden in its maze of confused drapery as a fieldmouse in
a nest of coloured ribbons.'

And it is this mysterious property of the word to body itself forth at
certain moments into a creature of almost sentient powers (as when in
war-time the knowledge of the password may prove a matter of life or
death, or the answer 'I do' before the marriage altar may signify a lifetime of happiness or unhappiness or the plea before the bar of justice
'guilty or not guilty' may mean imprisonment or freedom, and perhaps,

more significant than any of these instances, the potency of the true word, text, or hymn to an intensely religious people like the Egyptians in their *Book of the Dead* so often referred to in 'The Ondt and Grace-hoper' upon which depended life everlasting or doom),—it is this power of the word to become for the mind of man a bridge, a mediator, divine reason, protector, or saviour which is the secret seed of this song of songs to the Logos, *Work in Progress*. . . .

And it should be obvious now in what sense it is just to say that the 'Anna Livia Plurabelle' Fragment is not a description of a river, but the River Liffey, palpitating with the 'chittering waters', 'liffeying waters', and the sense too in which 'The Ondt And The Gracehoper' Fable is not a description of insects but an airy, buzzing, fluttering word-insect, 'Floh and Luse and Bienie and Vespatilla'. . . . And if we remember that as in the case of the novel or any other work of fiction the problem of setting the limits of the 'story' in time and space must face the author we shall soon realize that since there is no 'beginning' nor 'end' to universal history, the usual straight line construction of a novel like *Ulysses* is inadequate to the purpose. . . .

To fit this universal 'history' with its *quasi* circular structure, 'the lubricitous conjugation of the last with the first', suggesting the infinite into a finite frame, since humanity is of time and space and the 'story' *must* have a beginning and an end, the author shall set about to rummage among philosophical writers with their theories of history and discover in Vico's *Scienza Nuova* and in the dialogues of Bruno certain specula-tions on the origins of the world and human society which shall furnish him with the frame of the 'finite story' in the four cardinal ideas of the Neapolitan, 'the lightning look, the birding cry, awe from the grave, overflowing on the times' and in the ideas of Bruno approximating the doctrines of his teacher that the universe is infinite and everywhere the same; that its centre is everywhere, *ubique totum,* and nowhere, and that it is all centre or all circumference. . . .

The author's next problem must be the creation of a method of character construction to give the work the proposed universal nature. . .

In the significance of numbers to the human mind the Dubliner finds a clue for the creation of a system of number–character–entities. History furnishes abundant material to crowd a great part of racial experience even within the limited classification of the number entities selected by the author of *Tales Told of Shem and Shaun*. . . .

It should be noted perhaps, that the ideal reader for whom the author labors is not a unilingual, insular being, but rather that mythical creature who, tempted by a few lucid pages, may continue in the pursuit of unlocking the secret of this, linguistically, the most difficult work extant. . . .

. . . Perhaps, too, the Dubliner writes his 'history' not alone for the applause of his contemporaries, since according to the modern chronicler's theory, certain words, symbols, and poetic vagaries are like the flaming stars which are invisible to the eye, because their light has not yet reached the earth. . . . '*Habes aures et num videbis?*' . . .

TALES TOLD OF SHEM & SHAUN

August 1929

---

229. Editorial, *New York Times*

23 August 1929, 20

Some fragments of another work of genius which Mr. James Joyce is slowly perfecting have been published in London. They show him as a fashioner or creator and transformer of language. He continues on a great scale the method of Lewis Carroll. Not infrequently he employs the metathesis system which the Oxford undergraduates so long and affectionately attributed to Dr. Spooner. But his new strange tongue is not the perfume and suppliance of a moment. It is constant, elaborate, voluminous. The beginner has no trouble with such simplicities as 'weight a momentum'; but there must be at least 160 seconds in a minute before we can read at sight a passage like this, cited by the *Spectator* and apparently relating to the operation of describing 'an aquillitoral dryangle on a given strayed line'. The theme is easy, but some of the language surprises by himself. . . .

[quotes from p. 296]

If we may say so without irreverence, this looks sleazy, broken, interrupted by surrenders to intelligibility. Compare it with the first stanza of 'Jabberwocky':

> 'Twas brillig, and the slithy toves
>   Did gyre and gimble in the wabe;
> All mimsy were the borogoves,
>   And the mome raths outgrabe

Under so worthy a master, Mr. Joyce's studies ought to be as fruitful as his terminology is satisfactory. If he could but combine with that

the mystic and mighty thought which Miss Gertrude Stein has manifested in such a classic as 'Certainly the union of oxygen with ostriches
is not that of a taught tracer,' the ultimate form would be married to
the ultimate content. Then nothing but conservatism and decline could
be expected of 'revolutionary' literature. Mr. Joyce's purpose is not
humor. His is the deep melancholy common to inveterate readers and
writers. All words look shabby or sick to him. He hates them. He must
have a new lot. To weary word-'slingers' the product of his Paris
factory may bring encouragement and hope.

The *Congressional Record*, translated into Jabberwocky-Joycese,
would double its circulation in a week. . . .

230. Michael Stuart on the sublime

1929

Extract from 'The Dubliner and his Dowdili (A Note on the
Sublime)', *transition*, No. 18 (November 1929), 152–61.

Work in Progress is the ultimate pole in that tendency to objectivity
in European letters which seeks to approach the condition of an element
of nature recording like the winds upon the rocks and the trees the
history of the human soul in its progress through the world. To establish
a field of reference between the Dubliner's creation and that broader
field of literature which influenced it and which in turn must suffer to
be influenced by that revaluation of values which every new work of
art imposes upon the past it is vital to note its limitations, if the 'graph'
is to be considered for something more than another 'Ayenbite of
Inwit.' The critic's office, the truism may be repeated by arrangement
with the publishers, is to bring into play those ideas which will aid the
'common reader' to a comprehension of the work itself, its relation to
literature as a whole of which it is both the child and the parent, and

perhaps, also, to consider the work in the light of general ideas to which literature more nearly than other arts must always be related.

If we are not overawed by the majesty of words and apply to 'Work in Progess' the critical canon contained in the mock Joycean Latinity of the Geometrical Fragment which echoes in part Bruno's belief 'that everything can only come to a knowledge of itself through a contrast with its opposite'—'quodlibet sese ipsum per aliudpiam agnoscere contrarium', we shall but follow the author's own guiding principle for the illumination of his dream-world, a principle holding true as well in other categories than literature. This criticism by contrast will justify itself largely on the ground of aiding us to understand what the work is by showing us first what it is not. . . .

Something of a strange, out of the world sense is communicated by the work as a whole, 'Metamnisia was all sooneone coloroform bruen,' the effect of a humanity abiding in a familiar planet, and yet, in some respects, if we but look at these shades attentively, so unlike anything found among other living or imaginery creatures. . . .

To the readers of '*Vera Historia*,' the Latin lyricists, Boccacio, yes, and the juvenile masterpiece *Alice in Wonderland* the non-ethical world of 'Work in Progress', ringing with laughter, may prove a welcome refuge from the too facile literature of a restless age brimful with the struggles, complexes, conflicts of a low order. And the lovers of the sublime in literature may find there something to their taste also. . . .

'Sublimity is an echo of the inward greatness of the soul.' Attentive readers of the 'Mookse and the Gripes' will realize something of the great-heartedness of the author who notwithstanding the spurns of the unworthy seeks to reconcile the warring element in human nature in his fable. The artist's creed which laughs both at dogma and at heresy may prove, after all, the highest form of wisdom, since it is founded at the basis upon sentiment. And perhaps in that millenium where the 'political man' and the 'economic man' shall be regarded in the same light as our shadowy ancestors of the paleolithic or Magdalenian periods, and Dublin discovers something or someone of Dublin greater than Phoenix Park, Wellington Monument, or Guiness's Brewery, and literature and the arts achieve in the eyes of 'homo Vulgaris' to the dignity of 'politics' or 'business' Joyce's 'joyicity' like Oberon's mid-summer madness shall be known at something of its true worth. . . .

231. Hamish Miles, review, *Criterion*

October 1930, x, No. 38, 188–92

Extract from a review of Stuart Gilbert's *James Joyce's Ulysses, Anna Livia Plurabelle, Tales Told of Shem and Shaun, and Haveth Childers Everywhere.*

Portrait of the Artist left the reader with a sense of a prologue; *Ulysses* followed with an air of finality. And then? At the moment of writing, Mr. Joyce's *Work in Progress* remains a question-mark. Here are three publishers, offering three fragments from this at prices ranging from one shilling to four guineas; but nothing is vouchsafed us regarding the length or shape or subject of the complete work. *Ulysses* suffered in some ways from its publication in unrelated fragments in the old *Little Review* days; *Work in Progress* probably suffers more from its present mode of publication, in these volumes or in the late *transition*, as we are evidently to move there in a less tangible world than Dublin or Mr. Bloom's mind. But there is enough to show that a work of curious complexity and erudition is in the making, capable of surprising musical effects and, perhaps, that *hallucination des mots* after which Rimbaud felt. There is no escaping the fact that the understanding of this work will call for immense reserves of patience, and unprovided with the theme and sequence of the whole, one cannot as yet begin to say whether or not the effort will repay one except in the possible benefits to be derived from sheer verbal athletics. Mr. Gilbert, it may be recalled, has published a brief commentary on the word-structures employed in one paragraph; without being really exhaustive, the explanatory notes occupy two-and-a-half times the space of the text selected. And, unless, I am mistaken, this passage is comparatively matter-of-fact alongside passages in, say, *Haveth Childers Everywhere*. If *Ulysses*, as some hold, shows Mr. Joyce to be essentially a writers' writer, its successor looks like turning him into a don's writer. But these various fragments have plenty of passages which show Mr. Joyce's extreme sensitivity in musical performance upon words. The closing page of *Anna Livia Plurabelle,* with the two voices calling faintly in the riverside dusk, is by now almost an anthology piece of the loyal vanguard; earlier comes a passage which remains in one's memory, where the Liffey is a younger stream. . . .

[quotes from p. 204]

But criticism in detail upon these fragments can only be of a tentative nature. Until *Work in Progress* is available as a whole, judgment must stand in suspense. . . .

232. Unsigned review, *Saturday Review*

10 December 1932, cliv, 629

These 'fragments from *Work in Progress*,' as Mr. Joyce's next book has been known for the past eight years or so, show the author of *Ulysses* to be, or to be posing as, stark, staring mad.

Ulysses had importance: that, at least, conferred by being longer than a telephone directory. It had the novelty of introducing the latrine to the drawingroom. However wearisome its tawdry belching, it was intelligible. The *Work in Progress*, if the fragments now offered are fair specimens, is not. This is not, or·perhaps rather, not only because we are what Mr. Joyce's numerous admirers regard as Philistine dunces, but because the words in which it is written have no meaning, save conceivably to the author himself. And for a human to chatter words that have no meaning to others is a sign of madness. It may be retorted that Mr. Joyce's ideas are so recondite and so, in the strictest sense, unutterable, that he has felt constrained to invent a new language wherein to express them. But this again is only another way of saying that he is mad, for vanity so overweening is madness. To make clear that this judgment does not come from personal prejudice or mere bumptiousness, it is only necessary to quote from the book. Here is one typical passage. 'The whool of the whaal in the wheel of the whorl of the Boubou from Bourneum has thus come to taon!' Here is another.

'Hic sor a stone, singularly illud, and on hoc stone Seter satt huc sate which it fitted quite poposterously and by acclammation to its fullest justotoryum and whereupon with his unfallable encyclicling upom his alloilable diupetriark of the wouest,' and so on till the end of the sentence half a page later.

'Twas brillig. and the slithy toves. . . .'

Yes, we know. But Lewis Carroll was writing nonsense. Mr. Joyce apes sense. And nonsense apeing sense is madness. . . .

233. D. G. Bridson, review, *New English Weekly*

5 January 1933, 281–2

This is the third selection of Mr. Joyce's *Work in Progress* to be published in this country. First of all came *Anna Livia Plurabelle*, which is probably the best of the three. Then came *Haveth Childers Everywhere*, which has the appearance of being slightly more ambiguous. Now we have *Two Tales of Shem and Shaun*, which are nearer, perhaps, to the first than to the second.

A great deal has been said about Mr. Joyce's later work, and a great deal more has probably been written. The number of honest folk who regard him as a genial-minded maniac, however, must still be far in excess of the number who do not. Yet it is surely time that an intelligent interest be taken in unusual work which has been published for an odd five years. . . . The obvious fact is that 'Work in Progress' (at least, those fragments of it which have appeared in England) should not be referred, as literature, to any other published literature at all. The approach to its appreciation should be rather through its music than through its sense.

But before proceeding to any consideration of its musical qualities it were advisable to consider Joyce's aim in writing the book in the first place. And it must here be stated that his expressed wish is that 'what I am doing should not be judged until it is completed.' But it is also permissible to quote his further remark that the fragments have 'a certain independent life of their own.' Accordingly it seems fair to suppose that so long as we do not concern ourselves with the contributory qualities of the fragments, but are rather content to examine them for the qualities common to every page of them published thus far, we shall be on ground which is fairly safe. The quality most obviously apparent is a seeming obscurity. A first reading of the opening sentence of 'The Mookse and the Gripes,' for instance, may suggest that the sentence is wholly devoid of meaning.—'Eins within a space and a weary wide space it wast ere wohned a Mookse.' But if the meaning is not at once apparent, it is there nevertheless. A child, indeed, would probably find little or no difficulty in the matter: what it did not understand, it would certainly take for granted. If the sentence is anyway apprehensible, it most obviously is possessed of a meaning. Now precisely how long it took Mr. Joyce to twist his fifteen words to their final shape, we do not know. But twenty pages of similar work, he assures us, employed him for twelve hundred hours. The full understanding (taking understanding to mean a coincidence of the reader's evoked flow of ideas with that of the author considering his work) would occupy the reader for the best part of his life. Every word, as a matter of fact, would have to be assessed on a varying number of planes of meaning,—the number sometimes being as many as ten or a dozen. Mr. Joyce's explanation of a typical phrase, as related by Mr. Sisley Huddleston, is this. 'His commentary was illuminating. I have no desire to misrepresent him, but as I remember he would take such a phrase as "Phœnix culpa," and would then explain. Now here you have a suggestion of *felix culpa*—the blessed sin of the early Church fathers—that is to say, the downfall of Adam and Eve which brought Christ into the world; and you have the suggestion, not only of the Garden of Eden, but of Phœnix Park in Dublin, and of Irish history with its wrongs and crimes, and you have the eternal way of a man with a maid, and you have . . .' Let that suffice for an explanation of Fiendish Park, muddy chrushmess, the Mookse and the Gripes, and the Ondt and the Gracehoper. The fact remains, that the closer the application to the text, the more and more words appear in their own original sense,— each with more rings of association than there are about Saturn. But the book holds more than acrostics, and the reader is well advised to disregard the meaning entirely for a while. That the 'aim' of the work is a process of enlarging and revitalising the language, we have the author's assurance. But the work is more than a mine for philologists.

Gerard Manly Hopkins once remarked, it will be remembered, that however awkward his verse might appear, it had only to be read with the ear to be appreciated. And the fact that Mr. Joyce has recorded a reading of the last four pages of *Anna Livia Plurabelle* is significant. To many, indeed, the recent broadcasting of the record brought an understanding of the work which they never before imagined possible. For whatever the value of his telescoped words, his associated ideas, his parallel planes of meaning,—the fact remains that the most important feature of Mr. Joyce's recent prose for the plain reader is its superb musical cadence.

For a full enjoyment of the *Two Tales*, then, the reader must empty his mind of all prejudice and opinion, reading the book for the first time impersonally. His first reading will at least supply him with a proper pronunciation (and this is important) for such unusual words as archunsitslike, infairioriboos, ishallassoboundbewilsothoutoosezit, pull-adeftkiss and oxtrabeeforeness. And no longer so likely as before to trip over words whose unusual 'shape' at first confused him, the reader is in a fair way to begin his real appreciation. . . . And now, reading the book *aloud*, the full beauty of the rhythm and the peculiar turn of the words is (or certainly ought to be) at once apparent and enjoyed. There is nothing in these *Two Tales* so lovely, perhaps, as the ending of *Anna Livia*, but there is a humour no less rich and an idiom no less fascinating. As the mind relaxes before the flow of the words, a succession of images is called up much as is the cinematic flow of images in a dream. The words call up ideas which are mentally visualised as either objects or events, each fading away into other patterns more complicated and surprising at every reading. For the words becoming ever more familiar to him, the associated ideas which they hold within themselves are loosed ever more freely and generously, until the reader's mind is almost overwhelmed by the visual imagery evoked. Then it is that the meaning begins to appear in its final simplicity. And always there is the superlative beauty of the onomatopœic and lyrical prose for accompaniment. It is this music, in fact, which is alone able to induce that mental quietude and detachment necessary to a full appreciation of the imagery.

The reading of these fragments is an experience not to be paralleled by the reading of any other book which has yet been published. The beauty of pure sound might be roughly paralleled in the reading of Homer (say) where the reader's knowledge of Greek was negligible: but such a reading would give none of the rich associations or imagery of the reading of Joyce. To *understand* the work,—that is to understand it consciously and of intent,—is hardly worth our trouble, if it is in our power to do so.

It will be argued, of course, as it has been argued already, that such a peculiarly aesthetic experience as the reading of *Work in Progress* entails is not worth our enjoying. But where the results of the reading are so incontestably delightful as are the results of a sympathetic reading of either *Anna Livia* or *Shem and Shaun*, we have small need to concern ourselves with the ethics of appreciation. That Mr. Joyce is a sincere artist as well as a genius goes without saying. That he thinks it worth his while to write the prose he does, should be our justification sufficient for reading it. Where our reading delights us, we have small cause to complain in any case.

Two Tales of Shem and Shaun is a book not only to buy: it is a book to enjoy and a book to memorise. Essentially it is a book to recite. . . .

234. E. Oldmeadow, review, *Tablet*

14 January 1933, clxi, 41–2

The word set at the head of this article ['Rot'] is rarely used in the school-boy's exclamatory sense, by decorous journalists. But it may—and to-day must—be used in its unsavoury old meaning.

There came to *The Tablet's* office the other day a book called *Two Tales of Shem and Shaun* by James Joyce. After a first glance at the contents, we felt ashamed of the publishers for associating their names with such Rot; but, on second thoughts, we are inclined to praise them. By publishing the so-called *Two Tales*, they will have helped to burst a bubble. For a decade there has prevailed among some decent readers a notion that Ireland has produced a superlative genius whose master-piece is held back from the public by a Puritanic and Philistine censor-ship. While we speak without exact knowledge of the price demanded, we can affirm the broad fact that Mr. Joyce's 'great' book is printed at somebody's press in Paris, and can be brought into England only by stratagem or stealth. Thus confined to malodorous channels, it has not come under the noses of ordinary, self-respecting persons, who have therefore taken upon trust the story that Mr. James Joyce is a writer of supreme gifts, and that all men of perspicacity would hail him as such if a few over-frank pages had not put his work on the black-list.

In order that our readers, who are certainly not vulgarians or fossils, may judge for themselves whether the hard word at the head of this article be or be not *le mot juste*, we will transcribe without altering or omitting one letter or comma the opening sentences of 'The Mookse and the Gripes,' which is the first of the *Two Tales*. Here they are: . . .

[quotes from p. 152]

As the words we here have copied out fill exactly one page of *Two Tales*, and as there are only thirty-two pages of type in the whole book, we are not unreasonable in saying that we have given a Joyce-sample of sufficient quantity; and we hereby add an assurance that the sample is equally fair as regards Joyce-quality. Open in the middle, and you will find: . . .

[quotes from p. 156]

The last sentence of all is this bit of lunacy or blasphemy:

In the name of the former and of the latter and of their holocaust. Allmen.

If it were not for the fact that certain English and expatriate-Irish critics are trying to foist this Rot upon us as Literature—by the way, Messrs. Faber & Faber describe *Two Tales* as 'Contemporary Classics' —*The Tablet* would leave such imbecile echolalia to the alienists. But the plot has gone so far that Messrs. Yeats & Shaw have already named Mr. Joyce as a man who must, as a matter of course, be one of the first and most honoured members of their 'Irish Academy of Letters'; and, whenever there is protest from any of us who retain our sanity and our respect for those minima of form and clarity without which neither Literature nor any other art could exist, we are told scornfully that we are dullards and backnumbers.

If readers of these lines will go back for a few moments to the longest of the three extracts printed above, we may be able to suggest an explanation of the Joyce Boom. Its vogue, we believe, is due to the fact that Joyceism subtly flatters the vanity of those critics who are mightily proud of having picked up odds and ends of knowledge. 'Eins within a space' is a silly variant on 'Once upon a time'; and 'ere wohned' means 'there lived.' Therefore, the belauder of this imbecility is flattered at the thought that he knows enough German to recognize *eins* as 'one' and 'wohned' as coming from the German verb *wohnen*, 'to dwell,' with, perhaps, a flicker of allusion to Samuel Butler's *Erewhon* as well. The *flabella* are the great fans used in papal processions; and it makes petty-minded persons feel quite learned when they can puzzle out 'flabelled his eyes, vaticanated his ears, and palliumed his throats.' To have written 'carburetted his eyes, rolls-royced his ears, and six-cylindered his throats' would have had just as much or as little sense in it. Mr. Joyce gives to dull dogs the priceless satisfaction of imagining themselves to be smart; and there is nothing more to it.

As Mr. Joyce, whose works are morally unclean as well as æsthetically monstrous, is not the only practitioner of these new methods, the time has come for plain, prompt speech. The answer to the clique-men who pretend to scorn or pity us for 'not understanding Joyce,' should be that life is too short and Literature too precious for something much worse than levity and affectation—namely, for outright Rot. . . .

235. Unsigned comment on T. S. Eliot and Joyce

1933

'Mr. Eliot and Mr. Joyce', *Everyman* (28 January 1933), n.p.

Whatever be the state of your interest in those two mystery men of letters, T. S. Eliot and James Joyce, you now have for the price of two half-crowns the mystery in your grasp.

A straw shows which way the wind blows, and two tiny books, *Sweeney Agonistes, Fragments of an Aristophanic Melodrama*, by T. S. Eliot, and *Two Tales of Shem and Shaun*, by James Joyce, both from

Messrs. Faber at two-and-six each, throw a sudden illumination down the obscure ways which their authors have chosen to travel. . . .

[discusses Eliot]

The first great difference between Mr. Eliot and Mr. Joyce is that Mr. Joyce has a sense of humour. This Mr. Eliot totally lacks. Wit he has of a sardonic sort, but he has never had a really good laugh in his life. But read Mr. Joyce's *Two Tales*, and I am a very bad prophet indeed if they don't give you your laugh of the year.

They are among other things an uproarious satire on the cheap sort of current literary stuff that so many of us are so often taken in by. Joyce should be taken regularly as a cathartic by critics. Take this passage: . . .

[quotes from p. 158]

Read that aloud, with as much dramatic expression as you are capable of, and after a while you will decide that it means quite as much as three-quarters of the stuff you normally read, besides being infinitely more entertaining.

James Joyce is one of the greatest satirists that has ever lived. And like all great creative spirits, he gives new life to old things.

After reading Joyce you will be given an entirely fresh sense of language. Words have a way of becoming mere sounds, without meaning. One of the functions of a great writer is to renew the life of words, to revive the sense of wonder and magic in words that have become conventionalized, to freshen the whole life-stream of language.

This is what Joyce is doing for us. Read Joyce, and you will come back to your novel and your magazine and your newspaper with a greed for reading, a delight in words that you have never had before. It will be like seeing England again after months in India or Africa.

Such pat little books as these two by Mr. Eliot and Mr. Joyce can hardly ever have been issued simultaneously before. What a contrast they make! One is thin, solemn, academic, negative, slightly self-important, morose; the other is hearty, full of laughter, bursting with vitality—and the onward and upward struggle of things. One, in fact, stands for death, the other for life in our generation. . . .

236. Frank O'Connor on Joyce

1930

'Joyce—The Third Period', *Irish Statesman* (12 April 1930), 114–16.

Mr. Joyce's reputation, such as it is, rests upon two books, the *Portrait of the Artist as a Young Man* and *Ulysses*. In the two other books that preceded these he was obviously handling material which he could not work; he was neither a great romantic poet not a great realistic story-teller, and his poems and stories were excellent only in their sensitiveness to form and style.

In the two biographical fantasies that followed, Ireland found its greatest artist. The *Portrait* was an astonishing advance upon *Dubliners*, but *Ulysses* was a still more astonishing advance upon the *Portrait*. With it one became aware of the artist's two obsessions, language and form. In *Ulysses* language became putty in his hands; he made it do things one had thought it impossible for language to do; at one moment it suggested the movement of waters, at another the stale air of a bawdyhouse; it was passionate, sentimental, maudlin, etiolated, violent, obscene and exquisite by turns. And in *Ulysses* form had become for Joyce as it became for some of the Irish poets, ritual. The book followed in outline the story of the *Odyssey*, and since Mr. Bloom was its Ulysses, Mr. Bloom must do what Ulysses had done, and so we have the Sirens and Cyclops and the rest of the Homeric paraphernalia. One of the scenes took place in a lying-in hospital, and the style had to show in microcosm the passage from non-being to being, from darkness to light, resuming from paragraph to paragraph the whole experience of mankind as reflected in English prose style. It was the form of a great artist who was also a pedant, who attached to form a significance that it has seldom had outside ritual.

In his latest work, reviled by friend and foe alike, Joyce has carried those two obsessions a step further, but the step is as big as that between the *Portrait* and *Ulysses*; it is Joyce of the third period, and the greatest of Irish artists has sailed off into a world where the atmosphere—for most normal lungs—is so rare that it is scarce liveable-in. Nobody quite understands the form; nobody in Europe is quite qualified to say what any particular passage may mean, and Joyce's critics ask in something like his own words, 'Are we speachin d'anglas landadge, or are you sprakin sea Djoytsch?'

That I think is not Mr. Joyce's fault. He is really not a lover of mystification, and he has done his best to make his meaning clear. I have before me a book of essays on his latest work by some of the young people who come under his influence [*Our Exagmination*]. Two or three of these essays—I am thinking in particular of Samuel Beckett's, Eugène Jolas' and Thomas McGreevy's—are very interesting, and with a little more detachment would have been first rate criticism; others are merely dull. (While, of course, one distrusts the philology of the writer who tells us that 'usqueadbaugham' is Gaelic for whiskey.) But good or bad, the ideas are Joyce's, and as such to be treated with respect.

His new work as I understand it is founded on the philosophy of Vico as Ulysses was founded on the *Odyssey*. Its very title *Work in Progress* resumes an idea of Vico. All the characters are ideal characters, that is to say, they may change name or substance at the artist's pleasure; they move in a world of ideal time and space, so that the background, Dublin, may become any place at any time. This sense of ideal characters existing in ideal time and space is conveyed to the reader by the language, which is almost entirely associative, so that a servant's fall from grace, as well as being a symbol of the fall into original sin, may also be an image of the battle of Waterloo.

> Boo-hoo, what'l she do?
> The general lost her maidenloo,

as Hosty sings.

This associative language is the reader's first and greatest stumbling block, because, since the ideas which it expresses are universal, it is necessarily derived from every activity of the human soul. It anticipates in the first place the break-up of the English language into dialects, a phenomenon that is already taking place slowly under our eyes in American, Scots and Irish literature—one has only to think of negro poetry in America or McDiarmid's experiments in synthetic Scots. It also anticipates the universalisation of language. Whether one can anticipate natural processes is a question that might very reasonably be put. Meantime it seems entirely futile for literary men to set Joyce's work aside as unintelligible; if a critic can tell us no more than the indigent humourists of literature have told us already he had far better be silent. The question is not whether *Work in Progress* is intelligible or unintelligible—no serious critic speaks to-day of the unintelligibility of Mallarmé's *Après midi d'un Faune*—it is whether *Work in Progress* is good or bad, readable or unreadable.

Can one appreciate Mr. Joyce's new work? I think one can, though for myself *Work in Progress* like *Ulysses* contains a vast amount of dead wood. I have never been able to appreciate Mrs. Bloom's soliloquy and many other passages in *Ulysses*—admirable no doubt in themselves—and I am certain that whole tracts of *Work in Progress* will remain for-ever outside the range of my interests. But I have got many things from it. I have enjoyed the Anna Livia episode with its haunting four-dimensional pattern; . . .

[quotes from p. 21]

And there are those brilliant phrases which only Joyce could have written, things that for their humour and melody haunt one's mind long after one has forgotten what they are about. 'Tempus figets.' 'Vigagoes intactas.' 'Rockquiem eternuel give donal aye in dolmeny.' As I remember them it seems to me that this book, full of verve and sparkle, is Joyce's happiest. Not that it is entirely divorced from the work of his youth, which gave one the impression that it was written in tears. Like everything else of his it is intensely personal, and people and things associated with his earlier books reappear. Cork is there with its 'straat that is called cork-screwed (a phrase that should delight any Corkman) . . . . the finest boulevard billy for a mile in every direction from Lismore to Cape Brendan, Patrick's if they took the bint out of the mittle of it.' Dublin, of course, is there under a thousand forms from the memory of a child's song

> Esker, Newcsle, Saggard, Crumlin,
> Dell me, Donk, the way to Wumblin

to 'the brodar of the founder of the father of the finder of the pfander of pfunder of the furst man in Ranelagh.' But the cruelty, I think, is gone and the humour being more abstract is kindlier, as though the quarrel with his 'poor little brittle magic nation, dim of mind' needed no longer to be expressed in the savage taunts of the *Portrait* and *Ulysses*.

Here and there too, we find the artist, breaking the silence to which he had pledged himself, emerging to indulge in a sly gibe at his critics.

By this new work Joyce has kept for himself a place among the greatest in literature to-day, and for his country a place in the mind of Europe. It would have been so easy for him, after *Ulysses*, to have been content with the position of an imitator of himself. Only the very great have that tirelessnes., that relentlessness, and beside it the question of whether *Work in Progress* will prove a gigantic failure, as some believe, or another masterpiece, as I hope, makes little matter. . . .

237. Herbert Read on classic or romantic

1930

'James Joyce: Romantic or Classic', *Cambridge Review*, li (13 June 1930), 488–9. Also appeared in *A Coat of Many Colours* (1945), pp. 145–8. Extract from a review of Stuart Gilbert's *James Joyce's Ulysses* (1930).

. . . The purpose of this note is not to follow Mr Gilbert in his analysis, which I find wholly admirable and immensely illuminating, but rather to question one or two general *assumptions* which he makes. Perhaps Mr Gilbert claims them as *conclusions* arising from his analysis, but that is the paralogism common to all defensive criticism—to set out with an unresolved assumption and to conclude, not in proving anything, but merely in making plain what was otherwise obscure—the subconscious desire to identify ideals and actuality.

On the grounds of the elaborate structural character of *Ulysses* Mr Gilbert assumes the classicism of Mr Joyce. He dissociates him from sur-realism and all such attempts to present 'a mere fantasia of the subconscious, the manifesto of those forces of disorder which riot in the background of the mind,' and asserts that 'in the seven years which Mr

Joyce devoted to the construction of this monument of literature, well-planned and strongly built, he never once betrayed the authority of intellect to the hydra-headed rabble of the mental underworld. *Ulysses* is, in fact, a work essentially classical in spirit, composed and executed according to rules of design and discipline of almost scientific precision.' The fallacy inherent in this statement is similar, it seems to me, to the notion that if you subject a congenital criminal to a term of imprisonment with hard labour, he will emerge a pattern of human virtue. All the evidence, it seems to me, tends to prove that Mr Joyce is a congenital romantic. *Dubliners* is not significant of much except a romantic interest in realism, and *Exiles* would not answer to any of the tests of classical drama. But these works apart, what is *The Portrait of the Artist as a Young Man* but that introspective self-projection which is the very type of romantic literature? Even if we read into it a certain ironic detachment, we must still remember that irony is only perverted sentiment, and the resort of disillusioned romantics. But the most complete evidence of Mr Joyce's essential romanticism is to be found in his verse—*Chamber Music* and *Pomes Penyeach*. . . . The truth is, that what matters in this distinction between romantic and classical is not the form, but the informing spirit. The only tolerable distinction between romanticism and classicism is that which relates itself to the distinction drawn by psychologists between introspective and objective types of personality. Romanticism is egocentric expression, classicism is the expression of impersonal values. It is true that all classicists are or have been in some degree romantic (they would not be human otherwise), and it is therefore possible to admit the early romanticism of Mr Joyce, and still claim a classical spirit for *Ulysses*. But I do not think this' claim can be allowed, because the necessities of objectiveness imply an ever-increasing tendency towards simplicity, clarity and universality. There is no obscurity in classic art. That is, if anything, its main disadvantage. The mind is so constituted that it likes to encounter a certain measure of resistance in its perceptions. Therein lies the justification of romanticism.

A certain type of romanticism seeks to express itself in a complication of forms. As a matter of fact, it is essentially the Northern, and more particularly the Celtic, type of romanticism. The true counterpart of Mr Joyce's *Ulysses* is not Homer's *Odyssey*, but the *Book of Kells*. . . .

Confirmation of this hypothesis of the nordic nature of Mr Joyce's romanticism is found in his latest work. The publishers of Mr Gilbert's book have had the courage to issue at the popular price of one shilling an episode from that *Work in Progress* of which large extracts have appeared from time to time in various esoteric magazines. *Anna Livia Plurabelle* is great fun for anyone who likes to take the trouble to puzzle out all its elaborate allusions and puns. And Mr Joyce, who has the sense of character (Leopold Bloom is as solid and immortal as any character in English literature) does manage to convey, across all his obstacles, the aroma and the lustiness of two washer-women by the Liffey. But we are a long way from clarity, simplicity and universality. In this method Mr Joyce again harks back to his Celtic or Anglo-Saxon ancestors, who had a device in literature known as kenning, the object of which was to hide the meaning of a phrase in the remotest possible allusion. Such kennings are comparatively simple, because they are the outcome of a naïve tradition. But Mr Joyce brings to the game all the resources of a very considerable learning and sophistication. The game is amusing, and there is a sense of reality behind it all. But it is the antithesis of classicism. . . .

238. Herbert Read on Joyce's influence

1930

'The High Priest of Modern Literature', *Listener* (20 August 1930), 296.

To explain the significance of James Joyce it is necessary in the first place to make a distinction between two literary publics. This is difficult, because any such division seems to imply some kind of snobism: the kind of snobism ridiculed as 'high-brow', for example. But the distinction between high-brow and low-brow really begs the question; from the point of view of the music-hall comedian and his friend, the man-in-the-street, all serious writing is high-brow. For the purpose of this enquiry I would like to assume that we are all high-brows. Then we still need a distinction between what we may call a craft-conscious public, and a public merely out for instinctive enjoyment. The latter forms the majority, and to it most works of art are addressed. But there exists this other public, perhaps only numbering a few hundreds in any country, for whom literature is not a question of the direct absorption of a synthetic product, the work of art, but rather the analysis of it. Some people like a machine because it runs smoothly, and ask no more; others will be seeing how it works. It is too this latter type that the work of James Joyce appeals. . . . But this is where the peculiarity of Mr. Joyce's method becomes evident. He is writing deliberately for the analysing public, and in his later work at any rate we may fairly say that the enjoyment is proportionate to the anlytical power which the reader can contribute.

The public can now obtain for one shilling an excellent example of Mr. Joyce's latest work (*Anna Livia Plurabelle.* Published by Faber and Faber.) In almost any single paragraph they will, if they persist, find a hundred shifting lights. . . .

To the first kind of reader I described, it will all look and sound like so much gibberish. But those who are analytically minded will get a good deal of enjoyment from the mental effort of keeping up with the agile acrobatics of the author. It is a legitimate form of enjoyment, but how, it will be asked, does it differ from the enjoyment of a really difficult and erudite crossword puzzle? Here I must confess that I am not sufficiently a partisan of Mr. Joyce's methods to answer with any confidence. I only know that if this gibberish is read aloud it does acquire an odd sort of impressiveness, akin to the impressiveness of poetry read in a foreign language we do not understand. Beyond this there may be some kind of formal structure analogous to the structure of a fugue in music, but it is not in any way obvious.

A comprehensive explanation of Mr. Joyce's art would have to follow his development as a writer. I think I have read everything that Mr. Joyce has published, and to me the extravagances of his latest work do not come as a surprise. I see them as a gradual development from his earliest work. I see them also as an outcome of his innate romanticism. I know that Mr. Joyce has been hailed as a classical writer, particularly by his commentator, Mr. Stuart Gilbert, but that is a classification which I cannot accept. It rests on the fact that *Ulysses*, Mr. Joyce's masterpiece, is based throughout on a close structural parallelism with Homer's *Odyssey*. The notion rests on a fallacy which identifies form and content; just as though we were to say that water poured into a vase takes on the form and properties of that vase. All the evidence it seems to me, goes to show that Mr. Joyce is really a romantic. His first stories, *Dubliners*, revealed that romantic interest in realism which comes from Norway rather than Greece; and Mr. Joyce's only play, *Exiles*, is a psychological drama far removed from the canons of classical drama. *The Portrait of the Artist as a Young Man*, published in 1916, is a work of great lyrical beauty, but it also belongs to that introspective mode of self-projection which is the very type of romantic literature. Even if we read into it a certain ironic detachment, we must still remember that irony is only perverted sentiment, and the recourse of disillusioned romantics. But the most complete evidence of Mr. Joyce's romanticism is to be found in his verse—*Chamber Music* and *Pomes Penyeach*. For example:

> The moon's grey-golden meshes make
> All night a veil,
> The shorelamps in the sleeping lake
> Laburnum tendrils trail.
>
> The sly reeds whisper to the night
> A name—her name—
> And all my soul is a delight,
> A swoon of shame.

Mr. Gilbert quotes this poem as evidence of Mr. Joyce's classical spirit, presumably because it is written in regular iambics! It is the same assumption as that which led him into claiming *Ulysses* as a classical work. The truth is, that what matters in the distinction between romantic and classic is not the form, but the informing spirit. . . .

By accusing Mr. Joyce of romanticism, I am not condemning him. It is not the business of the critic to take sides in this everlasting opposition of romantic and classic. His business is merely to identify and classify. With no other than a scientific intention, I find Mr. Joyce to be a romantic poet of the most extreme kind; he is so romantic that he has reduced his egocentricity to its last refinement, and evolved an art of which only he himself can be the full participant. But in the process he has so revitalised the current use of language, that no one interested in the art of writing from a craft-conscious point of view can afford to neglect his example and achievement. Mr. Joyce is the high priest of modern literature precisely because literature is a priesthood and has a sanctuary more inaccessible than the monasteries of Thibet. . . .

239. Philippe Soupault on Joyce

1930 (1943, 1959, 1963)

Extracts from 'Autour de James Joyce', *Bravo* (Paris) (September 1930), 16–17; later incorporated in *Souvenirs de James Joyce* (1943, 1945) (91 pp., a fragment from 'Anna Livia Plurabelle' in French translation, pp. 71–91). A fragment from this work was translated by Maria Jolas in *James Joyce Yearbook* (1959), ed. Maria Jolas, pp. 126–9. Another fragment appeared as 'James Joyce' in his *Profils Perdus* (1963), pp. 49–70.

The present text is translated and extracted from the *Bravo* article (1), from the *James Joyce Yearbook* (2), and from *Profils Perdus* (3).

(1) . . . Thus am I not indifferently proud to state that I have met in my life two men whose genius seemed dazzlingly brilliant to me. These two men are Pablo Picasso and James Joyce.

. . . As for James Joyce, he is the one who is courageous enough to propose to all those who endeavor to write to forget their methods, their routines, and to finally dominate literature and to find again a new vision.

The name of James Joyce bursts forth like a storm. In the Old and the New World he arouses the most lively quarrels. All those who are for the Paralyzing tradition, all those who fear all that is new, endeavor to have believed that all of Joyce's work is a joke, or further that it is snobism! But others who are more clear-sighted simply declare that this writer finally brings a brilliant light and frees literature from all the absurd bonds which time, criticism and professors had so well constructed that they were ready to choke and kill literature.

There is nothing to doubt. The genius of James Joyce, even for his worst detractors, leaves no doubt. In order not to use the word genius, his most faithful enemies treat him as a monster. . . . In essence, it is only a question of understanding. . . .

Soon his name will represent a powerful force for us because the influence of Joyce is only beginning to be felt. It will bring through the violence of its current status all the allusions which at the beginning of the twentieth century threatened to paralyze literature. It is not necessary to be a prophet since it is only necessary to be clear-sighted in order to distinguish the importance of James Joyce and of his work. This work is only comparable to an immense conflagration.

(2) . . . For the faint-hearted and more easily discouraged, for those who are still alive and who go to make up our epoch, I shall attempt to sum up what, in my opinion, constitutes the greatness and 'density' of Joyce: Joyce created a world. . . .

To my knowledge, no writer has ever subordinated his life to his work more completely than did Joyce. At the cost of real suffering, which I witnessed, he accepted a condition of permanent slavery, a slavery of both mind and body, that was complete. I can still see him, during one of the days that I spent with him, tortured by a word, constructing, almost rebelliously, a sort of framework; questioning his characters, turning to music for a more fictitious dream, a more vivid hallucination; and finally dropping exhausted onto a sofa, the better to hear the word about to spring shining into being. . . .

The most striking thing about this phenomenon which, in the scientific meaning of the word, is one of the purest to be found in literary history, is its unity. Joyce's first work foreshadowed and prepared his maturity. What was to be definitely achieved in *Ulysses* had already been attempted and approached in *Dubliners*. In these fifteen short stories, the reader, the author and the principal character are one. The author does not stoop to lie. He also rejects what we disparagingly call *literature*. No falsity of attitude, no trickery, no ambiguity; only the most absolute good faith. . . .

The value of this nearly forty-year long experiment to the victorious completion of a work which constitutes one of the highest achievements in all literature cannot be sufficiently stressed.

(3) . . . It is suitable then to remember that for the reader who is no longer detached from the author but associated with him, it is important to read *Dubliners* before *A Portrait*, then finally to come to *Ulysses* and to end with *Finnegans Wake*. Let's repeat an earlier statement: Joyce created a world and this world in only accessible to us if we know how to humbly obey the wishes of the author. . . .

I had the occasion, at the time when I was translating with him, or rather when he was translating with my help, to see and to hear worked out a fragment of *Finnegans Wake*, the episode of 'Anna Livia Plurabelle.'

[see No. 191 for a fuller account of Soupault's work on this translation]

These translating gatherings lasted three hours. They were exhausting. Joyce was never satisfied with the results. I have never, however, met a man who was such a sure, faithful translator. It was necessary for him to consider words as objects, to draw them out, to cut them, to examine them under a microscope. He persisted and never surrendered. This was not out of 'conscience' nor of mania; it was the application of a pitiless method. It was a question of a 'matter' so moving, so rich, so new, so evasive also that it was necessary never to let go, not even for a second. And I remain persuaded that to the cause of his fellow-translators Joyce restrained himself, that he pitied them. When he worked alone, he was even more uncompromising. He would let himself be submerged in the tide of ideas, projects, remembrances, comparisons, imaginations, sounds, descriptions, odors . . . In the midst of this whirlwind, he maintained a *sang-froid*, and his critical sense, fearing the laxness which would cause him to accept the almost, the nearly so, never relaxed. When I wish to describe his state while he was working, I can not escape from this cliché: body and soul. Before my eyes Joyce, his index finger raised, saying nothing, repeating a word, a phrase, criticizing, rejecting, taking back an entire fragment, destroying pages already on the point of being printed. . . .

Paris helped him to end *Ulysses*, to write *Finnegans Wake*. Never, to my knowledge, had any work of this type been attempted and achieved. *Ulysses* seemed a superhuman endeavor. When one will be able to study and to read with the care that it merits, one will be persuaded of the exception grandeur of the last work of Joyce. Let us not conceal the fact that for today's readers the difficulty of reading is very great. The reading of *Ulysses* could be made easier with some commentaries. A book would be necessary to help the well-intentioned reader who would wish to approach *Finnegans Wake*. It is only with time that the reader will be able to, if not with ease, at least with simplicity, read this great work. It is so many years ahead of the time in which it was written. It is the privilege of certain geniuses to be able to advance upon the states of mind and the intelligence of their contemporaries, and it is thus a price of fame. . . .

James Joyce was not unaware of this fact. He did not say, like Stendahl, that he would be understood 'later,' but believed that he would only acquire readers slowly, and he wanted to exact from them an effort equal to his own. He did not scorn his readers, never seeking to flatter their taste for facility. He was not writing for the 'happy few' because he did not estimate that his books were reserved for the élite. He unceasingly enriched his art, imposing on all that he attained a rigor and a certitude which excluded hesitation and misconception. Joyce had a horror of misunderstandings and almosts. For his, and consequently for his readers, there was no middle term.

240. Austin Clarke on Joyce

1930

'James Joyce', *Everyman* (15 May 1930), 486.

Not so many years ago Mr. James Joyce was an ill-paid teacher of English in Trieste. To-day, as the author of *Ulysses*, he has become a European figure. . . . Notoreity has given dangerous curiosity to the writings of Joyce. But his revolutionary art is an influence working, for good or bad, in the minds of younger writers. Coteries have been formed to explain the enigmatic work of Joyce. 'Consciousness-stream,' 'cerebralist' are among the high-flown words used to enlighten us regarding this writer who delves into the twentieth-century mind and has always called a spade by its improper name.

The Portrait of the Artist as a Young Man is the key to Mr. Joyce's later work. In that astonishingly frank portrayal of the adolescent mind we see sensitive youth struggling through the terrors of religious unbelief to art, and no detail of the clash between immature idealism and the ugliness of matter and sexual development is spared us. Here are the tortuous agonies of the half-mediæval Catholic mind which we find in Huysmans. Against a drab Dublin background Stephen Dedalus pursues his thoughts and dreams: . . .

[quotes from ch. 5]

Ulysses is, ostensibly, the record of a day spent by a Dublin Jew, but never were twenty-four hours so packed with astonishing consciousness. Through the worldly, gross, but cheerful, mind of Leopold Bloom we see and hear the throning and idiomatic life of 'the seventh city of Christendom'. . . . James Joyce, in a forced telescopic style, shuts the experience of a chapter into a few sentences. That is to say, he works as a poet rather than a prose writer, loads every rift with ore, and follows the associative method to its extreme limit.

1930: *Ulysses*

Ultimately this is the method of Rabelais, who joyously poured out his enormous catalogues as though they would never end, delighting in the fecundity of life and the vast quantity of objects in the mediæval world. In his gigantic horseplay Rabelais turned the whole vocabulary topsy-turvy, twisted, invented words, punned with sounds and ran up and down the echoing galleries of rhyme. With the painful intensity of a modern, Mr. Joyce tries to capture that imaginative significance and wealth of words which were lost to the English language with the decline of dialect. He follows every sound echo, invents words, plays as Shakespeare with dreadful puns.

What is one to make of the following typical passage from his later work? . . .

[quotes from p. 199]

Such an extract suggests the philological jokes of Lewis Carroll, and readers may see in it but nonsense, or crossword puzzles. But Mr. Joyce is attempting, not successfully perhaps, to do a great number of things at the same time, to give us the indiscreet meditations of a Gargantuan washerwoman as she rubs and wrings the dirty linen of Dublin, to compress and make words as idiomatic as slang, to hide geographical references and to express in sliding sentences and by onomatopœia the River Liffey flowing seaward.

Much nonsense has been written by admirers of *Ulysses* and there have been silly imitations. Mr. Joyce draws upon his early memories of Dublin life for every detail, and what appears to be unintelligible or profoundly mysterious turns out to be but a minute localism. His endless and accurate detail, the kaleidoscopic word pictures, give a phenomenal and inexhaustible air to his work. The ultimate value of Joyce's intensive method will be questioned, but to dip into *Ulysses* is to step from the safe pavement into the very dizziness of mental traffic. . . .

241. G. K. Chesterton on Joyce

1930

Extract from 'The Spirit of the Age in Literature', *Bookman*, lxxii (October 1930), 97–103.

This unsociable quality in the intellect, which can coexist with so much superficial sociability or herding in the habits, is the most outstanding fact about really able writers in recent days. One of its manifestations is a verbal eccentricity in works of a talent that goes beyond the eccentric. It is something like the secret language that is invented by a child. *Ulysses* contains a number of very queer words; though perhaps none queerer than Ulysses. For the comparison is curious in itself, seeing that throughout a prolonged pagan epic Homer manages to be very pure in very plain language, while Joyce manages to be very coarse in very esoteric language. There are whole passages, of the sort on which the moral argument turns, which are dark to the point of decency. He has been compared to Rabelais, but the very comparison should be enough to show us vividly the difference made by the Spirit of the Age. It is the whole force of Rabelais that he seems to roar like ten thousand men; that one of his giants is like a multitude turned into a man. What he roars may not always be very distinct or intelligible, any more than the roar of an actual rabble or mob; but we know that what is being shouted is something quite normal and human, even if it be what some would call bestial. But we do not feel, or at least I do not feel, that James Joyce ever speaks for anybody except James Joyce. We may call this individuality or insanity or genius or what we will; but it belongs to its time because of this air of having invented its own language; and moved a little further away from anything like a universal language. The new Ulysses is the opposite of the old Ulysses, for the latter moved amid ogres and witches with a level-headed and almost prosaic common sense, while the former moves among common lamp-posts and public houses with a fixed attitude of mind more fantastic than all the fairy-tales. I am not here either adequately praising or adequately criticizing this much controverted work; I am merely using it as an illustration of the isolation of one mind, or even of one mood. Rabelais sometimes seems confusing, because he is like twenty men talking at once; but Joyce is rather inaudible, because he is talking to himself. . . .

242. Paul L. Léon and Joyce

1930

Extracts from Lucie Noel [Léon], *James Joyce and Paul L. Léon: The Story of a Friendship* (1950), pp. 7, 8, 10, 15, 17, 44–6.

Delivered in part at the Meeting of the James Joyce Society, 18 November 1948.

James Joyce and Paul Léon met in 1928. It was the beginning of a friendship that was to last twelve years and would have certainly continued had they lived. . . .

He fully appreciated Joyce's achievement as a writer, defending it tooth and nail when the occasion arose, but he was more interested in Joyce as a person. . . .

Those who knew my husband well often wondered why anyone as self-sufficient as he was, with serious interests and intellectual work of his own, should have been willing to devote so much time to Joyce. Frequently, when the question was put to Paul, he would answer:

'I am most interested in watching Joyce's process of creation. He has me look up words in various languages, and his mental process and the metamorphosis of language he indulges in are most fascinating to witness. . . .'

My husband was as aware as was Joyce of the latter's mission in the field of experimental letters—that no one had ever written a *Finnegans Wake*. But one day I overheard him say to Joyce:

'Sir, this may be genius, maybe this is art, I grant you all that, but please don't ask me to understand it.'

When he would tease Joyce in this way about *Finnegan*, Joyce would accuse him of not taking his mental acrobatics seriously enough. But Paul, whose memory was brilliant, could quote entire paragraphs of Joyce's work, and correct offhand any misquotation he might read or hear. . . .

1930: *Work in Progress*

Despite his poor eyesight, it always seemed to me that Joyce was very conscious of color. I remember his asking me in the early years of our friendship to name colors, their shades and ranges. We talked of the rainbow and of prisms, and he made notes. I asked him why he wanted all that information, and he told me that in *Ulysses* he had made use of children's games and that now, in *Work in Progress*, he intended to use colors. . . . It was, I suppose, inherent in the day-by-day relationship between Joyce and my husband that the latter should seldom have made any generalizations about the value of his friend's writing. What he had to say came out in private discussions of details with Joyce himself, and perhaps in the private correspondence which is now in the Dublin Library. His attitude, however, is indicated in the following letter to his niece, Mrs. Olga Howe, written May 23, 1930:

My dear Olga,

Many thanks for your quickly sent note—so short and so sweet enclosing the By-stander's opinion of Joyce. It might be he is right on the whole except for one or two things. I read an article on 'Joyce working' in some American paper to which he seems to refer in which all the details of how, where and when he works were given: white cloths, red pencil, huge sheets of paper—I am glad to say I have never seen him working if the description is correct. Besides I have here the typescript of his new book which I am afraid is worth millions because all the alterations are done in my handwriting—had they been done in his I am afraid nobody would have understood anything. . . .

Now as to his work it might be sheer nonsense, and I am careful telling him my opinion every evening after work. Though I seem to share the opinion of the reviewer in as far as I do not understand anything at all about it I still think some theory can be worked out. At present my latest based on 'ipsissima' verba is approximately as follows: When St. Patrick went to baptise Ireland he found some difficulty to explain the sense of the Holy Trinity when suddenly his eyes fell on the ground where he saw a most commonplace little flower, trodden by the people, dirtied by the animals which had a three-leaf forming a single one. He took it and showed it to the people who shouted: Credimus, Credimus!

Now does not every word we use represent a Trinity: it has a sense, a sound, a power to evoke pictures. One does not feel it as rule unless 'something goes wrong , i.e. either the sense is stupid, or the picture obsolete, or the sound false. Would it not be possible to write a book where all these three elements of literature are segregated and dissociated? A device can be used, a most commonplace banal device to prove it: a pun. Hence in the description of the river Liffey there are in the text the names of 600 rivers and in the description of Dublin, some 500 names of places, cities, lord mayors, etc. etc. Naturally all this was known before, but the adjustment done by great authors was done unconsciously, I wonder if there is anything wrong in attempting to make this process of reconstruction of the LOGOS conscious?

Now the last part is the Obscenity. A thing I have been unable to swallow myself until I discovered that it was a peculiarly Anglo-Saxon pruderie that made him apply this device.

To all my objections he answered—'it is not my fault that God has made the same organs serve two purposes.' Hence the basis of Anglo-Saxon pruderie is apparent: people do not do certain things in public because they could be mistaken for something else. Such argument naturally is beyond me, as I would any day any time rather do what I call 'deliver a cake' in public than conjugate the verb which sounds very much like 'fortification' but has nothing whatever to do with it. Why, I do not know exactly, but the theory that I could disclose would be too long to dwell upon right now.

This is altogether enough—I am afraid too much, even for what it is worth—so I am taking the stand when I read:

> But I waged love on her and spoiled her undines

that it is good to remind people that while their heads touch heaven their feet are often in the mud. It happens so often. . . .

243. Rebecca West on *Work in Progress*

1930

'James Joyce and his Followers', *New York Herald Tribune Books* (12 January 1930), 1, 6.

. . . They [the *transition* group] are engaged in transactions on such a large scale that, where they make losses, these seem pretty heavy; but the losses are counterbalanced by the gains, which also are true to the scale. This is so, too, in relation to the creative process in which they are most interested; that is, the workings of Mr. James Joyce's genius.

At present there might be suspected to be a heavy loss sustained in that quarter, because it appears more than possible that in *Work in Progress* he is following—if not a blind alley—for no path along which a genius travels can remain that for long—but an avenue hardly wide enough for the army of his powers. One cannot come to any final opinion on the subject until the whole of the book has been published. . . .

Quite possibly some features will appear in *Work in Progress* in its completed form, which will remove all the objections that at present rise up against it in the mind of any reader outside the cult. But since his own followers insist on discussing it at the present stage, and since if he does remove these objections, he will practically stand everything that is known about the human mind upside down, it is worth while stating them.

The distinctive attribute of *Work in Progress* is that it is not written in English, or in any other language. Most of the words that James Joyce uses are *patés de langue gras*. . . . They are 'portmanteau' words such as Lewis Carroll invented when he wrote 'Jabberwocky': ''Twas brillig and the slithy toves Did gyre and gimble in the wabe.' They are chosen, often but not always, in the sly, punning spirit that looks for disguises by which forbidden things may leer and sidle past the censor; so that very frequently by their grossness they recall Leopold Bloom out of *Ulysses*, great embodiment of the repressed side of man. They are

534

sometimes strung together in sequences that do not obey the ordinary laws of syntax.

The common accusation against the result of these processes is that it is incomprehensible. It is nothing of the sort. . . .

The main objections that make one, in spite of the fact that one is entertained, wonder whether James Joyce is not misapplying his genius in using this new form are three, and one of them involves this very question of effort and time. . . . But if Mr. James Joyce is to take ten, or twenty, or thirty years packing allusions into portmanteau words; and if his readers are to take twelve (since a cipher takes longer for a stranger to read than for its inventor to write) or twenty-five, or forty years unpacking these allusions out of the portmanteau words, it is impossible to avoid the suspicion that troops have been marched up a hill and then down again. . . .

Another objection, which certainly cannot be resolved until 'Work in Progress' is complete, is esthetic. . . . It would seem that the intellectual effort required to unmake James Joyce's words into their constituent parts would perpetually be splitting up the attention and breaking up the state of unity in which the mind must be to accept, say, his personification of the life of a river, the stream of creation. One remembers that there was in *Ulysses* a curious demonstration of Mr. Joyce's failure to appreciate the effect on the mind of simultaneous presentation of objects on different planes. The parallelism between *Ulysses* and the odyssey which James Joyce carefully contrives by sending Stephen Dedalus through incidents that correspond with the Odyssean wanderings is justified by him and his followers as being designed to afford a contrast between the Manichean spirit manifested by Joyce and the Greek spirit manifested in Homer. But it does nothing of the sort, because there can be no real contrast between its esthetic rendering of the Manichean spirit and its purely factual references (through these correspondences) to the Greek spirit, of which the intellect is invited to remember as much as it can, but which is never esthetically recreated. The two are almost as widely divided in their appeal to the attention as the printing on the page and the page numbers. At present *Work in Progress* seems to be invalidated by more diffused addiction to the same error; but we shall see.

There are two other objections, which both have reference to psychology. It is impossible to discuss James Joyce without frequent references to psychology, since nearly all of his recent subject matter and much of his technique he derives from his knowledge of Freud and

Jung. The first point on which one would like to be satisfied is whether the main function he is trying to make the word perform is not one which is properly performed by the image in the mind for which the word is only a counter. . . . It is Joyce's theory that if words are so handled as to recall meanings they had in the past we will go back into the experience of the race in these bygone phases, and revitalize the words and ourselves by knowledge of these eternal and recurrent processes. But this does not seem to be necessary, if, as Freud and Jung hold in their different ways and to different degrees, the mind of man inherits in his unconscious the collective mythos of mankind and is perpetually in touch with it. That view cannot be considered irrelevant in this connection, because James Joyce has himself accepted it. The aim of this book is to make the unconscious conscious; and it represents the unconscious as a storehouse of primitive myths. It appears clumsy and uneconomical, then, to use obsolete words in order to bring the past to the present when an image spontaneously springing up from the unconscious will do the same thing with much more dynamic force.

The other objection to *Work in Progress* concerning the word has also to do with James Joyce's psychological sources. Obviously, he got this idea of the word-paste from the Freudian and Jungian analyses of the puns people make in dreams. These are resolved into their constituents when the dreamer practices free association on them. . . . Now, why does James Joyce invent these words? Has he a naive faith that since free association shows the direct connection between such a word and the unconscious the invention of such a word by reversing the process of free association will automatically drive a connection down into the unconscious? Surely not. He must have entirely created the psyche which he is expressing; he must have before him its conscious and its unconscious and be completely aware of its contents and their relationship. Every portmanteau word he invents must have its causal connection in one of the mythological figures he describes. Then why is there no sense of clarity, of the gratification that comes from comprehension, such as pervades an analysis that is successful in coping with its subject matter in the same way, and any work of art, such as *King Lear* or *The Divine Comedy* that has resolved the matter in the terms of its age? Is it because James Joyce feels a disposition, when in doubt, to create an effect of disintegration because the most satisfactory creation of his genius up to this date has been Leopold Bloom, the disintegrator? Or is there some new sort of clarity that will appear in the completion of *Work in Progress*.

I would not myself stake a penny on any of my objections. I state them only because it seems to me of interest to consider what points James Joyce will have to make if he is to quell all resistance in the minds of his age who are looking for the inheritor of art and would like to find it in him. Can one think of any other writer concerning whose work such interesting considerations arise? . . .

244. Stuart Gilbert on Joyce's growth

1930

Extract from 'The Growth of a Titan', *Saturday Review of Literature*, vii (2 August 1930), 17–19.

. . . Thus, indeed, almost *verbatim*, several of Joyce's earliest critics described *Ulysses*—as (to quote an Irish writer) 'an assault upon divine decency as well as human intelligence,' or (according to the *Dublin Review*) 'a devilish drench . . . sin against the Holy Ghost.' It has been truly said that a prophet is not without honor save in his own country and in his own house!

And now we have *Work in Progress* (the provisional title of Joyce's still unfinished work, over half of which, however, has appeared in the pioneer review *transition*), an assault, the critical pontiffs affirm, on literary decency as 'devilish' as the attack on divine decency which shocked Mr. Shane Leslie. Given the plainspokenness of *Ulysses* and the verbal audacities of *Work in Progress*, it is perhaps not surprising that Mr. Joyce has been hailed in certain quarters as a 'literary Bolshevist,' whose object and delight is to blow sky high all conventions, social and artistic.

But, if we consider Mr. Joyce's work as a continuous whole, from the formally impeccable set of poems entitled *Chamber Music* to his latest experiment, it will be clear, I think, that his progress is one of evolution not revolution—but an evolution so speeded up that, at first sight, it looks like the holocaust of tradition, a wanton 'scrapping' of past discoveries. For while (as the Victorian sang) normal literature broadens slowly down 'from precedent to precedent,' the Irish writer progresses by leaps and bounds, taking with unflagging zest hurdle after hurdle of literary achievement. . . .

The *Portrait* is a tale of evasion, a spiritual echo of that oft-told theme, the prisoner's escape from captivity. *Ulysses* marks a further stage of evolution and *Work in Progress* yet another milestone, far beyond *Ulysses*, on the rocky road to freedom. For now the constraints not only of nationality and religion, but also of language, are broken through and our 'hawk-like man' is freely soaring sunward, beyond and above the nets flung at his soul to hold it back from flight.

But (if I may be pardoned the *cliché*) his liberty is not license. The kind of freedom to which young Dedalus aspired was not that harum-scarum extroversion of the 'subconscious' which is, or was till yesterday, the last word in modernity. No, like nature herself, like the achievements of science, Joyce's progress is always towards a richer synthesis of life, a greater altitude of flight and wider horizons. As his work develops, we find a growing interest in form, a finer tesselation of thematic patterns, and a closer linking up of style with subject, till of *Work in Progress* one may literally assert *le style c'est le thème*.

Already in *Dubliners* (an early collection of short stories), the ferment of that symbolical symmetry, so characteristic of Joyce's later writing, was at work. . . .

[quotes from 'Grace']

The *Portrait*, too, is more than the story of a keen-witted and sensitive boy, the struggles of adolescence, and, at last, escape. In it we find as well the ordered evolution of a philosophy, of an attitude to the jumble of events and sensations we name experience. The young man encounters life 'hot for certainties,' an answer to the eternal question: What does life *mean*? The Church offers a solution, but intelligence and sensibility conspire to reject it. Next philosophy flatters the intellect—yet, for all its parade of logic, gives but a 'dusty answer.' From dust of philosophy and ashes of religion Stephen Dedalus turns to that dynamic, vital synthesis of experience which he finds in the 'beauty of order,' the artist's cosmic vision. . . . The search for absolute truth, most hopeless of quests (unless, like the scientist, one limits it to mere phenomena or, like the priest, to a set of dogmas) is over for him. It is only in ordered beauty—like the Venus of Milo, of no time and of all time—that Stephen's soul can find repose. On that discovery the chronicle of the young artist's struggle towards self-realization ends. He is now ready for the creation of that ordered pageant of human life, ancient and modern, that is *Ulysses*.

Ulysses has been so often dissected, defended, or decried by writers of all nations that it is needless for me to dwell on its theme. . . .

At first sight *Ulysses* may seem a chaos of riotous imaginings, a betrayal of order, of decency, of all that evolution has achieved to raise man above his fellow animals. But a closer study shows that each word is used as exactly as in a scientific manual, always with the same connotation, and that *Ulysses* is linked together by an all-pervading rhythm, just as each part of the body—and here we see why Joyce has related each episode to a bodily organ—is joined to all the others by a vital synthesis, a complex of nerves and muscles. *Ulysses* is, in fact, the most 'symbolical' book ever written (the most intensely 'living,' too), for it is a small scale miniature of the universal macrocosm. . . .

James Joyce's *Work in Progress* is the highest hurdle he has yet 'taken,' surpassing even *Ulysses* in scope and complexity. It is assuredly the most curious and intricate book the world has seen. Less than half the size of its predecessor (to judge by the parts which have appeared in *transition*), it will comprise an epitome or synthesis of life richer even than that of *Ulysses*. Difficult reading, no doubt, but so scintillant with humor that, even if the reader can only penetrate the uppermost of the layers of meaning, superimposed (like cinematic images) one upon another, the mere sound and look of the prose, its verbal antics, are a delight in themselves. The basic idea is (as in *Ulysses*) a theory of re-currence, moulded, most probably, on the Italian Vico's 'cycle of history'; the dimensions of time and space are telescoped and we see, like gods or as in dream, all history in the flash of a moment. As the Chinese poet wrote a millennium ago: 'True indeed is that saying of the Wise Men, "A hundred years are but a moment of sleep."' *Work in Progress* has the aspect of a dream and is written in a dream language. We are shown a panorama of city, field, and forest, seen dimly beneath a moon darkened ever and again by scudding clouds, the landscape of a vision. Sometimes the texture lightens to a tissue of rippling gossamer, vaguely reminiscent in its superficial aspect of that Wonderland to which Alice has led so many happy children and happily unsophisticated elders. Such a passage is the 'pastoral' of Jaun the Irishman, in which he gives a company of twenty-nine (for it is leap year) pretty girls a musico-floral version of a birdland nocturne:

[quotes from p. 450]

The passage goes to the lilt of a frolicsome Irish song. Here 'l'Alouette' refers not only to the lark but to a Dublin firm, and 'Adelaide' (for reasons concerning Jaun's career) to the Australian capital as well as the famous song. The nightingales have turned naughty and *beneath* has grown nocturnal. Almost every word is nuanced so as to recall the *motifs* of the passage—music, birds, and flowers. In 'twittynice black-budds' we hear the twittering chatter of twenty-nine *jeunes filles en fleurs* and the echo of a familiar nursery rhyme. 'Numerous' is changed so as to suggest poetic 'numbers' and *numerosus* (Lat: *musical*); 'varia-tions' is Italianized (Italian forms, the language of music, have been prepared for in the context) and yields 'fairy' plus 'odes.' A few lines before Jaun spoke of 'solfanelly' (Italian matches, with a hint of the 'tonic solfa') and this, combined with the word 'tonic,' gives the clue to the next sentence, 'I give, a king, etc.' This sentence is a translation of the notes of the scale (*do, re, mi, fa,* etc.) as an Italian understands them. (The note *si*, for instance, is the Italian 'Yes.') The word 'echoed' has been wedded to the French *éclosion*, the blossoming of a flower, a posy of birdnotes rippling up the scale.

The lightness of the rhythm befits the theme of this passage which (like all *Work in Progress*, all epic poems) is meant to be read aloud. Here is much more than a mere word game, the exploitation of puns or 'portmanteau words'; it is a new method of handling language whereby such a 'dead' word as 'twenty-nine,' a mere enumerative, is reanimated by the transfusion of vivid meaning. The numeral skeleton is apparent, but it is clad with the attributes of life. . . .

[quotes from p. 502]

The question is often asked: What is the 'story' of *Work in Pro-gress*? A complete answer is obviously impossible till the entire work has been published and we can see exactly how, as in *Ulysses*, each component fits into place. Meanwhile certain aspects are already apparent. The symbolism is on a vaster scale and still more intricate than in *Ulysses*. The characters have multiple personalities (they are akin, perhaps, to the Platonic 'ideas') and, according to the context, the light is thrown now on one facet, now on another. . . .

'Hopelessly obscure' has been the verdict of most critics up to date (the same was said of *Ulysses* at first). Obscure, yes—but not hopelessly so, and not more so than any synthesis of life which, rejecting the short cuts of abstraction, gives a living picture of its theme and deals with personalities, not axioms. And—another shock for the wiseacres!— all over its vast panorama flicker the lambent lightnings of a character- istically Irish and Rabelaisian humor. Nothing is here of highbrow gravity and the note of tragedy is rarely heard. (Nor, despite appear- ances, was *Ulysses* an 'epic of despair,' for the protagonist is Mr. Bloom, a Falstaff, and the 'Hamlet young man,' Stephen Dedalus, plays second fiddle to him throughout).

For those who look the facts of life and history squarely in the face there are but two alternatives—tears or laughter. Each brings to the Great War which humanity is waging against death, despair and decay, on a front that is never 'All Quiet,' the outlook of his own temperament. The Irishman Joyce has the spirit of the Sammies, Tommies, and *Poilus* of the front line, and gaily hums as the banshies keen around his observation post, 'Pack up your troubles in your old kit bag And smile, smile, smile!'

HAVETH CHILDERS EVERYWHERE (HCE)

June 1930

245. Padraic Colum, review, *New Republic*

'From a *Work in Progress*', *New Republic*, lxiv, No. 824 (17 September 1930), 131–2. The same article appeared in *Dublin Magazine*, vi, No. 3 (July–September 1931), 33–7.

In his late thirties James Joyce recast the most used of literary mediums, the novel; he recast it with *Ulysses*. He is now recasting the novel more radically, and he is recasting language as the medium of writers who know that what they write should tend toward poetry.

In his late forties, then, he is engaged in the most heroic effort that is being made by any writer of our epoch. His *Work in Progress* represents that effort. It is not completed, but already it has had effect: language, writers have been shown, is evocative as well as descriptive. And narrative can be made to tell us about other than diurnal happenings. As narrative, *Work in Progress* is more like a piece of mythology than it is like a novel; it seems to me to have a likeness to that curious fragment of Central American mythology that we call the Popul Vuh. *Haveth Childers Everywhere* is the third fragment from *Work in Progress* to appear in book form: already there have been published *Anna Livia Plurabelle* and *Tales Told of Shem and Shaun*.

Haveth Childers Everywhere is to be compared with *Anna Livia Plurabelle*. The latter is about a river and about river civilizations; specifically, it is about the River Liffey. The former is about a city, about Dublin. And as the book about the river had the rhythm of flowing water, the ripple, the sweep, the still spread of the river, this third fragment has in its rhythm the blare of the city. The river was incarnated in a woman, Anna Livia; the city is incarnated in a man, H. C. E.

Considered as a man, H. C. E. is the boss man—in every situation—

he is Adam, he is Abraham, he is the Duke of Wellington, he is Daniel O'Connell. In his origin he is Norse, for Dublin was founded by Vikings and Norse merchants. . . . As he appears before us in the present fragment, he is Everyman, for he is answering to the charge that is brought against all of us—call it Original Sin or the Fall of Man. Something has happened in a garden, in the city park, and he is protesting his detachment from it. And in the course of his defense he brags of all that he has accomplished—all that Dublin has done. . . .

[quotes Joyce's belief that history has no validity as found in his essay 'James Clarence Mangan']

. . . In other words, history is not a denial of reality when it is known as mythology. It is mythology of this kind that we have in *Work in Progress*. In *Anna Livia Plurabelle*, James Joyce introduced hundreds of river names as verbs and nouns and adjectives. In this fragment, which is about the metropolis, he introduces hundreds of words derived from names in other cities to describe scenes and events— 'madridden mustangs and buckarestive bronchos' appear in the last passage of *Haveth Childers Everywhere*, passages that describe the city's transportation.

A rhythm which has a scriptural powerfulness bears everything along. . . .

[quotes from p. 532]

A reader who is not prepared for this development in Joyce's writing will protest that these are meaningless successions of words. I can get, such a reader may say, a sense of rhythm, I can feel that somebody is talking loudly and compellingly. But what it is about I do not know. . . .

[an explanation of the passage]

. . . But why, it will be asked, has James Joyce found it necessary to use this arcane language? Briefly, because *Work in Progress* deals with the night life of humanity, that dream life which is the one-third of our mortal career. The language of the day cannot be the language of the night; another language has to be found to render this state. And, as any of us know who have caught ourselves in the stage between sleeping and waking, a number of memories and notions are imposed, one on the other, in our unwakeful condition.

Joyce finds his language in words in which a number of meanings are telescoped. We have all noted such words. . . . James Joyce has his words change as the situation changes. Thus, the Phoenix Park in Dublin becomes the Fiendish Park when H. C. E. offended or was framed up in it, and the Pynix Park when Athens, as one of the world's metropolises, was to give a name to H. C. E.'s city. . . .

In the medium that Joyce is establishing, poetry and humor have fresh reaches. Take the poetry of the passage which evokes the cathedral, with its bells, music and lights:

[quotes from p. 552]

And the humor of the passage describing those direful portraits— 'painted by hand' as we are always informed, but looking like photographs of wax figures that we see in provincial town halls:

[quotes from p. 550]

The effect that James Joyce is working for can only be realized in a complete work; he cannot achieve it by introducing such passages of poetry or humor into writing that is close to our norm. It is heroic of him and it is right on his part to make a complete departure and to put all his discoveries in an integral work. But to a man engaged in such heroic effort one might counsel prudence. It is not prudent on his part to bring into his work some private piece of knowledge or to over-elaborate some element of his meaning. I fancy I detect instances of both imprudences in *Haveth Childers Everywhere*. Take, for example, the description of the metropolitan cathedral already quoted. Besides all that refers to bells, music, color, anthem, there are references to local and national affairs. When he says 'to tellforths' glory,' one who knows Dublin remembers that the organ builders of the city are Telfords; one who knows Irish history remembers that a Norse chieftain put his wife sitting on the high altar of a cathedral, and so one gets the reference in 'she sass her nach, chillybombom . . . upon the altarstane.' But what has 'forty bonnets' to do with this? One suspects that this is some private understanding of Joyce's. And when he speaks of 'such gretched youngsters' we are delighted with a phrase that combines 'Gretchen' with 'wretched.' But why is it elaborated by adding, to 'I would not know to contact such gretched youngsters,' the cryptic words, 'in my ways from Haddem or any suisterees or heiresses of theirn, claiming by, through, or under them.' One has to work hard to get even 30 percent of understanding of *Work in Progress*. But even less than 30 percent gives one humor, poetry, a sense of mythological character, that one cannot get in any other writing of the present day. . . .

246. Michael Petch, opinion, *Everyman*

1931

'The Approach to James Joyce', *Everyman*, v (25 June 1931), 701–2. Petch refers to an earlier letter by F. B. Cargeege ['The Mystery of James Joyce', *Everyman* (11 June 1931), n.p.] in which these comments are made: 'Are there really people who imagine they can read this jargon? I simply do not believe it. Is it an amazing literary hoax? . . .

May I offer a little enlightenment to your correspondent, F. B. Cargeege? He states that *Haveth Childers Everywhere* is '*absolutely* incomprehensible,' and goes on to say that it has been foisted on 'us.'

I first started to read Joyce in the trenches. I began with the serial publication of *Ulysses* in the *Little Review*, going on to *Chamber Music, Exiles*, and *Portrait of the Artist as a Young Man*. Then I got *Ulysses* in one volume and have followed this up with *Work in Progress* in the pages of *transition*. I frequently dip into the pages of Joyce, always with pleasure, profit and an increase of understanding. I advise your correspondent to look up the copies of *Everyman* for May 15 and August 30, 1930.

Joyce is bound to leave traces on the speech of the men who follow after him. *Ulysses* carries to a much further point the qualities that began to appear in his earlier work; and, in consequence has been hailed as epoch-making in English literature: it closes an epoch in content and opens one in style. Any writer who attempts new arrangements of words or who employs more words of the English language than is customary is regarded by the obscure reader as insane.

Pitfalls of originality await the explorer, it is true; but, there are others. Words and phrases are things of fashion. Like clothes they descend in the social scale, until worn-out or discarded. Reliance on phrases clouds the intellect. Respectably married adjectives beget Victorian families of clichés, while an enfranchized imagination will grow athletic and inventive at exercise. If language is to be a living thing there must be innovations in grammar, spelling and syntax.

Joyce is labouring at the break-up of beautiful words in English, and busied with the erection of Polyglot word-structures. The reconstruction is both novel and stimulating. He takes the view that there is no hope for writing unless disintegration first takes place. . . .

Joyce is preoccupied with words (not sentences) spoken or sung, their music, their rhythm. He will devote many hours to the set *elaboration* of a single page, so it is manifestly impossible to apprehend his work at a single glance.

The last four pages of the shilling edition of *Anna Livia Plurabelle* have been recorded for the gramophone. Intonation does help. Mr. Gerald Heard has sensibly suggested that the reading should be seen, and the tone assisted by expression. He further points out that Mr. Joyce is 'attempting to charge language with overtones, harmonics and un-resolved chords so that for the ordinary reader to understand (if the author cannot deliver his message personally) it will be necessary to employ a trained executant, as the ordinary lover of music, to appreciate a score, must hear a good pianist render it.'

I am tired of hearing Joyce compared to Rabelais, who only play-fully and infrequently essayed neologisms. Joyce is doing the navvy work of the new language. He has grasped staggering possibilities that few seem to suspect. His composite vocabulary has more than a score of ingredients—all the living European tongues, a little of Asiatic, some Afrikaans—and Greek and Latin. I have also detected traces of idiomatic South American Spanish that would have eluded me, save for contact with the natives of Robin Hood's Bay, who sail regularly to the Rio de la Plata.

Joyce often has recourse to more than one language to construct a portmanteau-word, which would be detected more quickly by a poly-glot than a monolingual Briton, but even the polyglot would be dazzled by the facets of the resultant word—the seemingly effortless mingling of classic myth with Biblical incident—of pious apostrophe with implacable vendetta (in referring to the Invincibles 'O felix culpa!' becomes 'O foenix culprit!')

The initial thing to learn about Joyce is that he is the major droll of our time. Even with a knowledge of languages to parallel his own one would need a goat-like nimbleness of mind to follow his every caper.

His knowledge is profound; in addition to knowing the languages, he knows the literature, the folk-lore, the slang and the music of the same peoples.

The chorus-leader of *Work in Progress*—H. C. E. (here comes everybody) is synthetic and amorphous—the theme of the book is non-spatial, non-temporal. Joyce does not add one iota to human understanding—seeming to possess all human knowledge, he plays a light air over it. He does not bore his readers with a re-statement of familiar ideas. He transcends didacticism by combining or fusing references and associations, at the same time freeing them from topical and parochial limitations. He buries all the weeds of language two spits deep. He does *not* abandon dictionary interpretation of words but brings out all the meanings a word ever had, building a counterpoint of ideas, playing on latent rhythm, colour and smell.

On the first page of *Work in Progress* there is a word imitating the sound of a thunderclap, composed of syllables for the word for thunder in more than twelve languages, a word of ninety-four letters, a link with Æsop. This is the word:

BADALGHARAGHTAKAMMINARRONNKONNBRONNTONNERRON-
NTUONNTHUNNTROVARRHOUNAWNSKAWNTOOHOORDENENTH-
URNUCK

More lives are lived in towns than in country places, and while we have a large vocabulary of rural beauty we have but the slenderest æsthetic of cities, so Joyce tries to create out of the demotic words spoken in drab cities. He is sensitized to dirt and loves it for the sake of truth; forming new words in the Greek fashion of compound epithets—by telescoping grammar. Sometimes the concatenation is like a mighty collision between mammoth dictionaries.

While there is a plethora of fogged readers, there is perhaps hardly a sufficient number of obscure writers. An intelligent enquiring human being does not want to be given such all his life, but rather thrives on variety and a graded diet. Towards the end C. E. Montague came to question clarity and to love the recondite word. He even opened a small private mint and gave us such coin as 'aromatist,' 'futilitarian,' etc.

The books of the future may not be written as Joyce writes now; the mould may be discarded, the matrix not serve for other births, but it is serving its turn. . . .

247. Sisley Huddleston on Joyce and *Ulysses*

1931

Extract from *Back to Montparnasse* (1931), pp. 192–203.

James Joyce's *Ulysses* is naturally on the list of banned books, though many thousands of copies have been sold and carried into England and America. I can understand everything that is said against this monumental work; though I think whatever demerits are to be found in *Ulysses* are more than counterbalanced by its amazing merits. But let us admit, for the sake of argument, that there are grave ethical faults in *Ulysses*, which cannot possibly be countenanced by the authorities. . . . Here were some of Europe's most admirable critics declaring that a masterpiece had appeared—that a landmark in literature had been planted—that something profoundly original, something which would deeply affect subsequent writing, had been born from the brain of Joyce. The critics may, of course, be right, or they may be wrong. Yet there is a certain presumption in favour of their rightness. There is, at least, a doubt as to their wrongness. . . .

The trouble is that there are many people who are incapable of distinguishing between lewd lucubrations and *Ulysses*. I dare say many of them bought *Ulysses* for the sake of passages which, they had been told, were improper. How disappointed they must have been! For the passages they sought are so rare, and are so interwoven in the texture of the book, and are so meaningless by themselves, that the nasty-minded purchasers would find *Ulysses* dull reading, and think themselves swindled. . . .

Incidentally, I may take this opportunity of remarking that Joyce is by no means so incomprehensible as is assumed. There are passages which are doubtless incomprehensible; there are other passages which demand more attention than it is fair to ask from any reader, a wider knowledge than should be presupposed by a writer, and a process of association of ideas that cannot operate in identical manner in any two persons in the world. My own advice is to let these passages go—to read them aloud for their music, their obvious humour, their apparent sense, their curious suggestiveness; and not to search farther for hidden meanings. Yet if there are many such passages in Joyce's newer work, presenting linguistic difficulties for the pedagogic mind, there are, practically speaking, no such passages in *Ulysses*; and certainly anybody can understand *A Portrait of the Artist as a Young Man* without undue mental effort. *Dubliners*—a collection of short stories which, strangely, gave great offence, and was, I believe, publicly burnt—is simply written. . . . But without seeking controversy, I will merely say that, in my opinion, a great disservice has been rendered Joyce by the insistence, of many of his admirers, on an obscurity which, for the most part, is not present in his writing up to the publication of 'Work in Progress.'

Doubtless Joyce himself has not sufficiently discouraged this insistence on his obscurity. *Ulysses* can be read and enjoyed without any heed being paid to the nonsense of its parallelism with the *Odyssey* of Homer. The parallelism is far-fetched. The incidents in *Ulysses* which are supposed to correspond to the incidents in the *Odyssey* can only be made to correspond by a ludicrous effort.

There was some such parallelism in the mind of Joyce; but I suspect it to have been very vague, and I do not think it determined the order, the character, or the shape of the incidents. He told me about it at the beginning, and he elaborated it rather unconvincingly. I fully accept his account; but I do not feel that it is necessary for an understanding of *Ulysses* to demonstrate the parallelism in detail. The demonstration cannot, in my view, add to the interest or the artistry of *Ulysses*. . . .

If one were to make a comparison of Joyce and Lawrence, one would be bound to say that Lawrence stands for acceptance, and Joyce for rejection. Lawrence would find lust and all natural things good, while Joyce would find lust and all natural things bad; Lawrence rails against those who would suppress human or even animal instincts. while Joyce rails against those who would exhibit animal or even human instincts. There could be no greater contrast than that of these two men; and yet they have been inconsiderately bracketed together. This contrast will be appreciated by any one who has seen Joyce, the family man, in his family parties; and his very conventionality in living has resulted in unconventionality in writing. Joyce is the puritan who is shocked by the libertine; Lawrence is the libertine (in theory at least) who would shock the puritan.

Withal, Joyce is saved by a sense of humour. Perhaps the essence of Joyce is his humour. It saves him from ultimate disgust. It keeps him sane and sound in spite of his abhorrence for physical filth. What was it that Rabelais said? *Mieulx est de ris que de larmes escrire*—which may be roughly translated: It is better to write of laughter than of tears. So Joyce, obsessed by the banality, the beastliness, and the tragedy of things, endeavours to turn them into fun. We cannot forget what underlies that fun but neither should we forget the alchemy of his fun.

I sometimes wonder whether he takes those who take him too seriously as seriously as they take him. I sometimes wonder whether, in odd moments, he is not amused at the ponderous exegeses he has himself inspired. I sometimes wonder whether one author of a Joyce-yen exegesis has not his tongue in his cheek. And yet it is difficult to conceive of any one writing hundreds of thousands of words to perpetrate a gigantic joke. There must surely be two departments of the human brain. . . .

If *Ulysses* seems to present difficulties, what are we to make of the book that bears the provisional title of *Work in Progress*? Joyce complained to me that the critics who had been kindly disposed towards *Ulysses* professed that they could make nothing of the chapters of *Work in Progress* which Eugène Jolas boldly printed in *transition*. The public that cares for new and significant writing was also given the opportunity of judging Joyce's development by the separate publication in book form of various sections, of which the most satisfactory was that entitled *Anna Livia Plurabelle*. . . . I do not think anybody should stay to analyse all the words. What do they matter, apart from the atmosphere they create? The best known passage—which I have heard Joyce recite several times—needs no explanation. Night falls on the Liffey, and the washerwomen, who are talking across the river, turn into tree and stone, and their voices grow fainter and more remote, so that in the end we read: . . .

[quotes from pp. 215–16]

Nobody asks for a glossary. Nobody wants to know precisely what is meant by foos or ho. For that matter they are simple enough, but it is better that we should not occupy ourselves with them, as though Joyce's prose were a crossword puzzle. Throughout he reforms and deforms words; he makes audacious puns; he hides the names of rivers and other objects; and personally I do not think anybody should trouble to pick out all the meanings of all the puns or discover all the rivers. A general understanding suffices. Vico proposed in his *Scienza Nuova* the making of an ideal and timeless history, in which all the actual histories of all nations should be embodied, and Joyce takes for his material all that is timeless, and confounds myth and reality. Suppose we let it go at that, and grasp what we can grasp, and enjoy what we can enjoy, and not worry about that which escapes us because our knowledge does not happen to be the same as Joyce's knowledge, and our ideological associations are not the same as his, and our verbal processes are somewhat different? . . . Besides, I am not sure that Joyce himself could always, without ingenious afterthought, explain every word he coins. In short, Joyce, like the Bible, is, from a literary viewpoint, better without commentators. Theology doubtless has its place; and I suppose Joyceology has its place; yet I prefer the *Song of Solomon* and *Anna Livia Plurabelle* as they are—I prefer their direct appeal to the indirect appeal of learned pedagogues.

The commentators have overdone it; they have directed attention to the difficulties of Joyce's prose; I would rather read him simply. Underneath the surface there are doubtless incredible subtleties which we are not compelled to fathom; on the surface Joyce is as simple as Lewis Carroll, who can be understood by a child, and yet cannot be interpreted by a professor of language, when he writes:

> 'Twas brillig, and the slithy toves
> Did gyre and gimble in the wabe.

But I remember that Humpty Dumpty did tell us what was meant by brillig and slithy and toves and the rest. He added nothing; and the Humpty Dumpties who explain Joyce add nothing. . . .

248. Wyndham Lewis on Joyce

1931

Extract from Louise Morgan, 'Wyndham Lewis: The Great Satirist of our Day', *Everyman* (19 March 1931), 232 [231–3]; reprinted in *Writers at Work* (1931), pp. 43–52.

In the course of an interview Lewis makes several general comments on Joyce.

. . . In writing, the only thing that interests me is *the shell*. It's the actions and the appearance of people that I am concerned with, not the 'stream of consciousness' of any 'mysterious' invisible Within. I think the normal human attitude is physical, not mental.'

'You think Joyce's method is not normal then?'

'His method is romantic. The method preferred by me may be described as classical; it is objective, and rather scientific than sentimental. The classical is the form to which all romantic revolutions of style return. The romantic is a decadence, a constantly recurring decadence if you like, but a decadence.'

'The novel will not develop in the direction of Joyce then?'

'I think not, because his *inside* method is too limited to be a universal method. I have used the inside method occasionally, but only under special circumstances. It can be very effective when dealing with the extremely aged, with young children, half-wits, or animals. But for the most part I use the *outside* method. . . . The trouble with the "thought-stream" method is that it robs work of all linear properties whatever, of all contour and definition: it breaks up or dissolves their shells. The romantic abdominal *within* method results in a jelly-fish structure, without articulation of any sort.' . . .

249. Henri Fluchère on *Ulysses*

1931

'*Ulysse*', *Le Foyer Universitaire*, ii, No. 5 (May 1931), 1–6.

I have spent five or six years reading James Joyce's *Ulysses*. I have no shame in admitting that the admirable French translation . . . has just provided me with a month of diligent confrontations, rewarded by the solid satisfaction of having, thanks to it, penetrated to the heart of these labyrinthine corners where I was often lost. *Ulysses* is, without doubt, the most considerable literary event of the last ten years. As such, it has been the object of abundant controversies, the most varied in tone, ranging from the most passionate admiration to the absolute end of rejection. A masterpiece, immense book, a *summa*, some say: caco-graphy, the reign of the absurd, the sordid, the burlesque, 'unsmokable' contemplation, others say. I intend to arrange some of these impressions and if possible derive some ideas. . . .

[summarizes some earlier criticism]

Let us keep believing that *Ulysses* is a novel. It is a psychological development, a chronological analysis which wants to be exhaustive of the conscience of man, representing the normal man. Two points of view must be considered: as a document and as a work of art. I will, indeed, say 'work of art.' Because if the value (I was going to say scientific) of this work is not contested, it is its artistic value which is the object of the most vehement discussions and which, finally, will plead for or against it in the tribunal of the composite conscience of the public which judges as a last resort.

The Joycean method, or if you wish, the technique of investigation, composition, writing, is going to constitute the first level of our inquiry. The writer who wants to tell a story and paint a soul has, it seems, only two or three ways of proceeding. The simplest way is confession. He writes in the first person, and tells the events in which he has been involved, from his point of view, and he analyzes the sentiments which he has experienced. This is the subjective, direct method, which casts the most glaring light on the central hero, but can only conjecture about his confederates, since it only allows the author to speak of himself. The writer can, next, tell the events to which he has assisted, but only as a spectator and, after the exterior witnesses, reconstruct, in the indirect style, the development of this action. He will remain exterior to the narration. It is only through an artifice of presentation that he will pretend to offer the event which he tells to the adhesion of the mind of the reader. These artifices of presentation are multiple. The closest to the real (although not the most likely) is the epistolary artifice. The author is only an editor: he publishes the letters of characters in the action, and finds, there, the subjectivity of confession in some sort reduced. . . .

[six paragraphs of illustration of these points, moving toward a discussion of the interior monologue as practiced by Larbaud, Proust and Joyce]

. . . James Joyce is the great worker of interior monologue. *Ulysses* would not exist without it.

It is no longer necessary to believe that *Ulysses* is interior monologue from end to end. Joyce fades away before Leopold Bloom and the others. But he puts them in motion. He locates them, then he follows them, like the shadow follows the body, and as a faithful mirror, or infinitely sensible receiver, he records their gestures and all the disturbances of their secret consciences. If his characters speak, act, Joyce perceives and reproduces their words and gestures, but between a reply and a response, in the course of the succession of movements which unite the hand to the handle of the door, the flux of conscience is not stopped. . . . But such a method, flowing from the following consequences is the major grief of Joyce's adversaries . . . The method of investigation seems to exclude all other methods of composition. The result will be an indescribable chaos, the reign of fragments and discontinuities . . . This is the supreme defeat of the artist who devours himself. It leaves the way free to follies, to mystifications. Such an art is not durable; it is even unthinkable.

Not at all. Because Joyce composes. He composes with a rigor which can not be grasped by reading only a few pages. His method of composition, as might be expected, is in harmony with his method of investigation. The 800 pages of *Ulysses* have for a subject the single day of Leopold Bloom. The unity resides in him. Bloom, so fugitive as are his states of successive conscience, has a personality *à moi* in the sense understood by philosophers. He is led by dominant preoccupations which come back, like major themes, in the course of the development of his day. His gestures are logically prepared by other gestures, his thoughts and desires conditioned by unimpeachable antecedents, and as they are followed step by step, one increases in depth and in scope in the knowledge that one has of him. A piece of soap, a visitor's card, a refrain—we soon know their importance, and that nothing is left to chance. Bloom becomes more and more real, more and more familiar. In the multiplication of notations, across the apparent disorder of themes and incidents, is Bloom the advertising canvasser, the friend of Stephen Dedalus, the fickle husband, the 'average' man which we find on the day it pleases Joyce to choose—the calendar of his life in this appropriate frame which again reinforces the unity by its character of irrefutable unicity . . . One could almost say that Joyce conforms, paradoxically, to the three unities: Dublin, the sixteenth of June 1904, Bloom. . . .

[here follows a long discussion of the Homeric parallels, relying primarily on earlier criticism]

Joyce's modern style is not one of his least merits, that is in having known how to create his style. Because to write *Ulysses*, a particular style is needed. To tell the truth, there is perhaps in *Ulysses* the sum of all possible styles, beyond which this ingenious experimenter seems only able to knock himself against a blank wall. Each episode has its original style, its color, its rhythm, and appears expressible only with this color and this rhythm. Never has the English sentence been worked, kneaded, with a hand so vigorous and so agile; never has it carried within its flanks so much richness and so much power of evocation. Each character, each place, each hour of the day speaks its language, possesses its syntax, its vocabulary, plays its magic. The words, withdrawn from their ridiculous pretentions, are only docile instruments of the intellectual life and succeed in only carrying the color or concept of which the author charges them. An entire study would be necessary to bring about a true philosophy of language and of the artistic creation of which it is the supreme justification. A prodigious vocabulary, borrowed from all the 'cants' which is enriched again with the finds of James Joyce, all which takes human shape . . . in brief, a prodigious creation of a language which has never seemed better adapted to its object.

[article concludes with commendation for the translators]

250. A Fellow Dubliner on Joyce, S. Gilbert and Gogarty

1931

Extracts from 'A Fellow Dubliner', 'The Veritable James Joyce according to Stuart Gilbert and Oliver St. John Gogarty', *International Forum*, No. 1 (July 1931), 13–17. Also appeared in *transition*, No. 21 (March 1932), 273–82.

A review of Stuart Gilbert's *James Joyce's Ulysses: A Study* and Gogarty's comments in a letter to the reviewer. The review is of interest because of the critics' own comments, which have been extracted from the review proper.

Mr. Stuart Gilbert has written a book about James Joyce. Dr. Oliver St. John Gogarty has written a letter on the same theme. The letter is short and the book is long. But shortness and longness are not measures of wisdom. Mr. Stuart Gilbert is obviously a professional literary critic and he is obviously not an Irishman. He is too solemn for that. Solemnity is not an Irish quality. An Englishman can be naturally solemn. And a typical Irishman is profoundly serious but rarely solemn. Moreover, Dr. Gogarty has this advantage over Stuart Gilbert: He is a Dubliner himself. He knew Mr. Joyce intimately and he is said to be the medical student whom Joyce presented as 'Buck Mulligan' in *Ulysses*.

Before coming to discuss either the book or the letter it may be well to make a few prefatory remarks here for the benefit of foreign readers. . . .

Mr. Joyce's literary pedigree therefore comes of first class stock. And nobody can doubt his intellectual ability. Joyce has a command of the English vocabulary which is very rare. And he has written very commendable prose in *The Portrait of the Artist as a Young Man*; but it just fails in that quality which would make prose what is called first class. Mr. Joyce can also write good lyrics, as you will find if you read

Chamber Music. The following lyric, from that collection, I remember by heart. . . .

[quotes 'Strings in the earth and air']

There would be no sense in calling attention to *Ulysses* here except for the fact that some responsible English writers have been praising Mr. Joyce's work in a superlative way recently, and this recent movement has come to the aid of a cabal of spurious literary people who have been trying for the past nine years to push *Ulysses* on the public—and especially on the foreign public—as the greatest masterpiece of modern English literature.

Mr. Stuart Gilbert is the latest of the responsible writers. His book is very formidable and very solemn. It runs into four hundred octavo pages. It is all about *Ulysses* and we are told by the author that it has been written under the supervisional collaboration of Mr. Joyce himself. Was Joyce pulling Stuart Gilbert's leg? The main thesis of the latter seems to be that Joyce is the modern counterpart of Homer. Mr. Stuart Gilbert tells us naïvely that the Irish are the descendants of the ancient Achaeans, who were Homer's people. Therefore Joyce is the Nth. great grand-child of the blind Achaean poet. . . . But Mr. Stuart Gilbert wants to find an historical pedigree for the author of *Ulysses*. Or was it the author of *Ulysses* himself that put the idea into the ear of Mr. Stuart Gilbert? Not unlikely; for in *The Portrait of the Artist as a Young Man* Mr. Joyce is already thinking of himself in the light of a pre-destined hero or genius springing from a great race whose history extends far back into the heroic past. . . .

Let me open a parenthesis here on the question of Mr. Joyce's classical scholarship. One of the characteristics of *Ulysses* out of which much capital has been made is the teeming display of classical allusions, especially Greek. Joyce is constantly pulling the long Homeric bow in order to astonish the uninitiated; and he has succeeded to some extent, especially with the Americans, where classical learning is not very widely cultivated. I was once given a book written by a Californian, Mr. Paul Jordan Smith, on *Ulysses* [*On Strange Altars* (1924), pp. 14–34]. Naturally I didn't read it; because even the most scholarly Californian could tell me nothing about *Ulysses* or Dublin that I had not known long ago. But I dipped into the book at anyrate and one of the first features that caught my eye was a long panegyric on the classical learning of James Joyce.

God help us. One might as well praise the poor galley slave for the welts on his back and admire them as an excess of muscle. In the Ireland of my time and Joyce's we were the galley slaves of classic learning. . . .

Let nobody think that here an attempt is being made to discredit the literary abilities of the author of *Ulysses*. As a *tour de force* in the use of the English language *Ulysses* is an object for just and honest admiration, even for wonder.

[quotes from the Calypso episode, pp. 66–9, 67–70]

That sort of writing is claimed to be Mr. Joyce's principal contribution to the enrichment of English literature. His *claquers* are constantly telling us that it is the only successful attempt that has ever been made at an exact transcription of the stream of consciousness of the individual. Very well. Let us grant them their claim. Does that make *Ulysses* worth while? The stream of consciousness that is here transcribed is a very muddy stream. Throughout the whole book the same kind of transcription goes on—broken words, broken phrases, a jamboree of senseless syllables here and a race of long-sounding words there, the latter having meaning in themselves but no meaning when strung together. But let us suppose that they actually transcribe Bloom's stream of consciousness. Does this faithful transcription of Bloom's stream of consciousness make *Ulysses* a monument of English literature? Or does it make *Ulysses* literature at all?

The stream of Bloom's consciousness, as transcribed by Mr. Joyce, is a very muddy and putrid stream. It is the stream that flows from a diseased mind—Bloom's—as you will easily recognise if you examine similar transcripts of the senseless chatter indulged in by certain types of lunatics in insane asylums. And here, by the way, it may be said that *Ulysses* is not a document that stands alone. The pathological records in the archives of lunatic asylums are its companions. . . .

When Mr. Stuart Gilbert's book on *Ulysses* first fell into my hands, and I was asked to write about it and about Mr. Joyce, I sent a letter to Senator Gogarty and mentioned some of the opinions which I have now expressed here. I asked Gogarty, in parenthesis, if he would be so kind as to write me a little lyric. A few days afterwards I received the following document. It is Dr. Gogarty's contribution to the argument; and I have not asked his permission to publish it; for, though he is an extremely clever man, he is very modest—with all his bounce—, as you will realise if you will read about him in George Moore's *Hail and Farewell*. . . .

'For you, a man of our race', he writes me, 'there is no excuse for falling into the trap which deceived so many Englishmen and which shall have them execrating him who set it when they suspect the deception, or, rather, become aware of their own shortcoming which hitherto they have sublimated at the expense of Scotland—dullness. For Joyce is a joke. No Scotsman could be so fooled. And you Irish!'

I am not trying only to imply that his books are but that he himself, by the sustained seriousness of his attitude in the face of absurdity, in face of the execrable, is a joke by reason of his preposterous pose or rather by his serious acceptance of the preposterous. I don't consider him a poseur. So you must not seek for criticism in him nor resistance. He recites, he recoils, he drivels. I see an American calls this latter part of him 'The Tragedy of the Unconscious'. Unconsciousness of humour is always a tragedy. Be careful or I will compare you to Mussolini, with his Leviathan lack of humour. . . . There never was such a Joker—such, as John Elwood would say, an artist—in the sense of artifex—as Joyce. And none the less Joyce for keeping his face. Why should a jester have to lead the laugh? Are all the audience dummies? Why, except for the sake of erudition, compare him to Swift? He has no *Saeva Indignatio*. He lies down with the abandoned and howls *Holy Murder* . . . He is not a mocking Dante but a mockery of him: all Dublin is his *Inferno*. It is, as he sees it, damnable enough without demonstration other than its existence. . . .

251. Harold Nicolson on the significance of Joyce

1931

Extract from 'The Significance of James Joyce', *Listener* (16 December 1931), 1062; 'The Modernist Point of View', *idem* (23 December 1931), 1108–9.

The entire first article is devoted to Joyce; Joyce is mentioned only briefly in the second article. These articles are derived from Nicolson's B.B.C. talk on Joyce (see the Introduction, p. 24).

People who think about James Joyce divide themselves roughly into three classes. There are those who regard him as a writer of improper literature. There are those who regard him as a technician of vast originality. And there are those who regard him as a prophet, clad in sackcloth and ashes, prophesying nihilism.

There is, in the first place, what some people call the 'ugly' side of Joyce. Obviously, there must be some reason why a writer of Mr. Joyce's distinction and integrity should, with such deliberation, dwell on subjects, and employ expressions, which it is customary in this country either to ignore or to record only in a delicate ambiguity of phrase. Obviously also a writer of Mr. Joyce's scholarship and serious-ness would not have devoted seven years of his life to writing a book with the intent to shock his readers. There must be some other explana-tion for Mr. Joyce's frequent references to realistic subjects, for his persistent and very detailed employment of words which are not drawing-room words. I think this explanation is as follows.

Mr. Joyce, as happens with most men of genius, reacted violently against his own early education, which took two forms—the discipline and the conventions of a Jesuit school, and the prevailing literary atmosphere. The former imbued Joyce with a sense of original sin. People who have no sense of original sin seldom write books which contain violent or obscene expressions. . . .

Mr. Joyce, in the second place, reacts against the literary atmosphere which prevailed during his most impressionable years at Dublin. . . . It was against this tenuous, this uncorporeal unreality that Joyce reacted. His reaction was extremely violent. He seized the muse of Irish romance by her pallid neck, dragged her away from the mists and wailings of forgotten legends, and set her in the sordid Dublin streets of 1904. In so doing, he did well.

There is a third explanation also for Joyce's realism. Mr. Cyril Connolly, in an article which he contributed to *Life and Letters* in April, 1929 [No. 185], made the interesting discovery that Joyce was, in fact, a mediævalist. There is much to be said for this intelligent paradox. . . . It would not be too far-fetched even to indicate how such a temperament finds an outlet in the Rabelaisian love of words—finds in the living language of the streets the pullulating life which is absent from the thin wisps of sophistication which serve for higher culture. The Rabelaisian coincidence is certainly a formative feature in Mr. Joyce's habit of thought.

There is a fourth explanation of Mr. Joyce's cruder realisms. He is essentially a comprehensive, and not a selective writer. In one of his novels he has taken a single day out of the life of his characters: this limitation of time provides him with the opportunity for a great extension of detail. He records everything which, during that day, happened to his main characters. And owing to this determined inclusiveness, he tells of many things which the selective writer would omit.

Behind all these, as it were accidental, causes lies a far more deliberate explanation. Mr. Joyce has formulated a perfectly definite theory of the function of a creative artist. The artist, to his mind, should aim at an æsthetic state in which 'the mind is arrested and raised above desire or loathing'. He considers this state, or *stasis*, to be the only possible mood in which what he calls 'proper' art can be produced. 'The feelings', he writes, 'excited by improper art are kinetic, desire and loathing. Desire urges us to possess: loathing urges us to abandon. The arts which excite them, pornographical or didactic, are therefore improper arts'. 'The artist', he writes again, 'remains within or behind or beyond or above his handiwork, invisible, refined out of existence, indifferent, paring his finger nails'.

Let me try to explain what Mr. Joyce means by this. He means that great art is as a mirror reflecting life: that the great creative artist should have no purpose in his mind beyond this purpose of accurate reflection. And that the moment any message, or even comment, is introduced there is a disturbance in the mirror, and art becomes what he calls 'improper'.

At moments Joyce becomes almost overpoweringly difficult to read, and, as such, almost overpoweringly dull. Yet this obscurity has its justification. Mr. Joyce is, above all, a pioneer in technique. He is, as such, disconcerting. He endeavours to abandon the inferential for the suggestive. He adopts the pattern and suggestiveness of music rather than the logical narrative of what we have hitherto regarded as English prose. His effect—and it is potent enough—is contrived as much by the interruptions in understanding as by the continuities of understanding. It is thus a mistake, when reading Joyce, to try to understand him. You must abandon yourself to receptivity: you must not expect a lesson or a story: you must expect only to absorb a new atmosphere, almost a new climate. It may take you some time to become acclimatised to Joyce. But when once you have achieved that absorption you will find that he has profoundly modified the shape of your observation.

Let me now examine some aspects of his technique. Mr. Joyce in the first place, is interested in what is called 'the stream of consciousness'. He endeavours, that is, to reproduce the simultaneity and multiplicity of the thought-stream. He realises that most of our thoughts proceed by association rather than by inference. He tries, therefore, to record these thought-processes in terms, not of continuity, but of association. Let me illustrate what I mean. Joyce wants to describe a man walking along the beach.

[quotes from the beginning of the Calypso episode, p. 38, 37]

Then Mr. Joyce has perfected the silent soliloquy or internal monologue—a device first attempted forty-four years ago by M. Dujardin in his *Lauriers sont coupés*. The internal monologue is thought before it is arranged into a logical sequence, it is a slow motion picture of thought. Until Joyce arrived, fiction had been the narrative either of external action or of conscious thought: Joyce extended the scope of fiction by adding to it the whole vast territory of sub-conscious thought. By so doing he may have confused our understanding, since with most of us understanding is little more than the recognition of the habitual. But he has added enormously to our capacity of observation; once you have absorbed the Joyce climate, you begin to notice things in your own mind which had never occurred to you before. And to have given to one's own generation a whole new area of self-knowledge is surely an achievement of great importance. . . .

Superficially we might say that the dominant note in modernist literature was one of criticism of, and reaction against, all that had preceded it. True it is that the modernist regards all Victorian theories, and all reversions to the Victorian formula, as suspect and compromising. True it is that the modernist is, to a certain extent, out to destroy what he regards as the timid self-delusions of his fathers. . . .

A further element introduced into modernist literature by the disillusion of the War generation is the element of contrast. This, especially in the poetry of T. S. Eliot—a writer who has had a deep influence on his generation—has created a constant preoccupation with the contrast between what we feel and what we should like to feel. . . .

This contrast between the desired and the attainable, between the unreal and the real, is even more emphatic in the work of James Joyce. Here you have a writer of great genius, tremulous sensibility and dynamic originality. Joyce is constantly preoccupied by the painful contrast between the unreal and the real, between literature and life. He knows that both are equally important. In order to underline that importance, he sometimes renders to life the things which belong to literature. For this cause he has been much misunderstood. People have not fully realised the strong purposiveness which lies at the root of all Joyce's work. . . .

252. Stuart Gilbert explicates *Work in Progress*

1931

Extract from 'A Footnote to Work in Progress', *Experiment* (Cambridge), No. 7 (Spring 1931), 30–3. Later appeared in *Contempo*, iii (February 1934), 4–5.

For his *Work in Progress* James Joyce employs at once a new literary form and a new technique of words; hence the difficulties in its perusal. The form of *Work in Progress* (so far as can be judged from that portion of the work—a little more than half—which has so far been published) may be likened to a carefully planned and exactly ordered fantasia, based on a set of ancient but abiding folk-tunes. For it is the paradox of this work to be at once fantastic and extremely symmetrical; nothing could be further from the super-realist 'free writing,' yet a reader's first impression is one of confusion, a vivid welter of ideas and free associations. A baroque superstructure hides the steel frame beneath.

The effect is one of polyphony; themes flow one above the other as in a fugue; the printed words represent a series of cross-sections, chords. Syllabic sounds are treated as units which can be moulded or reassembled so as to convey a host of meanings in a single vocable. A slight vowel change may suffice to add the required nuance, or—and this is where the plain reader is apt to stumble—the basic word or root is sometimes deformed out of easy recognition.

Ulysses was the epic of a day; *Work in Progress* is a nocturne, the stuff of dreams. The time dimension falls into abeyance, as in dreams; personalities far removed in time are merged in each other and, similarly, the scene of action is at once specific and world-wide.

The passage now reprinted in *Experiment* is taken from the opening pages of *Work in Progress* and was originally published in *transition*, No. 1 (April 1927). Its texture is comparatively simple and its humour exoteric. In the first paragraph we discover the gigantic protagonist, the strong man of any situation, a Vercingetorix, Adam, Sitric Silkenbeard (the Danish King of Duboin), Noah, Dunlop of the Tyres, Peter the Great, the 'Boss' of a big modern brewery, newspaper, etc. Two of his nonce-names are Here Comes Everybody and H. C. Earwicker (*alias* Persse O'Reilly). The initials H.C.E., once familiar as those of a pompous minister in Gladstonian times (Hugh Childers Erskine), often serve to indicate his presence, as in *Hic cubat edilis*. One of his many avatars is the Hill of Howth, near Dublin (there is an allusion to this in the word 'Whooth?'). Besides him we find Anna Livia Plurabelle, his river wife, the eternal feminine, one of whose vehicles is the Dublin Liffey; A.L.P. is a gay little old woman who trips along to a lilt of rollicking dactyls. . . . Satirists, moralists, reformers, all alike are mocked by the phantoms of their meliorism; the primal matter, a Proteus, contrives to slip through their fingers and leave them gaping at panther, snake or watery mirage upon the barren beach of Pharos . . . it was left to the author of *Work in Progress* to weave a spell to bind the old man of the tides, a grotesquery corrival with the cosmic harlequinade. . . .

253. George Moore to Louis Gillet

1931

Letter to Louis Gillet (20 August 1931), quoted in *Claybook for James Joyce*, by Louis Gillet. Translated by Georges Markow-Totevy (1958), pp. 32–3. Also in *James Joyce* by Richard Ellmann (1959), p. 631.

It was kind indeed of you to send me the number of *La Revue des Deux Mondes*, containing your article on Joyce 'Mr. James Joyce et son nouveau Roman *Work in Progress*,' [*Revue des Deux Mondes*, lxxxiv (August 1931), 928–39], and it is my pleasure to congratulate you on having achieved an article on a literary subject as well considered as an article by Sainte-Beuve. I am lost in admiration of the thought that you have put into this article and it required thought and consideration and reading and re-reading to disentangle Joyce's metaphysics. I say metaphysics for Joyce's book has nothing to do with art, nor yet science, so I suppose it must be metaphysics. Art is concerned with what the eye sees and not with the thinking mind. To the mind life is but the dreaming of a shade, but our actions arise from the belief that it is a great deal more than a shade and history will continue to be written notwithstanding Mr. Joyce's protest. I am by temperament an artist, that is to say by temperament one who is interested on appearance; a metaphysician only in the belief that the appearance may be illuminated faintly by a moral conception, but oh so faintly! With Joyce it is just the opposite. There are no appearances in Joyce; it is all syllogism. I am not quite sure of the meaning of the word syllogism, but I hope it will serve my present purpose. Joyce was in England some time ago. He had recovered his sight to some extent and lost his speech. I always heard of him in Dublin as one of the most garrulous of men. Now, he sits as silent as a mummy. He dined with me two nights and I had to make conversation all the time, which was tedious, and when I asked him to tell me how the action or the thought of *Ulysses* was advanced by associating the minor acts of Bloom with the acts of *Ulysses*, he answered 'I see I am on my defence.' I apologized. And by the next post I received a primer explaining all the mysteries of *Ulysses* and learnt from it that when Bloom smokes a corpulent cigar the reader is obliged to think of the Greek wanderer who blinds Polyphemus with a fire-hardened stake. I wrote to Joyce telling him that up to the present I had looked upon myself as a competent judge of a work of art and failing completely to discover the literary effect aimed at in the analogy of Bloom and his cigar and the wanderer's fire-hardened stake, I concluded that one of us had a blind patch in his mind somewhere. Which of us it is it would be an affectation for me to decide. . . .

254. Michael Stuart on Joyce's word creatures

1931

Extract from 'Mr. Joyce's Word Creatures', *Colophon*, Part 7 (1931). Also appeared in *Symposium*, ii (October 1931), 459–67 (from which the present text is taken).

Thus far the Dubliner has given life to three Universals in *Work in Progress*: the Word-River in the Fragment entitled *Anna Livia Plurabelle*, the Word-Insect in *The Ondt and the Gracehoper*, and the Word-City in *Haveth Childers Everywhere*. These three Fragments correspond to the three principal characters of the universal history which *Work in Progress* is intended to be. The names under which these three heroes occur most frequently in the story are Anna Livia Plurabelle, Earwicker (H. C. E. or Here Comes Everybody), and Shem and Shaun, a duel personality born from the marriage of A. L. P. and H. C. E.

We may note from the subjoined analysis of the verbal elements in *The Ondt and the Gracehoper*, selected because of its brevity and effectiveness, the following significant points. The language of this Fragment consists of a mosaic of seventeen tongues, English serving as the basic element with which the other idioms are interwoven. Names of insects and insect-members, references to Egyptian religious symbolism, and to the four principles of the development of human society as laid down by the Italian jurist, Vico, are the material from which the author creates his fable. The tone of this Fragment is satiric to the point of ribaldry; the impression of the whole is that of some airy Word-Creature ready to take wing.

A word on the plan of *Work in Progress* is relevant to the poetic problem set for himself by the author, affording simultaneously a view of the writer's general development. The Dubliner's art witnesses a steady progression from the Individual to the Universal. Indeed, the spiritual essence of scholasticism is so deeply imbedded in the roots of his soul that it manifests itself in his mature works in an all-pervading fashion.

All of the self-created complexities in *Ulysses* and *Work in Progress* resulting in ornamentation of structure, language, and character-creation arise undoubtedly from a compelling soul-need familiar to theologians of weaving a rich network of detail around the thread of an idea, a trait most noticeable in Gothic architecture and in the work of medieval book-illuminators. There is not a similar case in modern literature in which the problem inherited by scholasticism from ancient philosophy is resurrected to such a vigorous life as in the works of Mr. Joyce. We may note something of this fact in the three stages of his creative activity: the tendency to describe flesh-and-blood individuals as in *Dubliners, Exiles*, and *The Portrait* with the significant occurrence of unity of time and place in *Exiles;* secondly ,the tendency to universalize by suggesting as in *Ulysses* the existence of the aggregate, the City, and beyond the City, humanity; and lastly, as in *Work in Progress*, the tendency to disregard the life-story of individuals now merely named and remembered as the shadows of a dream 'in the palace of dim night' to create Universals as the characters of his story. In *Ulysses* as in Mr. Joyce's last work the reader often becomes aware that the action is being revealed through the mind of one of the characters, creating simultaneously the double effect of the subjective and the objective, so that a familiarity with each of these vast Gothic structures gives one the sense of some omnipresent Aristotelian divinity thinking his world into creation.

In *Work in Progress* the author has set himself the task of writing a miniature *universal* history as recalled by a sleeping Dubliner in a series of dreams lasting from about eight o'clock in the evening till four in the morning. Here, in a nutshell, is the whole scheme of the work. The chief poetic problem in this nocturnal world history is the creation of Universals. Unless *The Ondt and the Gracehoper* suggests a winged creature and *Anna Livia Plurabelle* a flowing river, the author has failed. It is the author's intention that the Creature or Thing embodied in each Fragment shall not be a description of an insect or a river but the verbal image of the Thing or Creature named. With Joyce the Word is life-giving, the Word is laughter-making (not the situation or character-description as with Rabelais or Cervantes), the Word is the all-in-all. A parallel to this magic evocative power of the word is to be found only in the Egyptian *Book of the Dead* and the *Popol Vuh* of the Central Americans. According to the followers of Osiris, not only the proper word, but also the manner, the tone in which words were pronounced meant success or failure for the soul seeking life eternal. In reading *Work in Progress* it is the tone of the voice, the manner of pronouncing aloud each word that will unlock to the reader the meanings of a word or a phrase.

The Ondt and the Gracehoper is a variation of the fable about the industrious ant, the champion of time, and the lazy, light-headed grasshopper, the champion of space. The contention between the two insects is interpreted according to tradition, although the sympathies of the author are evidently on the side of the 'gracehoper . . . who was always jigging a jog, hoppy on akkant of his joyicity . . . making ungraceful overtures to Floh and Luse and Bienie and Vespatilla . . . or . . . striking up funny funereels with Besterfather Zeuts, the Aged One. . . .' And, of course, 'the impossible gracehoper' comes to the sad end of the 'spindhrift,' 'sans mantis, sans shoeshooe, feather weighed animule, actually and presumptuably sinctifying chonic o' despair. . . .' The assiduous ant, 'boundlessly blissified,' reproves the Gracehoper, 'a darkener of the threshold.' Today as ever fables are written to point a moral for the human kind. Here (inter alia) the ant may stand as the symbol of any contemparary antagonistic to the time-spirit, whether a writer of 'volumes immense' or philospher or worldwide genius who cannot 'beat time. . . .'

[quotes and then analyses the first two pages of *The Ondt and the Gracehoper*, pp. 414–15]

255. Eugène Jolas, homage to Joyce

1932

Extract from 'Homage to James Joyce', *transition*, No. 21 (March 1932), 250–3.

. . . James Joyce reached the half-century mark in February of this year. It is a mile-stone in the literature of the world.

Joyce dominates his age as few writers have done. He has revolutionized literary expression. He has shaken the static world of phenomena to its foundation.

His work is not big in quantitative output. But *Dubliners*, written in his early twenties, followed by the *Portrait of the Artist as a Young Man* and *Ulysses*, created before he was forty years old, represent a gigantic architecture of a subjective-objective cosmos. Any one of these works would have sufficed to make the reputation of a great writer.

The as yet untitled *Work in Progress* is now being added by him to his life-work. A herculean task. A work without parallel in modern literary history. The English language here reaches heights not achieved since Shakespeare.

A life without sensational events is the background of this creative production. A life of exile for the most part. A life devoted exclusively to the flights of the spirit. A life of solitude, of pessimistic withdrawal.

From the moment he first tried to get a public hearing, there developed a sullen resistance against Joyce. He would never compromise. The publication of *Dubliners* was held up, when Dublin respectability seemed to be menaced. It was suppressed in Dublin after many delays in publication and it was not until several years later that it saw the light of day in London. The *Portrait of the Artist as a Young Man* aroused the fury of ecclesiastical cliques. *Ulysses* was considered to have inaugurated the 'sewage epoch', and was banned in America and England, to the everlasting disgrace of the intelligence of both countries. *Work in Progress*, during its publication in *transition*, was received for the most part, with catcalls and hisses.

Only a short time ago, both England and America once more played true to form. When Mr. Harold Nicholson. who had been invited by the British Broadcasting Company to speak before the microphone on the subject of current literature, suggested a discussion of the work of James Joyce, every attempt was made to prevent his carrying out his intention [No. 251]. After certain humiliating obstructions—which resulted in a sabotage of his first lecture—Mr. Nicholson was finally allowed to give the talk, on condition that he make no mention of *Ulysses*. . . .

Mr. Joyce's reputation on the continent has grown by leaps and bounds during the last six years. The translation of his works into the principal European languages—particularly the French rendition of *Ulysses* by Auguste Morel, with the assistance of Valéry Larbaud and Stuart Gilbert; which was published by Mlle. Adrienne Monnier—has started a plethora of critical estimates in almost every country. He is now profoundly influencing European writing.

About James Joyce, the artist, however, I should prefer not to go into details here. Many violent battles have already been fought around his name, and *transition*'s attitude is sufficiently well-known for me to forgo any further commentary.

But on his fiftieth birthday, I should like to say how much *transition* sympathizes with his titanic work and feels proud to have helped distribute his last creation. It seems appropriate, therefore, that *transition* make itself the mouthpiece of his friends in sending a message of greeting and admiration. . . .

256. Elliot Paul, comment on Joyce

1932

Extract from 'Farthest North: A Study of James Joyce', *Bookman*, lxxv (May 1932), 156–63.

. . . The manuscript of *Work in Progress* which I hoped to secure for publication in *transition*, I learned, had already been rejected by T. S. Eliot and Ezra Pound, who had been among his staunchest supporters in the days when fragments of *Ulysses* were beginning to appear and to be suppressed.

Later I came to realize that at no point in James Joyce's career has he been satisfied with his own work. Stephen Dedalus's pronunciamento that the errors of an artist are portals of discovery expresses more bravado than its author has ever possessed. It will be recalled that in the lying-in hospital scene of *Ulysses*, Stephen (who, of course, is Joyce) was deeply chagrined when Buck Mulligan reminded him that he had given the world but one slim volume of verses. The volume in question may well have been *Chamber Music*. Those verses were strictly conventional in form and remarkable for their lyric beauty, but they seemed to indicate rather a cautious talent, content to apply itself within narrow limits, than the scope which has characterized Joyce's later work. To him, they must have seemed rather an indictment than a measure of his abilities.

In *A Portrait of the Artist as a Young Man* Joyce followed an artistic pathway which his imitators have proved to be nothing short of disastrous for lesser men. An autobiographical novel specializing in childhood and adolescent impressions, however brilliantly it may be written, is a nerve-racking task for its author and Joyce felt the sordid atmosphere of his home and the unhealthy nature of his education too keenly not to suffer acutely in writing of his early life. . . .

The effect of youthful visions of hell upon his almost morbid imagination can best be estimated by a reading of the *Portrait*. By the time he had reached the dramatic night-town episode in *Ulysses* the long legendary history of man's descent into the inferno had become as comical as it was terrible to him and in that passage his wit flares and crackles like some huge unearthly pyrotechnical display. Although his readers have difficulty in recognizing the fact, an endless irreverent discussion as to the nature of original sin pervades *Work in Progress*. The significance of the thunderbolt, as Vico interprets it, driving primitive man into the cave, is especially meaningful to Joyce, who dreads it so thoroughly whenever threatening clouds obscure the sky.

It is easy to understand how a man like Joyce, so well grounded in literary tradition and familiar with the epics of all the principal languages, feels almost desperately anxious about the course he has chosen in breaking completely with past methods of writing. His career has been characterized by a series of experiments, each on a larger scale than the preceding one. At no point, I repeat, has he been complacent or cock-sure. It was not economic pressure nor a thirst for more glory which led him, after *Ulysses*, to embark upon the much-ridiculed *Work in Progress*. Progressively, since he was in school, he has been getting further out of touch with life and more and more intrigued with words. He knows that what he is doing now may be appraised as mere laboratory work, but some perverse curiosity within him drives him northward as his old companions, one by one, turn back toward the good safe temperate zone. It seems to him possible, at least, in view of the changes now in progress in the world, that the English language, much modified and expanded to admit all the other languages which have contributed to it or which border upon it, will become universal. Also he sees interesting relationships between the myths of various times and lands. So his prose has grown complicated, obscure and is almost completely dehumanized, like the abstractions of modern painting and music, and in a single sentence he jumbles together four or five languages. Many critics who have shown good judgment in other matters say that Joyce has gone crazy, others insist that he is fooling away his time. Actually, he is miles farther from insanity than many other men, past or present, who have accomplished a masterpiece before reaching the age of fifty. He has shown no tendency to seek a mental narcotic and has as little evangelical zeal as he had in the days when his aloofness from Irish politics earned him the censure of many of his countrymen and contemporaries. If *Work in Progress*, which sometime is to have a name, is judged to be worthless as literature and merely goes down as a philological curiosity Joyce will be disappointed but eventually will recover, I am sure. . . . *Ulysses*, in spite of its superficial parallel with the *Odyssey* and the numerous devices by which its author conveyed states of being and of feeling which hitherto had proved too difficult to be expressed, was essentially a realistic book, and it has a tang and an earthiness which can never be achieved by a synthesis of legends and of languages in which the material is second-hand. Joyce knows this very well, and it troubles him; but, like a prospector who has found a mine and lost its ownership, he cannot live upon the steady income of praise his past performances have earned him so he wanders on and on, not always hopeful but never quite discouraged. . . .

257. Desmond MacCarthy on the postwar novel

1932

'Le roman anglais d'après-guerre', *Revue de Paris*, xxxix (May 1932), 145–8 [129–52].

An examination of James Joyce's work would require many tunings and an analysis which could only be rendered intelligible by quotations. Since I am obliged to proceed superficially, the best thing to do is to proceed briefly. His influence is limited to writers or to virtual writers. Because opinions vary as to the value of his work, one can not doubt the extraordinary virtuosity and originality of Joyce. He began as a realist with *Dubliners*, and when it pleased him could evoke concrete subjects; he had at his service, besides, an immense vocabulary, a power of description as intense as that of Huysmans. During the war he published *A Portrait of the Artist as a Young Man* which presents us most profoundly with the soul of an adolescent; we can catch a glimpse of the insights of the interior world and hear bits of conversations through the sombre, thick, stuffy curtain of the diverse dispositions of the mind. There is beauty in this book, that of dawn fighting clouds and rain; and also horror similar to that of true childbirth. And the creature that came into the world was not the perfect and free artist, but a mutilated being, solitary and sullen.

Stephen Dedalus, the hero of *A Portrait*, is the second most important character in *Ulysses*.

Whatever may be the judgment of the future about this novel, whether it agree with that of some young authors and English critics who know that *Ulysses* is the masterpiece of the modern novel, or indeed that in spite of the extraordinary gifts of the language of its author, it is only an impostor, one can not doubt in any case that this is an original and most extraordinary work. That it can be read from one end to the other, certainly not, except by those who are interested in literary technique, or by those who have so absolute a faith in the author that they are ready to force his book, like a thief forces a safe, knowing that it contains a treasure. *Ulysses* was published in Paris and is still forbidden in England for reasons of obscenity. Obscene in the lewd sense it certainly is not; in truth, it would be rather too lugubriously the contrary, but it is seeded with words which it is forbidden to print, and there is in it a preoccupation with the body and its functions which is enough to arouse the disgust of the ordinary reader. Some have said that here was the modern epic poem, describing it as 'a comic and emancipatory vision of the entire modern world.' It is the story, extraordinarily developed, of a day in the life of a man, a Jewish advertising canvasser, which is to say that it proposes to bring beyond his conversations and unexpected encounters with other men all that has happened to him, through his mind. Different turnings of style are employed with the greatest skill in translating the different states of consciousness and the thoughts of Bloom; and the incidents which happen follow the order of events remotely analogous to the *Odyssey* . . . I do not see, truly, that these add to the interest of the book . . . The plan seems to have been employed to superimpose a sort of form on materials which, by their nature, are essentially formless. I have not sufficiently studied *Ulysses* to be able to express an opinion about its value. One finds in it pages a precision and a mastery so powerful that it is regretful to think that there are others which are extremely devoid of interest. But two things are certain: first, that *Ulysses* has shown the way in which the new novel has been moving for ten years; and that it has also shown the way or several ways that it will follow— who knows for how long? One could have believed that *Ulysses* was an end and that it would be impossible to penetrate farther into the contexture of the conscience. The author is now trying to write a book

in which he uses a language of his own invention . . . made of fragments of different words, often of different languages, and of deformations in the form of onomatopoea. It is, naturally, incomprehensible,
although by the third or fourth reading one begins to discover a vague
sense in it.

What is certain is that the comparison that has been made between
Joyce and Rabelais is deceptive. It is true that Joyce, like Rabelais, has a
great taste for words and a remarkable aptitude in using them; a love of
analogies and of assonances which, in his case, attain this particular
mental aberration which is called echolalic. He lets himself loose in a
flood of repercussions, some word plays and alliterations which, here
and there, burst from the mind, or forms a brilliant assemblage of
vocables but which, more often than not, only produce a prolonged
murmur which is not addressed to the intelligence. He launches a
quantity of obscene words and a tumult of scholarly words. When this
remark is made, and it is noted that the author of the *Life of Gargantua*
and that of *Ulysses* were born parodists, the first of general ideas, the
second of literary methods, we will have exhausted what they have in
common. From the point of view of intellect, it is truly impossible for
the two authors to be more different.

Although in appearance the most fantastic of men, Rabelais was also
gifted with as great a good sense and as formidably solid a mind as it is
possible for a man to have. Behind the buffonery and his great talent as
a story teller is hidden the philosophy of common sense and sprightly
stoicism. On the other hand, the background of verbal torrents of
Ulysses is a hallucinated sadness and a morose delight. The essential
character of the spirit of Rabelais is his boldness; he considers the body
with amusement and not with horror. *Ulysses* strikes me, as it has struck
others, as a product of suffering, of an almost unbearable oppression.
'Dedalus' allows the reader to measure how profound the mark impressed in the mind of the author of *Ulysses* was—through the course of his
youth there is the superstitious horror of the body and of love. In spite
of the sharp precision of his sentences, and his flashes of beauty and his
sardonic laugh—things which everyone can appreciate—the author of
Ulysses gives me the impression of an enslaved mind, rather than an
intrepid spirit.

258. John Eglinton on the early Joyce

1932

Extract from John Eglinton (W. K. Magee), 'The Beginnings of Joyce', *Life and Letters*, viii (December 1932), 400–14. Later appeared in his *Irish Literary Portraits* (1935), pp. 131–52.

. . . Joyce is, as all his writings show, Roman in mind and soul; for, generally speaking, to the Romanized mind the quest of truth, when it is not impious, is witless. What he seemed at this period I have attempted to describe, but what he really was is revealed in his *Portrait of the Artist as a Young Man*, a work completed in Trieste just ten years later. . . .

From this point [1908–9] Joyce becomes for me, in retrospect, an heroic figure. He had 'stooped under a dark tremendous sea of cloud', confident that he would 'emerge some day', 'using for my defence the only weapons I allow myself to use, silence, exile and cunning'. Pause on that word 'exile', a favourite one with Joyce. Why was it necesssry for him to conjure up the grandiose image of his rejection by his countrymen? Ireland, though famous for flights of wild geese, banishes nobody, and Dublin had no quarrel with her Dante; . . .

His mind meanwhile retained some illusions: for example, that he was a poet. He has, in fact, published more than one volume of poems; but I will take Æ's word for it that most of them 'might have been written by almost any young versifying sentimentalist'. Another illusion was that he could write, in the ordinary sense, a novel; for *A Portrait of the Artist as a Young Man*, which took him ten years to write, is no more a novel than is Moore's *Confessions of a Young Man*. In style it is, for the most part, pompous and self-conscious, and in general we may say of it that it is one of those works which become important only when the author has done or written something else. That Joyce should have been able to make *Ulysses* out of much the same material gives the book now an extraordinary interest. It tells us a great deal about Joyce himself which we had hardly suspected, and both its squalor and its assumption wear quite a different complexion when we know that the author eventually triumphed over the one and vindicated the other. Genius is not always what it is supposed to be, self-realization: it is often a spirit to which the artist has to sacrifice himself; and until Joyce surrendered himself to his genius, until he died and came to life in his Mephistopheles of mockery, he remained what Goethe called 'ein trüber Gast auf der dunklen Erden'.

I confess that when I read *Ulysses* I took Stephen Dedalus (Joyce himself) for the hero, and the impression seemed justified by the phrase at the end of the book when Stephen falls asleep: 'at rest, he has travelled'. The commentators, however, all appear to be agreed that Mr. Leopold Bloom is Ulysses, and they refer to the various episodes, 'Nausicaa', 'The Oxen of the Sun', 'The Nekuia', and so forth, with an understanding which I envy them. All the same, I am convinced that the only person concerned in the narrative who comes out as a real hero is the author himself. . . . A thousand unexpected faculties and gay devices were liberated in his soul. The discovery of a new method in literary art, in which the pen is no longer the slave of logic and rhetoric, made of this Berlitz School teacher a kind of public danger, threatening to the corporate existence of 'literature' as established in the minds and affections of the new generation. . . . They say that Joyce, when he is in good humour among his disciples, can be induced to allow them to examine a key to the elaborate symbolism of the different episodes, all pointing inward to a central mystery, undivulged, I fancy. *Ulysses*, in fact, is a mock-heroic, and at the heart of it is that which lies at the heart of all mockery, an awful inner void. None but Joyce and his dæmon know that void: the consciousness of it is perhaps the 'tragic sense' which his disciples claim that he has introduced into English literature. But is there, then, no serious intention in *Ulysses*? As Joyce's most devout interpreters are at variance with respect to the leading motive we may, perhaps without much loss, assume its seriousness to be nothing but the diabolic gravity with which the whole work is conducted throughout its mystifications. Yet the original motive may have been quite a simple one. Near the centre of the book, in that chapter known as 'The Oxen of the Sun', which, in Mr. Stuart Gilbert's words, 'ascends in orderly march the gamut of English styles', 'culminating in a futurist cacophony of syncopated slang', there is a passage over which the reader may pause:

[quotes from the 'Oxen of the Sun' episode]

. . . Bloom, therefore, is an impersonation rather than a type: not a character, for a character manifests itself in action, and in *Ulysses* there is no action. There is only the rescue of Stephen from a row in a brothel, in which some have discovered a symbolism which might have appealed to G. F. Watts, the Delivery of Art by Science and Common Sense. But the humour is vast and genial. There are incomparable flights in *Ulysses*: the debate, for instance, in the Maternity Hospital on the mystery of birth; and above all, I think, the scene near the end of the book in the cabmen's shelter, kept by none other than Skin-the-Goat, the famous jarvey of the Phœnix Park murders. Here the author proves himself one of the world's great humorists. The humour, as always, is pitiless, but where we laugh we love, and after his portrait of the sailor in this chapter I reckon Joyce, after all, a lover of men.

When Joyce produced *Ulysses* he had shot his bolt. Let us put it without any invidiousness. He is a man of one book, as perhaps the ideal author always is. Besides, he is not specially interested in 'literature', not, at all events, as a well-wisher. . . . As for Joyce, his interest is in language and the mystery of words. He appears, at all events, to have done with 'literature', and we leave him with the plea for literature that it exists mainly to confer upon mankind a deeper and more general insight and corresponding powers of expression. Language is only ready to become the instrument of the modern mind when its development is complete, and it is when words are invested with all kinds of associations that they are the more or less adequate vehicles of thought and knowledge. And after 'literature', perhaps, comes something else. . . .

259. Henry Daniel-Rops on the interior monologue

1932

Extract from 'Une Technique Nouvelle: Le Monologue Intérieur', *Le Correspondent*, No. 1664 (January 1932), 281–305.

A lengthy essay on the 'interior monologue' as used by Edouard Dujardin, Valéry Larbaud and Joyce. The article begins with a historical résumé, including Joyce's statement that Dujardin, not he, had first used the new technique, and the influence the technique had upon young writers of the time. The second part of the article is given over to Joyce (pp. 291–8), and the final part (pp. 298–305) to the advantages and disadvantages of the technique.

Having posed the question of knowing whether this new technique constitutes a real benefit for literature, it is, without doubt, indispensable to examine closely a text or else this essay will be useless. A very close analysis of this stylistic method will show, I believe, to the attentive reader the remarkable interest that he will find by losing himself in this strange prose, where, for the first time, the spirit seems to take flight, lacking points from which to return. I certainly do not flatter myself in such an analysis in providing a complete elucidation of the infinite mysteries which a page of interior monologue contain, especially when that page is written by a master like Joyce . . .

[quotes Philippe Soupault's comments on the difficulty of translating into French the *Anna Livia Plurabelle* section of what was then known as *Work in Progress*; see No. 191)

I have cited this commentary to show how many difficulties one encounters when approaching Joyce. These difficulties are three: the thought, the expression, and the language are equally upsetting to penetrate. In studying the last two, we will be at the heart of our subject, but we will leave out one important aspect of the work: the ideological and thematic conception . . .

Thought, in Joyce, is no less complex than the expression. In *Ulysses*, for example, we could not say that it had a unique subject, on which the book was constructed. There are a certain number of subjects, super-imposed, overlapping, and intimately mixed, one upon another. A development will be on one level and in one sense, but also on another level and on another sense . . . It is, perhaps, a superhuman task [to unravel all the complexities], it is, perhaps, very simply absurd in the eyes of some, but it is a work which warrants our industry.

The new work of James Joyce, the *Work in Progress*, is not now available to us in its broadest design, but we are assured that its design is no less vast than that of *Ulysses* and that its construction is no easier to penetrate. . . .

Without doubt the monologue has constituted, even as a technique, an enrichment of literature. It has, in its introduction into our literature, a triple benefit.

The first is that it has contributed a bridge to fill the gap between discursive psychology and the heavy, French novelistic productions before the war. . . .

By using the monologue, the novelist's sincerity becomes total. The writer identifies himself with his character and the novel can only be made (if it is written entirely in this form) from the point of view which the hero has personally recognized. . . .

On the other hand, concerning the profound recognition of its essence, the monologue, I believe, permits the attainment of goals which the older techniques would not allow to be approached. . . . The monologue allows one to know thoughts in their germinal stages. . . . And in placing the reader at the point where the thought is still not formed, the monologue certainly reveals something totally new. One often has the impression while reading the pages of James Joyce that reality is not something fixed or defined . . . one which we live, but a metaphysical creation of our senses, a nightmare if one wishes, a night-mare of half-urgings and beginnings. . . .

260. Thomas Wolfe comment on *Ulysses*

1932

Thomas Wolfe, in a letter to Julian Meade (1 February 1932), in *The Letters of Thomas Wolfe* (1956), ed. Elizabeth Nowell, pp. 321–2.

You ask again if I look upon writing as an escape from reality; in no sense of the word does it seem to me to be escape from reality; I should rather say that it is an attempt to approach and penetrate reality. This I think is certainly true of such a book as *Ulysses*: the effort to apprehend and to make live again a moment in lost time is so tremendous that some of us feel that Joyce really did succeed, at least in places, in penetrating reality and in so doing, creating what is almost another dimension of reality. . . .

261. Carl Jung, letter to Joyce

1932

C. G. Jung, in a letter to Joyce (? August 1932), in *Letters*, ed. Ellmann, Volume III, pp. 253-4, and in Ellmann, *James Joyce*, p. 642.

Your *Ulysses* has presented the world such an upsetting psychological problem, that repeatedly I have been called in as a supposed authority on psychological matters.

Ulysses proved to be an exceedingly hard nut and it has forced my mind not only to most unusual efforts, but also to rather extravagant peregrinations (speaking from the standpoint of a scientist). Your book as a whole has given me no end of trouble and I was brooding over it for about three years until I succeeded to put myself into it. But I must tell you that I'm profoundly grateful to yourself as well as to your gigantic opus, because I learned a great deal from it. I shall probably never be quite sure whether I did enjoy it, because it meant too much grinding of nerves and of grey matter. I also don't know whether you will enjoy what I have written about *Ulysses* [*Ulysses*: Ein Monolog', *Europäische Revue* (Berlin), viii, No. 9 (September 1932), 547–68; later included in his *Wirklichkeit der Seele* . . . (1933) and translated later as *Ulysses, A Monologue* (No. 262)], because I couldn't help telling the world how much I was bored, how I grumbled, how I cursed and how I admired. The 40 pages of non-stop run in the end is a string of veritable psychological peaches. I suppose the devil's grandmother knows so much about the real psychology of a woman. I didn't.

Well I just try to recommend my little essay to you, as an amusing attempt of a perfect stranger that went astray in the labyrinth of your *Ulysses* and happened to get out of it again by sheer good luck. At all events you may gather from my article what *Ulysses* has done to a supposedly balanced psychologist.

262. Carl Jung on *Ulysses*

1932

Extract from '*Ulysses*: ein Monolog', *Europäische Revue*, viii
(September 1932), 548–68. Later appeared as '*Ulysses*', in *Wirk-
lichkeit der Seele*, iv (Zürich, 1934), and was translated by W.
Stanley Dell for the Analytical Psychology Club, Spring 1949;
it is now part of the *Collected Works of C. G. Jung*, Volume 15
(*The Spirit in Man, Art and Literature*) (1966), translated by R. F. C.
Hull, pp. 109–32.

The Ulysses of my title has to do with James Joyce and not with that
shrewd and storm-driven figure of Homer's world who knew how to
escape by guile and by deed the enmity or vengeance of gods and men,
and who after a wearisome voyage returned to hearth and home. In
strongest contrast to his Greek namesake, Joyce's Ulysses is an inactive,
merely perceiving consciousness; a mere eye, ear, nose, and mouth, a
sensory nerve exposed without choice or check to the roaring, chaotic,
nonsensical cataract of psychic or physical happenings, and registering
all of this in an almost photographic way.

Ulysses is a book which pours along for seven hundred and thirty-
five pages, a stream of time of seven hundred and thirty-five days which
all consist in one single and senseless every day of Everyman, the completely irrelevant 16th day of June 1904, in Dublin—a day on which, in
all truth, nothing happens. The stream begins in the void and ends in the
void. Is all of this perhaps one single, immensely long and excessively
complicated Strindbergian pronouncement upon the essence of human
life, and one which, to the reader's dismay, is never finished? Perhaps it
does touch upon the essence of life; but quite certainly it touches upon
life's ten thousand surfaces and their hundred thousand color gradations.
As far as my glance reaches, there are in those seven hundred and thirty-
five pages no obvious repetitions and not a single hallowed island where
the long-suffering reader may come to rest. There is not a single place
where he can seat himself, drunk with memories, and from which he

can happily consider the stretch of road he has covered, be it one hundred pages or even less. If he could only recognize some little commonplace which had slipped in where it was not expected. But no! The pitiless and uninterrupted stream rolls by, and its velocity or precipitation grows in the last forty pages till it sweeps away even the marks of punctuation. It thus gives cruelest expression to that emptiness which is both breath taking and stifling, which is under such tension, or is so filled to bursting, as to grow unbearable. This thoroughly hopeless emptiness is the dominant note of the whole book. It not only begins and ends in nothingness, but it consists of nothing but nothingness. It is all infernally nugatory. If we regard the book from the side of technical artistry, it is a positively brilliant and hellish monster-birth.

I had an old uncle whose thinking was always to the point. One day he stopped me on the street and asked, 'Do you know how the devil tortures the souls in hell?' When I said no, he declared, 'He keeps them waiting.' And with that he walked away. This remark occurred to me when I was ploughing through *Ulysses* for the first time. Every sentence raises an expectation which is not fulfilled; finally, out of sheer resignation, you come to expect nothing any longer. Then bit by bit, again to your horror, it dawns upon you that in all truth you have hit the nail on the head. It is actual fact that nothing happens and nothing comes of it, and yet a secret expectation at war with hopeless resignation drags the reader from page to page. The seven hundred and thirty-five pages that contain nothing by no means consist of blank paper but are closely printed. You read and read and read and you pretend to understand what you read. Occasionally you drop through an air pocket into another sentence, but when once the proper degree of resignation has been reached you accustom yourself to anything. So I, too, read to page one hundred and thirty-five with despair in my heart, falling asleep twice on the way. The incredible multifariousness of Joyce's style has a monotonous and hypnotic effect. Nothing comes to the reader; everything turns away from him and leaves him to gape after it. The book is always up and away; it is not at peace with itself, but is at once ironic, sarcastic, poisonous, disdainful, sad, despairing, and bitter. . . .

263. L. A. G. Strong on Joyce

1932

L. A. G. Strong, *Spectator*, cxlix (9 December 1932), 844.

Of Mr. James Joyce's works I have read, with admiration and profit, the *Portrait of the Artist as a Young Man*, *Dubliners*, several poems, and *Ulysses*. I have also read *Anna Livia Plura-Belle* (and listened to Mr. Joyce himself reading from it on a gramophone record), which, though difficult, has left a clear and beautiful picture in my mind. I say this only to show that I approach any new work of Mr. Joyce with a sincere and painstaking desire to understand it. *Two Tales of Shem and Shaun*, however, is beyond my ken. . . .

[quotes from p. 156]

This is too difficult for me. All the same, I can make something of the following: . . .

[quotes from p. 159]

There is not space here to go into what Mr. Joyce is attempting, not only with words, but with their associations, public and personal. He is a writer of undoubted genius, and any experiment of his commands respect. Even so, I am suspicious of these tales, not because of the much which I do not understand, but because of the little which I do. It seems to me that Mr. Joyce, in his passage from literature to music, has strayed into a no-man's-land which belongs to neither. . . .

1933

264. A. Lyner on music and Joyce

1933

'Music and James Joyce', *New English Weekly* (19 October 1933), 16–17.

Where are the writings of James Joyce likely to lead us? The opinions or judgments of those who accuse him of all the offences—spiritual, moral and social—can with the greatest safety to humanity and art be put aside. They are of no critical or other value.

What Mr. Joyce set out to do is no guarantee of his success. It was new—the least of its virtues—but not unexpected. Exactly what is the problem Mr. Joyce set himself? It is composite. Firstly the mechanics— what Mr. Clive Bell would not like me to call significant form—of his writing, which also contains two problems; one, the philological extension of the language, by the use of slang and linguistic distortions; two, the eradication or suspension of time. This latter is the most exacting and vital problem of the associative method of writing, the real solution of which is music.

From the purely scientific psychologic point of view, the human consciousness is timeless. . . . It is into this timeless world that Mr. Joyce would transport us. How far he does so is the measure of his success.

From the artistic point of view—the view that concerns Mr. Joyce— it is a very dangerous world for the writer. In incompetent hands the method can become purely fanciful and imaginary, pointless and absurd. Virginia Woolf is an instance. She has failed entirely to solve her problem, and is writing something without either life or artistic vitality. I refer particularly to *The Waves*. . . . We are being told much about the music of Mr. Joyce's prose, and not in that general indefinite way in which 'music' is so often used. We are even being taught how to read it. And to prove the point beyond dispute, Mr. Joyce has recorded portions of his work. Also we see in the latest portions of his work, which are available, the long, strange, 'musical' words. Reading them gives us the pleasure that children get by just making sounds. Already people are beginning to see that the pleasure obtained from reciting his prose is much the same as that obtained from hearing the sounds of a language incomprehensible to them—which is a short remove from listening to music. It is as near as some people ever get. These should at least be thankful for Mr. Joyce.

With these facts in mind we can begin to answer our original question: 'Where are the writings of Mr. Joyce likely to lead?' In regard to art, of course. Its effect, if any, on our future mental outlook and literature is not so readily apparent. Like the true artist, he is not concerned with that—which is the only way that anything ever 'gets across.'. . .

One fact emerges which gives us a clue. The timelessness of his writing. Here, of course, I do not refer to the accidents of environment and social influences which 'date' a work, nor to the period confined externally between the beginning and end of a work; but to the time-lessness of the registered incidents in the latter period. In this respect it is like music, and completely unlike any literary production that has pre-ceded it. . . .

But if it is a characteristic of music to lose identity, then it is inevitable that Mr. Joyce's music will either be bad music, or not music at all, so long as he uses words which have, no matter how he twists or distorts them, a connotation, an identity, definite and rigid, as compared with a note of music. They are too inelastic. It was probably a subconscious realisation of this as well as his expressed desire which led him to use words and languages as he has done. But words hold on to their identity, and, being to the eye that must read them, so manifestly separate, have a disintegrating effect as well on his work. Again a sub-conscious realisation of this may have led him to make records.

Thus Mr. Joyce's prose, though leading us towards music, can never attain that end. The inherent difficulties and incompatabilities of his medium must ultimately prove the experiment a failure. His work, however interesting, falls between music and conceived literature. It is nondescript, and is not to be catalogued or fixed in any tradition. That is certainly an achievement. And that also is the only attribute he shares in common with Rabelais, in spite of some guesses we have heard.

Posterity, with a wider understanding, a larger spiritual life, and a greater sensibility, may appreciate to the full the implied qualities of Mr. Joyce's work. It is also the privilege of posterity to make or unmake at will. But in spite of internationalism, and the extended leisure to be created by machines, I am not inclined to credit posterity with these very necessary qualities. . . .

265. Mirsky on bourgeois decadence

1933

Extract from Dmitri Petrovich Mirsky, 'Dzheims Dzhois', *Almanakh: God* 16 (Moscow), No. 1 (1933), 428–50. Translated by Davis Kinkead as 'Joyce and Irish Literature', in *New Masses*, x–xi (3 April 1934), 31–4 (from which the present text is taken). See the reply by James Farrell (No. 288).

James Joyce and Marcel Proust are the leading representatives of the literature of the decadent bourgeois culture of the West. But of Proust, the Parisian, the portrayer of the upper layers of this society, one might say if he did not exist the Marxian critic would have to invent him. Joyce is not so pure an example of this type. He has, in addition, certain special characteristics, due to the fact that he was born in a colonial country. If a writer is to be classified by his characters, their locale, their period, then we should have to say that Joyce is the literary representative of the Irish petty bourgeoisie as opposed to that middle bourgeoisie which come into power in the new-born 'Irish Free State. . . . No less important is his attitude towards his material and the way he uses it. In his relation to his material Joyce is an apostate-emigrant. He has run away from the reality which produced his material. . . .

[a biographical sketch is followed by a brief discussion of Irish literature]

Along with this dreamy nationalism we have a special kind of cosmopolitanism, a desertion of Ireland for the continent and England, an effort to escape from their provincial hole, to get away from their landlord-merchant bourgeoisie and join the general Western culture of the cosmopolitan bourgeoisie. The most notable of these deserters was Joyce. His predecessor was John M. Synge. . . .

[a long discussion of Synge]

. . . A poverty-stricken intellectual, he [Joyce] wandered over Europe for a long time, earning a bare existence by giving English lessons. At first he was strongly influenced by the Irish Renaissance, as his book of poems, *Chamber Music*, shows. But in *Dubliners* he has already begun to free himself from this inheritance. *Dubliners* is a book of stories of the most prosaic life of the Irish capital, by its very subject sharply veering away from the mythological romanticism of the poets of the 'renaissance.' Here Joyce belongs to the school of the leading cosmopolitan writers—Flaubert, Maupassant, and the Anglo-Irish Flaubertian, George Moore.

Joyce was at this time working on an autobiographical novel, *A Portrait of the Artist as a Young Man*, in which he settles his accounts with his Irish education. This novel is the umbilical cord connecting the naïve provincial student with the world aesthete who beats the French at their own game. The style, strangely enough, is that of the renaissance. *A Portrait of the Artist as a Young Man* is more Irish, more youthful, more romantic than *Dubliners*. Whereas in *Dubliners* Joyce used a foreign medium, in *A Portrait of the Artist as a Young Man* he again reverted to his Irish roots and got rid of them once and for all. *A Portrait of the Artist as a Young Man* is the logical forerunner of *Ulysses*. . . . But in his period of maturity this changes to a perfect expression of the biological defeat of an idle, culturally refined, imperialistic bourgeoisie. Thus traits which originate in the rebellion of the petty bourgeois intellectual against an uncultured bourgeoisie become, in another historical setting, traits common to the international capitalistic culture of this period. . . .

It is unnecessary at this time to discuss the 'story' of *Ulysses*. The style, however, deserves comment. *Ulysses* is written in several different keys, to take a figure from music. These 'keys' give the story, as it were, a new dimension, a new coefficient. One chapter differs from another not only in content but also in style. And this style is subtly connected with the content.

In the matter of coining new words and deforming old ones, and in the variety and virtuosity of his style, Joyce has no equal. . . .

We should also observe the ending of *Ulysses*. Like *War and Peace* Joyce's novel ends with a woman as the incarnation of the eternal, unchanging, elemental life of the flesh. . . . For Joyce the triumph of the female, Marion Bloom, is the triumph of mysterious forces, of that which will remain living when men, the lovers of decay and death, have been completely swept away by history. It might seem that the book ends on a note of reconciliation as Marion at the end is swept by a flood of poetic thoughts. But this lyricism is not a reconciliation of the author with her but her own complacence in the triumph of the female, satisfied if she gets her male—'one as good as another.' For Joyce this ending expresses the triumph of middle-class Ireland, which has no need for Bloom with his timid desires and hankering for culture and offers Stephen only the bed of a dissipated bourgeois philistine. On the European stage the ending of *Ulysses* signifies the triumph of the vital bourgeoisie over the decadence represented by Stephen and Joyce. It is quite obvious that under other historical conditions the point of view of such people as Joyce would not have had a wide appeal.

Ulysses is the end of Joyce's artistic expression; the triumph of Marion is his final word. Since *Ulysses* Joyce has been writing ten years. Selections of his work have been published under the title of *Work in Progress* and a number of short pieces have appeared—*Anna Livia Plurabelle, Haveth Childers Everywhere*. This is pure nonsense, the work of a master of language writing nothing. The theme is again Ireland, but a completely unreal Ireland—a mixture of nonsensically-stylized conversations of ordinary Dubliners, with mythological frills. Russian futurism went through this period of nonsense in its earliest stages. . . . In Joyce this nonsense comes at the end of a brilliant but aimless career. In *Ulysses* Joyce exhausted his material. He subdued the English language to his will. He created the monumental super-Babbitt, Bloom. And at the zenith of his victory he voluntarily surrendered his vantage points to the vulgar female—Marion. There was nothing more to do. All he had left was naked virtuosity and he carried it further and further, smearing up language and sense into a kind of formless, meaningless mass.

We may ask ourselves whether Joyce offers a model for revolutionary writers. The answer is that his method is too inseparably connected with the specifically decadent phase of the bourgeois culture he reflects, is too narrowly confined within its limits. The use of the inner monologue (stream of consciousness method) is too closely connected with the ultra-subjectivism of the parasitic, rentier bourgeoisie, and entirely unadaptable to the art of one who is building socialist society. Not less foreign to the dynamics of our culture is the fundamentally static method in which the picture of Bloom is composed, and around him the whole novel. The novel is colossal, grandiose—there is no denying it— and in our time, when the slogan is 'Build a Magnitostroy of Art,' it may be tempting to imitate its huge contours. But Magnitostroy is not merely a gigantic thing; it is also growth, work, aim—a part of the revolution. *Ulysses* is static. It is more like Cheops than Magnitostroy.

In the matter of word creation unquestionably Joyce surpasses anything that has been done in Russian literature. . . .

There remains still the most fundamental element of Joyce's art, his realistic grasp, his amazing exactness of expression, all that side in which he is of the school of the French naturalists, raising to its ultimate height their cult of the *mot juste*. It is this exactness which gives Joyce the wonderful realistic power in depicting the outer world for which he is famous. But this has its roots on the one hand in a morbid, defeatist delight in the ugly and repulsive and, on the other, in an aesthetico-proprietary desire for the possession of 'things.' So that even this one realistic element of Joyce's style is fundamentally foreign to the realism towards which Soviet art aims, namely a mastery of the world by means of active, dynamic materialism—with the purpose of not merely understanding but also changing the reality of history. . . .

266. Emeric Fischer on the interior monologue

1933

Extract from 'Le Monologue Intérieur dans l'*Ulysse* de James Joyce', *La Revue Française*, xxviii, No. 3 (25 March 1933), 445–53.

The article begins with generous quotations from Valéry Larbaud's 'Preface' to *Gens de Dublin* (1926) and from Edouard Dujardin's *Le Monologue Intérieur* (1931), and draws the distinction between intellectual discourse and pure dream in the interior monologue.

In the reverie the thoughts, the images, unfold in the same way as the conscious, exactly as in the interior monologue. They follow one after the other, striving for the pleasure that their unfolding procures on a plane which Bergson has called horizontal. Because, if the effort exacts pain and if it is tiring or even distressing, the spontaneous development of images is made of witty delights and sometimes, we see this in Ulysses . . . physically. This is the relaxation of witty forces of the mind, obeying the most rudimentary sensations, the most hidden instincts, pursing its operations in extension and superficial knowledge and not in intensity and depth.

But if the object of the interior monologue is that of reverie, its form is that of discourse, whereas Joyce's interior monologue includes the possibility of a logical development. . . .

[quotes from the Penelope episode, p. 723, p. 738, and from a comment on the passage by Daniel-Rops in *Le Correspondent*, No. 259]

Thus the interior monologue offers us the unfolding of thought under undifferentiated forms, not only developed and synthetic. . . .

Ulysses can be read with passion without intellectually understanding the text. In this case, we identify ourselves completely with the character, our imagination lays hold of his sensation, his pleasure, his reminiscences, and we live with him, we dream with him. The prolonging of the interior monologue in our imagination will provoke pure reverie.

But we can read *Ulysses* objectively also. The interior monologue is, then, addressed to our intelligence and we often must painfully decipher its obscurities and establish its correspondences. Because the interior monologue in its fragmentary incoherence includes, as we have seen before, all the logical structure and grammatical armature of thought. But it is up to us, or rather up to our intellectual effort to find them, to develop them and to assimilate them. In order that the continuity of thought be established, two subjects are necessary in Joyce: the character whose thoughts are taken on and the reader who develops and organizes the engaged thought.

Without doubt, this is a unique attempt in the history of letters, that of associating to such a point the effort of the writer and that of his reader. The synthetic, virtual, implicit thought of the interior monologue must be prolonged and spread out in the mind of the reader in order to become explicit, actual and clear, in order to become a living and efficient reality.

Joyce has, then, tried to bring about the dissociation of the elements of thought without having brought harm to its unity. This unity is established through the logical construction of scattered elements, operated by the reader.

It is only by this reconstruction that we attain the plenitude which arrives in understanding all the grandeur, all the importance and the novelty of this work.

. . . In what exactly consists this synthetic thought which Joyce proposes to grasp in long pages of his *Ulysses*, and which seems to be anterior to the reverie and to the organized discourse? The interior monologue makes us think of the reverie by the apparent absence of cohesion and effort. But in the true reverie associations can be produced at will, while in *Ulysses* all is ordered and coordinated in terms of a logical, ulterior development.

[again quotes from Daniel-Rop]

The entire problem is included in the synthetic thought of Mrs. Bloom and in the development which results from it. In the monologue of Mrs. Bloom nothing indicates to us, at least visibly, the relationship which unites the two elements which are simply juxtaposed, conforming to their development in the mind. However, this relationship exists there already, in a latent state, since once the interpretation is given all becomes clear, comprehensible and organized. Of what does this relationship consist?

It consists in this: Mrs. Bloom considers an exterior fact, what Mrs. Riordan tells her about the tremblings of the earth. This provokes in the mind of Mrs. Bloom a reaction which is manifested not only through this thought—'pay us a little good time first'—that is, before the end of the world, but also by the following thought: 'what a hell the world would be if all women were of this type!'

Thus, the elements from which Mrs. Bloom's thoughts arise are not uniform and do not have the same value. Some represent impressions, remembrances, perceptions; the others, judgments and reactions. The mind by not passively submitting, causes these impressions to react more or less violently against them. The thought oscillates constantly between the impression received and the reaction provoked.

We could say that this is a true dialogue which is even engaged within the mind, of which the questions are formed by impressions and responses, by reactions or conversely. The interior monologue is the synthesis of questions-answers, of impressions-reactions, which are uniformly juxtaposed in the mind. The effort of the reader consists in dissociating its development, classing the elements which come forth from an impression, separating them and situating them according to their respective places.

In the interior monologue we find the interior dialogue which seems to be the origin of all spiritual life. Its prolonging in the intelligence becomes logical discourse and in the imagination pure reverie.

[traces these apparently paradoxical views in Gerhardt Hauptmann]

Joyce presents thought to us in the state when it is still a compact mass and not yet separated, articulated, or organized into sentences. This is why the punctuation is totally suppressed in the monologue of Mrs. Bloom.

[concludes with the thesis that the interior monologue is actually an interior dialogue which is the beginning of all psychic manifestations]

267. Pound on *Ulysses* and Wyndham Lewis

1933

Extract from 'Past History', *English Journal*, xxii (May 1933), 354–5 [349–58]. Reprinted in *College English*, xxii (November 1960), 81–6.

. . . The parallels with the *Odyssey* are mere mechanics, any blockhead can go back and trace them. Joyce had to have a shape on which to order his chaos. This was a convenience, though the abrupt break after the *Telemachiad* (Stephen's chapters) is not particularly felicitous, I mean that to the reader who is really reading *Ulysses* as a book and not as a design or a demonstration or a bit of archaeological research, this chop-off gives no pleasure and has no particular intrinsic merit (tho' it has parallels with musical construction and can be justified by a vast mass of theory). . . .

Joyce has made, to date, 3 contributions to literature that seem likely to *be there* for as long as any of the rest of it. His last decade has been devoted to experiment, which probably concerns himself and such groups of writers as think they can learn something from it. It can hardly be claimed that the main design of his later work emerges above the detail. . . .

Mr. Wyndham Lewis' specific criticism of *Ulysses* can now be published. It was made in 1922 or '23. 'Ungh!' he grunted, 'He [Joyce] don't seem to have any very new point of view about anything.' Such things are a matter of degree. There is a time for a man to experiment with his medium. When he has a mastery of it; or when he has developed it, and extended it, he or a successor can apply it.

Ulysses is a summary of pre-war Europe, the blackness and mess and muddle of a 'civilization' led by disguised forces and a bought press, the general sloppiness, the plight of the individual intelligence in that mess! Bloom very much *is* the mess.

I think anybody is a fool who does not read *Dubliners*, *The Portrait*, and *Ulysses* for his own pleasure, and—coming back to the present particular and specialized audience—anyone who has not read these three books is unfit to teach literature in any high school or college. I don't mean simply English or American literature but *any* literature, for literature is not split up by political frontiers.

I can not see that Mr. Joyce's later work concerns more then a few specialists, and I can not see in it either a comprehension of, or a very great preoccupation with, the present, which may indicate an obtuseness on my part, or may indicate that Mr. Joyce's present and my present are very different one from the other, and, further, that I can not believe in a passive acceptance.

In judging the modality of another intelligence one possibly errs in supposing that a man whose penetrations and abilities exceed one's own in a given direction shd. at least equal them in some other. In other words, the times we live in seem to me more interesting than the period of what seems to me reminiscence—which (to me) appears to dominate Anna Livia and the rest of the Joycean curley-cues.

I am, at 47, more interested in work built on foundations wherein I have laboured, than in that produced by Mr. J's imitators, and feel that this is justified on human and critical grounds. . . .

268. Robert Cantwell on Joyce's influence

1933

'The Influence of James Joyce', *New Republic,* lxxvii (December 1933), 200–1.

In the rush of current critical debate, including the discussions of Marxian criticism, the really dominant literary figure of modern times has suffered a curious neglect. *Ulysses* was completed in 1921. In the years since then there have been literally hundreds of novels written in its shadow, and while a considerable body of criticism has grown up around Joyce's work, it has been largely interpretation, defense or attack, rather than an attempt to get at the meaning of the widespread acceptance of Joyce's ideas and methods. Yet even a passing acquaintance with recent fiction makes it clear that Joyce's work has left a deeper, a more readily perceptible mark, than that of any of the masters of the immediate past—certainly a deeper mark than has been made by Proust or Gide or Mann, and certainly, despite the recent attempt of champions to read a depth of meaning into his career, a deeper impression than has been made by the novels of D. H. Lawrence. Unlike most literary influences, which—by definition—must be intuitively recognized rather than measured and substantiated, that of Joyce can be clearly traced through the tangle of modern writing, primarily because the technical discoveries he has made have been so widely adopted—and it must be remembered that the echo of a phrasing or of a method gives only a hint of what has gone on behind the scenes, barely suggesting the extent to which other aspects of a writer's work and life have dominated the imaginations of his followers.

For the sake of convenience, his influence can be separated into its three aspects: the influence of his technical discoveries, of the general attitude toward experience most eloquently expressed in his work, and of his personal career. The separation is arbitrary. . . . But to consider Joyce's technique. In the ten years since the publication of *Ulysses* novelists have modified and reworked and experimented with Joyce's methods with a persistence unlike anything in literary history. . . . The results of Joyce's influence, unfortunately, spoil this analogy, but the processes are roughly similar. It began almost as soon as *Ulysses* was published. Even F. Scott Fitzgerald paid his tribute in a section of *This Side of Paradise* and Herbert Gorman wrote *Gold by Gold* when the first copies of Joyce's masterpiece, smuggled in through underground channels and distributed in secret, were reaching the always limited audience in this country.

The spread of Joyce's technical devices has constantly increased, and not only in the sense that more writers have employed them. They are being used more skillfully and with greater discrimination. A comparison of the recent novels of Edward Dahlberg, William Faulkner and James Farrell, for example, with such very early attempts as those of Fitzgerald or Gorman or Melvin Levy, does more than establish the relative talent of these authors. It clearly illustrates the *process* by which Joyce's methods are becoming incorporated into the cultural equipment of our time. To call this imitation is superficial; what we are really witnessing, if the whole broad field of advanced contemporary fiction is viewed, is a period in which the methods Joyce developed are being studied and tested, their applicability to different kinds of situations guaged, their possibilities explored. . . .

In what particular ways are Joyce's methods superior for communicating the complex phenomena and the involved psychological relationships of the modern world? It should be remembered that no other novelist has introduced formal changes so daring or so imaginative. . . .

But for Joyce and no doubt for others who never reached a solution—the modern world, even the modern world of Dublin in 1904, presented scenes and relationships too complex to be packed into this framework. It is enough to point out, as one example, Joyce's attempts to capture in prose those complex mechanical sounds which are so heavy a part of modern urban life, and which writers of the past, never having heard, felt no need to express. Joyce did not arrive at his methods without a search through others. He wrote lyrics, a realistic play, stories, and experimented—in *Portrait of the Artist as a Young Man*—with a kind of reminiscent, analytical, free-association-of ideas-and-impressions writing, suggestive of Proust, before he hit upon the multiple methods of presentation employed in *Ulysses*. It seems clear that he quickly recognized the limitations of these forms and consciously sought for something more inclusive, something that would enable him to draw into his fiction more of the complexities of contemporary experience, to introduce that dissonance and contrast evident everywhere around him into the very detail of his work—in place, let us say, of the unity of tone or mood which characterizes *Portrait of an Artist* and for which such writers as Proust and James, who also desired to enlarge the scope of the novel, made their sacrifices. In *Ulysses* he worked out such a form, inclusive, varied, permitting the language to come ever closer to the actuality, This, I think, is what the writers who have followed him have sensed; they have recognized that under the lens of his methods all the overworked scenes of realistic narrative, like drops of water under a microscope, are suddenly seen to be teeming with unsuspected life; the pauses and silences whose meaning could barely be guessed, the nuances of moods, the emotional responses which are scarcely reflected in speech or gestures or facial expression—all this, it can be seen now, is packed with infinite voiceless dramas, with dramas which yield less fully to any other method of presentation, or cannot otherwise be stated at all.

The character of Joyce's innovations, then, their flexibility and peculiar fitness for reaching into more varied aspects of modern life, would adequately explain the reasons for his influence if other reasons were lacking. But here it should be pointed out that by far the majority of novelists who have followed Joyce have been imaginatively stirred by Stephen Dedalus rather than by Leopold Bloom, have written of, and emphasized more than Joyce himself, the dilemma of the artist in societies dominated by bourgeois standards. This has led to the neglect of other aspects of his work, even though he has concerned himself to an extraordinary extent with questions of the relationship between art and politics, of the artist's social role—with the very questions, in short, that are now being discussed in terms of revolutionary criticism. And he has dramatized his own decisions with greater eloquence, with more wit and audacity and scholarship and with more intense labor than the holders of opposing points of view have so far displayed.

It is impossible to analyze this part of his work in detail here, but to reread *Ulysses* and *Portrait of the Artist as a Young Man* now, when the excitement and novelty of Freudian interpretation of literature have worn down, is to be impressed with how much and how deeply the Irish revolutionary movement enters into his work, how it runs in a clear red line from his first stories and how it finally disappears in his last. . . .

[illustrates this point in all the works]

. . . But Joyce was not an esthete in the sense that we now use the term, nor does Stephen, unlike our esthetes, bluntly refuse the alternatives to his position. He knows what the conflicting points of view represent, and though he jeers at them, it is clear that he has thought deeply about them and what kind of action would be demanded of him if he accepted one of them. What he really builds up after he leaves the revolutionist is a vision of neutrality for the artist in social conflicts, and he provides an esthetic for it, a theory, outlines its way of life and, in the following scene of his lyric inspiration, pictures its rewards as eloquently as the artist's intangible rewards have been stated.

It would be easy for a Marxist to prove that such neutrality is in fact impossible, that it works to the advantage of the dominant class, but this is aside from the point; the Marxian novelists and critics have not dramatized their convictions so compellingly as Joyce has dramatized his. There remains the question of Joyce's personal career. He has withdrawn, he has not taken sides, and in the thirteen years since *Ulysses* was finished we have had only the few troubling fragments of *Work in Progress* to show whether his choice was right. Leaving aside the question of the

quality of this work, limiting ourselves to the question of Joyce's influence on his contemporaries, there is no doubt that there has been as
real a drawing back from *Work in Progress* as there was response to
Ulysses; there has been an attempt on the part of his followers to suspend
judgment, with all the uncertainty and search in other places which
that effort implies. Perhaps *Work in Progress*, as such disparate critics
as Edmund Wilson and Herbert Read believe, will belong with the
greatest of human poetry; the point that is relevant here is that the
course Joyce has followed seems to have led to a strained and meager
production, a lack of the unequivocal great work that might have been
expected to follow *Ulysses*. To some of us it seems even more tragic; it
seems that we are watching the greatest living master of prose at his task
of breaking up the language in which he won our respect.

How much have we lost because Stephen drew back from the revolution that attracted him, rebuffed by the first bluntness of intelligence
he found or by an occasional stare of terror he saw in the eyes of those
with whom he would have had to throw his lot? . . .

269. G. K. Chesterton on eccentricity

1933

Extract from 'On Phases of Eccentricity', in *All I Survey* (1933)
pp. 52–5.

For instance, what is hailed as a new style or a new school in literature
often consists of doing as a novelty what a Victorian did long ago as a
joke. Thus we have, in Mr. James Joyce or Miss Gertrude Stein, the
coining of new words by the confusion of old words; the running of
words together so as to suggest some muddle in the subconsciousness....
[p. 52]

Thus I have a purely intellectual doubt of the future of fads, and even of fancies, unless they are treated frankly in a fanciful manner. I do not think any such experiment succeeds in twisting the tradition of language out of its common tendency. I can easily believe that a book like *Ulysses* is a striking and original book in its place and time; like *Sartor Resartus* in its place and time; But I do not believe that Mr. Joyce has added a new range or direction to literary expression, any more than Carlyle succeeded in turning the English language into a bastard barbaric version of the German language. . . . [p. 55]

270. Eugène Jolas, explication

1933

Extract from 'Marginalia to James Joyce's *Work in Progress*', *transition*, No. 22 (February 1933), 101–5.

The principal criterion of genius is the capacity to construct a mythological world. In creating the saga of Anna Livia Plurabelle, James Joyce has given us the modern idea of Magna Mater, the super-occidental vision of the Anatolian Cybele, of the Egyptian Rhea. In the fragment being published in this number of *transition*, he presents the modern saga of the infancy of mankind.

Every effort to force the work of James Joyce into a literary-historic mould has heretofore been a failure. By the time the critics had caught up with *Ulysses*, identified it, and neatly pigeon-holed it into the category of naturalism, his new work had already progressed beyond all academic sign-posts, having no reference-point other than a *visionary* quality of invention. *Work in Progress* is, if we must indulge in identification, anti-naturalist, and, on the positive side, mythological. For it is primarily the story of mankind and the universe. The first mantic myth written in our age. A cosmography in hierophantic terms. . . .

[four paragraphs of explication of pp. 219ff. follow here]

A new development of Mr. Joyce's linguistic experiments can be noted in this fragment. His attempt to reproduce the language of children is particularly felicitous. In the girls' address to Shaun, we notice grammatical deformations that approach infantile stammering. He attempts a primitive syntax: 'He possible he sooth to say notwithstanding he gaining fish considerable to look most prophitable out of smily skibluh eye'; 'Is you zealous of mes?'; 'He relation belong this

remarkable moliman'. That he is following the most modern philological researches can be deduced from the passage: 'But up tighty in
the front, down again the loose, drim and drumming on her back, and a
pop from her whistle what is that, o holytroopers?' This is a picaresque
illustration of the theory expressed by Sir Richard Paget in his 'The
Nature of Human Speech' (At the Clarendon Press, S. P. E. Tract No.
XXII) in which the acoustics of speech is studied from a new angle.
We have here again a reference to the rainbow motif, it being in this
particular passage an attempt to sound-describe the word heliotropes
from the viewpoint of Sir Richard Paget's idea of gesture.

Notabene: we might observe here, the re-occurence of Mr. Joyce's
preoccupation with the irrationalism of numbers. Seven, being the
symbolism of space-time, emerges here—as it does throughout the
book—in the seven colors of the rainbow, (the seven names of the
Floras), while four, the number of mystic space, can be found in
numerous allusions, such as the passage: 'No more turdenskaulds
(No more thunder), Free leaves for ebribadies (Free love for everybody), all tinsammon in the yord (All canned goods in the earth), with
harm and aches till Farther alters (with ham and eggs till the end of the
world.)'

Into the mythological texture the author sometimes weaves bits of
autobiographical material, making particular allusion to the tragedy of
exile. . . .

The mythological symbolisms used include numerous past and
living references. . . .

In this passage of *Work In Progress*, the author returns once more to
Vico's cyclical conception of history. 'The same renew.' The triune
evolution: theocratic, heroic and human, is the basis of the work. The
fear felt by primitive man is still in us. The thunder-motif in the
invocation to the 'Loud' is based on Vico. It is, however, obvious, that
Mr. Joyce is not in the least interested in demonstrating any theory. He
is merely following a vision of his own: the sense of the pre-historic and
the historic as one great stream. It is interesting, in this connection, to
observe that M. Lévy-Bruhl, the French sociologist, has come to some
definite confirmations in his own researches. The primitive mentality,
according to him, is characterized chiefly by the pre-logical function of
the mind. He finds—as did Vico—that the basic emotion which impelled
man to create his gods and myths, is fear, or rather, apprehension. In
his recent book *Le Surnaturel et la Nature dans la Mentalité primitive*
M. Lévy-Bruhl develops the idea still further. The German meta-

physician Martin Heidegger has also found apprehension to be man's principal impulse.

An inkling of the author's most definite belief can be found in the final prayer. He looks at the universe with cosmic humor, creating a world of symbols, building a 'witchman's funnominal world. . . .'

271. Ronald Symond on *The Mookse and the Gripes*

1934

Extract from 'Third Mr. Joyce', *London Mercury*, xxix (February 1934), 318–21. Also appeared in *Living Age*, cccxlvi (April 1934), 160–4.

A weird and unsteady star has swum into the ken of modern literature, in the person of the Dublin Wanderer, Mr. James Joyce, whose strange and fascinating voice comes to us over the water in accents which grow more and more bizarre. Twice already has his style undergone changes which are almost tantamount to metamorphoses of the man himself. *Dubliners* and the *Portrait of the Artist as a Young Man* were plain enough, dressed in English as she is spoken at home. *Ulysses* was written with a different ink and by a different man. Once again has the restless genius said 'good-bye to all that,' and in his latest *Work in Progress* he carries the tendencies which were inherent in *Ulysses* to such fantastic development that the famous odyssey now seems, by comparison, to be written in a style of smooth lucidity.

We have only to read the first sentence from one of the published extracts of this work, *The Mookse and the Gripes*, to realise that here is a voice utterly strange and unique: 'Eins within a space and a weary wide space it wast ere wohned a Mookse.' What on earth is this?—asks the common reader; and he will have to keep his nose well down to the text to find an answer for himself. Critics, both English and foreign, have been at work on Mr. Joyce, but none of them can 'place' him. Whether they like his work or not, none can question his uniqueness. There is no possible placing of a composite Gilbert, Lewis Carroll, Rabelais, Dante, Bruno, Dean Swift, Coleridge, Freud and Vico, who combines this multiplicity of personality with a soft and subtle brogue as Irish as anything which ever came out of Dublin, a sublime indifference to time and space, and a habit of passing in and out of the dreamland of the subconscious as many times as his fancy may dictate. What a zeit for the goths—to use his own phrase—is this chameleon of literature, who invents his own language as he follows his adventurous path.

Is it the rational mind, that small portion of an iceberg which shows itself above water, or is it the whole mass, four-fifths of which is hidden in the tenebrous deep? Whether or not the third Mr. Joyce sees human nature steadily, he certainly sees it whole, in this sense. He is the spokesman of dreamland, the projector of our mental and spiritual chaos in the raw. He deliberately eliminates the rationalising and filtering process, and, though his technique is meticulously careful and his effects most subtly worked upon, he makes no attempt to speak the language of our waking consciousness. Rather does he deliberately immerse himself in the fairyland of subconscious chaos, and let his rich mind run amok on paper with the licence of a nightmare. He does not seek, either subjectively or objectively, to impose an order upon the phenomena of experience, but allows them to flash by in all their kaleidoscopic confusion. . . .

The characters of *Work in Progress*, in keeping with the space-time chaos in which they live, change identity at will. At one time they are persons, at another rivers or stones or trees, at another personifications of an idea, at another they are lost and hidden in the actual texture of the prose, with an ingenuity far surpassing that of crossword puzzles. . . .

[analyses the changes in identity]

The story of Anna Livia is perhaps the best known of the extracts which have been published in England. In this curious and baffling prose poem the entire text, from beginning to end, is charged with the hidden names of rivers, introduced by distortion of common words in such bewildering profusion as to give the context a fishy and watery flavour. Not only hundreds of river-names, but all the vocabulary of the water-side is inextricably jumbled in the medium of speech. . . .

Another favourite trick of the author is to convey meanings additional to those of the literal sense. By distorting the words in a phrase, he introduces a supplementary motif, blending two or more associations. Let us take an example, and see what we can make of it. Mr. Joyce tells us, of a rascally fellow named Glugger, that 'He dooly redecant allbigenesis henesies. He proform penance.' Now it appears that this penitent 'recants the Albigensian heresies'; but at the same time there is a suggestion that he 'decants all the Guinness and Henessey's.' Does it mean either, or both, or neither? Does Mr. Joyce wish to imply that the gentleman's repentance was partially dictated by the expansive influence of good Irish liquor, and that the *pro forma* penance was just a piece of boosy blarney? Is this why the phrase itself contains a flavour of alcohol, a whiff of the cork? Maybe it is, but what sort of literary fare is this? What will the purist call this doubly-flavoured pabulum? Neither fish nor fowl, nor yet plain meat, but 'beef cut with a hammy knife!'

Although the whole of *Work in Progress* is coloured throughout by Mr. Joyce's elfish and acrobatic humour, and invested everywhere with double and treble meanings or suggestions, there is no characteristically 'joycean' style. The gamut of his effects ranges from jagged staccato to the smoothest and most delicate rhythms. . . .

[illustrates this point by quoting from p. 244]

But what does all this jesting mean? Mr. Joyce laughs at *everything*. He is sometimes sombre, sometimes crude, but never serious. He can hearken to the still sad music of humanity, and reproduce it with most touching delicacy. But always, always, there is present that almost inhuman genius of humour. Mr. Joyce could outdo Hamlet. He could hold up his own skull and jest about it. His whole universe is a great phantasmagorial comedy, and he the great prophet of the comic sense of life. But methinks this prophet doth protest too much. There must be deep unshed tears behind all this uninterrupted laughter—he would not be human else. This most sensitive of men, brave voyager in the dark depths of human consciousness, must know and feel something of the wholly tragic, must have corners of his consciousness which are too serious for speech.

How, then, are we to appraise or understand the divine and profane peculiarity of Mr. Joyce? His text is obscure beyond all reasonable bounds, but we need make no mistake upon one score: he has colossal gifts. He has at his command a thousand twangling instruments, an encyclopaedic scholarship, great depth of poetic feeling, abundant courage, and all the sensibilities of saint and sinner. No living writer has the half of his equipment, and few have dug so deep into the dangerous but fecund depths of dreamland and the subconscious. Is this third stage the final stage of his development, or is there to be yet a fourth Mr. Joyce? Is this fantastic mine of twisted lore, this philologist's medley of the dreamlife, with its flashes and sparks and liquid lullabies, his last word, or will he pipe to our spirits other ditties of a different tone?

For my part I want to hear a fourth Mr. Joyce. Amazed, amused, and sometimes enchanted, but more often utterly puzzled by the third Mr. Joyce, I rise unsatisfied from *Work in Progress*. I marvel at it, but cannot bow down before it. I cannot comfort myself that I am competent to understand one-half of its contents, being insufficiently highbrow for its hybrid scholarship. Nor do I feel that any such accomplishment would add substantially to my joy in its perusal. But one thing emerges clear. There are potentialities in Mr. Joyce beyond the dreams of Æschylus, together with a craftsmanship unparalleled to-day. Here is a singer who might bring all heaven before my eyes, dissolve me into ecstasies. *Work in Progress* brings me multicoloured chaos, a whirlwind out of which there come dark Rabelaisian rumblings, a laughter as of disembodied goblins, pirouettings of the pixies and enchanting snatches of flute-melody, but out of which there speaks no steady and still small voice that I can hear. . . .

MIME OF MICK, NICK AND THE MAGGIES (MIME)

1934

272. G. W. Stonier, review, *New Statesman*

22 September 1932, viii, 364

. . . One cannot read far in Mr. Joyce's new book without discovering that its whole method is based on dreams. The characters are at the same time persons and landmarks of Dublin; every scene is played on a revolving stage; and the individual words of Mr. Joyce's prose convey two or more simultaneous meanings, which strike the imagination at different levels. He plays on our sub-consciousness in a multitude of ways, now echoing a forgotten passage, now half-suggesting a thought while our attention is directed elsewhere. The fact that no *single* meaning can be extracted from any paragraph has probably disturbed readers more than the actual difficulty of his verbal inventions. There is only one way of reading the later Joyce, and that is to go by the sound and the rhythm, which are simple enough, and let the meanings look after themselves. We must read passively, but at the same time Mr. Joyce expects of his reader the sort of acuteness which will spot a *double entendre*. If a music-hall audience can appreciate sexual jokes in this way, there is no reason why educated readers should not be capable of catching the allusions, historical and topical, which are embedded in *Work in Progress*. We may miss a good deal—Mr. Joyce's fondness for Dublin and modern languages may baffle the outsider—but what emerges is slapstick raised to the status of art; and, indeed, as a master of ribald poetry, Mr. Joyce has few equals in literature.

The Mime of Mick, Nick and the Maggies begins, then, in a Dublin theatre—'Every evening at lighting up o'clock sharp and until further notice in Feenichts Playhouse (bar and conveniences always open).' A number of characters are introduced after the manner of the newspaper serial—'and now read on here'—but most of them do not reappear. The playhouse fades; it is perhaps a summer evening, and the fairies and gnomes and principals of pantomime jig through the dusk, ending on a tableau.

> The flossies all and the mossies all they drooped upon her draped brimfall. The bowknots, the showlots, they wilted into woeblots. The pearlagraph, the pearlagraph, knew whitchly whether to weep or laugh. For always down in Carolinas lovely Dinahs vaunt their view.

Bits of nursery rhyme, doggerel, popular songs waft them away. Dublin becomes Eden; from a chorus of sprites whose names spell the word Raynbow we come to the house of Amanti and the names of advertisers. So it goes on, at a good pace, this mad midsummer night's dream. If there is a mime at all, after the first few pages, it is the mime of words, which tumble into strange postures and dance through catalogues of colours, sweetmeats, bawdy prayers, Dublin slang, till at last 'by deep request' the curtain drops. In the meantime, as usual, Mr. Joyce has given us a bit of everything from Adam to Mademoiselle of Armentières, and however difficult an exercise it might prove for the précis-writer, this 'cosmological fairy-tale' is rich in satire and pure magic. The delight which one finds in words like 'mother-in-lieu,' or such a phrase as 'making a bolderdash for lubberty of speech,' is sharper than the ordinary pleasures of prose. The scenes, the landscapes and characters of Mr. Joyce's fantasy are squeezed into animated words.

Reading the fifty pages of this new 'fragment'—so carefully written and written over—we are reminded, with awe and almost with horror, of the parent work, that vast snowball trundling down some hidden slope, of which this is merely a chip thrown into the sky. How many thousand *Micks* and *Anna Livias* has it gathered up in its course? And when will it reach the bottom? The reviewer forsees a day when he, too, will be expected to go out with a search party, ice-axe and Vico in hand, to examine the new landmark and scratch his initials in the ice. Meanwhile, he is content with a crystal or two.

The Mime of Mick, Nick and the Maggies, though not so good as *Anna Livia Plurabelle*, is a fair specimen of its author's prose. It contains, by the way, for those who have the true crossword mind, scriptural references on pages 3, 7 and 32, etc.; an acrostic on p. 16; advertisements of skin foods and hair tonics (reversed) on p. 38; a quotation from *Ulysses* on p. 34; and rhymes and ribaldry *partout*. . . .

273. Malcolm Cowley on religion of art

1934

Extract from *Exile's Return* (1934), *passim*. Appeared as 'Religion of Art', *New Republic*, lxxvii, No. 996 (3 January 1934), 218 [216–20] (from which the present text is taken).

. . . James Joyce also presented us with a picture of the writer who never repeats himself. From *Chamber Music* through *Dubliners* and *A Portrait of the Artist*, each of his books had approached a new problem, had definitely ended a stage of his career. *Ulysses*, published in the winter of 1921–22, marked yet another stage. Although we had not time in the busy year that followed to read it carefully or digest more than a tenth of it, still we were certain of one thing: it was a book which could, without abusing the word, be called 'great.' . . . Can a writer of our own time produce a masterpiece fit to compare with those of other ages? Joyce was the first indication that the question had another answer than the one we had learned in school.

Pride, contempt, ambition: these were the three qualities that disengaged themselves from all his writings. Toward the end of *A Portrait of the Artist* they stand forth most clearly. . . . He had pride, contempt, ambition—and these are the qualities which continue to stand forth clearly from *Ulysses*. Here once more is the pride of Stephen Dedalus that raises itself above the Dublin public and especially above the Dublin intellectual public as represented by Buck Mulligan; here is the author's contempt for the world and for his readers—like a host being deliberately rude to his guests, he makes no concession to their capacity for attention or their power of understanding; and here is an ambition willing to measure itself, not against any novelist of its age, not against any writer belonging to a modern national literature, but with the arch-poet of the European race.

And now this poor boy from the twentieth century had conquered his Peru and created his work of genius. We were not among the enthusiasts who placed him beside Homer, but this at least was certain: except for Marcel Proust there was no living author to be compared with him in depth, richness, complexity or scope. His literary career was an example for younger writers; his ambition dignified our lesser ambitions. But obviously he had written *Ulysses* at a price—just how much had he paid in terms of bread and laughter? How did a man live who had written a masterpiece?. . .

274. John H. Roberts on religion to art

1934

Extract from 'James Joyce: from Religion to Art', *New Humanist*, vii (May–June, 1934), 7–13.

There can be no sympathetic understanding of James Joyce's *Ulysses* without seeing it in direct relation to its origin in Joyce's autobiographical novel *A Portrait of the Artist as a Young Man*, where the discussions on religion and art so prepare the way for *Ulysses* that the latter is truly a sequel to *A Portrait*, not merely because Stephen Dedalus appears in both, but because *Ulysses* is the actual application of the ideas that in the earlier book are only explained.

It must be clear from the beginning that Stephen Dedalus is to be identified with Joyce himself and that the name of the old Greek artificer has been chosen for a purpose as a symbol of the creative spirit. In *A Portrait* we see how this spirit gradually becomes aware of itself; in *Ulysses* we see what it achieves.

The most important single influence at work on Dedalus is the Roman Catholic Church. But the relationship between Catholicism and the embryonic artist is exceedingly complex. Born into the Church, trained by the Jesuits at Clongowes Wood College and Belvedere College and later at the National University, Dedalus-Joyce is steeped in the ritual of his religion. His emotional being is sunk deep in the Roman Catholic faith. . . .

But strongly contrasted with this emotional tug toward spirituality is the intellectual repudiation of it. From early childhood Dedalus is aware of the squalor of Ireland, of the filth and poverty of Dublin, so vividly opposed to the wealth of the Church. His rational mind comes to accept his father's statement that the Irish are a 'priestridden God-forsaken race.' He acknowledges to himself the call of the flesh and thereby becomes unable to acknowledge the call of the spirit. . . .

And thus Dedalus frees himself from the Roman Catholic Church. But it is the irony of his release that in spite of intellectual emancipation, his inner (and more emotional) self is never altogether free. Between his inherited religion and his self-constructed liberty he must always waver. . . . In the opening section of *Ulysses* he is suffering remorse of conscience because he refused, at his mother's death-bed, to pray for her soul. Such a consistent and stubborn loyalty to his own precepts would be unimportant if it were not for the fact that he must forever pay for it with dark misgivings and despair. Dedalus is now more truly lost than if his soul were in the Roman Catholic hell.

It is out of this sense of loss, of frustration, that Joyce writes *Ulysses*, the theme of which concerns Dedalus's search for a father and Mr. Bloom's search for a son. It has been said that *Ulysses*, more than any other work of art, expresses the disintegration of the postwar generation. That may be true; but it does more than that. It portrays the wanderings of the two souls in search of the spiritual salvation that they can never find, for although during the course of 'Bloomsday,' the paths of Dedalus and Mr. Bloom cross and the two strays finally meet, there is for them no peace. . . . In the modern version, there is only bitterness, for to Joyce, who has found himself at odds with human-kind, the final adjustment that Homer believes in, never occurs.

There is, however, a kind of vicarious adjustment that Joyce does believe in, for while it is impossible for Dedalus ever to be at ease with his fellow men and their institutions, it does become possible for him to find an individual integrity in the creation of a work of art. The hopeless career of Dedalus in *Ulysses* represents the everlasting conflict between Joyce and organized society; but *Ulysses* itself, as a thing created by Joyce, becomes the compensation that the artist can some-how shape and forge out of his own being and out of his awareness of what life is. It is the creation he becomes capable of only after he has torn himself free intellectually from 'social and religious orders' and which is engendered by that very sense of ultimate emotional defeat which is the ironic accompaniment to his sense of victory. It is in this way that *Ulysses* is truly the sequel to *A Portrait of the Artist as a Young Man*.

A more exact relationship between the two novels becomes clear when we realize that *Ulysses* is itself a concrete expression of the aesthetic theory of tragedy stated in the earlier work. To understand this theory one must realize that it has been arrived at in Dedalus's mind only after the artist has escaped the 'nets of nationality, language, and religion.' It is based on a re-examination of the Aristotelian concepts of pity and terror, in which re-evaluation Dedalus comes to the conclusion that the tragic emotion is essentially static, that it *arrests* the mind and, in a suspension of all volition, succeeds in uniting the mind with human suffering and its cause. . . .

The work of art thus produced must, Dedalus continues, show three qualities that he borrows from Thomas Aquinas. The first is its 'wholeness', by which he means its discreteness, its quality of being something whole by itself. *Ulysses* admirably illustrates this aspect of the theory, for the book manages to be beautifully self-contained. It asks for no response other than comprehension. . . .

The second quality is 'harmony,' which is concerned specifically with technique. As most articles and volumes on *Ulysses* deal primarily with its technical problems, there is here no need of adding another to the already large number of such studies. But it should be pointed out that every detail of the complicated method of the book illustrates Joyce's concept of 'harmony,' by which he means the ordered arrangement into which the various factors of the novel fall, the pattern or design which is formed by this arrangement, and the sense of rhythm (or relation of part to part) in the structure. . . .

The third quality is 'radiance'. Whereas 'wholeness' and 'harmony' are aspects belonging to the work of art and are put there by the artist to be perceived by the critic or observer, 'radiance' seems to denote something that happens to the mind of the artist when in the creative process he has seen, felt, and achieved 'wholeness' and 'harmony'. . . . It is one of the supreme moments vouchsafed to the human race; it is the only justification for art.

Does *Ulysses* create this moment? There can be no doubt but that it did for Joyce; the only question is whether or not it does for us. The

answer seems to be that it can if we will let it. But we must rise beyond
desire and loathing in order to reach that stasis where our response is one
of comprehension rather than prejudice, where we grant the artist his
own vision and allow him to transmute 'the daily bread of experience
into the radiant body of everliving life'. The remarkable decision
handed down by Judge Woolsey in the *Ulysses* trial must always stand
as a landmark in our progress toward such an attitude, for in that
decision the law asks of an artist only that he be sincere and honest. . . .

That is all. It would seem to be enough. It is useless to ask for more.
For Joyce is not a prophet; he has no message. He is the pure artist. He
has come to grips with life and with himself. His effort to free himself
from the bonds of humanity and religion has made him only more
acutely aware of the everlasting hold that humanity and religion have
upon him. This knowledge tempts him to no sociological theories; nor
does it lure him into the manufacturing of cures. It has merely made
him understand the spirit of life itself as he has experienced it and given
him the compulsion to shape out of this knowledge his art. At the very
end of *A Portrait of the Artist as a Young Man*, after Dedalus has learned
to know himself, he utters the cry that is the immediate anticipation of
Ulysses: 'Welcome, O life I go to encounter for the millionth time the
reality of existence and to forge in the smithy of my soul the uncreated
conscience of my race. . . . Old father, old artificer, stand me now and
ever in good stead.' This is the final key to *Ulysses*, for that astounding
book is the statement of all that Joyce knows about himself and about
life; in its perfected artistry it is the unfettered communication of the
vision of a fettered soul. In this paradox lies the significance of Joyce's
work. Art is his release. The chains of existence never dissolve; but in the
very finality of their hold they make possible and necessary the creative
act which transmutes the agony of living into a divine and Olympian
comprehension that is beyond good and evil. . . .

275. A Communist on Joyce

1934

Extract from V. Gertsfelde, 'A Communist on Joyce', *Living Age*, cccxlvii (November 1934), 268–70.

The All-Union Writers' Congress has witnessed many revaluations, particularly of foreign writers, and the name of James Joyce provoked the most heated debate of any. Karl Radek, with his usual ruthlessness, expressed the opinion that Joyce's defects so overbalanced his merits that he could be safely rejected *in toto*. Others, however, held more moderate—and, we believe, fairer—views, notably V. Gertsfelde, a Soviet critic whose speech we reproduce below:

'Joyce's method is definitely experimental, and we cannot deny the writer the right to experiment, even if we question the value of his experimentation. Joyce's method, which is very unusual both from the æsthetic and the intellectual point of view, has led to the formation of a school in which we must include the names of such writers as John Dos Passos. Radek [No. 278] is entirely justified in saying that this school is a dangerous one, not because its teachings are petty, stupid, or inadequate—as one might suppose from Comrade Radek's report—but, on the contrary, because this school has so much to offer.

'What, then, is the danger? It consists in this: though one may learn a great deal, one may also unlearn many valuable things in Joyce's school. For instance, a devotee of Joyce who wishes to describe his hero looking out a window will no longer rest content with the following sentence: "Leaning on the window sill, he looked out over the immensity of the fields. Everything irritated him—that house over there, the fact that the peasants had set fire to the forest, the shed on Krivaia Street that blocked his view, and the fact that he himself was as irritable and cross as a doddering, finicky old man." The Joycean writer would have his hero looking at the fields and examining his own consciousness at the same time. He would attempt to fathom the phrase, "everything irritated him," and he would relinquish the false simile of the old man for looking out of the window. . . .

'This danger, moreover, is far greater to the western than to the Soviet writer, who is shielded by the Marxist point of view and the intense control of the reading public over its writers. The danger is not that the writer's mind will focus on the dung-heap—or, to put it more subtly—on the "inner life." Joyce's vision of man is not the result of his artistic method; rather has the method developed as the most adequate tool to reveal man as Joyce sees him. This conception, moreover, is the direct result of the capitalist system, the details of which Joyce presents so profusely without ever revealing the forces at work behind the scenes. But, if Comrade Radek thinks that Joyce's method is suitable only to the Joycean concept and discards the form with the matter, he is making a mistake. There is unquestionably a relation between the two, but it cannot be expressed by a simple equation sign. And it is far more important to cast light on the social influences at work on Joyce's art.

'These influences are very complicated. The power of the bourgeoisie to-day is largely dependent on its ability to hide behind a screen of pseudo-democracy, religion, and mysticism. In the realm of ideas this smoke-screening is carried out to a high degree of perfection. The bourgeoisie succeeded in transforming science and art into a mystery; consequently, scientists and artists become "neutral" people whose mysterious and spiritual depths no ordinary mortal can fathom. These men were placed above the slings and arrows of the populace; only their peers practising the same speciality could hope to judge them.

'Several of these priests recognized Joyce—we know that from the press. The readers who were not content with half-baked critiques had to admit that, if they did not understand Joyce, they had only their own ignorance to blame. And, indeed, they did not have the Joycean microscope at their disposal. In this way, the orders of the bourgeoisie are carried out. A writer produces a book that the initiated alone may evaluate. Many admirers of James Joyce will find the Fascist "Leader" idea right after their own hearts. . . . The revelation of men in relation to the outside world, in relation to the past and the future, is undesirable from the bourgeois point of view. If light must be cast, then let it be the light of a projector, which does not illuminate but blinds. In this way Joyce acquires social significance. He promises his audience that he will lead them to the depths that they long to fathom, but he excludes those things the penetration of which might lead to the revolution.'

V. Gertsfelde does not, however, challenge Joyce's sincerity and artistic integrity. Though he may serve the bourgeoisie by his partial presentation of contemporary life and his failure to use his art for the revolutionary movement, still does he show the decay of the present system. Though his microscope limits its field, it penetrates and reveals the disease that ails our world. In this way it may turn other, younger writers toward the revolution, and Joyce's supreme artistry may yet serve the cause of the proletariat. V. Gertsfelde's point of view is not unique; it expresses a Soviet tendency that the growing power of Fascism has intensified—the willingness to accept as friends those who are not enemies, though they be not Communists. . . .

276. Frank Budgen on Joyce

1934

Extract from 'Further Recollections of James Joyce', *Partisan Review*, xxiii (Fall 1956), 530–44. Later appeared as *Further Recollections of James Joyce* (1956).

. . . The cosmology, hagiology and the sacraments of the Christian religion are built into the façade of *Ulysses* and *Finnegans Wake* for all to see, but it might perhaps one day profitably interest a theologian to inquire how far the rejected doctrines of the Churches pervade the inner structure of those works. For example: Is there a Manichaean leaning in Joyce's 'spirit and nature' duality? Does he in his treatment of the mystery of fatherhood affirm or deny the consubstantiality of father and son? And what of the major theme of *Finnegans Wake*—the Resurrection?. . . .

It has often been said of Joyce that he was greatly influenced by psychoanalysis in the composition of *Ulysses* and *Finnegans Wake*. If by that is meant that he made use of the jargon of that science when it suited the purpose of his fiction, or made use of its practical analytical devices as when Bloom commits the *Fehlleistung* of talking about 'the wife's admirers' when he meant 'the wife's advisers,' the point holds good. But if it is meant that he adopted the theory and followed the practice of psychoanalysis in his work as did the Dadaists and the Surrealists, nothing could be farther from the truth. The Joycean method of composition and the passively automatic method are two opposite and opposed poles. If psychoanalysis cured sick people, well and good. Who could quarrel with that? But Joyce was always impatient or contemptuously silent when it was talked about as both and all-sufficient *Weltanschauung* and a source and law for artistic production.

'Why all this fuss and bother about the mystery of the unconscious?' he said to me one evening at the Pfauen Restaurant. 'What about the mystery of the conscious? What do they know about that?'

One might say that both as man and artist Joyce was exceedingly conscious. Great artificers have to be. As I saw him working on *Ulysses* I can testify that no line ever left his workshop without having been the object of a hundredfold scrutiny. And I remember my old friend August Suter telling me that in the early days of the composition of *Finnegans Wake* Joyce said to him, 'I feel like an engineer boring through a mountain from two sides. If my calculations are correct we shall meet in the middle. If not . . .' Whatever philosophy of composition that indicates, it is certainly neither automatic nor convulsive. . . . There was a good deal of the surefootedness and toughness of the mountain goat in Joyce's own composition and more than a little of the relaxed vigilance of the cat. . . .

I have commented elsewhere on Joyce's reactions to the criticisms of Clutton Brock and H. G. Wells, but his remark when I mentioned Wyndham Lewis's criticism of *Ulysses* is worth recording: 'Allowing that the whole of what Lewis says about my book is true, is it more than ten per cent of the truth?' . . . .

With regard to the language used by Joyce, particularly in *Finnegans Wake*, it is sometimes forgotten that in his early years in Dublin Joyce lived among the believers and adepts in magic gathered round the poet Yeats. Yeats held that the borders of our minds are always shifting, tending to become part of the universal mind, and that the borders of our memory also shift and form part of the universal memory. This universal mind and memory could be evoked by symbols. When telling me this Joyce added that in his own work he never used the recognized symbols, preferring instead to use trivial and quadrivial words and local geographical allusions. The intention of magical evocation, however, remained the same. . . .

277. Alec Brown on *Ulysses* and the novel

1934

Extract from 'Joyce's *Ulysses* and the Novel', *Dublin Magazine*, ix(January–March 1934), 41, 49, 50 [41–50].

Joyce's *Ulysses* is generally accepted as a most original contribution to the novel; even a landmark. It may be useful to examine the truth of this assertion; and, if we can, see in what the work is a landmark, what this landmark is significant of.

Ulysses is interestingly written; it grips. It is also long in comparison with the ordinary novel; and size, if it does not too much diminish quality, is impressive to us. But there are other novels which have achieved bulk together with a reasonably high level of quality; and there are many more still, even among works which are quite admittedly of lesser import and ephemeral, that grip the reader. That is the prime quality of the thriller, so that interestingness, as well as bulk, must be rejected as claims to originality or landmark quality.

That the mere bulk or the interestingness cannot be reasons for claiming the work as a landmark does not, though, necessarily mean that these qualities have not contributed something towards the resultant landmark quality. The reasons for that quality may be, but need not be, complex. But before we look for a complex reason we should examine possible simple reasons.

But before proceeding to what seems the crux of the matter, reference must be made to the pure form of the work. There has been some talk of the adoption by Joyce of a scheme, a framework, such as that rhythm employed in the *Odyssey*, which is a sequence of themes (somewhat rondo-fashion) in the development of a straight narration, similar to the rhythm that Professor Myres, in his book *Who were the Greeks?*, analyses on some Greek pictorial vases. It is difficult to see how the use of such a framework, on which to build the exposition, say, of Bloom's twenty-four hours, can be regarded as an important innovation. . . .

We have now come to a *result* of *Ulysses* which may prove, not at all because of any bulk or thrillingness, or even notoriety, but because of its special merits, to be a landmark. Joyce, in *Ulysses*, brought inner narration to such a point that by it destruction of normal, or outer, narration was finally completed. But out of the ruins come two things: an awareness of the dangerously corroding action of inner narration, which may make a healthy normal narration possible, and the possibility of a special new form, the prime purpose of which is not to narrate. In short, Joyce has shown that inner narration is not narration at all, but either an adjunct to proper narration or a new thing.

It is curious, indeed, that this culumination of the first age of the novel, in the triumph of inner narration, came just at the point where the main interest of mankind is no longer in individual matters, but social matters. But it is curious only on first thoughts, for on closer examination we see how characteristic of the development of a form this is. We may throw further light on the significance of *Ulysses* as a landmark, for we may note, in conclusion, that in this final destruction of the novel which contained the canker of inner narration we have merely the final throes of individualistic narrative art. It is necessary to destroy in order to rebuild; Joyce helps destroy the bourgeois novel; it remains for others to rebuild.

It may be suspected that the fragments of *Work in Progress* which have already appeared are part of Joyce's further attempts to develop narration—presumably along inner, really non-narrational lines. The fragments, indeed, do appear to be in a form which is certainly not the novel, which certainly has none but an illusive concern with narration, and proceeds from that land which is probably not only incognita, but even mythical—the mind. But it would be neither fair nor profitable to treat of mere fragments of a whole in the question of style. The most we can do at present is examine the mere language of them, for it is very striking. But when we do this it appears that, in his eagerness to develop inner narration farther than its ultimate expression (as in Mrs. Bloom's soliloquy) Joyce has quagmired himself on an excursion which is not an excursion in narration at all, but a mere function of the English language, as used by a Dublin man who has sojourned some time in Central Europe; and that is a problem, not of style or narration, but of linguistics, which can better be dealt with elsewhere. . . .

278. Ernest Boyd on Joyce's influence

1934

Extract from 'Joyce and the New Irish Writers', *Current History*, xxxix (March 1934), 699, 700 [699–704].

To many people the recent removal of the censorship ban on James Joyce's *Ulysses* will seem to be the most important event in the history of contemporary Anglo-Irish literature. . . .

Outside Ireland itself, this quintessentially Irish and local study of Dublin life has evoked somewhat extravagant enthusiasm and highly exaggerated claims for its importance. The distinguished French critic, novelist and translator, Valéry Larbaud of the *Nouvelle Revue Française* [No. 118] pitched the note when he declared that, with *Ulysses*, Ireland had made her re-entry into European literature. It is true, Mr. Joyce has made a daring and often valuable technical experiment, breaking new ground in English for the development of narrative prose, although the extension of the method, as exemplified in the published portions of *Work in Progress*, may well give his admirers pause. But the 'European' interest of the work must of necessity be limited to its form, for its content is so local and intrinsically insignificant that few who are unfamiliar with the city of Dublin thirty years ago can possibly grasp its allusions and enter into its spirit.

Essentially *Ulysses* is a continuation of the studies of certain Dublin types first adumbrated in the superb volume of short stories, *Dubliners*, and in that fine novel, *A Portrait of the Artist as a Young Man*, neither of which excited anything like the furore in esoteric circles which greeted *Ulysses*. Much has been written about the symbolic intention of this work, of its relation to Homer's *Odyssey*, to which the plan of the three first and last chapters, with the twelve cantos of the adventures of Ulysses in the middle, is supposed to correspond. Irish criticism, on the other hand, is more impressed by its simple realism, photographic in detail and documentation, while admitting the power of Joyce's bewildering juxtaposition of the real and the imaginary, the commonplace and the fantastic. He is the first, and perhaps the last, Irish Expressionist, showing a certain kinship with the Germans Walter Hasenclever and Georg Kaiser.

To claim for this book a European significance denied to W. B. Yeats, J. M. Synge or James Stephens is to ignore its genesis in favor of mere technique, and to invest its content with a mysterious import which the actuality of the references would seem to deny. James Joyce is endowed with the wonderful, fanstastic imagination which conceived the fifteenth chapter of *Ulysses*, a vision of a Dublin Brocken, whose scene is the sordid underworld of that city. But he also has the defects and qualities of the French Naturalists of the Zola school, which prompt him, for example, to catalogue all the various street-car lines and to explain with the accuracy of a guide-book how the city obtains its water supply. His eroticism, too, so misleadingly advertised by the censors, will be revealed as oscillating between mocking Rabelaisian ribaldry and the contemptuous and disgusted horror of the body which makes Swift the authentic precursor of this typical expression of Irish asceticism. As Judge Woolsey says in the decision prefacing this edition, 'In spite of its unusual frankness, I do not detect anywhere the leer of the sensualist.' Thus, the hopes of a certain type of reader are fortunately doomed to disappointment. . . .

279. Karl Radek on Joyce's realism

1934

Extract from 'James Joyce or Socialist Realism?' in *Contemporary World Literature and the Tasks of the Proletariat*, a report delivered at the Congress of Soviet Writers, August 1934, pp. 151–4; later appeared in *Problems of Soviet Literature* (1935), ed. A. Zhdanov *et al.*, 152–5, 157 [150–62] (from which the present text is taken).

See the reply by James T. Farrell (No. 288).

. . . Searches for a new form have begun. There are two names which best express the new ways by which bourgeois artists are attempting to create major works of art. One of these is Proust. . . .

The other hero of contemporary bourgeois literature, though he is not widely known even to bourgeois readers, is James Joyce, the mysterious author of *Ulysses*—a book which the bourgeois literary world, while reading it but little, has made the object of loud discussion.

What is the peculiarity of Joyce's method? He tries to depict a day in the life of his subjects motion by motion—the motions of the body, the motions of the mind, the motions of the feelings in all their shades, from conscious feelings to those which rise up in the throat like a spasm. He cinematographs the life of his subject with the maximum of minuteness, omitting nothing.

Thought is crocheted to thought; if the thought leads off at a tangent, the author hastens to follow it up. His hero, while drunk, is assailed by hallucinations. The author breaks off his story in the middle and reproduces these hallucinations. More than eight hundred pages are taken up with one day in the hero's life.

We will not dwell on the extraneous matter that is woven into Joyce's work, on how he encircles the actions and thoughts of his heroes with an intricate cobweb of allegories and mythological allusions, on all these phantasmagoria of the madhouse. We will examine only the essence of the 'new method,' by which naturalism is reduced to clinical observation, and romanticism and symbolism to delirious ravings.

What is the basic feature in Joyce? His basic feature is the conviction that there is nothing big in life—no big events, no big people, no big ideas; and the writer can give a picture of life by just taking 'any given hero on any given day,' and reproducing him with exactitide. A heap of dung, crawling with worms, photographed by a cinema apparatus through a microscope—such is Joyce's work.

But it is sufficient to consider the picture that he gives, in order to see that it does not fit even those trivial heroes in that trivial life which he depicts. The scene of his book is laid in Ireland in 1916. The petty bourgeois whom he describes are Irish types, though laying claim to universal human significance. But these Blooms and Dædaluses, whom the author relentlessly pursues into the lavatory, the brothel and the pothouse, did not cease to be petty bourgeois when they took part in the Irish insurrection of 1916. The petty bourgeois is a profoundly contradictory phenomenon, and in order to give a portrayal of the petty bourgeois, one must present him in all his relations to life.

Joyce, who is alleged to give an impartial presentation of the petty bourgeois, who is alleged to follow every movement of his hero, is not simply a register of life; he has selected a piece of life and depicted that. His choice is determined by the fact that for him the whole world lies between a cupboardful of mediæval books, a brothel and a pothouse. For him, the national revolutionary movement of the Irish petty bourgeoisie does not exist; and consequently the picture which he presents, despite its ostensible impartiality, is untrue.

But even if one might conceive for a moment that the Joyce method is a suitable one for describing petty, insignificant, trivial people, their actions, thoughts and feelings—although tomorrow these people may be participants in great deeds—then it is perfectly clear that this method would prove utterly worthless if the author were to approach with his movie camera the great events of the class struggle, the titanic clashes of the modern world.

A capitalist magnate cannot be presented by the method which Joyce uses in attempting to present his vile hero, Bloom, not because his private life is less trivial than that of Bloom, but because he is an exponent of great worldwide contradictions, because, when he is battling with some rival trust or hatching plots against the Soviet Union, he must not be spied on in the brothel or the bedroom, but must be portrayed on the great arena of world affairs. Needless to say, trying to present a picture of revolution by the Joyce method would be like trying to catch a dreadnought with a shrimping net.

Just because he is almost untranslated and unknown in our country, Joyce arouses a morbid interest among a section of our writers. Is there not some hidden meaning lurking in the eight hundred pages of his *Ulysses*—which cannot be read without special dictionaries, for Joyce attempts to create a language of his own in order to express the thoughts and feelings which he lacks?

This interest in Joyce is an unconscious expression of the leanings of certain Right-wing authors, who have adapted themselves to revolution, but who in reality do not understand its greatness. . . .

Socialist realism means not only knowing reality as it is, but knowing whither it is moving. It is moving towards socialism, it is moving towards the victory of the international proletariat. And a work of art created by a socialist realist is one which shows whither that conflict of contradictions is leading which the artist has seen in life and reflected in his work. . . .

280. Frank Swinnerton on Joyce and Freud

1934

Extract from 'Post Freud', in *The Georgian Scene* (1934) pp. 415–19; the *Georgian Literary Scene* (1935) pp. 332–5.

If Lawrence was unsophisticated, Joyce is the reverse. One can trace his steady progress in sophistication from the close realistic studies contained in *Dubliners*, impressions mostly of squalid life in a city, through the quickened reminiscence of *Portrait of the Artist as a Young Man*, to the extended and often very brilliant display of *Ulysses*. Only hard-headed Irishmen and cosmopolitan Jews are as sophisticated as he, or could have written anything in such an idiom as that of *Ulysses*. . . .

Joyce has some of the traits of the sophisticated journalist or *entre-*

preneur. Being an Irishman, he is master of an inexhaustible pen. His knowledge of the life of back streets, of saloons, the lewd thoughts of maidens, the doings at Catholic seminaries in Ireland, of foul old men, and a thousand other disagreeable matters, is extensive and peculiar. He rarely soars above the base; but the base is known to him without mercy. He can lay his hand upon its heart and feel the very beat of it. He can imaginatively enter it and be of it, so that the reader of what he writes may well feel that this is at that moment the whole of life. And as he has progressed in sophistication he has also progressed in his own quite special technique, which has not yet reached its end, although it has long passed the instantly intelligible. He carries a kind of literary postimpressionism as far as any man has yet done—farther than any other writer except Gertrude Stein. Sometimes he writes in a series of jotted shorthand notes; sometimes as if he overheard and recorded a dialogue between strangers; sometimes in wild fantasy; sometimes in a jumble of disconnected thoughts. The jumble is his mainstay in some of the best passages in the book called *Ulysses*. . . .

[quotes from the Calypso episode, pp. 68, 69]

Now to a quick mind, self-observant, ready to catch notes and take them, to sight contradictions in mood and response, and to explore memory, the concoction of such a jumble is not difficult. The method is familiar enough in scraps of impressionist fiction. What gives Joyce's jumble its peculiar merit is his wit and the frequent malicious precision of his exposure, which goes deeper into soliloquy than the work of any other writer. . . . He has not, I think, a truly creative imagination but abnormal cleverness, in which he takes a virtuoso's delight. Those words of Lawrence's which I have quoted put the matter over-strongly. Though they are so amusing, they represent the puritan's point of view. But they have a penetration natural to Lawrence's literary criticism. Lawrence, though it was his way to see the defects of other authors, rather than their qualities, made no mistake in the nature of the defects, and in a phrase summed up what most of us would take pages to express, even if, at the end of them, we reached the same conclusion. . . .

[the next paragraph is deleted from the 1935 version of this essay]

Ulysses, for example, which seems to be as much of a jumble as some of the reflections contained in it, is an elaborately constructed work upon the model of Homer's *Odyssey*. A long book has been written pointing out every parallel between the *Odyssey* and *Ulysses*. It is made a point of by all those who highly esteem Joyce as a writer, that his longest book is a modern work, based upon the *Odyssey* but dealing with only eighteen hours in time. Just why a book should be important because it is based upon another book, I do not know. I suppose the point is that Joyce is a great scholar who has studied the *Odyssey* whereas other people might suppose him to be merely a novelist. In the same way, there is said to be some magic in its concern with eighteen hours of time. I do not understand that, either. The time stunt is no better than any other stunt; it may need some ingenuity for its employment, but it is not essential for art or meaning. It is a convenience, an attractive condensation; nothing more. I should know this, for it was a book of my own which began the timestunt fashion. Far too often, nowadays, some ingenuity of technique is given the blessed name of art. So, as far as I can tell, neither the time scheme of *Ulysses* nor its debt to the *Odyssey* gives the book any special claim to attention. It must stand upon its more positive merits.

Those merits, as I have suggested, are the merits of virtuosity. Nobody has ever presented the thoughts of a vulgar woman such as Mrs. Bloom with such terrible convincingness. They have the air of being complete and unerring. . . . On the whole, however, when one abstracts one's admiration for performance, there is little enough in the book which can justify the adjectives of its admirers. It is quite empty of idea, although it is packed with ideas. It is also packed with the most brilliant mimicry known to me; mimicry and impersonation. If mimicry and impersonation made great literature, *Ulysses* would be a great book. It seems to me to be a hotch-potch. The fact that it cannot yet be published in England, and the fact that after being pirated in America it is now available there, have given it adventitious attractions for the amateur of letters. It has, in the same way, been something of a key book for rebel authors in both countries; and while many of those who applaud it have never read it through, and could not with understanding read it through, they have taken their position as defenders of courage against the squeamishness of mankind, and cannot withdraw.

What Joyce has is this great knowledge of the seamy side of life and and character. He has unrivalled power to represent the thoughts and feelings of some very odd people. He has a literary manner which ranges from the Rabelaisian to the Meredithian, and has between those extremes a large area of clever, ingenious, sophisticated impressionism which at its best is of amazing virtuosity and penetration. If he had remained the realist of *Dubliners* (but he could not do that, for his is essentially an egotistical talent), he might have had high standing as an objective realist. He now has high standing as a psychological realist. I should not, however, rate him higher than that; and it will be understood that I am commenting solely upon the claim made by respectable critics that *Ulysses* is a great book, and the author a fixed star. To my mind he is a very able man, but not different in kind from other able men; only more brilliant and ruthless than they, and with a preference for what H. G. Wells has styled the cloacal. In that field he is a past-master.

As to his latest experiments, I can say nothing. I do not find them entirely unintelligible; indeed, the words seem to me to swim at times into great vividness of picture or communication. But the ultimate meaning of such writing escapes me. . . .

281. Richard Thoma on the dream in progress

1934

'Dream in Progress', *Contempo*, iii, No. 13 (February 1934), 3.

So there is music in the names of rivers, but a reading of *Anna Livia Plurabelle* is proof there is more. No one will deny Joyce is a super-punster, but Cocteau is always right and he has written :'Sans calembours, sans devinettes, il n'y a pas d'art sérieux . . . Tout chef-d'oeuvre est fait d'aveux cachés, de calculs, de calembours hautains, d'étranges devinettes.' It is easy to say Nile to one's self, or Amazon, or even Congo—and thereby mentally conjure up vivid lands and sunburst flowers and poison; but Joyce is not satisfied with that. Joyce is a classicist. With Anna Livia before him, who does not come to the realisation that he has felt the tigris eye, that he has known the gangres of sin or that he has suffered from neuphrates? I speak of men. Who does not remember that he has heard a savage green voice in himself: Oronoko!—and who does not recall the lazy human mañana of his own reply: Garonne, garonne . . . first thing in the marne . . .

These questions are addressed to the elect. One cannot be concerned with the ignorant, though one must remain horribly conscious of their fat wormy presence, . . . No doubt the ignorant worship propulsion but cannot abide transport. They accuse Joyce, on their wild reckless rocketing east and west and roundabout, of *tours de force*. Some retrogress so far as to call them *tours de faiblesse*. Joyce cannot be read on trains, they say. Airplanes abhor Joyce. They will never see Joyce *is* a train, a monastery. No doubt the truth of the matter is in *tours d'ivoire*, rare and inviolable and therefore valuable and admirable. But the ignorants' ignorance is exasperating and I wish I could wipe them off the face of the earth—along with a few others. The inevitable conclusion is that the acceptance of motors requires only an act of hypocrisy on the part of the world while the acceptance of Joyce requires an act of faith in one's self. . . .

And there Anna Liffeys by, attracting the seas and the rivers, acting magnetically upon the fleuve Amour and the Styx alike, drawing their plural talents into her pregnant belly. It only takes a moment and the result is a poem. Why should it take longer? The existence of all our earth is but a second to any god and that that second is centuries long has nothing to do with time. There is everything rotten in clockwork.

The poem is Anna Livia. It is a poem for the awake. Joyce has been accused of 'rising above his medium.' This is a lie. When one rises above one's medium, one enters a new state—no longer the one one 'rose above.' By his use of language, Joyce does not enter a 'dream state' but a state for composing dreams for the awake by welding together a previous dissociation of impressions. Joyce is always a poet and therefore awake. The ridiculous 'dreaminess' poets are condescendingly discredited with must be denied once and for all. Let it be understood once and for all that only poets are awake, aware. The rest of the world is unbroken sleep. The world will only waken when it hears the poets' trumpets. That is, the rest of the world will never be broken; it will never waken, because poets don't use trumpets. Indeed, in order to hear each other, poets must stroke irrawaddying in their ears.

For us the riddle is eternally resolved: the eggs came before Joyce but Joyce broke them up and turned Humpty Dumpty into Hamlet. . . .

282. Edith Sitwell on prose innovations

1934

Extract from 'Notes on Innovations in Prose', in *Aspects of Modern Poetry* (1934), pp. 215–17.

. . . Language had become, not so much an abused medium, as a dead and outworn thing, in which there was no living muscular system. Then came the rebirth of the medium, and this was effected, as far as actual vocabularies were concerned, very largely by such prose writers as Mr. James Joyce and Miss Gertrude Stein. Prose writers, naturally, scarcely come into the scope of my book; but as the anarchic breaking up and rebuilding of sleepy families of words and phrases, for which Miss Stein is responsible, must, in the future, affect poetry very greatly, it will not be amiss to examine them. The most interesting account of this revolution, as far as I know, is contained in an essay by Mr. Eugène Jolas 'The Revolution of Language and James Joyce' (*transition*, February 1928). This essay, indeed, is of acute interest and importance. . . .

Mr. Jolas says of Mr. Joyce: 'In *Ulysses* and in his still unnamed novel (he) was occupied in exploding the antique logic of words. . . . In his supertemporal and multispatial composition, language is born anew before our eyes. Each chapter has an internal rhythm differentiated in proportion to the contents. The words are compressed into stark blasting accents. They have the tempo of immense rivers flowing to the sea. Nothing that the world of appearance shows seems to interest' (*Note:* There I do not agree, E. S.) 'except in relation to the huge philogophic and linguistic pattern he has undertaken to create. A modern mythology is being evolved against the curtain of the past, and a plane of infinity emerges. The human being across his words becomes the passive agent of some strange and inescapable destiny. . . .'

To see Mr. Joyce's style at its most beautiful, to share with him his recreation of our old and outworn visual world through the word, we cannot do better than to quote this intensely lovely and strange passage from *Three Fragments from Work in Progress*. . . .

283. Dorothy Richardson on Joyce

1935

'A few facts for you . . .' *Mercure de France*, cccxlvii (August–September 1963)' 128 [127–28].

From a letter written to Sylvia Beach (15 January 1935).

. . . An interesting point for the critic who finds common qualities in the work of Proust, James Joyce, Virginia Woolf and D. R. is the fact that they were all using the 'new method' though very differently, simultaneously.

Proust's first volume appeared in 1913 while D. R. was finishing *Pointed Roofs*. She preceded J. J. and V. W. but they were writing their books when hers appeared. . . .

284. L. A. G. Strong on the novel

1935

Extract from 'The Novel: Assurances and Perplexities', *The Author, Playwright, and Composer*, xlv, No. 4 (Summer 1935), 112, 114–15 [112–15].

An intellectual weekly recently invited its readers to imagine Henry James receiving as a gift James Joyce's *Ulysses*, and offered prizes for the best accounts of his reaction. The winning competitors made the master salute many merits, but they hazarded also a bewilderment at the work's apparent lack of form. Actually, the question set is a profound one. It raises in their sharpest form the issues perplexing the contemporary novel. It demands a re-valuation; and forces us to ask whether the old standards are valid to measure new work. . . . Stephen Dedalus, the artist whose *Portrait . . . as a Young Man* had already been given to the world, is one type of fine sensibility: Bloom, *l'homme moyen sensuel*, is another. They are the 'mirrors', advantageously placed to reflect not only the experience but the scene: and theirs, to start with at any rate are the 'adopted, the related points of view.'

[Mr. Strong's quotations are from R. P. Blackmur's *The Art of the Novel*]

. . . To condense the aim of *Ulysses* into a few words is not easy . . . the whole work to be an epic of man's fall from grace, the slow staining of a perfect morning by the corruption of day, cast in a form—a structure—parallel to the *Odyssey*, which shall not only keep the vast mass of material within bounds, but afford opportunity for criticism of contemporary life by the comparison between the original incident and its Dublin counterpart. To compass this large and complex object he has had to forge new tools. The edges of his naturalistic scene have been continually shading into reality of another kind. He has had to record not only what is happening in space and time, but what is happening in the timeless unbounded world of the mind, and, often, to record both at the same moment.

To do this he has been obliged to extend the powers of language. . . .

Joyce is revealed to the careful student of *Ulysses* as an extremely, perhaps an excessively, deliberate artist, with a respect for tradition no whit inferior to James's. Moreover, paradoxical though it must seem, their views coincide in a number of instances. Where does the difference lie? How far would James be right in regarding, as the winners of the competition made him regard, Joyce's *chef d'œuvre* as formless?

That he would regard it as formless seems certain: yet its form is almost pedantically determined. There is a real sense in which *Ulysses* fails, in which its author has bitten off more than he can chew: but his effort has enlarged the scope of the novelist's art. He has not been content with a success inside the accepted limits: he has preferred to fail, if fail he must, on the scale of Tolstoi. James's objection to *War and Peace* was not that it tried to do too much, but that Tolstoi did not succeed in carrying out what ought to have been his aim with regard to his material. He did not proceed by the laws James thought essential. A super-Tolstoi might have brought the thing off; but such a being was unlikely. To the aim of *Ulysses* he would probably have made a similar objection; but he might well have decided in addition that Joyce was trying to do too much. With all his subtlety, he might have shrunk from so vast a curiosity, such merciless pursuit of the human mind to its depths. He would have hated the book's enormous superstition and have been shaken by its coarseness, all the more because he would have unerringly realised the fastidious writhing mind at the back of it. Seeing all this, he would simply not have understood it.

I believe that the crux of the difference between James and Joyce lies in James's definition of experience. He defines it as 'our apprehension and our measure of what happens to us as social creatures.' Obviously, this definition would no more suffice the author of *A Portrait of the Artist as a Young Man* than it would have sufficed Blake. In the larger work, Stephen and Bloom are conscious enough of their social inadequacy, but their real trouble, the Agenbite of Inwit, the worm that never dies, has to do with their relations with eternity. It is in his awareness of this, and in the subtleties and complexities of experience that arise from it, and in the subtleties and complexities of the writing in which he seeks to record that experience, that Joyce's work, with all its faults, transcends the rules of the game as understood by Henry James. . . .

635

285. L. A. G. Strong on Joyce and new fiction

1935

Extract from L. A. G. Strong, 'James Joyce and the New Fiction',
American Mercury, xxxv, No. 140 (August 1935), 433–4 [434–7].
Also appeared as 'What is Joyce Doing with the Novel?' *John
O'London's Weekly*, xxxiv, No. 881 (29 February 1936), 821–2,
826 (from which the present text is taken).

Novelists may be divided roughly into two classes, the traditional and
the experimental. The traditional novelist is one who finds existing
methods of expression adequate for what he has to say. He may add to
the tradition, but what he adds will be a mannerism, a new way of
using the accepted tools. He has not needed to forge tools of his own.

The experimental novelist, on the other hand, finds the existing
tools inadequate. His difficulty resembles the poet's. Both are ahead of
their time. Language lags behind perception, being merely an agreement to give certain names to things which we see often enough to
agree about them. But the poet and the experimental novelist are seeing
new things, about which there is no general agreement. The existing
language is inadequate to convey their discoveries. . . .

I suggest that among the things demanded of the reader by, for
instance, James Joyce in his later work, is an extension of this capacity,
which will enable him to comprehend a still larger unit, the paragraph. . . .

With Joyce words have always had a value in themselves, apart from
their value as the names of things and qualities. He has more than a
poet's, more than a singer's, sensitiveness to them: more than a priest's.
The key passage comes from his early novel, *A Portrait of the Artist as a
Young Man*:

[quotes from ch. 4]

There are in this the germs of the vocabulary and technique of
Ulysses, the hieratic concentration on words themselves of *Work in*

Progress, the evocative rhythms of *Anna Livia Plurabelle*, the associative multi-lingual stuff, the dream vocabulary of *Work in Progress* as a whole; and something besides. Joyce's feeling for words, whether he is conscious or not of the fact, is magical. The words are the material for an incantation. Here again the clue is in the *Portrait of the Artist*, in the religious scenes, where the Latin words exercise upon the fainting heart of Stephen Dedalus their more than symbolic meaning. Here, from angles so widely different that each would recoil in indignation, Joyce and Yeats meet: Yeats with his magic, Joyce with his superstition.

Over *Ulysses*, as over the earlier work, broods the sense of sin, that terrific spiritual legacy which the Catholic Church irrevocably leaves her children. *Ulysses* is a great Catholic novel. The blasphemies that turn the short-sighted against it are the desperate gestures of a man doomed to accept, with his spiritual entrails if not with his intellect, certain Last Things. The whole book is the agonized attempt of an artist to bring all life within his scope, aware that his effort is also a religious effort, and agonized because, while his genius bids him accept his own interpretation, he cannot escape from the interpretations of others. The Catholic artist knows that none other is better equipped to face and portray life in all its aspects, but he is tortured by the problems of expediency.

Joyce's words, then, are his ritual, his incantation, and he is as serious in their use as any priest. In many of the scenes in *Ulysses* they are governed by theory, as where, in the lying-in hospital, the language moves to the New World to celebrate the arrival of the new life. This variation in language, and the Græco-German combinations of words, and the boldness of association, are the main contributions of *Ulysses* to the art of the novel. Joyce's avowed purpose is so to reconstruct Dublin, in the compass of a single day of June, 1904, that if the city were swallowed in an earthquake a reader of the book would find a perfect record of what had gone. More than photographic description is needed for such a reconstruction. Magic is necessary: and magic proceeds by incantation.

How Joyce's technique of incantation may be used is shown in *Anna Livia Plurabelle*, particularly in the closing paragraphs. . . . The appeal is not to the conscious mind, but to the mind in dream, which is reached by a series of gentle, inadequate calls to the lulled senses. No image is so sharp as to project from the silvery twilight: each makes its faint tinkling impact, and fades blurred into the dream, into the music of the whole crepuscular incantation.

Effects of such delicacy obviously cannot be attained without precision somewhere: and Joyce is one of the most precise and pernickety of artists. He is throughout *Work in Progress* essaying a dream language. *Ulysses* dealt with day. *Work in Progress* deals with night. If in day-time language must change to suit its theme, then the language of night-thinking, that series of apparently illogical leaps by which we progress in dream, must likewise be suited to the activities it describes. . . .

The real difficulty Joyce has put in his readers' path is not word puzzles, nor erudition, nor Dublin lore, but the fact that he is asking them to *unlearn* something: to study a page as a picture and not as a series of logically connected images arranged in lines from left to right. Faulkner and Isherwood have asked readers to rearrange their ideas of order in the telling of a story. Joyce asks it in the page, the paragraph, the sentence.

Where will all this take us? Are we at the opening of a new tract of country, or up a *cul de sac*?

Joyce has, of course, exercised a profound influence on the practice of subsequent novelists, but it has come through *Ulysses*. The later technique has found few imitators. It is not a general technique, but a very special set of tools forged for a special purpose. The word-amalgams have been copied, but to little purpose, and generally by people who do not know what either they or Joyce are at. This has been the general trouble, as regards imitators—that these new methods are hard to understand. Most readers, most novelists, and more critics have been standing back, waiting for the work to be finished, or, failing that, waiting to see what the other man is going to say about it.

There is no disgrace in that. To get the hang of a revolutionary technique requires time. When, two or three years ago, I was given one of the published fragments of *Work in Progress* in my weekly batch of novels for review, I frankly declined the adventure. To tackle anything of the kind at a few hours' notice is a folly requiring more courage than I could command. But, if one's mental muscles are not too stiff, one may twist round far enough to envisage certain new possibilities. One may even unlearn, painfully and temporarily, a fixed habit. The reader of poetry has an advantage here.

I have throughout been dealing almost exclusively in terms of Joyce for the simple reason that, up to the present, his influence in the experimental novel has been paramount. The use of monologue, which has been developed by Mr. Calder-Marshall and Mr. John dos Passos, derives from *Ulysses*. There is hardly an experimental novelist of importance whose work does not show a certain debt to Joyce. Even *The Waves*, so alien in atmosphere and temper from Joyce's work, suggests a widely different use of the same device. I have concentrated on Joyce because his work contains almost everything that has been and is being done in the experimental novel.

Even so, we are unlikely to be confronted with a spate of *Anna Livias*, a multitude of *Works in Progress*. Joyce's experiment may prove a dead end, though I do not think so. I do not believe that any writer of importance will follow him as far as he has gone into the recesses of a private associational mythology. But we are likely to see a great increase in flexibility in the use of language, a more poetic manner of writing, and a narrative method infused by the new theories of space and time. . . .

1936

286. James Joyce and Gertrude Stein

1936

Harry Beardsley, 'James Joyce *vs.* Gertrude Stein', *Real America*,
vi, No. 5 (February 1936), 43, 76–7.

. . . Singers of the Stein Song have coupled her name with that of
James Joyce—frequently to the disparagement of Joyce—as leaders in
the development of a new technique of expression. Even to one who is
not a whole-hearted Joyce enthusiast, it seems presumptious to mention
the two in the same breath. If Gertrude Stein has a literary twin, that
twin most certainly is not James Joyce. . . .

Joyce, in *Ulysses* has written a really important work, and successfully carried out daring experiment in the use of English language. He
has evolved a technique of expression, which if not wholly original, is
at least the most complete embodiment of theories he and others have
experimented with—a technique that bears indisputably the stamp of his
individuality. His work is not always easy reading; indeed it is frequently
involved, verbose, and boring. Nor is it always easily comprehended
even by readers possessing the necessary keys to its interpretation.

To understand *Ulysses*, one must be familiar with the classics, with
the geography of the city of Dublin, with the previous works of Joyce,
with several languages; and one must know the life history of the
author and something of the psychological workings of his mind.

Without these keys, much of the allegory and allusion of *Ulysses* is
meaningless. It may be questioned whether a work with such an involved pattern—a work that demands so much of the reader—can be
ranked as a great piece of literature. Time alone will enable us to find
the answer.

By one standard, however, *Ulysses* is entitled to rank high in contemporary literature. Any work is entitled to be judged from the following

standpoints: (1) What was the author's purpose in writing it? (2) How well has he succeeded in what he set out to do?

In considering the author's purpose, we can do no better than to accept the verdict of Judge John M. Woolsey .of the U.S. District Court of New York, who ruled that *Ulysses* was a work of literature, not of pornography, and should not be barred from the United States. The Judge may reasonably be considered free from the log-rolling of literary cliques, a man of mature judgment and judicial temperament, and one with no axes to grind.

Almost any fair-minded person reading *Ulysses* must concede that Joyce achieved what he set out to achieve.

Certainly his characters come to life in his pages; certainly we are shown the innermost workings of their minds; certainly he presents them by means of a technique radically different from the conventional novel form; certainly that form is developed with great skill and ingenuity; certainly the style of writing is distinctive, unusually effective, and frequently characterized by grace and beauty.

That Joyce is a skilled literary craftsman must be obvious to anyone who reads him. One does not have to approve of the style he has developed in *Ulysses* to pay tribute to the skill he has displayed.

Granting that there is much that is obscure, much that is tedious, one must also recognize that there are numerous passages of brilliant and beautiful prose, and that he is consistent and purposeful in everything he has written. While many of his coined words appear meaningless, many others are startlingly effective, and most of them appear possible of interpretation once the proper key is found. In short, the coined words are not haphazard combinations of syllables but deliberate and purposeful inventions. Joyce has worked out a formula and has adhered to it. Setting himself a difficult assignment of writing he solved his problem successfully. As a laboratory experiment in the mechanics of expression, if in no other respect, *Ulysses* is a highly successful, and stimulating work. . . .

287. Thomas Wolfe on *Ulysses*

1936

Letter to Maxwell E. Perkins (15 December 1936), in *The Letters of Thomas Wolfe* (1956), ed. Elizabeth Nowell, pp. 585–6.

. . . A great book is not lost . . . There are always a few people who will save it. The book will make its way. That is what happened to *Ulysses*. As time went on, the circle widened. Its public increased. As people overcame their own inertia, mastered the difficulty which every new and original work creates, became familiar with its whole design, they began to understand that the book was neither an obscene book nor an obscure book, certainly it was not a work [p. 585] of wilful dilettante caprice. It was, on the contrary, an orderly, densely constructed creation, whose greatest fault, it seems to me, so far from being a fault of caprice, was rather the fault of an almost Jesuitical logic which is essentially too dry and lifeless in its mechanics for a work of the imagination. At any rate, now, after fifteen years, *Ulysses* is no longer thought of as a book meant solely for a little group of literary adepts. The adepts of this day, in fact, speak somewhat patronizingly of the work as marking the 'end of an epoch,' as being 'the final development of an outworn naturalism,' etc. etc. But the book itself had now won an unquestioned and established place in literature. Its whole method, its style, its characters, its story and design has become so familiar to many of us that we no longer think of it as difficult or obscure . . . [p. 586]

288. James T. Farrell, reply to Mirsky and Radek

1936

Extract from *A Note on Literary Criticism* (1936), pp. 83-5, 97-106, 109.

Pages 83-5 are a reply to Mirsky's 'Joyce and Irish Literature' (No. 265); 97-107, 'James Joyce or Socialist Realism', from 'Contemporary World Literature and the Tasks of the Proletariat', a report delivered at the Congress of Soviet Writers, August 1934, pp. 151-4, and 'Problems of Soviet Literature', edited by A. Zhdanov *et al.*, are a reply to Karl Radek's criticism of Joyce (No. 279).

. . . We can gain a further sense of the confusion in this aspect of the critical problem by considering the views of D. S. Mirsky on James Joyce. After describing the social and ideological backgrounds and the personal history of Joyce, and proving that Joyce was introduced as a figure into the world of the international bourgeoisie by two millionaires, Mirsky asks the question whether or not Joyce offers any model for revolutionary writers:

[quotes from Mirsky]

These quotations reveal the widespread confusion that has accompanied the applications of such categories to literature. Mirsky assumes such a direct tie-up between economics and literature that he finds Joyce's exactitude in description to be an acquisitive and an æsthetico-proprietary desire for 'things'; and that Joyce's utilization of the interior monologue is too closely connected with a parasitic element of the bourgeoisie to be usable by revolutionary writers. Such discoveries enable Mirsky to legislate for writers at wholesale on what will or will not influence them. . . .

. . . Radek contends that 'it does not lie within the power of bourgeois art to imitate the realism of Balzac, who endeavored to paint a picture commensurate with the epoch in which he lived. For a full picture of life as it is would be a condemnation of moribund capitalism.' He goes on to cite Joyce as an example. . . .

[quotes extensively from Radek]

Radek then concludes, among other things, that Joyce's method is unsatisfactory for the presentation of themes of class struggle; Balzac and Tolstoy are more appropriate models for the Soviet writers. In rebuttal of disagreements with his interpretation, Karl Radek says: 'All that appealed to Joyce was the medieval, the mystical, the reactionary in the petty bourgeoisie—lust, aberrations; everything capable of impelling the petty bourgeoisie to join the side of revolution was alien to him.'

The basis of this criticism is, I think, that Joyce failed to write what Radek, retroactively, desires him to have written. Radek is applying not criteria of judgment but standards of measurement; these standards of measurement relate to class phenomena, and he is proving Joyce a bourgeois writer and then condemning him because he is not the kind of bourgeois writer that Balzac was. Radek applies the standard that a writer must treat the whole of the life of his characters. But Joyce did not treat the whole of the life of the petty bourgeoisie. No writer can succeed in presenting all of life nor all of one class in a book or even in many books. A writer does not surmount all the limitations of his time, his heritage, and many other humanly and socially qualifying factors and conditions. Radek's criticism is of a type that is irrelevant and unreasonable.

One of the ideological and social backgrounds of Joyce's work is Irish nationalism, to which we find him antagonistic. His revulsion goes back to the Parnell episode, which shook Irish history and bitterly split the Irish nation. Instead of condemning Joyce, however, it would be more fruitful for us to investigate this antagonism as it is refracted through his work, by making a genetic approach to its sources. Such an approach would provide us with an emotional awareness of this feature of Irish life; and it would furnish us with much illustrative information.

A second ideological source in Joyce is Roman Catholicism, which connects closely with Irish nationalism. Ireland is a Church-ridden country, and the clergy played an important—and infamous—role in the Parnell case. Ireland is strongly Catholic, belligerently Catholic, furiously Catholic; and, whether or not the reactionary elements of the petty bourgeoisie appealed to Joyce, his attack on Catholicism in Ireland has banned his works from his own country and made him a pariah.

Has a Marxist, then, any right to take a position like Karl Radek's on Joyce? Is a Marxist warranted in judging from so philistine a viewpoint while failing to consider the relation of Irish Catholicism and nationalism to Joyce's work?

Finally, the relation of Joyce to Irish literature must be considered; there we find him among the first to utilize the urban life of Ireland as the material for Irish writing. In the main, his predecessors utilized material from native folklore, from the life of the peasantry, and the like. This fact was a tremendous step forward in the history of Irish literature. All such factors are ignored by Radek in order to enforce a blanket condemnation. . . . And further, there is the fact that Joyce has influenced several writers who have to some extent treated the national revolutionary movement; and it is not unsafe to prophesy that, when and if a novel dealing with the revolutionary movement in Ireland is written so as to satisfy Mr. Radek's thesis of socialist realism, it will be shown to have been influenced—most likely profitably—by Joyce's *Ulysses*. . . .

COLLECTED POEMS

December 1936

289. Review, *New York Herald Tribune*

1936

Horace Gregory, 'Fifty Lyrics by the Author of *Ulysses*,' *New York Herald Tribune Books* (13 December 1936), p. 8.

So much has been written of James Joyce since 1922 that the present collection of his fifty lyrics scarcely needs an introduction. And yet despite this knowledge fourteen of the poems published in the exquisite slender volume make their first appearance in book form. . . . The present occasion is more like a belated tribute to the author of *Ulysses* than the publication of a first edition, and as if to commemorate the event the small book contains a reproduction of the delicately modeled crayon portrait of James Joyce by Augustus John.

To reread the poems is to recall the rich associations of literary history during the last thirty years and to be aware that the poems of *Chamber Music* owe their existence to young Stephen Dedalus, who leaned over the turrets of Buck Mulligan's tower, gazing outward to the sea, on a certain memorable summer morning in 1904. The poems were to wait another three years for publication, and their author's long exile from Dublin had not yet begun. To read *Chamber Music* in 1936 is to see how closely young Dedalus followed in the wake of W. B. Yeats's 'tragic generation,' and is again heard speaking to Buck Mulligan: 'History', Stephen said, 'is a nightmare from which I am trying to awake.' And from this remark the thirty-third poem of *Chamber Music* seems to follow:

[quotes the sixth poem, 'I would in that sweet bosom be']

As from a great distance the lyric seems to echo the prevailing mode of a late Victorian twilight which held William Morris's refrain of an

646

'idle singer of an empty day.' In Joyce's early poems the mode remains unbroken, yet I believe that there is warning of a time to come in the closing lines of 'I heard an army' [xxxvi]:

> My heart, have you no wisdom thus to
> despair?
> My love, my love, my love, why have
> you left me alone?

In *Pomes Penyeach* the images of fear increase; 'black mold and muttering rain' descend and

> Ghostfires from heaven's far verges
> faint illume,
> Arches on soaring arches,
> Night's sindark nave. ['Night piece']

The nightmare of history is re-entered and as it closes the melodic clarity of Joyce's line seems to deceive the ear; the verse is no longer the very antithesis of the prose in *Ulysses*. The poet who was once Stephen Dedalus is no longer gazing seaward from a Dublin tower. Again at the close of *Pomes Penyeach* 'A Prayer' is said and, though the words are spoken with the clear reverberations of late Elizabethan music, the mode of the 1890s is replaced by the style of Joyce's later prose, which had become an influence greater than any single poem in contemporary literature.

And for the end of the fifty lyrics there is another prayer in 'Ecce Puer,' which is in celebration of a new-born child and may be read, perhaps, as an epitaph, a last message, echoing the cry of a dying generation with *ave atque vale*:

> A child is sleeping:
> An old man gone.
> O father forsaken,
> Forgive your son.

290. Horace Reynolds, comment,
New York Times

1937

'James Joyce's Poetry does not Suggest *Ulysses*', *New York Times Book Review* (10 October 1937), 4. This critic begins his review by 'placing' Joyce in terms of his independence of the Irish literary renaissance.

. . . That independence is reflected in this verse: when his fellow-poets were following Yeats's call to write of Ireland, he turned back for his models to the Elizabethan and Carolinian lyric.

Joyce's determination to be 'unconsortable'—obvious today in his resolve to write only in a language of his own making, an idiom unsullied by any other's use—his eschewal of the Celtic Twilight later protected him from any suspicion of being in Yeats's hair when that poet wrote bitterly of his 'imitators': 'But was there ever dog that praised his fleas?'

Yet in spite of all rejection and negation, the Irish mode is manifest in this book: one does not easily absolutely deny one's blood. It is here in the last poem in *Chamber Music*:

> I hear an army charging upon
> the land,
> And the thunder of horses
> plunging, foam about their
> knees,

which reminds one of Yeats's 'Hosting of the Sidhe': 'Caolte tossing his burning hair and Niamb calling *Away, come away*.' It is here also in the moan of the vowels, in the Irish fondness for keeping one vowel open all through a lyric:

> All day I hear the noise
> of waters
> Making moan,

> Sad as the sea-bird is,
>   when going
> Forth alone.
> He hears the winds cry
>   to the waters'
> Monotone. [xxxv]

But for the most part for all that they come out of the Irish landscape these lyrics are more Elizabethan English than Irish Renaissance. All are slight in thought, sentimental in feeling the young poet seeking in remembered moods of love a solace for hurt pride. What gives them distinction is an almost glass-like perfection of form, fastidious use of 'elegant and antique phrase,' including the polysyllable, a subtlety of cadence which haunts the ear. Melancholy as a Chopin Prelude, these lyrics like George Moore's sentimental Lady of the Fountain, sing their sorrows to the moon. *Chamber Music* was first published in 1907. The handful of lyrics published twenty years later under the title *Pomes Penyeach* show little change. The wind in the grass, rain falling on the black mould, a birdless sky at twilight—such landscapes evoke an evanescent mood perfectly expressed and cadenced:

> And, gathering, she sings an
>   air:
> Fair as the wave is, fair, art
>   thou! ['Simples']

Little of Joyce's abundance has gone into his verse. These collected poems are no fat volume but a thin book of only fifty lyrics, not one of which overruns its page. But they will doubtless be long read, both for their delicate attenuated music and because they were written by the author of *Ulysses*. That a man whose prose is so contrapuntally many-voiced should write lyrics which are simple song, a melody piped on a single pipe; that he who has led the vanguard of the novel should in his verse linger behind in the asphodel fields of Fulke Greville and Sir Philip Sidney—such antitheses pose a pretty critical question. Perhaps it means that *Ulysses* was achieved only by deliberately sinking the sentimentalist in the satirist, that these lyrics, which are sometimes little more than an exquisite sigh, are to James Joyce what Swift's 'little language' was to the author of *Gulliver*.

291. Irene Hendry on Joyce's poetry

1938

'Joyce's Alter Ego', *Washington Square College Review*, ii, No. 2 (January 1938), 17.

James Joyce today is in the position of a man who sits quietly contemplating the monument his followers have erected over his still-unoccupied grave. His famous 'stream-of-consciousness' style of writing has had a greater attraction for aspiring novelists than perhaps any other. He is the foremost experimenter in prose technique of his time, and in spite of imitators and rival experimenters he is still the master. He has, nevertheless, ceased to be an important force in modern literature. Literature now is turning outward and upward, and Joyce, who still looks inward, probing among the Freudian shadows of Humphrey Earwicker's subconscious, has become a name with a purely closet prestige. He has been left so far behind that this book of his poems . . . has received virtually no notice from the metropolitan reviewers, although it adds a new angle to the portrait of the man that is already known to the public.

Joyce's poetry, consisting of only fifty brief lyrics, has none of the complexities, obscurities and the massiveness of his prose. The poems in the *Chamber Music* section, those earliest in composition, are chiefly variations on the traditional themes of youth and fleshly love and the finely-spun desolation of its denial. They are delicate and musical, but— with the exception, perhaps, of the final poem in the group, which has stronger imagery and a more moving presentation of emotion in its picture of a symbolist army charging out of the sea upon the shore— they are little else.

Pomes Penyeach, while their subject-matter is similarly circumscribed, show a greater individuality and a greater subtlety in their rhythms; one can find here and there a suggestion of the Joyce of unforgettable prose. In such poems, particularly, as 'On the Beach at Fontana' and 'A Flower Given to My Daughter,' there is the same simplicity and dignity of feeling that places the stories of the *Dubliners* collection beside the best of Chekhov and Thomas Mann:

[quotes the poem]

'Tilly,' 'Nightpiece,' and 'A Memory of the Players in a Mirror at Midnight' are sensitive tapestry patterns, worked with the precision in the choice of the exact word that is one of the characteristics of Joyce's meticulous craftsmanship and that is probably responsible for the metamorphosis of Molly Bloom's vernacular into the strange dream-language of *Work in Progress*. 'A Memory of the Players in a Mirror at Midnight' is the most graphic, with sharp, flesh-and-blood imagery and a dramatic blending of realism and symbolism:

[quotes the first stanza]

There is music in these poems—music and depth of feeling and a perfection of phrasing. They reveal sensitive lyrical gifts where one might not have suspected them. But they are ephemeral, comprising only the mood of the moment and rooted only in a limited personal emotion. One can only say that Joyce's accomplishment in verse is slight; although its vitality has been mummified in its obscurities, and although no one may care any longer to pursue its method to a decadent extreme, it is difficult not to see the more substantial shadow of *Ulysses* in the background.

292. Mary Colum on Joyce

1937

Extract from *From These Roots: The Ideas that have made Modern Literature* (1937), pp. 348–9.

. . . On the publication of *Ulysses*, it was considered by many that it was not possible in literature to carry the expression of the unconscious further and have it keep any intelligible pattern. However, Joyce's new puzzling book, *Work in Progress*, is an attempt to carry the revelation of the unconscious life many stages further than in *Ulysses* and much further than any other writer has dreamed of bringing it. Proust said of the opening chapter of *A la Recherche du Temps Perdu*, 'I have tried to envelope my first chapter in the half-waking impressions of sleep.' But Joyce, in this latest work, tries to depict the whole night-life of the mind, and the result, I am afraid, will be intelligible to a very limited number of readers. In *Work in Progress* he is influenced by Novalis's and Mallarmé's theories of the sounds of words, and the work has, in its best-known passage, reproduced so effectively, through the sonority of his words and sentences, the effects of falling night and fluttering river-water that, without the words being even intelligible, the reader can know what the passage is about if it is read aloud and falls on the ear as music does. There are specific points in technique in which it is difficult to believe that any writer can go beyond Joyce. One is the skill with which he evokes a scene, an atmosphere, a personage, a group, without ever once describing them or giving a hint as to who they are or where the scene takes place. He is a master of the evocative method, and if the reader compares the opening of *Ulysses* with the opening of Sinclair Lewis's *It Can't Happen Here*, he will observe immediately and inevitably the difference between the two methods, the evocative and the descriptive. Joyce's mastery of the interior monologue is the second point in his technique in which he is likely to remain unsurpassed, and for this mastery he undoubtedly owes a great deal to Freud. . . .

293. Æ on Joyce and *Ulysses*

1938

Extract from George Russell (Æ). *The Living Torch* (1938), ed.
Monk Gibbon, pp. 139–40.

He is creating a psychological following who are trying each to evolve
a language of his own, as he is doing. I wonder do master and pupils
ever meet? Do they ever speak to each other in the language they use
when speaking to the public? How enchanting it would be to listen to
such a conversation!

I feel a little sadly about Joyce, who has an astonishing talent, which,
in spite of my chastening recollection of unintelligibles of the past who
became merely obvious to a generation who succeeded them, I feel he
is burying in a jungle of words; and the burying is none the less effective
because all the weeds in that jungle of words, which spread so prolific-
ally over the grave, have been carefully selected. One suspects with
Joyce some truly profound idea, some dark heroism of the imagination
burrowing into the roots of consciousness, the protoplasmic material
for literature, where there are strange blurrings and blendings of words,
moods, passions, thoughts in a mysterious mush. Normally these are
transfigured into the intelligible by their manifestations in speech or
literature. But Joyce does not desire in his later work to allow that
transfiguration to take place or allow the murky chaos to lose its formlessness. He desires to give us that murky chaos itself. . . . I wish he had
tried to penetrate into the palace chambers rather than into the crypts
and cellars and sewars of the soul, and written after *Ulysses* the effort of
his hero to rise out of that Inferno through a Purgatorio to a Paradiso.

294. A Marxian view of *Ulysses*

1938

Extract from R. Miller-Budnitskaya, 'James Joyce's *Ulysses*' (translated by N. J. Nelson), *Dialectics: A Marxian Literary Journal* (New York), No. 5 (1938), 6–7, 10–11, 25–6 [6–26].

Ulysses was designed to be, like Dante's *Divine Comedy* and Goethe's *Faust*, an all-embracing encyclopædia of the philosophy, politics, religion, science and art of its entire epoch, an encyclopædia expressed in terms of images. This most mature work of bourgeois art of the epoch of imperialism, in which the course of development of that art is summed up and brought to a close, turns, however, into a self-negation of all contemporary Western civilization.

Ulysses is permeated with political, religious, national and racial hatred, a hatred which turns into the deepest disgust for humanity, comparable only to Gulliver's in his travels to the land of the Houyhnhnms. This bitter, destructive nihilism, due in part to the wounded nationalism of the Irish bourgeoisie and its hatred for the English monarchy, might have introduced a revolutionary tendency into *Ulysses*; but Joyce's anarchical proclivities degenerated into a peculiar iconoclasm, into pessimism and misanthropy. In his hatred for modern Western bourgeois culture he turned back to forms preceding the epoch of imperialism, to ancient mythology and mediæval scholasticism.

All of Joyce's writing, from *Dubliners* to *Work in Progress*, centers about Dublin, Dublin 'the quintessence of Ireland,' the city incandescent with religious disputes and political dissensions, the oppressed city seething with pent-up fury. A characteristic feeling of mingled love and hatred for his native city, particularly intense after his exile, runs through all of Joyce, a bitter, derisive hatred for his country and his countrymen interwoven with a desire to glorify and perpetuate Dublin. . . . Now his whole art is applied to celebrating his native town, though his feeling for Dublin, its squares and stews and beery streets, is as different from the provincial quality of Irish patriotism as it is like to the pagan sentiment of birthplace, to the tag '*dulces moriens reminiscitur*

Argos,' of Virgil and Theocritus, the feelings of Sophocles for Colonus and Odysseus for Ithaca.

This contradiction in Joyce's art corresponds to his social and historical background. The last decade of the nineteenth century and the beginning of the twentieth was a period of bitter conflict in Ireland between the petty bourgeois intelligentsia—at the time the standard-bearer of Irish national culture—and the Irish bourgeoisie. When the revolutionary wave receded to its lowest ebb, the Irish intelligentsia crystallized into a distinct social group. Unable, under the prevailing historical conditions, to find outlets for the expression of their creative talents, they reverted to individualism, pessimism and all sorts of oppositionary sentiments, thus coming into conflict with the Catholic reaction and bourgeois philistinism. This conflict was further intensified by a relentless hatred for the English bourgeoisie and every manifestation of its political and cultural domination, as well as by a hankering after the Continental, a desire to coalesce with cosmopolitan, all-European bourgeois culture.

Ulysses is an elaborately detailed description of a weekday in the life of one Leopold Bloom, a petty philistine Dublin Jew, an advertising solicitor by profession. The action takes place in the city of Dublin on June 16, 1904. The principal characters are Bloom, Stephen Dedalus, a young poet, and Bloom's wife, Marion. . . .

[a discussion of these characters follows here]

Joyce's word-building is based upon the antithesis between the national and the cosmopolitan in his art. His language is an attempt to convert English, by Irishizing it, saturating it with Dublin folk dialect, and tracing the roots back to their ancient Celtic and Scandinavian origins, into a peculiar pan-European Esperanto. Such is the foundation of Joyce's stupendous philological work culminating in *Work in Progress*. Joyce's word-building here becomes a form of expressing his myth-building, his reversion to the prehistoric legends of Dublin, to the original sources of Celtic and Scandinavian mythology, to the pagan animism of the Scandinavian North.

Thus Joyce, who received no recognition in his own country and who suffered persecution in the new and the old world alike, Joyce the master of formal, cosmopolitan, bourgeois 'radical' art of the epoch of imperialism, is closely bound to the national culture of the Irish bourgeoisie against which he took up arms.

The whole stylistic structure of *Ulysses* is contradictory. Designed to reveal the subconscious, to bring to the surface the primeval element in human psychology, and to establish the supremacy of the irrational, this novel is distinguished by the iron logic of its construction. . . . The complex symbolism in *Ulysses* is based in part on the Freudian conception of the role of the irrational in the human psyche; it is employed as a method of revealing the subconscious through the medium of artistic images.

At the same time one of the outstanding characteristics of *Ulysses* is its perfect structural harmony; it is a complete system, following its own rules, in which every detail has been planned, co-ordinated and tested with almost scientific precision.

While Joyce's recognition of the irrational is bound up with his Freudian trend, the rational and constructive elements in *Ulysses* are due to the influence of mediæval and scholastic philosophy.

Ulysses contains a whole series of separate styles, each in strict conformity with the central idea, the philosophical content and the emotional coloring of the particular episode in which it is employed. Occasionally the same episode contains a succession of several auxiliary styles against the background of one basic style. Through all this encyclopædic multiformity two main principles stand out, two main stylistic lines that often interweave, based on the socio-historical and philosophical paradox of *Ulysses*. These are, first, symbolism, ensuing from Joyce's mediæval, scholastic trend, and second, naturalism, which is permeated with Freudism.

In his symbolism, revolving chiefly about Stephen, Joyce gives expression to his desire to invest Ireland with a halo of romantic hero-ism, to glorify her by means of pagan mythbuilding and the symbols of the Catholic church. Joyce's naturalism, on the other hand, as represented in Bloom, gives expression to his feeling of banishment, his hatred, and his desire to expose the sordid pettiness of contemporary bourgeois life in his native land. . . .

Ulysses is the culminating point and converging terminal in the development of the two great styles of nineteenth and twentieth century bourgeois art: psychological realism, which later developed into decadent naturalism and impressionism, and the neo-romantic symbolic style. And Joyce's naturalism and symbolism signify the disintegration of bourgeois art.

Joyce has had an incalculable influence upon all contemporary bourgeois formalist literature; his Weltanschauung and his technique have become the æsthetic bible of his disciples and apologists. The contemporary psychoanalytic novel follows closely in the footsteps of *Ulysses*, where Freudian philosophy, Freudian symbolism and Freudian methods found their most perfect literary expression, where the psychology of the 'average man' is subjected to the most minute, painstaking microanalysis. Here the Western philistine is portrayed on a huge canvas, in every detail, and, deliberately, in slow motion. And it is this average philistine, in his naked abomination, that Joyce has proclaimed the real master of life, the sole possessor of the wisdom of our age, the modern Ulysses, the mentor of the poet and philosopher Stephen Dedalus.

Joyceism is a most reactionary philosophy of social pessimism, misanthropy, barrenness and doom, a hopeless negation of all creative, fruitful forces. Joyce beckons backward, to the gloom of mediævalism, to ecclesiastic and scholastic methods of thinking. He glorifies the principle of sex as the primeval, elemental force of the mind and the universe, he enthrones the subconscious as opposed to the hostile intellect. The fundamental element of Joyce's philosophy, however, that which underlies his whole world view, is his tendency to destroy the laws governing the material world and the human mind, his desire to turn being into chaos, his conception of the universe as a potent stream of sexual energy pouring forth into emptiness, into non-existence.

Joyce's wordbuilding, in which he engages ostensibly for the purpose of creating new linguistic systems, is profoundly antagonistic to the idea of language as a reflector of the objective material world. In reality it leads to the destruction 'from within' of the English literary language. It means the breaking up of English into its simplest elements, a return to the language of primitive chaos.

Joyce's prose not only marks the destruction of nineteenth-century bourgeois styles and the disintegration of literary English; it signifies the disintegration of the image in literature. In his latest creation, *Work in Progress*, which carries further the destructive tendencies manifested in *Ulysses*, Joyce constructs his prose and his rootbuilding by direct regression to primitive forms of thinking. The myth form expresses the ancient animistic view of the world, denoting a return to inarticulateness, to a chaotic, pre-logical form of consciousness. Here it results in the disintegration of the image, forming the tie that binds Joyce's prose to primitive thinking. Joyce's famous interior monologue, used so extensively toward the end of *Ulysses*, is in reality a return to that monotonous flow of inarticulate perceptions that characterized primitive consciousness; it is an attempt to penetrate to the very beginnings of language, to the dawn of articulate speech. Here again Joyce follows Freud, who sought his symbolism in the sacred books of antiquity and in the habits of savages, in the final analysis a reversion to the psychology of primitive man.

In these tendencies Joyce is allied to the contemporary 'radical' current in bourgeois painting, where similar tendencies have resulted in a trend toward 'themelessness.' It is the quest for the primeval, the turning to savage, primitive art as the elixir that might help to revive bourgeois culture. The reactionary significance of these 'modernist' seekings is quite clear. They are based fundamentally upon a repugnance for the creative and organizing power of the intellect, upon a loathing of the objective material essence of the external world, upon a rejection of physical and historical laws. They give expression to an anarchic desire to destroy, to turn the universe into chaos, in a word, to the pathos of suicide of contemporary bourgeois civilization. . . .

295. Eugène Jolas, homage and commentary

1938

Extract from 'Homage to the Mythmaker', *transition*, No. 27 (May 1938), 169–75.

. . . This complex, this enigmatic work [*Work in Progress*] has challenged contemporary speculation as no other book has done for a long time. Its fragmentary appearance will probably have militated against an immediate acceptance, but the reader has doubtless now been prepared through *transition* and the exegetical efforts of *transition* writers. There have been a few indications in the past fifteen years sketching the ultimate silhouette.

We know that Mr. Joyce's ambition has been to write a book dealing with the night-mind of man. We have already followed most of the purgatorial, multiple characters, blundering through their larval and anthropological transmigrations. . . . Examining with new eyes Mr. Joyce's revolutionary conception of the paragraph, we have tried to keep in mind that the dramatic dynamic is based on the Bruno theory of knowledge through opposites, and on the Vico philosophy of cyclic recurrence. . . .

In *Work in Progress*, the pre-logical or pre-conscious mind of the ancestors is continuously at work. Mr. Joyce presents his phantasmagoric figures as passing back and forth from a mentality saturated with archetypal images to a contemporary kinesis, from the past of childhood memories to a vision of future construction.

History being, in his earlier words, 'a nightmare' Mr. Joyce gives us the multi-dimensional idea of Time in sleep. His conception of Time is born out of his deep sense of race parallelism. It has relations with the newest discoveries of physical science as well as with oneiromantic experiments. The Joycean idea is cosmic Time, a collossal vision that negatives Bergson's theory of *durée*. . . .

One of the chief myths which *Work in Progress* treats exhaustively and with glacial objectivity is that of original sin. The myth of the fall of the angels: the idea of the 'diabolical principle': the gnostic-mystic idea of the demi-urge; the antithetical dynamism of good and evil. . . .

The opposition of Catholic puritans is not shared by the highest ecclesiastical authorities, and it might be of interest to hear what the *Osservatore Romano*, world-organ of the Vatican, has to say about James Joyce. In a recent issue of that famous newspaper (Oct. 22, 1937), we find the following reference to him in an essay on modern Irish literature:

> And finally James Joyce, of European fame, iconoclast and rebel, who after having sought to renovate the old naturalism, attempted in *Ulysses*, to translate plastically the inner reality, and, who, in *Work in Progress*, in an experiment, both oneiric and linguistic, is seeking to open up new paths for the expression of human sentiments.

The Catholic Church is apparently far removed from the philistinism and hypocrisy of some of the orthodox literary critics of Dublin, London and New York.

It is now more than ten years since I read the first version of *Work in Progress*, then a comparatively small manuscript. I had the privilege of seeing it grow bit by bit, of watching its expansion at close range. In Mr. Joyce's word-alchemical laboratory I have had the pleasure of glimpsing the amalgamations he made of his journeys into the unconscious of mankind.

The publishing of any one of the seventeen fragments in *transition* has always been an event in the editorial life of the review. It was not the simple process of taking over from the author a completed manuscript, but required the active collaboration of members of the *transition* staff, of friends and sympathizers. It was necessary to go through a number of note-books each of which had esoteric symbols indicating the reference to a given character, locality, event, or mood. Then the words accumulated over the years had to be placed in the segment for which they were intended. . . .

'This book', he sometimes says, 'is being written by the people I have met or known'. Sometimes he hardly seems to be listening to the conversation around him. Yet nothing escapes his prodigious memory, whether the dialogues be in English, French, German, or Italian. It may be a slip of the tongue, a phantasmatic verbal deformation, or just a tic of speech, but it usually turns up later in its proper place.

Only absolute indifference to the sociological habit of thought could make possible such a devotion to the purely creative *élan*. Joyce does not take sides. He tells the pessimistic story of mankind's internecine war with a smile of irony and sometimes pity. He presses seconds into interplanetary aeons by looking at everything from a 'funnominal' perspective. He has no 'ethical' axe to grind. Yet is it not a fact that all his characters—beginning with with those in *Dubliners* and continuing through *Work in Progress*—are people of the lower social strata, the so-called proletarized lower middle-class, the poor white whose struggles in the never changing world of Cain and Abel, or Shem and Shaun, he presents with the detachment of a whimsical understanding? The martial antinomies of life are the elements with which he deals. In lowly puns, irrational junctions, cross-currents from more than forty languages, we see the child-play of 'The Mime of Mick, Nick and the Maggies', the legend of the 'Mookse and the Gripes', the myth of 'Anna Livia Plurabelle', the fantasia of 'Shem and Shaun', the grotesque of 'Haveth Childers Everywhere', the fable of 'The Ondt and the Gracehoper'—all of them folk of the common, human run, yet made sublime by the creative imagination of a poet.

Work in Progress is 'a compendium, an encyclopedia of the entire mental life of a man of genius', a definition which Wilhelm Schlegel posited, more than a hundred years ago, for the novel of the future.

Soon the Book of Proteus will appear in its entirety. We who have watched it grow, hope that there will be ears to hear and rejoice at the fabulous new harmonies of this All-World Symphony! . . .

FINNEGANS WAKE

May 1939

296. L. A. G. Strong, review, *John O'London's Weekly*

5 May 1939, xli, No. 1,047, 168

By a fortunate chance, I have just been re-reading *Ulysses*, and the experience is particularly valuable for an approach to *Finnegans Wake* the completed volume of what has hitherto been known as *Work in Progress*. Not only are very many allusions, names, and even rhythms carried over from the earlier book to the later, but *Ulysses*, that immense and final proof of Mr. James Joyce's greatness, inspires the reader to tackle the tremendous difficulties of *Finnegans Wake* in the strengthened belief that Mr. Joyce must know what he is about. A novelist of genius would be unlikely to spend seventeen years in the composition of a gigantic crossword puzzle.

Since it has taken seventeen years to write, seventeen months would not be an unreasonable time to ask before reviewing it. All I can do at short notice is to give some indication of the scope of this vast and difficult book, plus a hint or two about the way in which it is written. . . .

Finnegans Wake deals not with day but with night. It is an attempt to pursue the mind into the inner activities of sleep and dream. It carries on the same allusions, the same Dublin lore, into a labyrinth; into the new complexities of thought and language which a dream world compels. . . .

Joyce does not hesitate to delve into this [HCE] Dubliner's most local memories, nor for that matter into his own erudition; though, for the general reader, the local references will perhaps be the most difficult. In the approach to one section, for instance, I was considerably helped by the fact that I could remember some of the advertisements inside the Dublin trams when I was a child. . . .

And music—which cannot help recurring in any study of Joyce—brings us to the second clue. . . .

It is essential, if we are going to understand *Finnegans Wake*, to listen to its paragraphs as if they were music, to repeat them over many times to ourselves, before we attempt to subject them to logical prose analysis. The appeal is less to the conscious waking mind than to the subconscious mind, the mind in dream. It is the appeal of poetry rather than that of prose: and we can completely defeat our powers of comprehension if we start pulling these paragraphs to pieces before we have listened to them and allowed them to make their half-hypnotic effect upon that part of our mind to which music speaks.

Joyce is a magician for whom words have always held a magical importance. We can trace the development of his magic from the celebrated passage in *A Portrait of the Artist as a Young Man*, where Stephen Dedalus on the sea shore considers the effect of words upon him and their value for him, through *Ulysses*, to the final incantation of the work before us.

How this technique of incantation may be used is shown in the passage about Anna Livia, particularly in the closing paragraphs. By a dreamy, rhythmic movement, a gradual whispering of faint pictures, a scene, a mood, an impression is evoked, elusive, without detail, a glimmer of summer twilight, perceived by a dreaming mind that is at once a tree on the bank, a stone, an old woman talking to herself and to others, the river that is flowing by, the sky that floats reflected in it, and all that rivers and stones and trees and old women have ever meant to man. The appeal is, as I said, not to the conscious mind, but to the mind in dream, which is reached by a series of gentle, inadequate calls to the lulled senses. No image is so sharp as to project from the silvery twilight: each makes its faint tinkling impact, and fades blurred into the music of the whole crepuscular incantation.

Of the structure of the whole I do not yet feel competent to speak, but it would appear to follow the structure of the house in which the dreamers are sleeping, going room by room from basement to attic. A concluding quotation will show that not all of *Finnegans Wake* is hard to understand.

[quotes from p. 445]

297. Paul Rosenfeld, review, *Saturday Review of Literature*

1939

'James Joyce's Jabberwocky', *Saturday Review of Literature* (6 May 1939), 10–11. Another review by Rosenfeld appeared as 'James Joyce: Charlatan or Genius?' *American Mercury*, xlvii (July 1939), 367–71.

Long heralded and eagerly awaited, the new, two-hundred-thousand-word novel by the illustrious author of *Ulysses* proves to be a work not unlike *The Making of Americans* by Gertrude Stein and *Towards a Better Life* by Kenneth Burke. It is one of the latter-day abstract fictions in which the writing is not so much about something as that something itself. As in its relatives, in *Finnegans Wake* the style, the essential qualities and movement of the words, their rhythmic and melodic sequences, and the emotional color of the page are the main representatives of the author's thought and feeling. The accepted significations of the words are secondary.

Indeed, in the case of this new volume, the language approaches a condition of privacy. It is composed to a great extent of sonorous neologisms reassembling syllables and whisps of words derived from Irish, English, and American dialects and languages as related to English as Norse, French, German, and Italian are; and of portmanteau-words, etymological puns, Hibernicisms, and other humorous ambiguities. In some instances, these neologisms reveal themselves as clever and economical concentrations of two or more meanings. In many others, they remain unintelligible, and the author's drift is entirely elusive.

Yet it is possible that in future years this new language of Joyce's will grow less private. . . . Even now, certain pages, passages, indeed whole chapters of it make or appear to make sense: and in any case seem to convey their author's ideas and his characteristic boundlessly bitter, boundlessly sad, and still humorous feeling. One of them is the initial chapter, which loosely adheres to the old narrative form. . . . Another is the final chapter of Part I, the famous 'Anna Livia Plurabelle' chapter. It is a sort of gongoristic and onomatopeic prose-poem about life symbolized as a girl and the course and flow of a river. Still others are the drunken epithalamium in Part II, the Swiftian sections of Part III, and almost the whole of the brief and relatively lucid final portion, with its feeling of a sad awakening.

And as a whole the book conveys or seems to convey a meaning. To begin with, the narrative plunges us into some manner of timeless reality, in which the selves of the Norse founders of Dublin and the subject of the narrative (possibly H. C. Earwicker, an imaginary Dublin postman of the 1900s, possibly Here Comes Everybody or even the author himself) and the egos of Sir Tristram and of Dean Swift are contemporaneous and even interchangeable. . . .

And this timeless reality appears to be the scene of some evolutionary process. Interfused in substance though they are, the four parts are distinct and represent a progress. The first has a mythological atmosphere, the second an heroic and theological one (there is a suggestion of heroic drama and of theological volumes and their commentaries), the third a rationalistic and human character (a fable and a liberal sermon figure here), while the fourth is full of suggestions of preparations for action and creation.

Now, these four stages correspond to the four periods of human evolution according to the eighteenth-century Italian philosopher Giambattista Vico, whose name, like that of Giordano Bruno, appears throughout the book in various disguises. . . . we arrive at the following conclusion. It is that in all likelihood *Finnegans Wake* represents sleep half-satirically conceived as a recapitulation of the process by which life organized itself and society developed; and particularly the action of the mind of a sleeping individual whose monogamitic inclinations are struggling to harmonize themselves with vagabond and ascetic ones. This would not prevent its being a half-tender and half-savagely blasphemous picture, much in Joyce's spirit, of human life as a drunken dream.

Yet in the face of the wit and mysterious poetry with which the book is strewn, and all the reasons for foreseeing its future greater intelligibility, we close it without a great feeling of enthusiasm. . . . It is cold and cerebral in comparison with that of a veritable 'radical' like Gerard Manley Hopkins. The pressure of passion and driving necessity frequently seems absent. And too often we have the sense of repletion and a mark overshot. . . .

298. Louise Bogan, review, *Nation*

1939

Extract from 'Finnegans Wake', *Nation*, cxlviii (6 May 1939), 533–5. Also appeared in her *Selected Criticism: Prose and Poetry* (1955) pp. 142–8, 149–53.

Joyce has been writing *Finnegans Wake* for seventeen years. . . . A whole school of imitators has clustered around its linguistic and philosophical example, and its influence has been so strong that critics have been led to write of it in, as it were, its own terms. Something unheard of and extraordinary was happening to language, history, time, space, and causality in Joyce's new novel, and the jaw-dropping and hat-waving of the front-line appreciators were remarkable in themselves. Because this subjective, or rolling-along-in-great-delight-with-a-great-work-of-art, school of criticism has had its innings with Joyce's book, the plain reviewer might do well to approach the work at first with a certain amount of leaden-footed objectivity, remaining outside the structure and examining it from as many sides as possible.

Joyce himself, as we shall see, has given a good many clues to what the book is about. The first thing that strikes the reader, however, is the further proof of Joyce's miraculous virtuosity with language. *Finnegans Wake* takes up this technical skill as it existed at the end of *Ulysses* and further elaborates it. Then Joyce's mastery of structure and his musician's feeling for form and rhythmic subtlety are here in a more advanced— as well as a more deliquescent—state of development. The chief reason for the book's opacity is the fact that it is written in a special language. But this language is not gibberish—unless it wants to be. It has rules and conventions. Before one starts hating or loving or floating off upon it, the attention might be bent toward discovering what it is, and how it works. . . . Joyce is not writing as he is writing to cover up inexpertness. Prosodically, he is a master, as can readily be seen if he is compared with his apprentices.

He is a master-musician and a master-parodist. Here, even more than in *Ulysses*, Joyce brings over into literature not only music's structural forms—as exemplified by the fugue, the sonata, the theme with variations—but the harmonic modulations, the suspensions and solutions, of music: effects in words which parallel a composer's effects obtained by working with relative or non-relative keys. Phrases and whole passages are transposed from a given style, mood, tempo, signature into a more or less contrasting one. Certain proper names— Finnegan, Earwicker, Anna Livia, Dublin, Phoenix, Howth, James and John, Lucan and Chapelizod—reappear in truncated, anagrammatically distorted, or portmanteau forms. The night-river leitmotif reads, at its most normal: 'Beside the rivering waters of, hitherandthithering waters of. Night!' Its variants are numerous and remarkable. Joyce, the parodist, in *Ulysses* colored matter with manner with extraordinary effect. The number of styles parodied in *Finnegans Wake* is prodigious. But these present parodies differ somewhat from their predecessors; they are actually more limited. The punning language in which they are framed gives them all a mocking or burlesque edge (the prose poems, only, excepted). This limitation and defeat of purpose—for an immense book written in two main modes only is sure to grow monotonous—is the first symptom to strike the reader of the malady, to be later defined, which cripples *Finnegans Wake*.

Thus equipped, then, with his private vernacular, Joyce proceeds to attack what certainly seems to be every written or oral style known to man. A list of these styles would fill pages. The range and variety can only be indicated here. . . .

[Following paragraphs illustrate this point]

There is every reason to believe that a *complete explanation* of the whole thing will come, after a longish lapse of time, from Joyce himself. This happened, it will be remembered, in the case of *Ulysses* after about nine years. . . . There is nothing whatever to indicate that Joyce has any real knowledge of the workings of the subconscious, in sleep or otherwise. . . . The later versions of the fragments already published seem to be changed out of sheer perversity: a clause is omitted leaving nothing but a vestigial preposition; a singular noun is shifted to the plural, and the meaning is thereby successfully clouded. . . . The most frightening thing about the book is the feeling, which steadily grows in the reader, that Joyce himself does not know what he is doing; and how, in spite of all his efforts, he is giving himself away. Full control is being exercised over the minor details and the main structure, but the compulsion toward a private universe is very strong. . . . Joyce's delight in reducing man's learning, passion, and religion to a hash is also disturbing. . . . After the first week what one longs for is the sound of speech, or the sight of a sentence *in its natural human context*. . . . The book cannot rise into the region of true evocation—the region where Molly Bloom's soliloquy exists immortally—because it has no human base. Emotion is deleted, or burlesqued, throughout. The vicious atmosphere of a closed world, whose creator can manage and distort all that is humanly valuable and profound (cunningly, with God-like slyness) becomes stifling. . . . *Ulysses* was based on a verifiable theme: the search for the father. The theme, or themes, of *Finnegans Wake* are retrogressive, as the language is retrogressive. The style retrogresses back to the conundrum. To read the book over a long period of time gives one the impression of watching intemperance become addiction, become debauch.

The book's great beauties, its wonderful passages of wit, its variety, its marks of genius and immense learning are undeniable. It has another virtue: in the future 'writers will not need to search for a compromise.' But whatever it says of man's past it has nothing to do with man's future, which, we can only hope, will lie in the direction of more humanity rather than less. And there are better gods then Proteus. . . .

299. Unsigned review, *Times Literary Supplement*

6 May 1939, 265–6

Few, if any, books of our time have been so much discussed before publication as Mr. James Joyce's *Finnegans Wake*—the book which was described during its sixteen years of gestation as *Work in Progress*. Here we were to have something even more Joycean than the Joyce of *Ulysses*—the quintessence, the *ne plus ultra* of that style and that method which have had so considerable an influence upon contemporary literature. Mr. Joyce is perhaps easily first among the literary innovators of to-day who have deliberately turned their backs on tradition in the conviction that life as it is honestly seen by perceptive minds to-day demands for its expression a new technique—in his case even a new vocabulary and a new grammar. . . . *Finnegans Wake* shows him as almost savagely satisfied with the thrilling spectacle of life as he sees it in all its sordidness, its restless emotionalism, its inconsequence, its somnambulant absurdity. He does not desire to reform it, but to gratify his creative spirit in the expression of his impressions of it. His constructive purpose is to find a way satisfactory to himself of expressing the movement of life as he sees it, changing its texture and hue from moment to moment, a flux of sensations whose reality cannot be appreciated without a sense of the flux. To achieve his end he thinks it necessary to rid himself of traditional literary methods which, in his opinion, lend themselves to the very falsities of apprehension abjured by him. . . .

Words—strange, violent, fabulous words—are his joy and his bane. It is in the process of translating his vision into language that Mr. Joyce becomes so baffling. It is not merely that he has introduced strange words into his vocabulary. . . . But Mr. Joyce has turned everything upside down. He has twisted ordinary words into something different merely because he seems to like them better in Jabberwockian form. Far-fetched literary, philosophical, journalistic, or music-hall references which have leapt into his mind thrust themselves into the middle of his nouns and adjectives. His language twists and turns with every vivid idea that interrupts his own thought and must needs be reproduced for the reader. The result is what the sur-realists appear to aim at—an uprush of words and images from the subconscious imagination—we hear shouts of laughter or lamentation, shrieks of gaiety and sorrow, low mutterings of reflection, explosions, yet all set down with a kind of cold-blooded matter-of-factness so far as the translator, namely the author, is concerned.

A sympathetic and patient reader can get stimulation and entertainment out of such literature. But he will only get from it a fraction of what was in Mr. Joyce's mind. There is only one person who can fully understand and appreciate this stupendous work, or can tell us truly how splendid it is or is not; and that person is Mr. Joyce himself. For in turning his back on the languge of communication which we know and inventing a new language of expression he has presented insuperable obstacles to complete understanding. It is true, we are not required to understand in the sense that we could understand a logical thesis or a plain narrative. The comprehension asked of us is rather that with which we should expect to appreciate music, whose notes and chords do not profess to carry a precise meaning, yet in combination may produce in us both emotional and intellectual results. But even if we accept *Finnegans Wake* in this sense, it is still the case that the notation is unfamiliar, the scales alien. Mr. Joyce is of course abundantly justified if he is content with the satisfaction of art for art's sake, and a splendid audience of one. But in so far as he aims at communication—and why else publish a book?—how serious a drawback that he should require a method which interposes such barriers between his most appreciative readers and his own fertile mind. . . .

300. Padraic Colum, review, *New York Times*

7 May 1939, 1, 14

How, in two thousand words or less, is one to review a book which even a cursory examination shows to be unprecedented, a book of considerable length by a thoughtful and tremendously equipped man who has spent sixteen years writing it? The only thing one can do is to indicate the value of the work and to show a way of approaching it with lessened perplexity. I say *lessened* perplexity, for a certain perplexity cannot wholly be removed from a reading of it and the present reviewer freely acknowledges that there is much in the book that he is still seeking explanation for.

Language, nothing less than the problem of conveying meaning through words, is the first term we have to discuss in connection with *Finnegans Wake*. . . .

The problem of the writer of today is to possess real words, not ectoplasmic words, and to know how to order them. They must move for him like pigeons in flight that make a shadow on the grass, not like corn popping. And so all serious writers of English today look to James Joyce, who has proved himself the most learned, the most subtle, the most thorough-going exponent of the value-making word.

From his early days Joyce has exercised his imagination and intellect upon the significance of words, the ordering of words. . . .

Joyce approached the problem of the word not only as a writer but as a musician, a linguist, a man trained in scholastic philosophy in which definition and rigorous literalness are insisted on. And this concern with the word has brought him far as a literary technician. All writers are concerned with process, with trying to pass from what can be described to what can be activated. Most of us leave it at the stage of description. 'He sat there and listened to the music'; 'Sitting there, he listened to the music.' So we write, but we know very well that this sort of writing gives us nothing of the process—a man responding to music. Joyce, in his later books anyway, wants to deal only with processes. In *Portrait of the Artist* some one looks at the algebraic signs on a blackboard: he writes of 'the Morris dance' of these signs. In that phrase a historical process is presented: we have the activism of algebra, its Saracenic origin, the decline of the civilization it came out of to the point when Europe knew only its remnants as dancers and buffoons.

Accept what looks like Volapük on the pages, I would say to one who has got *Finnegans Wake*, and turn to the last section in the first part, the section that begins 'O tell me all about Anna Livia!' This section has been published and discussed; readers interested in literary development have an idea of what it is about. The reader who is not looking for usual connotations, for logical structure, can find something delightful here: he can experience the child's surprise at flowing water and all that goes on beside it:

[quotes from *Anna Livia Plurabelle*, p. 196]

It is about the Liffey, Dublin's river, Anna Livia. Anna Livia is also a woman; the women washing clothes on the banks are talking about her as a woman. It may entertain the reader who begins here casually to pick out the names of the world's rivers that are used in this narrative of Anna's bedding. 'O, passmore that the oxus another!' Her ravisher is the man from overseas, the Viking founder of Dublin. 'In a gabbard he barqued it, the boat of life, from the harbourless Ivernikan Okean, till he spied the loom of her landfall and loosed two croakers from under the titilt, the gran Phenician rover.' The croakers are the ravens of Odin; the Phenician suggests the hero Finn (who appears as Finnegan) as well as these first voyagers along the Atlantic, the Phoenicians. The story told in this episode is not local: it is the myth of river-civilizations. As the water flows night descends, death takes the place of life, the gossiping washerwomen are metamorphosed into a stone and a tree. And here we have a passage that has the evocativeness of music:

[quotes from p. 216]

On the tale of Anna Livia, the riverwoman, like flotsam and jetsam, are carried the names and deeds of remembered people, and histories and legends. A reading of this episode, will give one I think, a sense of Joyce's idiom and of the direction of this formidably original book.

The last chapter is about resurrection, the resurrection of the dead. Here let me inform the reader that the general idea of *Finnegans Wake* is in the philosophy of the seventeenth-century Italian Vico. History, according to Vico, goes from savagery to corruption which is death, and then to a new beginning: its figures are Polyphemus in his cave, Achilles on the battlefield, Caesar with his imperium, Nero playing the lyre and falling under the swords of his guards. Then the rude beginnings of a civilization. This last chapter is the one that I should recommend the inadequately instructed readers to turn to after the Anna Livia episode.

It begins with a sacred word three times repeated 'Sandhyas! Sandhyas! Sandhyas!' Then, instead of the trumpet, we have the radio call:

Calling all downs. Calling all downs to dayne. Array! Surrection. Eire-weeker to the wohld bludyn world. O rally, O rally, O rally! Phlenxity, O rally! To what likelike thyne of the bird can be. Seek you somany matters. Haze sea seat to Osseania. Here!

'Dayne,' of course, suggests daylight; also the Viking origin of the hero. One of his names is Earwicker, but the name of his country, Eire, is now inserted. 'Phlcnxty' suggests the phoenix, the bird of resurrection, and the mind is carried back to the fall of Earwicker, that occasion of sin that was in a garden, in the Phoenix Park. The book ends:

My leaves have drifted from me. All. But one clings still. I'll bear it on me. To remind me of. Lff. So soft this morning ours. Yes. Carry me along, taddy, like you done through the toy fair. If I seen him bearing down on me under whitespread wings like he'd come from Arkangels, I sink I'd die down over his feet, humbly, dumbly, only to washup. Yes, tid. There's where. First. We pass through grass behush and bush to. Wish! A gull. Gulls. Far calls. Coming, far! End here. Us then. Finn, again! Take bussofthee, mememoree! Till thousands-thee. Lps. The keys to. Given! A way a lone a loved a long the.

'Lff,' I take it, is Lif out of Eddas who survives Ragnarok and begins again the cycle of history. The keys suggest St. Peter. 'Me' and 'memories' are contained in the idea of the resurrection of the body. But why, it will be asked, has James Joyce to manufacture words of this sort, and who, in the name of Finnegan, are the people in his book?

Perhaps this is the place for me to insert two glosses of my own. Where I grew up in Ireland there were several boys who had uncles whose name was Manus. For many years I had the notion that the name was exclusively avuncular, that it was the property of the uncles. Then I learned that the Irish Manus was taken from the Scandinavian Magnus: thereupon a portion of Irish-Scandinavian history became real and present for me. Later I learned that the Scandinavian Magnus was from Carlus Magnus, Charlemagne, and the Carlovingian Empire became dimly seen, heard, felt, personified in some way; something remained of it in villages I knew, and the expression of that something would add to the present content of literature. To express it one would have to use words which, belonging to the present, could at the same time evoke the past.

Again, I got into a train, say, at Buffalo: men, women and children are in the coaches, reading, dozing, looking on the scenes they pass; I do not know where they come from or where they are going to. For a moment they are abstract human beings. One feels them as neither acting nor acted upon. But to evoke this feeling of actlessness one would have to form a language that would be removed from normal language which is about actions. In a minute, of course, one personalizes them, discovering that this is a salesman and the other is a teacher going to Florida. All the same, each has a life that cannot be expressed in the language of action; all the same, each has a life that has been molded by the mountain and the river, by Polyphemus, Achilles, Caesar and Nero.

Well, cursorily speaking, this is what *Finnegans Wake* is about. It is history made present through these vasty figures who sum up the race, who are also the mountain and the river of the land. The figures are not representational but are like figures in a tapestry that emerge, merge with each other and with natural objects. One sees Tristan become the Duke of Wellington, or St. Patrick, Anna Livia becomes Swift's Vanessa. The title of the book is from an Irish-American vaudeville song. It was a song about a hod-carrier who fell off his wall, who was thought to be dead, who was given a wake, and who, at the mention of whisky, resurrected himself. But the name Finnegan is the same as that of the national hero, Finn MacCool. And Finn means 'the fair-haired' and so might stand for all Nordic heroes.

He has fallen like Adam and like Humpty-Dumpty; he is accused of a crime that is said to have taken place in a garden, in Phoenix (for the purpose of the charge, Fiendish Park), he justifies himself by telling how he created a civilization for his Anna Livia. He is the boss-man in any situation and so he can be referred to as Adam or the Duke of Wellington or Daniel O'Connell. His woman is the river, but she is also the Little Annie Rooney of the song. And the man is Earwicker, but he is most often written of as H.C.E. or Here Comes Everybody. His sons as Shem the Penman and Jaunty Jaun; they are also Cain and Abel, the angel Michael and Satan.

Having read the Anna Livia episode and the Resurrection episode, the reader knows enough of the idiom and the plan to begin with the first chapter. Even if he does not understand all that is on any one page he will find sentences lovely in their freshness and their beauty and sentences that one can chuckle over for months. We have novels that give us greatly a three-dimensional world: here is a narrative that gives a new dimension.

301. Oliver Gogarty, review, *Observer*

7 May 1939, 4

It is easier to understand Mr. Joyce than to understand his later writings, which we will never understand unless we know something of Mr. Joyce. . . .

[a long biographical comment follows]

Joyce's language is more than a revolt against classicism, it is more than a return to the freedom of slang and thieves' punning talk. It is an attempt to get at words before they clarify in the mind. It is the language of a man speaking, trying to speak, through an anaesthetic. It is presumed to be the language of the Subconscious mind, whatever that may be.

When I think of the indomitable spirit that plodded on, writing *Ulysses* in poverty in Trieste, without a hope of ever seeing it published, I am amazed at the magnitude of this work, every word of which in its 628 pages had to be weighed, twisted, and deranged in order to bring up associated ideas in the mind. Though parts of it appeared from time to time during the last sixteen years in various magazines under the title of *The Work in Progress*, one chapter in particular, pages 196 to 216, appeared in book form, and is also recorded on the gramophone by the author. It is the most successful experiment in this strange style. 'Anna Livia Plurabelle' deals with the river Liffey rising in the hills and flowing through Dublin, lapsing with its history between two washerwoman, who stand on either side washing dirty linen until one becomes an elm tree and the other a stone. The names of about 170 rivers are suggested, and the effect of twilight falling on the flowing water is brought about by words that flutter like bats over the darkening stream.

Who were Shem and Shaun the living sons or daughters of? Night now! Tell me, tell me, tell me, elm! Night, night! Telmetale of stem or stone. Beside the rivering waters of, hitherandthithering waters of, Night!

Mr. Yeats confessed to me that this kind of prose made any other colourless.

But that is intelligible compared with the advance on it, if it may be so called (page 293) where a diagram is given entitled 'Uteralterance or the Interplay of Bones in the Womb.' The paragraph above it reads:

[quotes from p. 293]

This gives only a slight example of the method of comminuting words. The immense erudition employed, and the various languages ransacked for pun and word-associations is almost incredible to anyone unaware of the superhuman knowledge the author had when a mere stripling. In some places the reading sounds like the chatter during the lunch interval in a Berlitz school. Every language living and dead in Europe gabbles on and on.

But what is the motive force behind this colossal production? Finnegan's wake may be the wake, that is the funeral celebration, as well as the panegyric, of civilisation. Resentment against his upbringing, his surroundings, and finally against the system of civilisation throughout Europe, perhaps against Life itself which Finnegan may represent, created this literary Bolshevism which strikes not only at all standards and accepted modes of expression whether of Beauty or Truth but at the very vehicle of rational expression. This arch-mocker in his rage would extract the Logos, the Divine word or Reason from its tabernacle, and turn it muttering and maudlin into the street. It is impossible to read the work as a serial. It may have a coherency and a meaning. What is wrong with the meaning that it cannot be expressed? Ripeness cannot be all in this instance, nor can a myriad-minded man full of infinite suggestion satisfy the reader with suggestions alone. Perhaps it is wrong to look for a meaning where there is every meaning. It may be unmodern to expect sense. Lewis Carroll stopped short brilligly, but this goes on lapsing as everlastingly as Anna Livia. There is nothing new under the sun: it is only exaggerated. This is the most colossal leg-pull in literature since McPherson's Ossian. Mr. Joyce has had his revenge. . . .

302. Edwin Muir, review, *Listener*

11 May 1939, xxi, No. 539, 1013

Finnegans Wake, James Joyce's new book, has taken sixteen years to write; the burning question for a reviewer is how long it will take to read, if reading means understanding. In sixteen days it would be possible to go over the book and glance at the words, as fine a collection of words as anyone could wish for, in English, Scottish, Erse, French, German, Italian, Spanish and a number of other languages ranging in knowledgability to Finnish. After these come the portmanteau words, the puns, the distorted words and invented words; the Franco-German words and Anglo-Italian words, the dog Latin bedogged again and the pidgin English once more bepidgined. This is the 'night language' which Yeats said Mr. Joyce set out to discover. It is an enormous lingual feat; it does give the feeling sometimes that one is moving in a world where everything, including language and syntax and the principles of mental association, are different; it is an attempt never attempted before, which could only have been undertaken by a man of Mr. Joyce's genius and perseverance. To say that the attempt is either successful or unsuccessful, after the few days' grace given to a reviewer by the convention of reviewing, would be absurd; it is possible that any such attempt must be unsuccessful: I do not see how we can share Mr. Joyce's nights. But this book by all appearances describes his sleep-world in the language of sleep; and without being a sleep-reader, one must make what one can out of it.

The first impression you receive is an impression of style; even when you have very little idea what is being said, you know that only Mr. Joyce could have said it in that way:

> Wroth mod eldfar, ruth rodd stilstand, wrath wrackt wroth, confessed private Pat Marchison *retro*.

That might have come out of *Ulysses*, and it has the same imprint as the comprehensible parts of that encylopædic work. Another thing which connects this book with *Ulysses* is the great amount of verbal facetiousness:

> And of course all chimed din width the eatmost boviality.

Another thing is the enormous amount of detail for the sake of detail:

[quotes from p. 59]

And finally, like *Ulysses*, the book has an imposed framework of some kind, which is probably given in the first sentence:

> riverrun, past Eve and Adam's, from swerve of shore to bend of bay, brings us by a commodius vicus of recirculation back to Howth Castle and Environs.

There is a central mythological character called H. C. Earwicker, Here Comes Everybody, and various other names, who may well be the counterpart of Simon Bloom in the other book. There are countless historical references to such people as Awful Grimmest Sunshat Cromwelly, Stonewall Willingdone, Lipoleums, also known as Boomapart, and numerous private citizens of Dublin. There is, indeed, a strong resemblance between the day-world of *Ulysses* and the night-world of *Finnegans Wake*; one often feels that Mr. Joyce is working over the same material again, that long lost day in Dublin in 1904, from which Stephen Dedalus now seems to have disappeared.

The book is much more effective read aloud than to oneself, and produces sometimes a feeling of drunken incantation:

[quotes from p. 21]

There is an exorbitant amount of this storytelling without any story, an endless eddying of words that return upon themselves:

[quotes from p. 21]

There are occasional flashes of a kind of poetry which is difficult to define but is of unquestioned power:

[quotes from p. 25]

There is rarely any sense of urgent compulsion, except at the end, where it is possible that Mr. Joyce is speaking his own thoughts:

[quotes from pp. 627–8]

The cold mad feary father is the sea, but how many things the sea may mean in Mr. Joyce's sleep-kingdom I should not like to guess. The end of this book, like the end of *Ulysses*, is the best part of it, and no one can read it, I think, without receiving an impression of a strange sorrow and mourning over life. It is curiously simple and direct.

But as a whole the book is so elusive that there is no judging it; I cannot tell whether it is winding into deeper and deeper worlds of meaning or lapsing into meaninglessness. Anything can change into anything else. . . . The book has the qualities of a flowing stream, sound and rhythm; the rhythm is sometimes beautiful, as can be tested by reading certain pages aloud. How much Mr. Joyce has concentrated on this, and how much he has given way to his mere intoxication with language it would be hard to say; for long stretches the book reads like a long private joke, the elaborate blarney of an insatiable linguist:

[quotes from pp. 627–8]

There are parodies of the sagas, skits on almost every style of writing, enormous catalogues in the vein of Rabelais, snippets of folk-lore, echoes of music-hall songs, all slightly dissolved, all tending to flow into each other, and producing a continuous effect of storytelling while continuously avoiding the commission of a story. To dip into this flux for a little is refreshing, but to stay in for long is to be drowned, 'with winkles, whelks and cocklesent jelks', in Mr. Joyce's enormous Baroque moat. A reader might well cry 'Lifeboat Alloe, Noeman's Woe, Hircups Emptybolly!' . . . .

303. B. Ifor Evans, review, *Manchester Guardian*

12 May 1939, 8

Mr. Joyce's *Finnegans Wake*, parts of which have been published as *Work in Progress*, does not admit of review. In twenty years' time, with sufficient study and with the aid of the commentary that will doubtless arise, one might be ready for an attempt to appraise it. The work is not written in English, or in any other language, as language is commonly known. I can detect words made up out of some eight or nine languages, but this must be only a part of the equipment employed. This polyglot element is only a minor difficulty, for Mr. Joyce is using language in a new way. A random example will illustrate:

[quotes from p. 281]

The easiest way to deal with the book would be to become 'clever' and satirical or to write off Mr. Joyce's latest volume as the work of a charlatan. But the author of *Dubliners*, *A Portrait of an Artist*, and *Ulysses* is obviously not a charlatan, but an artist of very considerable proportions. I prefer to suspend judgment. . . .

What, it may be asked, is the book about? That, I imagine, is a question which Mr. Joyce would not admit. This book is nothing apart from its form, and one might as easily describe in words the theme of a Beethoven symphony. Those who have been privileged to discuss the work with Mr. Joyce suggest that he has been influenced by the proposal in Vico's *Scienza Nuova* to write an ideal and timeless history into which all ordinary histories are embodied. The clearest object in time in the book is the Liffey, Anna Livia, Dublin's legendary stream, and the most continuous character is H. C. Earwicker, 'Here Comes Everybody': the Liffey as the moment in time and space, and everything, everybody, all time as the terms of reference, back to Adam or Humpty Dumpty, but never away from Dublin. This seems the suggestion of the musical half-sentence with which the work begins:

riverrun, past Eve and Adam's, from swerve of shore to bend of bay, brings us by a commodious vicus of recirculation back to Howth Castle and Environs. . . .

One concluding note. Mr. Joyce in a parody of Jung and Freud ('Tung-Toyd') mentions 'Schizo-phrenia.' One might imagine that Mr. Joyce had used his great powers deliberately to show the language of a schizophrenic mind, and then he alone could explain his book, and I suppose, he alone review it. . . .

304. G. W. Stonier, review, *New Statesman*

20 May 1939, xvii, 788, 790

In an unfamiliar world one makes for the familiar. Turn to page 196 of Mr. Joyce's mighty work: the lovely *Anna Livia*.

. . . But it is silly to label Joyce a classic before his time, to take up a highbrow attitude towards his work. . . . But, besides being a humorist, he has a lyrical gift which rises high over the Binsteads, Beachcombers and music-hall comics. Occasionally in Binstead you will find a pretty verbal invention; I remember the Brighton gal brought up to the sounds of 'the cuckold and the martingales'—an anticipation of Mr. Joyce's method. In *Finnegan's Wake* we find this extravagant lovely invention everywhere:

[quotes from p. 159]

. . . The language with which Mr. Joyce now habitually deals is miraculously compressed:

[quotes from p. 17]

. . . There is more sound and sense than (for some reason) reviewers would have us believe, in Mr. Joyce's night-language. After all, they might have reflected, our greatest living prose writer doesn't spend seventeen years of his life in elaborating a language which no one will be able to understand. One can learn chinese and, with less difficulty, one can learn the word-signs of Mr. Joyce's new tongue. It does, in fact, if one reads him patiently and little by little, carry its own lucidity, and where the meaning fades music tides us over. The mistake is to read him as though he were writing the same language as Mr. Agate, Sir Hugh Walpole and Mr. Charles Morgan; he is not; that is the whole point of his book. If you are satisfied with the verbal thrills of the above revered writers then there's no need—indeed it would be foolishly risky—to have anything to do with Mr. Joyce. He writes for those who are tired of our ready-made literary cadences. And once again, as in the fragment *Anna Livia*, he has provided a wonderful ending:

[quotes from p. 627]

. . . For an unreadable book *Finnegan's Wake* turns out to be remarkably quotable. All it lacks is the warmth, the body, the human nature that make books like *Tristram Shandy* immortal. It is the superb verbiage of a man exiled, disillusioned and without a theme; and what a great pity that is. That is why I have quoted so much, from the 'illegible airy plumeflights' of the master of lyrical modern prose. . . .

305. Georges Pelorson, review, in *Aux Ecoutes*

1939

Extract from '*Finnegans Wake* of James Joyce, or the Book of Man', *Aux Ecoutes*, xxiii, No. 1096 (20 May 1939), 29. Also appeared in expanded form in *Revue de Paris*, xlvi (September 1939), 227–35 (from which the present text is taken).

I know nothing more striking than the work of James Joyce as incontestable proof of what is genius. It has the unusual character, this appearance of revolution which seeks certainties and with which it contents itself. But it is so complete, while at the same time so solitary, falling from the same weight, carried for nearly forty years by the same gravitation, that it appears like an absolutely closed and complete system, tracing its immutable course across the space of human creation and the human mind. I mean that all new work by Joyce is so strictly bound to the preceding works that its own movement also finds its place in the vaster movement.

[brief note about the earlier works]

With *Finnegans Wake* . . . we cross the threshold into night.

In this sense, it can be said, if one wishes, that *Finnegans Wake* is a complementary book and closes a cycle. It can be said on the condition that it is not forgotten that this work is itself a cycle in itself, the sleep cycle, the cycle of duration, drawing to the same feminine element of water its symbol. . . .

[quotes the first and last words, comparable to the monologue which closes *Ulysses*]

Such is the time of this action (if it is accepted that everything written down from the simplest novel to Descartes's *Méditations* necessarily involves an action): a closed duration or more exactly a sort of time finished, a duration of recurrence (recirculation).

[discusses the setting and the ballad of the title]

The action itself remains, properly, spoken.

On this point, the critic who, as here, ought to limit himself to a few pages, can not but avow himself conquered in advance. If *Ulysses* could pass for a novel, if the fact even that nothing happened in it (in the habitual dramatic sense) became the pretext for a sort of vast action of inaction, the same does not go for *Finnegans Wake*. We are not even in the presence of a semblance of a novel. Here neither the action (the intrigue) governs the characters nor the characters the action, for the good reason that action and characters remain without end in the position of creation, are never anything but changing projections of a more profound and hidden reality, have only value as symbols. This reality, I will call it Memory, if I were sure of being understood, is time. The master of the action, in this book, is in fact time, this enormous and cavernous belly where nothing is created which has not first been consumed, used up, submitted to endless digestions. A prodigious world of birth and return. A world where forms . . . reign, where life is never but furtive color, ephemeral proof of reality.

One of the particular functions of mythology is to name the forces with respect to their attributes. Thus it is with Joyce and his characters. Their names are only simple attributes, simple reflections translating an action whose roots penetrate straight to the depths.

[illustrates the various changes rung upon *HCE*]

Thus, then, is time, a perpetual creation and a perpetual return, which presides over the action, which *is* the fundamental action. In this closed circle what can happen which may happen which will not happen? [que peut-il se passer qui ne se soit passé, qui ne se passera?] All becomes episode. But necessarily, each episode, in itself, contains the entire time. And it is there, without doubt, that we have the character of this book: that it is nothing which may not be brought back to the totality of immanent Memory.

The book is divided into three parts and a sort of epilogue. But, again, one does not know how to underline the embarrassment which the usual words 'parts' and 'episodes' here cause the critic. I would like to use the terms 'circles' and 'segments', giving the idea better to that which Joyce himself holds tenaciously, that each part, each episode, is to itself alone a whole which is further *the* whole.

[The critic illustrates each of his 'circles', pp. 230–4: The first circle is divided into eight segments (typographically), in a sort of exposition of forms, a litany of attributes. The author sings the themes of his characters, the multiple echoes of each of his heroes which resound from one end to the other of this enormous closed cave of time. History and mythology are confused. The characters are mere reflections of man, across his memory. Man directs, through the grace of Joyce, this ample symphony of the unconscious . . . The reality of myth and history lives in us. Briefly, this is all the attributes which sleep in us, all this immense symbolical parade of the unconscious. . . .]

It would take a book to analyse this book. One would have to be Joyce to be able to translate it. A unique work, yet unmerciful. A work which, for the public, seems to isolate Joyce not only from the reader but from the rest of his work. And yet how necessary, how ineluctable. Wagner alone can furnish, if the worst come to the worst, an analogy of form, of 'event.' Spiritual fathers have been looked for. Joyce has generously given many keys: Vico, Bruno, Dante have been searched to find a framework. For my part, I do not think that it is necessary to love this book in order to find scholarly exegeses. And I do not believe that I betray Joyce by inviting the reader to lose himself in the book as is done in music. It is purposeful that the river remains the living, essential theme of the book. The entire book flows. To understand it one has, in truth, only to allow himself to be carried and to descend the course, often being on the point of sinking.

Even the language is torrential and carries you. All that is necessary is to listen, to hear oneself read. The language is so strictly bound to the depths of the book that it is both the earth and the sap. I mean that Joyce has drawn here as from a spring of thought. Not only does it express but it is expressed. . . .

[discusses the language]

The metamorphosis of the language is on an equal footing with that of the characters. The word play is made on solid roots, as the play of the characters gravitates around principles, of this sum of principles, which is closed time, immovable because of having no movement except circular, except to return. And that Joyce had to choose to express this gravitation and to make this supreme bond of language, the process of plays on words . . . could it be otherwise? Not only was it not necessary for this book to be the terrain of scholars but . . . it was necessary that he attain the man in the reader, that he strike straight to the heart.

306. Malcolm Muggeridge, review, *Time and Tide*

20 May 1939, 654-5

Mr. James Joyce's *Finnegans Wake* faces the reviewer with peculiar difficulties. In the first place he cannot read it, only battle through a page or so at a time without pleasure or profit. This would not, in itself, matter so much; but he does not know what the book is about. The dust-cover, which might be expected to help, says nothing except that *Finnegans Wake* has taken sixteen years to write, that it has been 'more talked about and written about during the period of its com-position than any previous work of English literature,' and that it would inevitably be 'the most important event of any season in which it appeared.' . . . Thus defeated by book and blurb, it is natural to cast a surreptitious eye at what other reviewers have had to say. . . . The usual line is that Mr. Joyce is a great writer, that for reasons best known to himself he has evolved a curious way of writing which bears little resemblance to the English language as commonly used, that so painstaking an effort is not to be dismissed out of hand, and that in any case gramophone records of passages from *Finnegans Wake* recited by Mr. Joyce have been found by competent persons to be delectable. . . .

Considered as a book, and considering the object of a book to be by means of written symbols to convey the author's emotions or thoughts to the reader, *Finnegans Wake* must be pronounced a complete fiasco. . . .

Idiocy has its charm; the distracted utterances of a dislocated mind seem to bear some relation to one another, to suggest a dim coherence like a faded picture; 'Come o'er the bourn, Bessy to me,' or, 'Pillicock sat on Pillicock-hill,' have an odd poignancy, relevance even, when Poor Tom says them, but only because he was supposed to be mad. . . .

To discover coherence in incoherence, form in formlessness, light in darkness, has been an everlasting pursuit. Mr. Joyce has reversed the process, looking for incoherence in coherence, formlessness in form, darkness in light. Words instead of straining to contain what has been dimly understood, to signify truth, strain to confuse. They desert experience and understanding, and signify only chaos, in the process inevitably disintegrating, ceasing to be words at all. Language which emerged from confused, meaningless sound, returns to its origins— painstakingly, laboriously returns, taking sixteen years over the process.

Here and there in *Finnegans Wake*, it is true, a mood may be sensed, an association of images or of words detected; but these are occasional flashes of coherence in an ocean of incoherence; mistakes, it almost seems, failures in Mr. Joyce's method. The effect of the whole is of impenetrable and despairing darkness—

[quotes from p. 298]

307. Alfred Kazin, review, *New York Herald Tribune*

21 May 1939, 4

Finnegans Wake is James Joyce's fourth book of fiction, and the first in which he does not formally appear as a character. Whether as the boyish 'I' who peers through the first stories in *Dubliners*, or the gangling, desperately proud Stephen Dedalus who bestrides *A Portrait of the Artist as a Young Man* and *Ulysses*, Joyce has played the paramount role in his own fiction. In a very real sense his books have been the saga of James Joyce; they have offered a confession, staggering in its concentrated intensity of the mind of Stephen Dedalus as agonist and lay priest, intellectual and lover, infidel and poet.

All writers, we say, are conditioned by their youth; they get their subject from youth's grievance, Joyce has been obsessed by his youth to the exclusion of all else. The world has always been for him the Ireland he has not seen for thirty years; God has always been the cultivated, inexorable, rather sadly remote God who presides over the Dublin intelligentsia. His subject has always been the Dublin of 1900–10; the people he knew in it, the superstitions and aspirations they shared, his universe. He has turned round and round in that universe as Dante suffered in the sight of God. Like the great Catholic spirits of the Middle Ages, Joyce has accepted the common experience of mankind as an abstraction. It is something he has known and pondered by instinct, a symbol among the paraphernalia of man's fate.

Alone among the artists of our time, therefore, perhaps alone in Europe since Beethoven wrote those last quartets that climax man's quarrel with life, Joyce has slowly and with relentless patience assumed the overpowering importance of his soul and written as if the world were well lost for art. Through blindness, war, poverty, neglect, the cackling of those who do not understand, the smug self-satisfactions of those who do not wish to understand, Joyce has followed his *métier*. Yet remarkable as his accomplishment has been, the terrifying isolation that has made him the writer he is seems today even more significant. For it has brought him, through one of those cycles that spell the biography of genius, from the longings of *Dubliners*, the limpid beauty of *Portrait of the Artist as a Young Man*, the herculean comedy of *Ulysses*, to the nightmare of darkness and immolation. That is *Finnegans Wake*.

No one has yet described *Finnegans Wake*. What we have had is an effort to fix the intention of the work, and none of the many interpretations and essays in Joycean exegesis that I have seen has gone beyond the rudimentary summary Edmund Wilson offered eight years ago in *Axel's Castle*. We know that the book presents a Dublin night, as *Ulysses* presents a Dublin day. The hero is a Norwegian living in Dublin, Humphrey Chimpden Earwicker (H.C.E., or Here Comes Everybody), who has been at various times a postman, a worker in Guinness's Brewery, an assistant in a shop. He is married and the father of several children, but he has been carrying on a flirtation with a girl named Anna Livia. As the book opens ('riverrun, past Eve and Adam's from swerve of shore to pen of bay, brings us by a commodius vicus of recirculation back to Howth Castle and Environs'), he is slowly falling asleep, and the great dream that is *Finnegans Wake* begins.

Now Joyce has tried not to describe the dream, but to present it. The conscious will is not only to capture the unconscious, but it is to anatomize it. Sleep is a great marsh of conscience, of desire; it is a corridor of fear in which men utter the words that were never spoken, resolve the hopes that were never offered. The sleeper is always alone, and though he may not figure in his dream, life spills out in his mind in a staggering and frightful confusion. A song may turn into a woman's face, an enemy assume the devil's horns. For Joyce sleep has no relation to time or space; it is a great void into which the names, the places, the objects, the associations, the tricks and caprices of mind, the whole stalking phantasmagoria of consciousness, filter through. It is as if a God were looking at life not as a chapter in history, or as a tableau of conduct, but as something stupendous in its disorganization, a clutching of many hands, a blind and mangled effort to rise from the slime, the great desire to assume identity.

But with this, Joyce (and this, I think, is the central drive of the book) has made of sleep an instrument of satire. Sleep not only reverses normal daily consciousness; it mocks it. Just as a child who has been cruelly hurt by some elder will dream of conquest and revenge, so for the mature mind sleep is the assertion of its dignity. The dream may often seem distorted, and even more agonizing than life, but it is a disordered formulation of the desire for order. In Earwicker's sleep, life becomes not only astonishingly fluid, but brilliantly free. The will has full dominion;

what has been restrained by law or shamed by custom suddenly breaks loose. There are no longer any castes, any bars; there is, above all, no conscious morality.

So Earwicker, dreaming of Phoenix Park in Dublin (where he made love to Anna Livia), is thrown into a world in which Wellington leaps out of his statue, the soldiers' monuments are dissolved into an army of fusiliers, the clothes he was wearing turn into goat and sheep skin, the desire for Anna Livia, the shame at desiring Anna Livia, is spun into a whirling carnival of fear and exaltation. For a moment the sleep rouses, sleep is shaken off, the language is stilted, legal, chill ('a baser meaning has been read into these characters the literal sense of which decency can safely scarcely hint'); but then the tempo slackens, sleep has taken possession again, the dream returns to that crucial evening in Phoenix Park. Earwicker's longing at this moment is to justify himself; it is not true, one hears him saying, he did nothing wrong. But the dream has confused the dreamer; fusiliers and Anna Livia are interchanged; the intervals of sense are blended. Thus we read: 'He lay at one time under the ludicrous imputation of annoying Welsh fusiliers in the people's park. Hay, hay, hay! Hoq, hoq, hoq! Faun and Flora on the lea love that little old joq. To any one who knew and loved the Christlikeness of the big clean minded giant H. C. Earwicker throughout his excellency's long vice-freegal existence the mere suggestion of him as a lust sleuth nosing for trouble in a boobytrap rings particularly preposterous.'

But how, you will ask, can Joyce know a dream? The answer, of course, is that he can't. In reality *Finnegans Wake* is a stupendous improvisation, a great pun. Even in sleep one cannot imagine an Irish-Norwegian brewer remembering words in a language he has never read, perhaps never heard. Yet Joyce sprinkles the book with agglomerations out of seventeen or eighteen languages. When we read 'quidam, if he did not exist it would be necessary quoniam to invent him,' the brilliant play on Voltaire's aphorism has no relation to Earwicker's conscious or unconscious experience. It is the sleep, in truth, not of one man, but of a drowsing humanity. All cultures have relation to it, all minds, all languages nourish its night speech. The brilliance of Joyce's display can seem almost too resplendent; we feel ourselves in the presence of a nature so superior in kind that the effect is blinding. Words take on dozens of associations, all equally firm, real, clever; the punning becomes a galvanic needle playing on the sloth and fat of conventional language and thinking.

But what, I ask you, are you going to do with 'As the lion in our teargarten remembers the nenuphar of his Nile (shall Ariuz forget Arioun or Boghas the baregams of the Marmarazalles from Marmeniere?). It may be, tots wearsense full a naggin twentyg have sigilposted what. . . .' Or that wonderful word on page 3, two lines long, which begins 'bababadalgharaghtakamminarronnonkonnbronntonner,' etc? As one tortures one's way through *Finnegans Wake*, an impression grows that Joyce has lost his hold on human life. Obsessed by a spaceless and time-less void, he has outrun himself. We begin to feel that his very freedom to say anything has become a compulsion to say nothing. He is not speculating on anything man may possibly know; he has created a world of his own, that night world in which all men are masters and all men dùpes, and he has lost his way in it. For extraordinary a feat of language and insight and learning as *Finnegans Wake* is, what may we expect to follow it? The denigration has been too complete; after this twisting, howling, stumbling murk, language so convulsed, meaning so emptied, there is nothing. This is night and this is sleep; and there is also the day. For it is always frightening to remember that sleep is an approximation of death.

308. Morley Callaghan, review, *Saturday Night*

27 May 1939, n.p.

For seventeen years, it is said, Joyce worked on *Finnegans Wake*, and it seems only fair that anyone writing a piece about the work should be given at least a year to get at its full value and meaning. I have been looking at the book for about a week. Therefore, all I can pretend to give is some first impressions gathered when first looking into *Finnegans Wake*.

The legend is that Finnegan had a fall and was thought to be dead, and there was a wake that lasted some time, and he suddenly awoke when he heard the word, 'Whiskey.' With the first line you plunge right into the dream or night world. There is no getting back to the objective rational world of the conscious mind. Not only is there no way of seeing things in clear related outlines, the whole rational or logical structure of language seems to be broken down. It is a little frightening. You are caught in this flow, you try desperately to catch the meaning, to get hold of something that is familiar to the day world which can serve as a guide. It is the apparent meaninglessness that is frightening, for the eye can catch nothing, yet the tireless anti-logical voice keeps sounding, and you have to listen; suddenly the sound itself begins to give a kind of hope or comfort. In this night world where all things are terrifyingly strange, the sense of music is retained.

It is possible, bit by bit, to become familiar with the dream structure, as nearly everyone has found out. . . .

Of course the dream flow is of the world of Dublin and Ireland. Much must necessarily be lost to a North American reader. But you must never lose sight of the fact that it is an Irish book. In fact, large sections seem to be written in Irish brogue. What seems so strange to the eye can be turned into something very familiar and comical to the ear simply by reading these passages aloud. . . . It is great writing. It is a new sensation in literature, a new way of looking at things perfectly realized, something that can be brought off only by a great master.

Since the greatness of the achievement can be grasped in the Anna Livia section, and in other smaller passages, the mind keeps hungering to grasp the same full meaning in the opaque passages. . . . Inescapably it comes to you that Joyce is conducting some great prose orchestration out of all the words from all the languages that have flowed through his Irish mind.

It gets that you can follow, or get used to the new word structure, and of all things, you find that again and again it is based upon the pun. There is great wit. And rarely does a page fail to offer some kind of a laugh. Parodies of all styles are here. The reader begins to get a curious satisfaction from this all pervading comedy. It is the lifeline that holds him to the rational world. It is as though the dreamer, out of whom this great flow of words comes, had a vast comic sense and every word was touched by it.

But this very play of words arouses some suspicion and wonder in the reader. Is Joyce actually attempting to produce the dream reality, or is he just using that structure again and again to orchestrate words for their own sake. Of course the answer might readily be that that was exactly what the dreaming night mind revealed in this book did: get drunk on words. But whatever the intention the result seems to be there over and over again: a literature feeding not on life but on words. . . .

309. Richard Aldington, review, *Atlantic Monthly*

June 1939, clxiii, n.p.

. . . Common honesty compels this reviewer to state that he is unable to explain either the subject or the meaning (if any) of Mr. Joyce's book; and that, having spent several hours a day for more than a fortnight in wretched toil over these 628 pages, he has no intention of wasting one more minute of precious life over Mr. Joyce's futile inventions, tedious ingenuities, and verbal freaks.

Such a book is either impudent or insolent; impudent, if it is merely an elaborate hoax; insolent, if it is serious and the author really thinks that the world has either time or inclination to master a new system of Jabberwock English merely to read one book.

The problem of *what* Mr. Joyce has to say in *Finnegans Wake* may be left to those who have time and energy to waste. The reader who takes up this book for the first time will at once be involved in the problem of *how* he says it. Mr. Joyce claims that he understands and can explain every syllable of the book. Doubtless, but who cares? Readers are not interested in what the author's words mean to him, but in what they mean to them. And what Mr. Joyce has written is 628 pages of pedantic nonsense. . . . This heavy compost is frequently infected with that lecherous suggestiveness of which Mr. Joyce is a master, which was defended in *Ulysses* as germane to the characters, but which here seems to have no purpose more interesting than the author's morose delectation. . . .

Such are the main ingredients of this ghastly stodge, repeated over and over again. The boredom endured in the penance of reading this book is something one would not inflict on any human being, but far be it from me to discourage any reader who prefers to use a perfectly good five-dollar bill to buy *Finnegans Wake* rather than to light a cigarette with it. (The latter course will give more lasting satisfaction.)

Translated into native Tasmanian, this book should have a well-deserved sale. . . .

310. Unsigned review, *Irish Times*

3 June 1939, 7

The writing of *Finnegans Wake* took sixteen years, short enough, perhaps, beside the stretch of time that could be spent in trying to understand it. For it must be said at once that this way, at least, Mr. Joyce gives full measure to the reader. Nothing moves, or appears, or is said as ever before in any book. It is endlessly existing in its impenetrability. . . .

The work is described as a novel, and although in their essence all the stories of the world may be here, there is no single story that one can grasp. It may be a novel to end novels; for, if there is shape at all, it is the shape of a superb annihilation—as of some gigantic thing let loose to destroy what we had come to regard as a not unnecessary part of civilisation. One feels its power, the kind of gleaming genius behind it, but no communication of anything is achieved, perhaps simply because it is just not intended. . . . There are moments of beauty, the measured sounds of lyrical prose which beat upon the ear, but which do not come into the understanding, and always an airy gesture beyond the words which make it, as if Mr. Joyce had greatly enjoyed doing all this despite the torture of the sixteen years' labour that it took. Yet pleasure never altogether reaches to the reader; he is faced with an acute bewilderment from the beginning, to the end, which is no end.

And what of the middle portion of this work of art? There is no middle either. It passes in one night, and the significance of night is upon it. It is the endless folding and unfolding of a dream. It makes its own space in which to have unlimited freedom to complicate itself. It is something alive only in its sleep, and from it comes a muttering beneath hundreds of thousands of subconscious words. The life that can leap from a page is never here, but there is another kind of energy, a fierce fluency which becomes a mockery of itself. . . .

The reader begins to reject constructively the formlessness which is all around him; he tries to find a way out, to relate to some kind of plan of his own, even one of these embedded pages. There are lingering lovely passages like flickers of gold. By following the small light they give there may be real illumination a little further on. But the light fails, and he is left to wander round and round in the maze. . . .

The author appears to be doing something which has no relation to the reader of a work of fiction; nothing coherent comes out of all these words; it is a game which only Mr. Joyce can play, for he alone knows the rules, if there are any. He will take a word and twist and turn it, and chase it up and down through every language that he knows—English, French, German, Gaelic, Latin, Greek, Dutch, Sanscrit, Esperanto. The sounds of words in infinite variety fascinate him. . . .

Detaching oneself from the book one tries to come to grips with the purpose of Mr. Joyce in writing *Finnegans Wake*, for there must have been some purpose behind all those sixteen years of labour. It can be only one of two things. It can be that he was engaged all that time on the compilation of a new and wonderful work on English, and that his notion of giving it the semblance of a form which baffles us, permits him to try out the results of his experiments with words without coming too close to the form of a dictionary of outlandish usage. He is learned and subtle in the ways of words, and he may have considered it necessary to do this service for the language, so as to release it from the clogging effects of conventional accumulation and its tyranny over mind in the construction which it has reached. Or he may have thought of taking up the duty neglected by the academicians of adjusting language generally to the new speeds of earth and air.

Thus, we may be face to face in *Finnegans Wake* with one of the great milestones of literature, and in this book a new language may have been born. If so, it will be necessary to learn it for ourselves without assistance, because to ask Mr. Joyce for a key to it would be to ask him to surrender all claims for *Finnegans Wake* to be considered a work of art. As such, this is its chosen expression. We may come to learn the language only by first realising what the book is about. And that is where Mr. Joyce has the advantage over the reader. . . .

The extent to which *Finnegans Wake* may begin to influence the English language will be the measure of its reality and the only proper test of its importance. The writer may come to it to dig for words amidst the ruins of the novel, but the form of *Ulysses* and the content of it which could be imitated are not here. This book could be imitated only by Mr. Joyce himself. It may appear, therefore, in the ultimate view, that, although after *Ulysses* he had no more to say, in *Finnegans Wake* he went on saying it. . . .

311. Harry Levin, review, *New Directions*

1939

'On First Looking into *Finnegans Wake*', *New Directions in Prose and Poetry* (1939), pp. 253–87.

This long article and the substance of a review of *Finnegans Wake* ['New Irish Stew,' *Kenyon Review*, i (Autumn 1939), 460–5] were modified and absorbed into Mr. Levin's *James Joyce: A Critical Introduction* (1941; revised and augmented edition, 1960) (see the Introduction, p. 28).

When we have mastered this book, we shall have found the answer to a question that T. S. Eliot and I. A. Richards have been asking each other for a good many years—the question of how far the special out-look and peculiar conditioning of an author need be shared by his readers. . . .

No Catholic reader . . . could appreciate Joyce; but there remains an additional doubt as to whether Joyce could be appreciated by a reader who is not a Catholic. We are left to choose, then, between failing to appreciate him altogether—an alternative which is now more widely and less seriously embraced than ever before—or understanding the most hypocritical suspension of disbelief that patient readers have ever been called upon to make. If we would enter here, we must abandon all hope of participating in the writer's experience or accepting his views. We must face, in the cold consolation of Mr. Richards' terminology, a veritable encyclopedia of pseudo-statements. We must remember, for the mild encouragement we may derive from Mr. Eliot's admission, that it is possible to appreciate Dante's language before understanding it.

For it is obvious that 'that ideal reader suffering from an ideal on-somnia' (120) to whom *Finnegans Wake* is addressed exists all too ex-clusively in Joyce's mind. He is either Joyce or nobody. Upon that nightmare—to which the reader, the writer, and the book are consub-stantial—you and I are merely intruders. How shall we justify our intrusion? Let us cold-bloodedly concede that this one book is of, by, and for its author alone. The only person for whom all the nuances click, for whom all the implications unravel, for whom the ultra-violet allusions shine brightly, is Joyce. But if this fact deprives us of an expectation, it also relieves us of a responsibility. If we cannot plumb the most absolute depths of the book,—and one of Joyce's clearest intentions was evidently to produce a work so rich and recessive that it could never be completely fathomed—we can take greater pleasure in its surfaces. If it withholds its darkest mysteries from everyone but its author, it is lavish with small rewards, unexpected confidences, and delightful souvenirs, which it scatters among the most casual passers-by. In spite of its proclaimed privacy, there is something for everybody in *Finnegans Wake*. It is, in Joyce's apt coinage, a *funferal*.

Both the philistine exasperation and the intellectual snobbery which have combined to envelop Joyce's reputation are based upon the same assumption—the assumption that Joyce is for better or worse a man with a message, a message which he has taken coyly diabolical pains to conceal. The critical issue is usually fought over the question of whether or not this message is ultimately worth the arduous process of decoding. It does not seem to have occurred to many of his admirers or detractors that this very process, viewed in another light, is the most enlivening and characteristic feature of his art. The substance of what Joyce has to communicate is easily reduced to a few stock attitudes and recognizable postures. It is his technique of communication which is really worthy of the prolonged attention it demands. Once this is realized, his style is no longer a succession of encrustations, but the very heart of the matter. And the process of reading Joyce is no longer a pedestrian business of cutting through to his meaning, but precisely the kind of effort which any good poem involves. It is still a 'game' or 'exercise' if you like, but so are many of the monuments of civilization.

It is a game, I am convinced, which any reader can play, although his inclination to do so will naturally vary with the amount of time and effort he finds it necessary to spend. At the outset, this expenditure appears vast enough to justify the laborsaving devices of exegesis which no doubt are now being laboriously accumulated. But such devices must virtually defeat their own ends, when Stuart Gilbert needs ten pages to furnish a purely verbal gloss for less than two pages of Joyce's text [in *Our Exagmination*]. Joyce is no friend to commentators; perhaps he recognizes that they have not done him the most friendly services. In one of the startlingly candid asides which he is continually addressing to the reader, he actually warns them off his premises: 'I don't want yous to be billowfighting . . . over me . . . wearing out your ohs by sitting around your ahs. . .' (453). Sometimes Joyce is so explicit and confidential a cicerone that the aid of an interpreter seems officious. 'Wipe your glosses with what you know' (304) is his genial advice.

Where there is so much to be seen, different witnesses will report different things. These notes of mine are offered not as a commentary or prolegomenon or even an adequate review, but simply as a tentative and unauthorized account of a first reading of *Finnegans Wake*. The only first-hand account of which I am already aware is that of Edmund Wilson, and it will be seen that my observations supplement his in some respects and complement them in others, although the emphasis differs considerably. Many such accounts, I trust, will be set down, published, and discussed, before we secure an authoritative interpretation of the book. If this one serves any purpose, it is for you to check against your own experience of the book, for verification or disproof.

The greatest obstacles to our understanding of *Finnegans Wake* are located not so much in our naivety and lack of special equipment as in the critical misconceptions we have artificially set up. To begin with, we approach the book from the wrong direction. Without pretending to rival Joyce's linguistic gifts or match his eccentric learning, those of us who have the curiosity to read him usually have enough in the way of languages and lore to limp along after him down those particular bypaths—what he perhaps would call 'a smetterling of entymology' (417). What he also takes for granted, and what we lack totally, is a thorough grounding in Irish life, in the streets and monuments, the sounds and smells, the pubs and stews of Dublin. Thus we completely miss the solid core of humanity at the basis of Joyce's work, and occasionally manage—by way of slight compensation—to catch hold of the fragments of his fantasy as they ramify outward. From our oblique point of view, what should be familiar seems utterly recondite and what should be recondite seems vaguely familiar. It is hard to imagine a situation better calculated to distort any critical realization of an author's intentions.

Beyond this initial distortion, the mere fact that we catch our first glimpses of the work through the dark glass of commentary is bound to foster a number of misleading expectations. Concretely, there are at least three misconceptions that threaten to shape our total impression of *Finnegans Wake*. The first of these is that, while not differing greatly in kind from the books we are accustomed to read, it happens to have been written in a rather queer language, and must therefore undergo the process of translation to which all foreign books—including the Scandinavian—are regularly subjected. The various studies of *Ulysses*, helpful as several of them have been, have encouraged the notion that Joyce had a 'story' to tell which was detachable, and which lost little by being summarized for the convenience of the busy reader. . . .

A second, and related, fallacy is that *Finnegans Wake* is a novel. Herein is the real reason for putting critical emphasis on the 'story' and brusquely attempting to extract a quintessential content from the morass of form in which it lies embedded. Our reading habits are so purely the product of a naturalistic tradition that our main concern is still with the literal subject-matter of a work, and not with its techniques of presentation and patterns of symbolism. . . . All the motley phantasmagoria of *Finnegans Wake* emanate, as we shall see, from a literal situation; but that situation is so slight, and Joyce's elaboration is so imaginative, that the reader who looks for a psychological novel may well feel that his efforts have been frustrated. That is, if his literary horizon is so bounded by the naturalistic tradition that poetry and humor are to him a matter of effort.·

Poetry and humor help us to overcome the third obstacle to the understanding of *Finnegans Wake*—a feeling, again definitely rooted in the background of Joyce's early writing, that it is a morbid, brooding, solemn book. Nothing could be farther from the actuality. Hard as it is to imagine a middle-aged Stephen Dedalus, the inescapable truth is that Joyce has entered upon a later period, a period of serene garrulity. The religious and domestic struggles so sensitively registered in *Portrait of the Artist* and *Ulysses* have been resolved; a measure of material security has been provided; more or less appreciated, more or less isolated, Joyce has had seventeen years of untrammelled freedom to cultivate his talent. . . .

The appropriate mood for reading *Finnegans Wake* is that elicited by the five books of Rabelais, or—to come nearer home with an Anglo-Irish parallel—*Tristram Shandy*. . . .

But, from first to last, it is the other great prose master of Dublin who has left his mark on every page of Joyce's book. The figure of Swift continues, in Joyce's mythology, to oscillate between the 'sosie sesthers' (3), Stella and Vanessa. The unmistakable voice of Swift breaks in when we least expect it (144), nagging Esther Johnson in as high a key as Yeats' *Words upon the Window-pane*. Her pet-name ('Ppt') is a constant interjection. The very cry of the whippoorwill is transposed to 'Moor Park' (359, 433, 449), the estate of Sir William Temple where

Swift suffered his early humiliations. Joyce's own spokesman, Shem, is clearly to be identified with Swift; at one point he is even called 'Mr O'Shem the Draper' (421). But Swift is more than a character in Joyce's book; he is a precedent for it. That is not as far-fetched as it sounds, when we recall the puns, jingles, and parodies that interlard Swift's occasional writing, the conscientiously recorded *clichés* of *Polite Conversation*, the 'little language' of the *Journal to Stella*, or the letters to Dr. Sheridan that look like English and turn out to be Latin.

Beyond their mutual fascination with language, beyond such masquerades and mystifications, Joyce and Swift have in common a controlled style and an uncontrollable imagination, a disposition to take trifles seriously and to trifle with serious things. More intimately, they seem to possess the same sharp eye for incongruities, the same sensitive ear for dissonances, the same delicate nose for ordures; the same dehumanized rigor in pursuing a point; the same unabashed familiarity in confiding details; the same strange blend of misanthropic sentimentality and humanitarian detachment. . . .

A Neapolitan contemporary of Swift's, and one who ultimately shared with him the doom of senile decay, is the other presiding figure over Joyce's work, 'the producer . . . Mr. John Baptister Vickar' (255), otherwise known as the philosopher Giambattista Vico. His *Scienza Nuova* was an ambitious and obscure treatise, combining a rather tame philosophical eclecticism with an exceptionally keen historical insight. For the first hundred years of its existence it was almost totally ignored. During the past century it has undergone an amazing series of posthumous adventures, at the successive hands of Michelet, Croce, and now Joyce. A philosophy which has room for such bed-fellows could only occupy a strategically placed half-way house between the mystical and the empiric, the traditional and the modern. . .

There is some significance, moreover, in Joyce's philosophical inclinations. These, while hovering somewhere near the outskirts of the Catholic tradition, definitely lean in the anti-scholastic direction. . . .

The feature of Bruno's system which seems to lend itself most readily to literary treatment is his doctrine of the reconciliation of antitheses, within the framework of an all-inclusive, perpetually, unfolding universe. Joyce himself furnishes a slightly intoxicated explanation of this doctrine (488), and it would seem to be the reason for the continual dichotomizing to which he subjects his characters. . . .

Joyce's relations with Vico are more explicit. The strongest link between them is the mythological fabric from which *Ulysses* is constructed. . . . In his twofold preoccupation with myth and language, then, as well as in his grandiose efforts to reformulate rhetoric as social science and to concentrate history into symbolic form, Vico paves the way for Joyce. And, in one sense at least, *Finnegans Wake* not only fulfills Vico's specifications, but actually confirms his theories.

This least questionable of Vico's theories can be stated in three words—'history repeats itself.' It is, in Joyce's phrase, 'a theory none too rectiline of the evoluation of human society and a testament of the rocks from all the dead unto some the living' (73). The actual pattern of the repetition Vico has worked out, and Joyce has followed with more symmetry than precision. . . .

On the basis of a very casual acquaintance with Vico, the extent to which Joyce follows him is not easy to determine. A few haphazard soundings—the use Joyce makes of the Viconian catchphrase, *pia et pura bella* (178, 610), or the frequent appearance of such legalistic themes as Moses or the Twelve Tables—indicate that one would have to be as deeply versed in the *Scienza Nuova* as Joyce is, in order to explore the question profitably. Meanwhile, it is clear enough, that Joyce adheres to the broad outlines of Vico's pattern. . . .

[Mr. Levin next discusses the relationship of Vico's phases of Civilization and the four sections of *Finnegans Wake*]

Before we can even start to read *Finnegans Wake*, we are confronted with a striking instance of the literal-minded ingenuity with which Viconian precept has been translated into Joycean practice. The book opens in the middle of things—in the middle of a sentence, as a matter of fact. For the beginning of that sentence we must turn to the end of the book. The final passage—if anything here can be called final—is a continuously flowing, eternally feminine soliloquy, not unlike the concluding chapter of *Ulysses*. But this time an even more elemental female than Molly Bloom is speaking; it is Anna Livia Plurabelle, the voice of the River Liffey, as she winds along her tortuous course from the nearby Wicklow mountains toward Dublin Bay, and finally rushes forth into the arms of her father, the sea.

The opening sentence marks this transition from the *Ewig-Weibliche* to the masculine principle, and 'brings us by a commodius vicus of recirculation back to Howth Castle and Environs.' Thus, at the very moment of our introduction to them, Joyce has reduced his hero and heroine to their least common denominators—the great castle that dominates the harbor from its promontory at the northern arm, and the little river that wanders across the city of Dublin. The rest is a series of episodes in the protracted romance between the 'lord of the heights' and the 'lady of the valley' (501). Henceforth they are to maintain their own cycle of relationships—a tree and a stone, a cloud and a hill, a river and a city. Together, they are ultimately reducible to our first parents, Adam and Eve. They comprise the city-building resourcefulness of mankind and the vital fertility of womankind. And, since no extremes of generalization are too far-reaching for Joyce, they are also civilization and nature, space and time, death and life. . . .

[here follows a lengthy discussion of Joyce's 'symbolic archetype', Howth Castle and Environs, and Joyce's 'composite method of characterization' (pp. 265–8)]

We have so little critical equipment for dealing with a complex piece of symbolic writing, that we may be excused for borrowing the terminology of the middle ages. Dante recognized that his own writing could be interpreted at four different levels, and it may throw some light on *Finnegans Wake* to consider it in those terms. Anagogically, it envisages the whole course of history, according to Vico's conception. Allegorically, it celebrates the topography and atmosphere of the city of Dublin and its environs. Literally, it records the adventures—or rather the nightmares—of Earwicker, as he and his wife and three children lie sleeping above his pub, and alcoholic slumber rehearses the events of the day before. Morally, it combines all these strands of symbolism into a single theme, which is incidentally the theme of *Paradise Lost*, the problem of evil and original sin. Finnegan, Earwicker, Adam, Lucifer, and Humpty Dumpty are involved in the same fall, and that fall is accompanied by a detonation of Vico's thunder.

Joyce pursues his theme farther than Milton in one important respect. His philosophical allegiances forbid him to think of a fall, except in terms of a subsequent rise (4)—whether it be conceived as historical renascence, theological salvation, or simply waking in the morning. . . .

Much of the material of the book is bound to remain speculative, until we chance upon the exact item of information that renders it concrete. Relationships are often clearer than significances, and many themes that are hard to identify are easy to recognize. For example, the four walls, the four provinces, the four directions form a chorus of old men—Matthew, Mark, Luke, and John. But this quartet frequently merges into a collective entity, the 'Mamalujo,' which in turn attaches itself to various personalities. 'Mamaluja,' which means 'mother-puddle' in Russian, definitely designates Joyce's heroine; elsewhere, when the old men are associated with Shaun, they bear the honorary titles of 'Shanator' (475). These, to be sure, are the most incidental details. Merely to keep a record of such minor correspondences and transmutations would require, in both reader and writer, 'a meticulosity bordering on the insane' (173).

Happily for both, there is no need for such a catalogue. Joyce's range of connotation is so heterogeneous, and his powers of invention are so resourceful, that they produce an effect of infinite variety. Yet, whenever we are in a position to scrutinize the variety, we notice that it is controlled by a few recurrent themes and a number of characteristic devices. Its myriads of minute particulars make up a handful of broad generalizations. The requirement for appreciating the book—it should be unnecessary to affirm—is not omniscience; it is an awareness of Joyce's rather limited preoccupations and an interest in his rather special technique. At this stage of exploration, a compass will be more useful than a chart. There is still a vast amount of exploring to be done before the tourists begin to arrive.

One of the peculiarities of Joyce's writing, which has been developing since *Ulysses*, is that you can scarcely understand a single page without knowing the rest of the book. The natural result of this tendency is the circular form of *Finnegans Wake*. . . .

With a few essential *Leitmotifs* in mind, and a nodding acquaintance with the philosophical pattern and imaginative situation of the book, the reader has no excuse for delaying further. It may be of some use to him, since the volume does not include a table of contents, to take his bearings from an informal series of page indications. He will observe, for what it is worth, that three of Joyce's sections are subdivided into unnumbered chapters. The first section contains eight chapters, the second and third contain four apiece, and the final section is not divided. . . .

[Mr. Levin here summarizes the book chapter by chapter (pp. 274-7)]

If anything is clear from this fragmentary summary, it is that the reader must expect digression instead of narration. The broad outline will be always before him and the crowded texture will be full of interesting details. But in the middle distance, ordinarily the center of the reader's interest, the action will be shadowy and capricious. . . . The real source of continuity, the only logical means of control, in 'this nonday diary' this allnights newseryreel' (489) is the flow of the language. Once we have conceded this, we have granted words a new importance. We realize that for Joyce they are matter, not manner. We begin to detach them and re-examine their syntactic, phonetic, and referential values.

The analogy with music is misleading, because it usually implies a limitation, not an expansion, of our means of expression. . . . Having laid down such vast reserves of potential association, he can easily and adroitly pun his way through 628 pages. The dream convention has given him license—along with a fluid imagery and a mercurial tone—for a systematic distortion of language. Psychoanalytic theory has invested these deliberate slips of the tongue with a special significance. Under cover of this drowsy indistinctness and these subconscious lapses, he has developed a diction that is actually alert and pointed, that bristles with virtuosity and will stoop to any kind of verbal trick. What are the ingredients of Joyce's 'mess of mottage' (183)? Some are auditory devices—rhyme, alliteration, assonance, onomatopoeia, spoonerisms. Others are largely typographical—acrostics, anagrams, games in which you go through a sequence of words by changing a letter at a time (142). Still others, less purely formal, weave groups of names into narrative—one still comes across examples of this *genre* in school magazines. . . .

Joyce's puns are more properly 'portmanteau-words,' for the component ambiguities have equal status and seldom coalesce entirely. Individually, they often contribute no more than the dream-like atmosphere of the *Silly Symphony;* 'Potapheu's wife' (193) merely lends a touch of domestic warmth to an otherwise chilling story. But the adjective 'lidylac' (461), for curtains, hits off just the proper lavender-and-old-lace nuance. . . .

'Portmanteau-words' and *double-entendres* are conveniently limited to two compartments; heavier luggage and longer phrases bring unlimited complications. Joyce's mastery of the various moods of discourse is like the talent of certain comedians for carrying on a perfectly convincing conversation in gibberish; only Joyce's 'double-talk' is not gibberish, but a serious discussion about something else. His accomplishment is necessarily based upon a secure command of the phraseology and intonation of popular speech. . . .

Usually, while the rhythmic structure is carrying you one way, the verbal complications are pulling you in another direction. You take the key, as it were, from the underlying sounds; but sudden substitutions and new associations are capable of changing it at any point; and it requires a conscientious ear to analyse the ensuing chords. . . . Far from conducting a campaign to disintegrate language, Joyce is willing to accept every word at its semantic value. Far from breaking down the norms of communication, Joyce's experiments—though many of them have not advanced beyond the laboratory stage—reveal possibilities of unlooked-for subtlety and almost microscopic precision.

But his habit of hinging the critical point of an episode upon a single elusive reference will raise more serious doubts. . . .

Naturally enough, *Finnegans Wake* has been greeted as a nocturnal sequel to *Ulysses.* Actually, Earwicker's stream-of-unconsciousness carries us so much farther than Bloom's stream-of-consciousness that we are beginning to get some notion of Joyce's ultimate destination. . . . There is still a recessive element of naturalism in *Finnegans Wake;* the Adam *motif* can be traced back to the style of the mantelpiece in Earwicker's bedroom, and Michael and Satan—or, for that matter, the heroes of Sebastopol—step out of a picture on the wall (559). Nonetheless, a novelist who takes such pains to plant his properties, and to establish coincidences, is a symbolist at heart.

That realism leads through impressionism to abstraction is one of the lessons that painting has taught literature. *Finnegans Wake* resembles one of those *collages* where bits of old newspapers are rather carelessly cut out and very ingeniously worked into the design. . . .

We may be applying the wrong critical category, when we try to measure Joyce by novelists and dramatists who were accomplished observers of human behavior. His resources of observation are largely auditory; apart from his incomparable ear, his range is not overwhelmingly broad. The personal qualities of his writing—from his earliest self-portraits to *Finnegans Wake*—are introspection, speculation, and an almost hyperesthetic capacity for rendering sensations. These are the attributes we look for primarily in poets. And his successes are the achievements of a poet—in arranging a verbal harmonics and touching off emotional responses. As a novelist he is, though not a failure, perhaps a bankrupt. He can no longer narrate; he can only elaborate. In a book compounded of so many of the stories that have continued to fascinate mankind, he has no story to tell. He merely effects a poignant kind of cross-reference.

Instead of telling a story, he assumes a situation. In spite of Stephen's demiurgic pretensions, in spite of Joyce's predilection for playing God, it would be less accurate to say of him than of most novelists that 'he creates a world of his own.' This is no disparagement of what he actually has created, but an effort to be specific about his achievements as an artist. These depend—to the vast extent of his awareness—upon an unqualified acceptance of the existing world. The play of allusions requires that everything be in its place. Echoes can only reproduce sounds. All his material is given, all his values are taken for granted, all his methods are deductive. . . . Joyce's art, at all events, is sculptural; his book, like his description of the Vatican, is 'chalkfull of master-plasters' (152). . . . But the final irony is, that, despite its fluid prose, it remains a static book. In retrospect, the warm flux resolves into something cold and stationary. The Ondt seems fated to triumph over the Gracehoper.

Among the acknowledged masters of English—and there can be no further delay in acknowledging that Joyce is among the greatest—there is no one with so much to express and so little to say. Whatever is capable of being sounded or enunciated will find its echo in Joyce's writing; he alludes glibly and impartially to such concerns as left-wing literature (116), Whitman and democracy (263), the 'braintrust' (529), 'Nazi' (375), 'Gestapo' (332), 'Soviet' (414), and the sickle and the hammer (341). The sounds are heard, the names are called, the phrases are invoked; but the rest is silence. The detachment which can look upon the conflicts of civilization as so many competing vocables is wonderful and terrifying. Sooner or later, however, it gives a prejudiced reader the uncanny sensation of trying to carry on a conversation with an omniscient parrot. *Quis expedivit psittaco suum* Χαιρε? Of an earlier effort to revive the spirit of Finn MacCool, of the Ossianic poems of James Macpherson, human prejudice spoke with Dr. Johnson: 'Sir, a man might write such stuff for ever, if he would *abandon* his mind to it.'

312. William Troy, review, *Partisan Review*

1939

'Notes on *Finnegans Wake*', *Partisan Review*, vi (Summer 1939), 97–110. Also appeared in *James Joyce: Two Decades of Criticism* (1948, 1963), ed. Seon Givens, pp. 302–18, and in *William Troy: Selected Essays* (1961), ed. Stanley Edgar Hyman, pp. 94–109.

Nothing could be less profitable than any attempt to offer a definite analysis or evaluation of the Joyce work at the moment. It is true that sections of it have been available for fourteen years; we have had time to become accustomed to its difficult language and technique; and there have been a number of tentative exercises in exegesis and interpretation. (The best of these are still those to be found in the symposium issued by Shakespeare and Company in Paris ten years ago and recently re-published in this country.[1]) But the work in its entirety has been off the presses only a few weeks; it is over six hundred pages long; and it is written in an idiom that can very easily create that state of panic which the mind experiences when, to recall a phrase of Proust's, it feels itself passing beyond its own borders. This last statement is not intended to be derogatory. It means simply that the impact of the book is such as to cause an extraordinary strain on the normal equilibrium of our faculties of response. It is not altogether a joke when Joyce refers to his '*funferal*' as designed for 'that ideal reader suffering from an ideal insomnia'. And since few of us can answer to the requirement we must follow the admonition to patience offered elsewhere in the text. What we must try to avoid are the facile and premature judgments that attended the publication of *Ulysses*, realizing that in the seventeen years that have elapsed since that event no single adequate interpretation of the central symbolism of the book has been written. Interpretation must precede evaluation; and, for several reasons that will become evident, the problems of interpretation in *Finnegans Wake* are beyond those presented by any modern work. If we have enough confidence in the task

---

[1] *Our Exagmination.*

on the basis of Joyce's other performances and of those sections of the present work that we have already learned to appreciate, we will be content to proceed for some time by what Yeats somewhere calls 'little sedentary stitches'.

The first and most obvious of the problems is, of course, that of communication. Here the most simple-minded explanation that can be offered is that Joyce is reducing language to 'pure music'. It is undoubtedly·true that the musical effectiveness of the style is quite overwhelming; there is nothing like it in contemporary writing. . . . 'Latin me that, my trinity scholard, out of eure sanscreed into oure eryan'. This is a line capable of being analysed as a quite acceptable example of the rare dactylic octometer—with a cæsura after 'scholard'. More often than not, Joyce begins with a regular metrical beat only to drop it suddenly for an effect of surprise: 'Drop me the/ sound of the/ findhorn's/ name, Mtu or Mti, sombogger was wisness'. The first two feet are perfect dactyls, the third a spondee, and then the line seems to dissolve into prose. The predominant foot throughout the work, however, is the more lilting, caressing anapest because of its closer correspondence to theme and subject. . . .

But this is still not to give justification to the charge that Joyce has reduced language to pure sound, which is to betray an unawareness of the functional interrelationship that always exists between sound and meaning in poetry. . . .

[the critic discusses the interrelationship between sound in meaning in music and in poetry]

In the extraordinary richness and variety of musical effect in his writing, therefore, Joyce is simply pushing to a high degree of development qualities that we find in all authentic poetry. And the same can be said of his manipulation of the content-meanings of words. Here the principal point to be made is that the poet does not use words for their past history alone. . . .

Is such a use of language what we usually describe as punning? Several of Joyce's reviewers have been content to leave the matter at that. But there are obviously puns and puns; we say that some are pointless, some make sense. Undoubtedly, Joyce allows a certain number of the pointless variety to creep into his book—if for no other reason than that pointlessness is one of the inherent capacities of the human mind. . . .

Is it possible that Joyce intends not only every word but the book itself to be an example of synecdoche? Let us look for what clues we may discover in the title. . . .

[the critic discusses Joyce's use of a part for the whole]

According to Vico, each of the three successive ages of history had its appropriate mode of communication: in the Theocratic period, it was the Hieroglyphic; in the Heroic, the Metaphorical; and in the Civilized, the Abstract. . . . Modern language, insofar as it is set down in print, is pictorial; and part of our response to the meaning of a word is our sense of its visual image. To this extent it also is hieroglyphic.

The point is worth making because Vico believed that in the period of 'the barbarism of reflection' that marked the final stage in the historical cycle language returned once again to the hieroglyphic . . . Since Joyce includes uproarious parodies of the first (the whole second episode of Part II) and examples of the hyperbole of the second (the sixth episode of Part I) we can conclude that the style of *Finnegans Wake* is compounded of the characteristic modes of expression of all three epochs of history.

The *form* of the work is, therefore, contained in each of its parts. 'In fact, under the closed eyes of the inspectors the traits featuring the *chiaroscuro* coalesce,' we are told on page 107, 'their contrarieties eliminated, in one stable somebody . . .' The problem of interpretation is the detection and labelling of these traits—symbols, images, motifs— and the reordering of them according to some logic of the mind. And this is a problem that is rendered almost hopelessly difficult by the very nature of the narrative method that Joyce has adopted.

It is clear that the center of everything is the dreamer, H. C. Ear-wicker; but while this citizen of Dublin is an individual character, highly particularized in many respects, he is also an archetype of the race. This is to say that his dream is conducted simultaneously on the two planes of the personal and the universal; and one is by no means always able to determine the exact nature of their 'coalescence'. . . .

But the exact nature of his crime is made known to us only gradually and by the most tenuous references throughout the text. In other words, the chronological method, in which effect follows upon cause, has been abandoned for what might be called the method of *simultaneity*. And it is a consequence of this method that effects may precede causes whenever they like because all that is recorded is the order of 'events' in the consciousness.

For the origin and development of this particular method we can discover three distinct influences: Vico's theory of the flux and reflux of history, Jung's conception of the collective unconscious, and Einstein's theory of relativity.

[the critic discusses each of these three influences and their place in *Finnegans Wake*]

Is it possible that *Finnegans Wake* represents a final stage in that long process of transcedence which has characterized Joyce's work from the beginning? In *The Portrait of the Artist as a Young Man* Stephen Dedalus passes through what might be called an initiation rite to emerge as an artist dedicated to the creation of the 'uncreated conscience' of his race. But this was not an adequate transcendence, in the sense either of primitive religion or of modern psychoanalysis, in which the individual always carries over elements of the old self into the new self that is restored to the world. Stephen had left behind all the old symbols of love and authority without discovering any new ones to take their place. The identification rather is with the *idea* of the role of the artist, which is simply one of projections of what Freud calls the Super-ego. *Ulysses* records in its opening episodes the insufficiency of the program of 'silence, exile, and cunning'. And the crisis to which his new spiritual isolation has brought him is not resolved until he is put into communication with Bloom, the representative of common humanity. Through his imaginative sympathy with Bloom he is restored to the state of grace which will make freedom of creation at last possible for him. Now the main difference between *Ulysses* and the present work is that where humanity is represented in the first by a 'coalescence' of universalized traits into a single figure existing in time and space, in the second these traits are diffused through time–space and coalesce finally only in the *pattern* of history. Humanity is impressive not in its actuality but in its immanence. And this becomes something comparable to the conception of the Divine Idea of the medieval theologians—that which is capable of taking on matter but is itself infinite in time and space. . . .

What is being suggested is that Joyce in this new work, like Yeats and Mann, seeks his salvation not in any escape from the present but in a transcendence of the present through the past. And the question of his seriousness, which has bothered some people, will be solved if we consider the piety that is involved in the energetic and still uncorrupted affirmation of life that is implicit in every movement of his writing. This is the seriousness of the greatest comedy, which always keeps in recollection the tragic knowledge that is at its base.

313. A. Glendinning, review, *Nineteenth Century*

1939

Extract from 'Commentary: *Finnegans Wake*', *Nineteenth Century and After*, cxxvi (July 1939), 73–82.

Mr. James Joyce's new work, *Finnegans Wake*, has had a bad reception in the English Press, judging by the reviews I have seen. It has been attacked as meaningless, drivelling, the work of a madman, 'a colossal leg-pull,' and so on; even his most sympathetic critic has described Mr. Joyce as 'a writer without a theme,' This is the more curious since, during the past sixteen years, most of the work has already appeared in serial form, and has been accompanied by a great deal of comment and explanation. In the circumstances, perhaps no apology is needed for drawing attention to what is already known about this extraordinary book. . . .

[discusses the Viconian structure, manipulations of language, purpose and technique, and method, pp. 73–78]

The obscurities of *Finnegans Wake* are partly due to its enormous range. No single reader could possibly recognise all the implications which have been worked into it. To grasp even the greater part of them his knowledge would have to include mythology in general, Irish history, papal history, the religious significance of numbers and colours, Dublin street-names, the Book of the Dead, the philosophies of Bruno and Vico, the careers of Swift, Duke Humphrey, Fin MacCool and Mr. Joyce, the names of most of the rivers and cities of the world, some fifty languages, and a great deal more.

That much of *Finnegans Wake* survives these difficulties is a tribute to Mr. Joyce's incomparable mastery of speech, of the evocative powers of words. In the first section there is a dialogue between two primitive men, Mutt and Jute, whose names relate them, characteristically, to the simple humours of the comic strip. . . .

[quotes from p. 16]

. . . There are implications in this dialogue which are beyond me, but though bits of foreign words and parodies of modern advertisements are worked into it, its whole texture never fails to suggest the primitive awkwardness of a social encounter in the Stone Age, the struggling, thick speech of two simple-minded giants to whom speech is a difficulty. The elements of the situation are physically present in the language, apart from its remoter implications.

The book is to be judged by the success with which this communication of essential qualities is maintained, and it must be said that in many places the communication breaks down. . . . Mr. Joyce is entitled to the benefit of a good many doubts till we have had time to become familiar with his completed work. Meanwhile, though there is much in it that is difficult, there is also a great deal that can be enjoyed. One has not to consult a reference book to appreciate the simpler humours of its constructions, such as its own account of itself in terms of food: 'once current puns, quashed quotatoes, messes of mottage', or its reference to psychoanalysis in the phrase 'jung and easily freudened.' Jaun's sermon is no more difficult than anything in Rabelais, and invites the comparison on any level. The fairy-tale imagery and streaming melodies of the Anna Livia section are accessible to anyone who can enjoy Hans Andersen and has an ear for music. Consider Anna in this passage, as she prepares to visit 'her furzeborn sons and dribblederry daughters':. . .

[quotes from pp. 207–8]

It is too soon to attempt a comprehensive judgment of *Finnegans Wake;* but it is clear that Mr. Joyce has created in it a medium which, in Mr. Eliot's words, is able 'to digest and express new objects, new groups of objects, new feelings, new aspects.' He has succeeded in restoring to language much of the vitality it has lost in this age of potboilers and newspapers; he has brought within its range states of feeling which have hitherto been inaccessible. . . .

One can allow many of the criticisms that have been made of this book: that it is pedantic, showy, unnecessarily obscure, and so on; and can still say that it has extended the tradition of literature. . . .

314. Review, *Dublin Magazine*

1939

Extract from A.C., Book Review in *Dublin Magazine* (July–
September 1939), 71–4.

The publication of this enormous work must, at least, satisfy curiosity
and speculation. . . . A few years ago a number of Mr. Joyce's disciples
and admirers published a symposium on the book entitled 'Our
Exagmination round his Factification for Incamination of Work in
Progress.' Mr. Joyce's experiments in word mutation became an
immediate influence.

The basis of Mr. James Joyce's new speech is the vernacular, and that
is the primary weakness of his choice. For when the contemporary cult
of the vernacular has passed, a multitude of books, including his own,
must suffer from the reaction. . . . The Dublin vernacular of *Ulysses*
had at least this advantage. It was, in the main, the traditional speech of a
good number of generations, the speech authenticated by country
idioms that came in with the hay carts. In his new work Mr. Joyce has
extended his range, a range symbolised by the introduction of Mutt,
Jeff, and other characters bound for oblivion. The intentions of *Ulysses*,
though at first puzzling, are now tolerably clear even to the general
reader. Into the events of a single day Mr. Joyce compressed the
idiomatic come-day go-day existence of Dublin. The intentions of
Finnegan's Wake also are tolerably clear. At any rate, one can grasp the
formula when one has dipped into half a dozen pages. Taking Dublin
once more as his milieu, he has endeavoured to symbolise the workings
of the nocturnal dream-mind. The history of Dublin from the earliest
Scandinavian settlements appears before us and at the same time this
city is all cities which man has built. So, too, the vague, shadowy or
grotesque characters which come and go are symbolic types, H.C.
Earwicker, Here Comes Everybody, Adam, Eve, Napoleon, and needless to say, the incomparable Anna Livia herself. The formula by which
Mr. Joyce achieves simultaneity and apparent universality of interest is

extremely simple in its origins, though difficult in its achievement. Most of those who have read the fragment 'Anna Livia Plurabelle' will remember that Mr. Joyce packed this onomatopoeic description of the river flowing towards the sea with the names of a hundred other rivers, hiding these names obscurely at times, suggesting them by double meaning or by the distortion of words. The same formula is employed throughout the book: for instance, in the lengthy epilogue in which we return once more to the Liffey flowing at dawn into Dublin Bay. This section begins with an invocation of the dawn-gods drawn from all mythology, Egyptian, Classic, Norse, Gaelic.

The actual synthetic language in which the book is written is, no doubt, an attempt to represent the sub-conscious, inarticulate depth of the mind in which it may be supposed the very roots of language can be found. Here again, however, the formula is simple in conception. Mr. Joyce does not appear to have any particular knowledge of comparative philology and, if we are right in judging by the work itself, his knowledge of German, French, Italian, Norwegian and Old English amounts to little more than a smattering. . . . His purpose has been to represent the confusion and apparent formlessness, I say apparent, of the dreamworld: and at the same time, to form for himself a medium thicker than ordinary English.

It is significant that during the last ten years or so all critics have chosen one passage as an example of Mr. Joyce's method. They have been helped, no doubt, by the gramaphone record which Mr. Joyce himself made and by the fact that the passage appears conveniently at the end of a section.

[quotes from pp. 215–16]

. . . The passage shows that Mr. Joyce is writing, as all good poets do, for the ear. It is romantic and, therefore, popular. And if one examines it, one finds that its romanticism is not particularly original. Even its wavering Celtic Twilight rhythm is a mere echo of what poets have done with more subtlety. . . .

Disassociation of ideas and the choice of the irrelevant rather than the relevant phrase have become so general as a mode that one can almost get into the state of mind in which meaning is not everything. Unfortunately, however, Mr. Joyce's new language seems to demand complete understanding. At a first glance he appears merely to present us with disassociation of ideas. Actually the formula upon which this language is based depends on a knowledge of what he means. The f~~~

ula is based on the pun, malapropism, and the deliberate distortion of words to secure double meaning. A pun must be shared to be enjoyed and every second word in this book is a pun. A first practical difficulty of course is that many of these puns depend on a detailed local knowledge of Dublin places and place names. . . . However, for the half dozen puns and spoonerisms which can be understood, there are hundreds to which we have no immediate clue. Here, however, is a fairly clear passage which indicates Mr. Joyce's punning and word-play:

[quotes from p. 17]

. . . It is unfortunate Mr. Joyce has not thought it worth his while to acquire even a smattering of Irish. The odd Irish words which he uses are rendered in the debased spelling of the Lover-Lever school. And he does not even apparently know the correct name of the Celtic sungod. Anyone can detect this stage-Irish undertone and one suspects that Mr. Joyce has gone merely to debased conventions of late Victorian times, the music halls and the ditties of Charing Cross Road. He has undone the work of the Irish literary revival and given us something as monstrous and ugly as the later-day Abbey brogue.

Assuming, therefore, that Mr. Joyce's language is meant to be understood, his book presents an insoluble problem to the reviewer. Calculating that two pages, by careful study, could be mastered in a single day, the entire book, which runs to more than six hundred pages, would take about a year to read in its entirety. . . . It is possible that many of Mr. Joyce's disciples may be secretly disappointed in the fact that this *chef d'oeuvre* is in effect and enjoyment a completely 'low-brow' work, showing a decidedly limited sense of humour and gigantic mainly in its trivialities, painstaking and industrious concentration on a very minor faculty of the conscious mind. But in the compiling of glossaries, commentaries, exegetical guides and fashioning of theories, the ardent among them may find something to do. . . .

315. Salvatore Rosati, review, *Nuova Antologia*

November 1939, ccccvi, 102-4

. . . *Finnegans Wake* takes a step forward. Just as *Ulysses* is a day in a man's life, the new book is a night. The rational control of the waking state, the circumstances of everyday life, are suspended during sleep; the subconscious has no values except those in the psyche itself, psyche in the psychoanalytical sense, that is, the Freudian censor. In such freedom, the flowing of the consciousness can expand and deepen until it touches the earliest roots of the mental life which are common to all humanity. Mr. Bloom was still a man; in *Finnegans Wake* there is to be sure a man (a vulgar man), and it seems to me, the ironic side of the book is extended to this very insistence upon individuality in such an unassuming form; but with him man in a universal sense is always present, more according to an historical universality than a philosophical universality. This seems to be confirmed by a fact which presents itself at first glance as an unlikelihood: if it could be understood, at best up to a certain point, that Mr. Bloom's Brain was so fertile in subtle associations and in scholarly memories, it would be far less easy to admit, without that universality of which we were speaking, such an historical memory, albeit unconscious, and such a faculty for transference, as those of which Finnegan gives proof, Finnegan who is no more than an inn-keeper.

All this is given in the book only slightly in the form of symbols; the universal value which they assume makes of the actions and the characters almost as many archetypes, obscured in a kind of musical rarification. Thus, the last section of the first part, the one which concerns the river Liffey and which is among the most beautiful pages of the book, has not so much a local reference to Dublin, as it figures forth the myth of the process of civilization on river banks.

[a discussion follows here of Vico's three cycles of history and their influence upon the structure of *Finnegans Wake*]

. . . But besides giving to a word a more pregnant meaning with such fusions and mixtures and new coinings, Joyce also wanted to obtain a particular musicality. An example from the many possible ones is the word 'manorwombanborn.' I believe it can be explained thus: to the word 'man' there is joined 'or,' because 'manor' means 'manor' or 'castle,' the principle of the male, stable, strong and turreted; a 'b' is added to the succeeding word 'woman' because 'womb' means 'womb'; thus the big-word means a being born both of the male principle and the womb of the woman, that is man in a universal sense. And let it pass when it is a question of these word-combinations; it is often very difficult to guess the meaning of pointed words which are entirely new or are derived from little-known languages.

Apart from the fact that a language formed in this way, and the absence of any reference to help a reader, generates sometimes an insurmountable obstacle, it must be noted that this newly elaborated prose of the book avails itself of all possible resources: assonance, alliteration, rhythm, so that no novel words, both old and new, seem to lose all meaning while retaining a musical value. Throughout the book, even the more intelligible and beautiful pages, suggestive signification is entrusted far more to the phonetic element than to the visual.

This contrast would be enough to exclude the simple strangeness. We have already said that Joyce is a good linguist. Anyone who has before him the very normal prose of his first books, notably *The Portrait of the Artist as a Young Man*, knows that many pages of Joyce, in so far as their writing is concerned, are among the most beautiful of modern English prose. Therefore the writer's abilities and understanding are beyond discussion. All that can be observed, at least, is that the words most laden with suggestiveness are the most habitual and that Joyce's method goes astray because of an excess of psychology. But even this is a matter of discussion especially if we reflect that the scale to which he is applied renders the undertaking new, notwithstanding the precedents. Moreover, it cannot be denied that Joyce has completed in language a new working [work, *lavoro*] of which it is not difficult to see that the influence even beyond the imitations, which there are, of certain of the most noteworthy aspects of his innovations (on Gertrude Stein and others).

Given the very long period of gestation of *Finnegans Wake*, we do not know if Joyce is about to give us other works, nor do we here feel like pronouncing up to this time a judgment upon all of his literary activity. We would only like to observe that in few instances has the intellectual, technical and scientific output of our time been assumed in an artistic function with an amalgam which may incorporate it working in as vital a way as Joyce has done. Because of this his work is to be considered an experiment which according to every probability will not be without effect. As for the rest, what he has assumed is by its very novelty and by its radical character a position which has escaped many particularistic discussions and admits only an equally radical attitude of consent or dissent.

CONTEMPORARY CRITICAL COMMENT

316. Sean O'Casey, letter to Joyce

30 May 1939

Quoted in Richard Ellmann, ed., *The Letters of James Joyce*, Vol. III, (1966), p. 442.

. . . My mind is still far away from the power of writing such a book. I wish I could say that such a power is mine. I am reading it now, and, though I meet many allusions, the book is very high over my head. A friend here (a painter) and I often read it (or try to) together; and I, it is fair to say, am better than he, and lead him into many a laugh and into the midst of wander and wonderland. It is an amazing book; and hardly to be understood in a year, much less in a day. I've had constant contact with you in *Dubliners*; in *Portrait of the Artist*, and in *Ulysses*—that great and amazing work. . . .

317. Dorothy Richardson, opinion

1939

Extract from 'Adventures for Readers', *Life and Letters Today*, xxii (July 1939), 47–9, 51–2 [45–52].

. . . Reaching *Finnegans Wake* we discover its author's signature not only across each sentence, but upon almost every word. And since, upon the greater number of its pages, nearly every other word is either wholly or partially an improvisation, the would-be reader must pay, in terms of sheer concentration, a tax far higher even than that demanded by Imagist poetry. And be he never so familiar with the author's earlier work, and in agreement with those who approve his repudiation of the orthodoxies of grammar and syntax, finding, when doubt assails, reassurance in the presence of similar effective and, doubtless, salutary heresies in the practice of the arts other than literature, the heavily-burdened reader of *Finnegans Wake*, hopefully glissading, upon the first page, down a word of a hundred letters—representing the fall that carried Finnegan to his death—into pathless verbal thickets, may presently find himself weary of struggling from thicket to thicket without a clue, weary of abstruse references that too often appear to be mere displays of erudition, weary of the mélange of languages ancient and modern, of regional and class dialects, slangs and catchwords and slogans, puns and nursery rhymes, phrases that are household words phonetically adapted to fresh intentions, usually improper, sometimes side-splitting, often merely facetious, incensed in discovering that these diverse elements, whether standing on their heads or fantastically paraphrased, apparently succeed each other as the sound of one suggests that of the next rather than by any continuity of inward meaning, and are all too frequently interspersed by spontaneous creations recalling those produced by children at a loss, bored to desperation by lack of interest and seeking relief in shouting a single word, repeating it with a change of vowel, with another change and another, striving to outdo themselves until they reach, with terrific emphasis, onomatopœia precipitating adult interference. . . .

Meanwhile the author, presumably foreseeing the breakdown of even the most faithful Joycean as likely to occur in the neighbourhood of the hundredth page, comes to the rescue in the name of Anna Livia, invoked by a parody of a well-known prayer ('Annah the Allmaziful, the everliving, Bringer of Plurabilities, haloed be her eve, her singtime sung, her rill be run, unhemmed as it is uneven'), with a chapter on the allied arts of writing and reading, here and there exceptionally, and most mercifully, explicit, preluded by a list of the hundred and sixty-three names given to Annah's 'untitled mamafesta memorializing the Mosthighest' (including *Rockabill Booby in the Wave Trough, What Jumbo made to Jalice and What Anisette to Him,* and *I am Older nor the Rogues among Whist I slips and He calls me his Dual of Ayessha*), and one day perhaps to be translated, annotated, and issued as a Critique of Pure Literature and an Introduction to the Study of James Joyce.

. . . Primarily, then, are we to *listen* to *Finnegans Wake*? Not so much to what Joyce says, as to the lovely way he says it, to the rhythms and undulating cadences of the Irish voice, with its capacity to make of every spoken word a sentence with parentheses and to arouse, in almost every English breast, a responsive emotion?

. . . Do we find it possible, having thus 'read' the whole and reached the end, a long, lyrically wailing, feminine monologue, to name the passion whose result is this tremendous effusion? Finnegan, the master-mason, and his wife Annie and their friends may symbolize life oɪ literature or what you will that occasionally call for mourning. For their creator they are food for incessant ironic laughter (possibly a screen for love and solicitude), mitigated only here and there by a touch of wistfulness that is to reach at the end a full note. Shall we remind ourselves that most of our male poets have sounded wistful? And the women? Well, there is Emily Brontë, who, by the way, would have delighted, with reservations, in *Finnegans Wake*. . . .

318. Léon Edel on *Finnegans Wake*

1939

Extract from 'James Joyce and his New Work', *University of Toronto Quarterly*, ix (October 1939), 68–81.

It seemed a little sad to many who read James Joyce's *Work in Progress* when it was appearing in *transition* that this great Irish genius should spend years fashioning an apparently exaggerated, if energetic, *jeu d'esprit*. They asked themselves why he refused to turn his pen to the world about him and concerned himself exclusively with the past. . . .

The answer is important. We are dealing, in Joyce, not with a reporter of immediate things, but with a devoted craftsman whose interest is the versatility and the universality of his *métier*. . . .

Of course he might have gone on writing other novels like *A Portrait of the Artist as a Young Man*. He might have done fifty or a hundred novels (like Mr Wells or Mr Bennett) or an endless series of plays (like Mr Shaw) in which there is constant reiteration of idea and constant revelation of the same personality. But Joyce does not seem to want to leave many pictures of his time. The process of turning out novel after novel does not excite him. He is a virtuoso who wishes to enlarge the writer's method and technique. He is a scientist in letters who likes nothing better than to rig out a new experiment. For him one book is but a sketch from which a larger canvas will grow, and each canvas is more ambitious than the last. In every sense Joyce is like a composer who essays many forms. He must write chamber music, overtures, piano compositions, and songs, but he must try his hand also at the symphony. James Joyce has so far written only one book in each form, and after more than thirty years he has published only seven books, two of them slender volumes of poetry. . . .

[a long literary history follows here, pp. 69–71]

Finnegans Wake must be read with the ear. It may not be a coincidence that Humphrey Chimpden Earwicker, the hero—if such a book can be said to have a hero—has been given that name and that Joyce substitutes forms of 'earwig' for it. . . .

[here follows a discussion of the 'plot', the Viconian structure, the language]

The book cannot be described adequately and it is too complex an organism for anyone to claim that he has penetrated to its depth and uncovered every meaning and every allusion. To understand the work sentence by sentence one would have to be able to go through the same series of mental associations in reading, as Joyce went through in composing. . . .

[compares five versions of *ALP* for changes in sound, imagery and meaning, pp. 75–8]

An understanding of *Finnegans Wake* lies in an understanding of the roles of the eye and the ear in this work. . . .

In *Finnegans Wake* Mr Joyce asks the eye to look at unfamiliar words and shapes on the printed page and expects it to communicate them to the ear. He asks the impossible. Only Mr Joyce's ear can catch all the sounds, all the beauties of his verbal fancies. The unprepared eye will invariably refuse to co-operate. Mr Joyce has put on paper a work that in reality should be heard, not read. That is why readers accustomed to having their eyes move comfortably and easily along the printed page find the book difficult. They trip and stumble. . . .

319. Mary Colum on *Finnegans Wake*

1939

'The Old and the New', *Forum and Century*, cii (October 1939), 158.

. . . Joyce's *Finnegans Wake* represents, for good or for ill, the very last word, up to the present and may be for a long time in the future, in the development of the novel. It is a step further in the revelation, in the understanding of Man the Unknown, the most unknown creature in the universe, than any we have had up to the present.

Finnegans Wake will be read by people who have an avid interest in what goes on in the mind and the emotions; it will be read by people interested in the renewal of language, in the sounds of language, and in the fantastic, unexpected word and idea associations that take place in the mind; it will be read by people interested in such things as the racial mind and the racial experience. But it will be read especially by those who have followed the way literature has been going for the past seventy years, for it represents the perfectly logical development of that way, and its influence will stretch far beyond the narrow circle of those who read the book. But I do not believe that that narrow circle will embrace more than a couple of thousand or that a single one of them will comprehend it totally—except, perhaps, some lonely and persistent reader on the banks of the Liffey who can retire indefinitely to an attic with a bottle of whiskey under one arm and a musical instrument of some kind under the other, to read of and ponder on an Earwicker who is himself and who contains all the past and future that is in himself.

Finnegans Wake is the revelation of the goings on in that part of the mind which contains the raw and confused materials of consciousness, and the events of the whole book take place in the minds of people who are in a state of dream, whether sleeping or waking. As we spend at least one third of our lives in sleep and over two thirds of it in some state of dream, it is fitting that some writer should devote himself to ex-

ploring what takes place in our minds and emotions during those periods; it is fitting, if we are to give any allegiance to the modern conception of literature as an attempt to portray the whole of man. . . .

320. Margaret Schlauch on Joyce's language

1939

Extract from 'The Language of James Joyce', *Science and Society,
A Marxian Quarterly*, iii, No. 4 (Fall 1939), 482–97.

It has by this time become a matter of common (not to say notorious)
knowledge that a perusal of the latest *opus* by James Joyce, *Finnegans
Wake*, lays an unprecedented task upon the reader. The technical
difficulties it presents have given rise in certain quarters to an expression
of humorous despair and to doubts concerning the author's sanity. A
critic writing in a scholarly journal [Joseph Prescott, 'James Joyce: A
Study in Words', *Publications of the Modern Language Association of
America*, liv (1939), 314] has suggested ironically that the next step after
the composition of such unintelligible discourse would be the publication of a volume of uninscribed pages which would render for all time
'the picture of the mind at that obscure moment in our embryological
past before we are ushered into the world of sensation and idea—in
short, the perfectly blank mind.' This extreme scepticism appears to be
unwarranted, however. Already some bolder spirits among the
reviewers have succeeded in throwing considerable light on the
method and intent of the book. Some have even made exaggerated
claims concerning its merits. It is not too early, I believe, to present here
some of the problems with which future criticism of this literary
experiment will probably have to be concerned. It is my purpose to
restate the technical problem with particular emphasis on the linguistic
devices employed, and in this connection to point out the long, witty

and comparatively lucid apologia for his method which Joyce has embodied in the text itself. (Curiously enough, this passage, which is the very heart of *Finnegans Wake* for a reader interested in its peculiar poetics, has been quite generally ignored by the reviewers.) I should like also to indicate how Joyce's ambitious synthesis of modernity is related to other attempts at the same sort of thing which use differing techniques; and, finally, to raise some fundamental questions—entirely apart from intelligibility—concerning its enduring value and pertinence.

The chief motive for Joyce's bizarre linguistic technique seems to be a revolt against one of the limitations of language hitherto assumed to be inescapable. It has been accepted as a necessary condition of speech that it must resemble a single melodic line in music, with the separate words succeeding one another in strict time sequence. . . . For the polyphonic interweaving of themes he tries to substitute polysemantic verbal patterns. The method is quite simple: you distort the words in a given passage so that they suggest at one and the same time not only the original normal ones but also another series of verbalisms which they now resemble. In order to convey these multiple phrases at once, it is important to respect the intonation of the whole as well as the individual words whose units of sound are being distorted. The procedure is therefore more complicated than a series of puns on individual words. Moreover, the words heard in overtone must be semantically related and must contribute to a single planned effect. . . . So Joyce shows us a single average individual lying asleep in Dublin: above him rise in vast concentric spheres the memories of all the earlier history and prehistory, the entire heritage of culture, which have made him as he is. Availing himself of the universal implications of his H. C. Earwicker, he has tried to pour through the man's sleeping consciousness all of past history and present civilization.

But does he do this? What he omits is for Marxist readers a matter of considerable moment. They will wonder whether their consciousness (even in sleep) is really so different from that of Joyce's *Everyman*. If so many conflicts and antitheses of universal history are to be included, why omit so extensively the tragic contradictions which press upon our very subconscious these days with clamorous insistence? It may seem strange to voice the demand that a structure already so top-heavy receive an additional burden; but it was the author's own choice to weight it so ambitiously. That is why we in our turn have a right to ask about the omissions. Out of the psychological maze of *Finnegans*

Wake there emerge many vivid impressions of the drabness of philistine Dublin, even the ugliness of its slums; again as in *Ulysses* Joyce has given us some unsparing satire of its lower middle class types: their gossiping meanness, their envy, their prurient curiosity, their transparant efforts at respectability. The only antidote is to be found, however, in heroic legends of the past and echoes of classical antiquity or medieval scholasticism. In this respect he resembles T. S. Eliot. So it is that Miller-Budnitskaya [No. 294] can speak with some justification of Joyce's 'reactionary philosophy of social pessimism.' However, the same technique might serve other more progressive purposes. It will do so in the future if it is really indigenous to our period. . . .

321. Louis Gillet on *Finnegans Wake*

1940

Extract from 'A Propos de *Finnegans Wake*', *Babel*, i (1940), 101–13. Translated by D. D. Paige as 'Joyce's Testament', *Quarterly Review of Literature*, i, No. 2 (Winter 1944), 87–99 (from which the present text is taken).

Everything Joyce did is important. His unique situation is well known: the extraordinary journey that this strange navigator took alone and (as the 'divine comic' says) *che fè Nettuno ammirar l'ombra d'Argo.* Somewhere there is a 'Joyce' Island, not easily located, for it moves about, exploring unknown seas, beyond all known lands. The scandal about *Ulysses* is still remembered. And now *Ulysses* is a classic. Would one dare say that this prodigious book appeared unreadable and barbaric? or that it was regarded as a shapeless mass and an indigestible farrago? It took me several years to absorb the shock and to succeed in understanding it. This recollection makes us circumspect. Let us be wary! *Finnegans Wake* is not easy reading. The labour of seventeen years cannot be absorbed in a day. Perhaps it is not for us but for the future to say the last word.

'There is no relation,' the author said to me one day, 'between *Ulysses* and my new book: one is day and the other night'. Let us take these words literally. . . . *Ulysses* begins in the morning at the hour when the city wakes and ends the following night in what the English call 'the small hours,' at the hour when mortals slip into sleep. *Finnegans Wake* extends from evening into morning. The two movements, the tonalities, are reversed. Day plunges into night. Night flows into dawn and into a sort of resurrection since it is, in addition, a Saturday night, the evening before Sunday (a Sunday in June or July, I presume, though I have not found the date indicated anywhere). The book is, on the whole, a new *Midsummer Night's Dream*.

But however different the two works are, they are nevertheless complements to one another. At bottom Joyce has never left the limits of his first book of poems, *Chamber Music;* all Joyce's themes are expressed in it. The material of *Ulysses* is the interior monologue, the complete representation of the consciousness of an individual, a complete image of his existence: psychological, visceral, practical, fantastic, intellectual, sentimental; the sum of his sensations, ideas, desires, velleities, caprices, perceptions, dreams, memories—all the diverse impressions which may, in the course of a day, traverse the field of consciousness. . . . In *Ulysses* there was already a distinctive rupture with the ordinary conventions of language, a plunge into the irrational, a return to the primitive and elementary, to chaos, outside the laws of syntax, approaching in some passages nightmares and delirium (the *Walpurgisnacht* at the bordello comes to mind) and ending, in the last part, with the wonderful revery and incomparable *berceuse* of Marion Bloom as she falls asleep.

Finnegans Wake starts us out along the same road, but a thousand paces from our starting-point or, rather, the starting point is at an infinite distance from the initial point. *Finnegans Wake* is about a man sleeping. The scene is the consciousness of the sleeper. Life is the dream of a shadow. Leopold Bloom, in the streets of Dublin, gave us the impression of a somnambulist. This time the last bonds are broken; the boundaries beyond external resistances are abolished; all the bonds with what is called reality have vanished. In the wrack of the world there is only consciousness at dream level, where the images and flotsam of wakefulness bob about. The universe is reduced to the condition of sleep. . . . Events released from the chain of succession whirl chaotically about on the surface of a continuous present, as a ball of mercury scatters in scurrying drops on a slate. Necessity and the reasonable world of cause and effect are avoided. Night comes into the soul as a deliverance. It lets loose a multitude of unknown forces, memories, instincts and leashed secrets which now are not held back. Everything is possible. The frontiers of personality disappear. When the darkening sky, swarming with millions of stars, alters ordinary objects for the sleeper, these objects are sensed only as a chaotic memory and are apprehended through a magic mist which transforms them like a prism and gives them body dreamstyle. One circumvagates in a world of marvels and metamorphosis. The images are summoned up, brought together and separated according to internal laws and the different attractions of the body-cells. They are no longer subject to the logic of time and place. Things lose their edges, their contours; they fuse or divide like elements of a soluble nature or an unstable composition analogous to that of music. The sole reality in this shower of shadows is that which goes on in the mind of the sleeper. . . .

[a broad summary follows here, pp. 89–91]

But this is not all. The central *motif* of all Joyce's work is the mystery of paternity, the mystery of the transmission of life, the rapport of the trinity made up of father, mother and child. But in this trio the wife is only an accidental element. This harmony, which Catholic piety expresses by the figures of mother and son as a Maternity which is sufficient in itself, Joyce sees rather as dependent upon men, an exclusively male mystery, passing from father to son and reducing itself to the mystery of Father (see in *Ulysses* the excellent meditation on *Hamlet* and the recognition of Stephen and Bloom, their complete spiritual, but not bodily, affiliation). The woman in this system (cf. the episode of the Sirens, Nausicaa, etc.) appears to be only an element of play, an embellishment, a variation, an adventitious and gratuitous caprice on the serious and masculine core of nature. . . .

But there is still more to this book. The sleeper, being the dream itself and being himself dreaming, finds that he is everything that he thinks; at the same time he is the substance and the consciousness of the universe. Every form and figure which enters into the tissue of his thinking life and shakes into gay life the limp vestments which hang in the cloister of his mind owe him being. He is, by turns and perhaps even simultaneously (since there is no longer 'time,' and succession here is only a manner of speaking), Adam, Duke Humphrey, the Viking founder of Dublin, Wellington (whose column is in Phoenix Park), Napoleon, Dean Swift (the lover of Vanessa), Tristan (the lover of Iseut), Finnegan (of *Finnegans Wake*), Dunlop, of Dunlop tires (why not, while one is at it?). It is clear that he is a particularly amorphous and extensible personality. After the work of Proust, we doubtless had our ideas on the constitution of the republic of Self tolerably enlarged. This new viewpoint has already gravely altered our conception of psycholgy.

But who does not see that it is a question of an entirely different thing for Joyce? In reality his epic is a metaphysic and an ontology. The sleeper is here a kind of protoplasm, a unique subject, a sort of central energy in which all phenomena and creatures are only diverse and multiple avatars, hypostases, as the gnostics say, incarnations comparable to those of Vishnu. He supports the universe as creation rests on the shoulders of the Creator. . . . The author teaches us nothing about the man, but confines himself to telling that he is all. Joyce treats him as the Eternal of whom we know nothing and who is perceptible only in his manifestations. The world is only a dream of God. *Somnium inebriati dormientis in crapula.* (Earwicker is the proprietor of a cheap pub.) All the beings proceed from his existence by proliferation and subdivision. He begets also sexes, individuals, fables and the events and topsawyers of history, multiplying them by oppositions and by dichotomy in an eternal infancy and fecundity of inexhaustible forms. And this creation is perhaps The Sin: disorder approaching the principle of identity, the irremediable trouble which disturbs rest and which explains the dream-insomnia of the sleeper.

Here, honestly condensed, one catches a glimpse of the general design of this great *Pourana*. Add, as has been often noted, the influence of the great Neapolitan thinker, G. B. Vico, and his ideas on the science of history, which he endeavours somehow to make into a synthesis, a history of histories. . . .

I believe that there is nowhere a more desolate view of our world and of the sheer emptiness of ourselves and things. It is a mockery (more tragic than Swift's) of the reality of the world and of those *lucky cocks, for whom the audible-visible-gnosible-edible world exists* (p. 88). The bitterness of this negation far exceeds the harshness of *Gulliver* and *The Tale of a Tub.*

It is only natural that Vico, as well as trying to write a unique history, should have dreamed of a unique language, a sort of mother language composed of the roots of all human idioms—a language which would be the common language of humanity. I do not know if this is where Joyce got the idea of the language which he set down, *with moltapuke on voltapuke* (p. 40), in order to write his *meandertale* (p. 18). I believe that he was drawn to it by the very form of his genius, by his prodigious verbal virtuosity, by the nocturnal quality of his subject and by this absolute absence of all reality, which permits words only to exist above a total void.

'I have put language to sleep,' the author told me in an expansive moment. He has put it to sleep, that is, freed it from the logical system of the chains of syntax and from constructive and grammatical masonry which, for the needs of practical life, weakens language by usage. Thus he has made a uniquely poetic instrument, a language of pure emotions, a creation of sentiment, a voice of profound life and the most secret truth, such as is sometimes believed to be perceived in dreams, in their stammerings. . . .

An epic like this, touching all the problems of life and existence, all the human and divine questions and based on the most denigrated form of the creative spirit, the pun, which Victor Hugo (Victor Hugonot, as Joyce says) calls the excrement of the human brain. What enterprise! What derision! The whole universe reduced to a perpetual punning! Doubtless, as everyone knows, there is a good deal of training and acquired skill in this art, as there is in cannon shots in billiards. The habit becomes a trick of which one is master only when he gets among specialists. But this is far from involuntary writing and automatic dictation and farther still from what is called the Language of the Night. On this point I am going only by my own experience: I have never noticed that I make more puns asleep than awake or that I have more wit sleeping than awake. But Joyce was forced by the nature of his subject to create his system of double and triple-meaning words, for his aim was to set forth in a single narrative all the histories and gods of the universe, to squeeze into it all science, philosophy and geography. Perhaps he could achieve this only by allusions and contractions, in pressing into each vocable the greatest possible number of meanings. This end could be reached only by a sort of multivalence or polyvalence capable of multiplying the power of relations and associations, of creating unlooked-for contacts and comparisons in each idea so that the text, already copious, is in reality three or four times longer than it appears. This single volume (as the brain of the author created it) is equal to the contents of a library.

I forego giving the idea of this *claybook*, which is at the same time a *livre à clef* and book of the Earth (a cosmic book, if you wish, and also the book of a man and human clay; the sigillate lands which serve as nourishment and the book that St. John eats in the *Apocalypse* are recalled). . . .

What complicates things is that Joyce works always with several languages (not just three or four, but seventeen or eighteen) and that without warning he passes from one to another or, rather, creates ingraftings, marriages and hybrids. *How miney combinaises and permutandies can be played on the international qurd*!

Doubtless all languages live by borrowing and gather into their vocabularies a crowd of foreign words. Rabelais did not hesitate to pepper his prose with Italian and German; the polyglot chapter on the indiscreet jewels is well-known. But the taste for play with mixed words, mi-parti (as in the old decks of cards Jacks were shown wearing one red and one jonquil sock), is a taste appropriate to Joyce. . . .

A text so charged with meanings, where the author creates each word and where it is necessary always to be hypercritical, becomes practically unreadable.

A strange decoction! A baroque cauldron in which all St. John's herbs simmer, an alembic in which the most bizarre chemicals are combined! Fundamentally, the book is what today we would call a farce. In Latin it would be called a satire (from the old word *sature*, a sort of mince-meat); it is a *bouillabaisse* composed by a prodigious artist and an astounding magician of language, but the partaker is bewildered at the result which comes out of the magic pot. Sometimes one has to read a page or even a single sentence several times in order to expiscate the meaning. But the whole work remains in great obscurity. For this reason one would like to see an interlinear text, or rather, a comparative edition which gives on opposite pages the text in two states: on the left the first sketch, still natural and relatively clear, on the right the definitive text, with all rewritings and erasures, regardless of how many notes and explanations are necessary.

It is difficult to express the mixture of admiration and irritation that the reader feels from this extraordinary and frolicsome joke. One is astounded at the resourcefulness of the writing, at the comic genius who breaks up words, alters spelling, disjoints, mixes, produces collisions and telescopings. . . .

And always, among all this, this unerring music, this ear, this sense of cadence and melody which make the prose of Joyce a source of delights, flights and pleasures without end, one is led in spite of himself, without knowing where and without anything more to ask, on this sea of enigmas, mirages, rhythms and caresses. One is ready to accept this liquidation of reason, of consciousness, of the artificial, this débâcle of sacred forms and hallowed verities, this chaffing ragout of all our illusions in a 'sonorous inanity' and a confusion of hilarious bacchanale.

One does not close the book out of discouragement and chagrin. The book falls from your hands. Because one does not see it clearly and gropes one's way along, perceiving only here and there a glimmering or an amusing detail, one is seized with impatience against this rattling of words, this logomachy. There are entire pages and groups of tens of pages in which it is impossible to discern the thread: the *inebbiated* author, as he says, seems to be seized by a verbal drunkenness, a vertigo of words, which makes him construct sentences which say nothing. . . .

Paris 1922–1939. One book in seventeen years. But what a book and what an adventure. A book of derision, nihilism and modesty, and, basically, of despair. *A collideorscape, a Jeeremy head sindbook.* During these seventeen years, through thousands of waking hours, the artist has patiently erected his derisory edifice, his architecture of prisms, dreams, caprices and nonsense, his *regginbrow* in the clouds, the only reality above the events of the world. With the disdain of a hermit or anchorite, he ignores the turbulent adventurers who fill the earth with their noise. He was content to make his salute, in writing and according to the rules of the Gai Sçavoir, the chronicle of eternity and the motion-less history of man. Everything is said and done, and everything remains to be done.

For all that has been done has yet to be done and done again. Eternal repetition, eternally useless, where there is only a sweetness and *motif* of confidence: *A youth in his florizel, a boy in his innocence, peeling a twig, a child beside a weany white stead. The child we all love to place our hope in for ever.*

Seventeen years: a single dream to fill in the interval between two wars. *Vanissas Vanistatum! O the vanity of Vanissy! All ends vanishing.* . . .

322. Walter Rybert on how to read
Finnegans Wake
1940

Extract from 'How to Read *Finnegans Wake*', *New Horizons,*
iii (November/December 1940), 14–19, 31.

Although more than a year has elapsed since its completion, James
Joyce's *Finnegans Wake* appears to be no more familiar to the reading
public than it was during its fifteen years' fragmentary appearance as
Work in Progress. The history of *Ulysses* is being repeated with all
indications that the same initial failure to comprehend will be followed
by the same gradual enlightenment, acceptance and ultimate acclaim,
but at a much slower pace. The work is yet known only to the few who
extend their hunt for literary fare beyond the beaten path. . . .

[discusses the critical reception]

It is not to be wondered that the book is unknown to otherwise
voracious consumers of the fiction market. The reviewers have told
them it is unintelligible. That the reading of *Finnegans Wake* is plenty
tough is undeniable. That it is unintelligible is not true. 'Given time to
read it,' is a *sine qua non*. Statements like these are the result of a prod-
ding, tyrannous deadline. Magazine reviews on the whole have been
somewhat, but not much, better than newspaper reviews. The best
have appeared in academic journals.

In this situation there is need for a lift for the average reader. Such is
here proposed. Under this magnanimous motive, furthermore, there is
an ulterior one. I have been a faithful reader of newspaper book pages
for years and I have rarely found an appraisal of a book therein to be
worth a tinker's dam. I have not forgiven their failure to tip me off to
Ulysses. Most of the stuff they recommend to their customers, to borrow
a word from the musicians, is pure corn. It may be good commerce but
it is bad criticism. I have had enough.

The first requirement in reading *Finnegans Wake* is a revision in reading habits. Be 'given time to read' is one, or 'take it easy.' It can't be done while hanging on a strap or sitting in a railway station. You've got to be where you won't be ashamed to laugh out loud, murmur 'ah!' or satisfy the desire to read something of what you've just discovered to an appreciative listener, preferably feminine. An easy chair, nothing else to do, are essentials. A pint of grog will be helpful.

Furthermore, it's not a matter of reading it 'as one would a foreign language, translating each word,' etc. etc. This is one thing that must *not* be done. If you have a scholar's yen for that sort of job, put it off until you have gotten what the book was jolly well made for—esthetic pleasure. You don't need Mr. Joyce's erudition any more than you need Herr van Beethoven's musical education in order to enjoy his Fifth Symphony. And you don't need to have been reared where they play cricket and drink Guinness instead of lager beer, as Mr. Ford Maddox Ford intimated. Just take a few tips from whatever erudition has been soaked up in the process of a middle-western education and proceed.

Rule number one: relax and read as though the parts you don't savvy do not matter. The book provides two elements, musical passages and humour, around which there is no mystery. It is richer in these elements than any other work, and the reader keeps on uncovering more of them each time he goes through it. This is no small part of the fun; the 'understanding' will come later. (The road to understanding is via esthetic perception and the first requirements include an ear and eye for musical prose. This is everyone's possession.)

Opening the book, we read:

riverrun, past Eve and Adam's, from swerve of shore to bend of bay, brings us by a commodious vicus of recirculation back to Howth Castle and Environs.

An examination of the components of this sentence will prepare the reader for much of what lies ahead. It will also acquaint him with the nature of the two major difficulties: the 'plot' and the manner of its telling. The 'plot' is a universal history of man as projected through a dream by a mind whose subconscious has at its disposal the lore of all literatures. The manner of its telling is one which exploits to the fullest extent the richest associations, the original meanings, the vocal and psychological origin of words, the association value of syllables, in fact, everything of esthetic value that language has acquired in the course of its evolution.

The first word provides a simple illustration of one of the devices in Joyce's narrative process: the economical mingling (mangling, if you insist!) of words or syllables so that they will suggest more than they do in their traditional employment. . . .

Anyway, we have rule number two, which is to free the imagination on all passages and think of all they remind us. Out of these we select what appears to be germane. Soon, to the reader's delightful surprise, he discovers the products of his imagination in future text and develops a lively interplay of mental receptivity and response never before dreamed of in fiction. . . .

What Joyce has given here is a whimsical presentation of the most interesting subject of speculation, progress. That human progress is not continuous but subject to an inner-destructive force that sends it back repeatedly to its rude beginnings has been argued heatedly down through all heathen and Christian civilizations. Oswald Spengler brooded heavily on this theme. Joyce's approach is the artist's one which presents it in its comic as well as its tragic light.

We now have, in this first sentence, a skeleton of the story. It is the barest outline of what is to come in this tightly crammed book: man's history, the rise and fall of his civilizations, his nations and his families. . . .

For the Viconian basis of *Finnegans Wake,* it will pay to read *An Exagmination of James Joyce,* a collection of papers by writers who have had considerable dope from Joyce himself. Suffice to say here that Vico suggested the writing of a universal history of man in accordance with his concept of it is as a continual recurrence of this cycle: Primitive man, frightened by thunder, develops the early stages of religion, animism. Society emerges, despotism evolves. The cave is the nucleus of the city, feudalism follows and is transformed into democracy. Democracy degenerates into anarchy, which is checked by a return to monarchy. The last stage is an internal breakdown, from which society starts anew.

Vico had some penetrating theories as to the origins of language, poetry and myth, all of which are exploited by Joyce. . . .

After getting the story outline from the first sentence and an idea as to the manner of telling, we immediately plunge into the dream of Earwicker, where we are astonished to find details concerned with the life of a man who appears to have been all places at all times and awfully hazy about where he happens to be at the moment. His vocabulary is immense, including that of dozens of languages living, dead, and not-yet-invented, plus the most complete collection of slang ever assembled, embracing expressions that were new on the streets of New York, Dublin, London, Paris, and Chicago, yesterday. Earwicker is Everybody who has been Everywhere, seen Everything and forgotten Nothing. As we join his exhaustive dream in the second paragraph, he is 'Sir Tristram, violer d'amores, fr'over the short sea.'

Such facility in projection and transference is a well known phenomenon in dream life and the unconscious mind. Earwicker's dream is more facile and far reaching than any ever thus put under analysis by Drs. Freud or Stekel, however. The question has been raised whether Joyce hasn't given his Dublin pub-proprietor character a symbolic repertoire that is beyond him. In this connection, Jung's theory of the collective unconscious comes to mind. . . .

It is the vast store of material that Joyce has drawn on that makes this book hard to read. But it is this, also, that enriches the work and gives it its singular quality. It is this which gives it more than any other book has got. This, of course, could result in just a vast jumble of tongues, a shaky tower of Babel, were it not for the fact that it is so precisely knitted together in the structure of the work. He has made all these details relate to one another.

Though Earwicker roams the universe, all his identifications with things apparently remote from his experience stem directly from his subconscious desires, his family life, his business, his livid history. We get glimpses of these things through his dream, obscure though they may be behind the symbols the unconscious mysteriously manufactures. . . .

In the handling of situations which Earwicker's dream brings forth, Joyce has made a special effort to make the telling fit the case. In the Jute and Mutt dialog, which is concerned with the awkward efforts of primitive man to convert his vocal powers into articulate speech, he has made it rugged, replete with primitive humour, and decidedly expressive of clumsy groping. . . .

In the process of reading, it has already been pointed out that there are episodes, even sentences, that can be enjoyed for themselves alone. How timely, in view of the present senseless wars throughout the world, are:'What clashes here of wills gen wonts, oystrygods gaggin fishygods,' and 'Arms apeal with larms, apalling, Killykilly: a toll, a toli.' What a beautiful deflation of military pomposity is :'This is the big Sraughter Willingdone, grand and magentic in his gold-tin spurs,' and 'This is his big wide harse.' . . .

[quotes from 'The Ondt and the Gracehoper', pp. 414, 415, 417]

This example will be enough to prove that there is plenty which is not of insurmountable difficulty in reading. All readers familar with the

Jabberwocky language in *Alice in Wonderland* can proceed easily. The principle rule is to keep on reading, moving over the sections that bother. These will come in time. It is more or less agreed that there isn't anyone who can get all there is in the work. Some will get this, others that. All will get more on repeated reading. It is a new book every time you pick it up. It will never be exhausted.

What Joyce has done is to pry the lid off the coffin in which writers of English have been busy nailing up their language since the days of Shakespeare. Somewhere, the craft of writing got off the principles of 'wholeness, harmony and radiance.' Sometimes the unity was achieved, rarely the radiance. What was intended to be radiance was in most cases superfluous ornamentation, an art that reached the consummate in Richard Wagner. We have also a good example in contemporary literature, that of the late Thomas Wolfe, through the empty shell of whose work the windy platitudes blow an awful racket.

It is rare that a work of art possesses a strong inner unity and an ornamentation radiating such varied forms. Problems of structure and ornament have wrecked many a well-intended work. The most notable failure in art is that in which ornament is plastered on. It is often surprising to find upon ripping off the tinsel that there is beneath it, after all, a work of art. . . .

Design whose ornament *is* that design and nothing else is the demand of the art of the future. Illustrations of how Joyce has accomplished this in his new work have been given. A re-reading of *The Portrait of the Artist as a Young Man* and *Ulysses* will show how this tremendous feat of engineering was worked out step by step, from the day when young Stephen Dedalus pondered: . . .

[quotes from ch. 4]

Authors have used words to describe. Joyce uses them to reproduce. The words as organized into a sentence by him become again the thing; often more than what could be presented by the thing. Consider all that is brought to the fore in 'Only a fadeograph of a yestern scene.'

As we proceed through *Finnegans Wake*, the realization grows that the text and subject matter are interwoven in a harmonious whole; that the story cannot be told otherwise. Life is a totality of change, constant motion, shifting appearances, which produces beauty through all the senses variously. It runs the gamut of gaiety, calm, sadness. It has been Joyce's purpose to reproduce all this with as close a reference to actual life as possible. . . .

Our commodious vicus of recirculation appears in a new light at the end of a long journey. The 'vicus' has progression; a progression that promises new discoveries if taken over the same route again. Keep on reading: 'A way a lone a last a loved a long the riverrun.' It is rich in rewards, this first of all books to encompass the whole of life, the finest work of art that we possess. . . .

323. John Peale Bishop on *Finnegans Wake*

1940

Extract from *Finnegans Wake, Southern Review*, v, No. 3 (Winter 1940), 439–52.

All that James Joyce has written is of a piece, for the material with which he has had to work has not been added to since he went into an exile thirty-five years ago. *Finnegans Wake*, in so far as it has to do with the world of observation, is made up of memories of Dublin. The men and women in it are, no less than those of his first book of stories, Dubliners. But they have long inhabited a city which scarcely exists apart from Joyce's mind. Their Dublin is the one the young Joyce knew, around the turn of the century, but no one who now went to the capital of Mr. De Valera could wholly find it. . . .

[quotes the opening sentence and explains it]

. . . It is enough for the moment to say that it not only clearly announces what *Finnegans Wake* is about, but that its very ambiguity forces us to consider how ambiguous are the relations of time and space, which is one of the important themes of this 'strangest dream that was ever half dreampt.' Every word is, as the physicists would say, a time-space event.

The Dubliners in this dream have little left them but the night-life of the mind and of the mind of a man who has long lived, and not only at night, in darkness. . . .

Joyce from the start was a poet; but in *Dubliners*, and through the *Portrait of the Artist as a Young Man*, his prose is submitted to the strictest discipline of Flaubert. He was still, when he wrote these two books, so close to his material that the realistic method is adequate to his demands. Where he surpasses any other follower of Flaubert, and indeed Flaubert himself, is the range of his prose, which he can on occasion bring close to the condition of music, without ever allowing it to destroy the conventions of realism. . . .

In *Finnegans Wake* it is the realistic element that is difficult to make out. Almost anything, Joyce says, can happen at night, and as to just what is happening throughout this long night we are deliberately left uncertain. On the other hand, the symbolic meanings, though they are many and complicated, and though the way of writing 'doublecrossing twofold truths and devising tingling tailwords' is so devious as to put the reader often in doubt, are certainly not impossible to follow. There are any number of passages that I am unable to elucidate; there are references so personal that they will be nothing to anyone but Joyce; there are others so remote that not one in a thousand will understand them. But darkness, and even pointlessness, are within Joyce's intention. 'A hundred cares, a tithe of troubles,' cries the Liffey, the river of life, as it is about to be lost and merged with the sea, 'and is there one who understands me? One in a thousand years of the nights?' This is man's history, and it must proceed in obscurity. But at last day dawns. And though at the end of the book the impression of any particular life in it may be dim, we should not be unaware of what Joyce conceives to be the truth of his history.

In *Finnegans Wake* Joyce has made an almost complete break with the Flaubertian tradition. . . .

. . . The language in which the work was written seemed to have been invented admirably to present the night life of the mind. And so it is. But if *Finnegans Wake* is taken to be as a whole the dramatic projection of all that passes through one man, now soundly, now fitfully sleeping, and once or twice starting into momentary wakefulness, it soon becomes not only unintelligible, but artistically impossible. Humphrey Cliveden Earwicker is not a person in the Flaubertian sense, though occasionally he appears as one. He is not an individual whom a dream is constantly transforming into someone else. He is an individual who must not be considered apart from the universal. His transformations are the essence

737

of his being, since everything in the book, including the words in which it is written, is constantly in the process of becoming something else. He can be sought on the realistic level, as can every other personage in the book; if he could not be found there we should not be concerned with his history. The common man includes all history; he is what he is because of all heroes and saints. What was, is. The divine, the heroic past is his human, his all too human, present. His is a spiritual night, not merely the night of Dublin. And Dublin is now Purgatory, as in *Ulysses* it was Hell. . . .

[analyses the structure, the language, and the multiple characterization]

. . . The truth about man is not to be found in his thought, but in his history. So the writing in *Finnegans Wake* moves incessantly through nonsense to poetry. The content always shows in the form, and when successful it is the form. It has been pointed out that what Joyce is doing here with words is what all poets have always done, and in particular what Shakespeare does throughout his latest plays: employ a sort of pun to make a compressed metaphor. But Joyce carries this process much further than Shakespeare did, and at the same time writes a work which is meant to be read, as the *Divine Comedy* is, not on one but many levels. Dante told Can Grande that his poem could be interpreted in four ways. I am not sure that the four would exhaust the number of ways in which *Finnegans Wake* may be read.

All this places an almost intolerable burden on the reader, no matter how patient he may be—and Joyce admonishes him to patience—no matter how accustomed he may be to literature that has departed from realism. For there is nothing in the form that Joyce has adopted to force him to stop at one point rather than another further on. Once the present-ness of the past has been admitted there is no saying how much of the past is to be adumbrated in any one contemporary event. Once it has been allowed that all is in a state not of being but becoming, words with the rest, there is nowhere that a man like Joyce, with his incompar-able mastery over words, is compelled to stop. And there can be little doubt that he has manipulated his text to its harm. . . .

And yet Joyce's form has served him well. For when we have come to the end of *Finnegans Wake*, we know that here is the past and the future of mankind. It is a history which restores religion and accords with science. Indeed, for the first time a poet has created for us a world which outwardly agrees with contemporary physicists, as inwardly it confirms the psychologists of our time. And yet it is so created that we

cannot escape the impression that it came into being, not through deri-
vation from what others have found, Joyce being almost blind and
largely cut off from outer sources of knowledge, but through contemplation alone. His mind in some ways resembles the medieval mind;
but the world he has imagined is our own. *Finnegans Wake* is probably
the most exasperating book ever written; but as a consideration of our
knowledge and as an exploration into the unknown it is worthy of the
great comic poet who wrote *Ulysses.* . . .

324. Max Rychner on *Ulysses*

1941

Extract from 'Reality in the Novel, Concerning *Ulysses* by James Joyce', *Die Tat* (18/19 January 1941); also appeared in *In Memoriam James Joyce* (1941), ed. Carola Giedion-Welcker pp. 32–6.

No work of literature between the two great wars challenged the intellect to the extent that *Ulysses* by James Joyce has. Right after its appearance, books, pamplets, and essays came out in vast numbers; these undertook to comprehend such a phenomenon and to establish a feeling of trust and understanding with the strange appearance of the novel.

The title itself signified a challenge: the novel has a thoroughly realistic texture; it is set in a definite time and place, on June 16, 1904, in Dublin—and it is supposed to represent an *Odyssey*. It does not center around an heroic epic with the early mystical background, but instead is more of a parody of works of recent times which stands in relation to Homer as Cervantes's *Don Quixote* stands in relation to the chivalric romance. It is the tragic and at the same time comic episode of an average modern metropolitan man whose life on an ordinary day is examined with unique exactness and close detail. Thus originates this chronicle of more than 1200 pages.

From Ulysses, the constantly tormented man, the hero of Troy and king of Ithaca, we know that he was a thrilling narrator and yet his fortunes have not been handed down in his wording of the novel but instead in the homeric frame. The day's events in the life of the hero in Joyce's *Ulysses* would spread out over two volumes so that nothing, so to speak, would stand out as important. He remains stuck in banalities. This is so that the writer doesn't clip out the triteness and banality; he even sets forth general, unimportant details. How the advertising agent of a newspaper, Leopold Bloom, brings tea to his wife in bed, how he bathes, etc., all this we find out in greater reality almost than Zola.

This is only a segment of the reality. In one scene we have three young men, who live in an old tower, wake up and ready themselves for the day: the one Buck Mulligan, a medical student, sings, full of mischievousness, out of the text of the liturgy and handles the shaving mug as if it were the holy receptacle of the Mass. A parody, yet with the eternal outlook upon the historical and spiritual reality of two Christian milleniums. With them the dull everyday reality of June 16, 1904 steps surprisingly, scintillatingly again and again into new relations and frames of reference.

[the critic discusses the funeral of Paddy Dignam, the Lying-in-Hospital and the prose styles used in each case]

This all at first seems like an ingenious amusement, the masterly bit of a late Alexandrine whose expressions stand at the disposal of the entire historical style. Yet it is important to reveal the deeper relationship of this style.

[quotes from Stuart Gilbert's *James Joyce* on the development of English prose in the 'Oxen of the Sun' episode]

. . . Everything is revealed or analysed in play and joyousness; the episode seems as an inverted Platonic banquet which is permeated by the spirit of Aristophanes.

Bloom sits oppressed and preoccupied with his thoughts at the party and waits until Dedalus breaks away. Memories of his dead son come to him and he senses in himself a growing inclination or attraction to Stephen Dedalus whom he begins to consider as a father considers his son, as Odysseus considered Telemachus.

Here we have touched upon a new, far-reaching theme of the work, the father-son problem. In this strange relationship during several night hours those constellations pointing into the greatness show themselves, which had been embodied in *Hamlet*, in mythology and religion in an inexhaustible sense of the language. Joyce refers to this because life constantly repeats these constellations, whose prototypes in religion and art are eternal. They are causative reality. Each new situation of life brings at the same time a recoil—Vico calls it *ricorso*—an earlier stage or a new connection of the stream of life at an earlier step whose provision or supply in strength, pictures, and thought are inexhaustible. An arbitrary day of an arbitrary man in an arbitrary city contains, exactly observed and each detail consistently planned, an unending abundance of relations to the Cosmos of nature and of the spirit. Nothing is isolated or separate; even the most singular, the most incomprehensible thing makes itself felt in countless connections which at first are unrecognizable, but reveal themselves in their darkness to sympathetic men.

Let us imagine a map on which Dublin is tied by lines with thousands of points to the entire world. To this system of reference of space, corresponding to a reference system of time, from June 16, 1904, on, thousands of moments of the past are joined to an enormous complex of sense. Joyce has constructed his *Ulysses* by this technique. Each action, every word of his characters has the sense of the day to day action and words and at the same time these actions and words conform to the great regularity according to the eternal repetition into which life is constantly ordered.

Even so each moment is pregnant with many possibilities for the future. This 'dumme Faktum' in the every day existence of an insignificant man becomes transparent in rational glimpses and allows the great figurations of the spirit to become recognized. This becomes there not great but significant. Out of his willfulness set free, it shares in the profits of the entire consciousness of the world like a colorful thread woven into a tapestry—a meaningful function acquired through greater association.

We can only touch here on a few points in *Ulysses*. Yet it is worth while to make authentic use of each point of his book as a stepping stone which constitutes a reference system of reality. Joyce has shown reality as well as created it. He has beheld its wealth by means of inspirational grief and sorrow and a feeling of victory. We can behold it, this reality, through his work.

325. Van Wyck Brooks on Joyce

1941

Extract from *The Opinions of Oliver Allston* (1941), pp. 199, 225–6, 228–9, 231.

See Dwight MacDonald's reply, 'Kulturbolschewismus is Here', *Partisan Review*, viii, No. 6 (November–December 1941), 442–51, which is not included here because of its length and because Mr. MacDonald would not allow 'cuts' made in the essay.

. . . Most of our critical writing deals with technical questions, and technical novelty, as it seems to me, is almost the only virtue it demands or praises. Not whether a writer contributes to life, but whether he excels in some new trick is the question that is usually asked. It is their formal originality that has given prestige to writers like Joyce, Eliot and Ezra Pound; and perhaps this is natural in an age of technics. But how can we ignore the larger questions involved in this drift of the modern mind? Obviously, it represents the 'death-drive,' as certain psychologists call it, the will to die that is said to exist side by side in our minds with the will to live. . . . There was James Joyce, the sick Irish Jesuit, whom Eliot described as orthodox, and who had done more than Eliot to destroy tradition. Had he not, in *Ulysses*, in his *Oxen of the Sun*, run through the whole of English literature, depreciating with his parodies its greatest authors, deforming every one of them, Gibbon, Burke, Goldsmith, Lamb, De Quincey, Dickens, Ruskin, Newman, Bunyan, Burns and a dozen others? What fools he made them seem, as he filled his travesties of their styles with trivial and salacious implications!—and all for the glorification of James Joyce. For what a big boy he must be to have put all these authors in their places! The past in all of Joyce's work went out in a bad smell, while Joyce settled down complacently in his 'snot-green' world; and yet Joyce was represented as defending tradition! Out upon this nonsense, Allston said. . . . Besides, in literature one had to remember the standard of health, and

Joyce was not at all concerned with this. His falsification of tradition had well-nigh wiped tradition out in minds that were already divorced from tradition: and it seemed to Allston that to reaffirm the true tradition was an indispensable task of the contemporary critic. . . .

. . . Did not these writers think of themselves as a 'vanguard'?—and what did this conception of a vanguard imply? Joyce referred to Ireland as 'the most belated nation in Europe.' Belated, Allston asked, in relation to what? Others, again, who denied evolution, spoke of the 'evolution of the novel,' which had reached its grand climax in *Finnegans Wake*; and, as Allston put it, evolution for evolution, which of these two was the more incredible? Did there exist such a thing as 'the' novel to evolve? . . . Was not James Joyce, for one, the ash of a burnt-out cigar, were they not all of them ashes of the eighteen-nineties, aside from the one matter of technique? And had they really possessed the 'sense of their age,' to which they were always laying claim? Or were they merely bats, as Allston said, that had flown in the twilight between the wars? . . .

CRITICAL OBITUARIES

326. Thornton Wilder in *Poetry*

1941

Extract from 'James Joyce, 1882–1941', *Poetry*, lvii (1940–1),
370–4. Separately printed by Wells College Press, Aurora, New
York, in 1944.

A critical obituary.

. . . Like Cervantes, he groped confusedly for his subject and his form.
The history of a writer is his search for his own subject, his myth-
theme, hidden from him, but prepared for him in every hour of his
life, his *Gulliver's Travels*, his *Robinson Crusoe*. Like Cervantes, un-
successfully, Joyce tried poetry and drama. Knowing the incomparable
resources of his prose rhythms one is astonished at these verses,—a
watery musicality, a pinched ventriloquial voice. Knowing the vital
dialogues in *Dubliners* and that electrifying scene, the quarrel at the
Christmas dinnertable, in *A Portrait of the Artist as a Young Man*, one is
astonished at the woodenness of his play *Exiles*.

Like Cervantes, he turned with greater success to short narratives,
and like him found in the dimensions of the long book, his form and his
theme.

Ulysses brought a new method into literature, the interior monologue. The century-long advance of realism now confronted this task:
the realistic description of consciousness. To realism, mind is a babbler,
a stream of fleeting odds and ends of image and association. Joyce
achieved this method with a mastery of fullness of illustration that
effaces any question of precursors. He alone has been able to suggest the
apparent incoherence and triviality of this incessant woolgathering, and
yet to impose upon it a coordination beyond itself, in art. . . .

We cannot know yet whether hate has buried this conception under
the debris of language analysed to dust or whether love through

identification with human history, through the laughter of the comic genius, and through the incomparable musicality of its style, has won its greatest triumph of all.

Joyce recommended this work to the world as his greatest, and it may be that when we come to know it, our gratitude for so many excellences in the earlier books will be exceeded by all that we owe him for this one. . . .

327. Cyril Connolly, *New Statesman*

1941

'A Note on James Joyce', *New Statesman and Nation*, xxi (18 January 1941), 59. Also in *Previous Convictions* (1963), pp. 269–72.

. . . In the next period of expansive leisure, when we can read again and reassess the past, he may well take the place which Henry James has lately occupied, that of the Forerunner in vogue, the fine product of a vanished and alien civilisation which by its completeness and remoteness stirs the imagination and so enters into communication with its successor. . . . In the years to come something really important could be written about him. Revolutionary in technique, yet conservative in everything else, so deadly respectable in his life, so fearlessly sensual in his writings, so tortured with the lapsed Catholic's guilt—the '*Agenbite of Inwit*,' so obsessed with his own youth that his clock seemed literally to have stopped on June 16th, 1904, and yet so determined to create a mythical universe of his own. We will never have the time, the security or the patience in our lifetime to write like him, his weapons, 'silence, exile and cunning' are not ours. I hope, but only for the time, to read through him and one day make a study of this literary anti-Pope, this last great mammoth out of whose tusks so many smaller egoists have carved their self-important ivory towers. . . .

. . . He was the leading representative in our time, and perhaps in all times, of the theory of literature as a pure art almost completely divorced from society.

Literature as a pure art approaches the nature of a pure science. And Joyce was also the great research scientist of letters, handling words with the same freedom and originality that Einstein handles mathematical symbols. The sounds, patterns, roots and connotations of words interested him much more than their definite meanings. One might say that he invented a non-Euclidean geometry of language; and that he worked over it with doggedness and devotion, as if in a laboratory far removed from the noises of the street. This does not mean that he neglected to present human beings in his novels. Stephen Dedalus and his father, Leopold and Molly Bloom, even H. C. Earwicker of *Finnegans Wake*, are figures that will not be forgotten. But they are figures that are analysed exhaustively in repose rather than being presented in action. And the side of them that held Joyce's interest was their subconscious—that is, the side that medical scientists like to deal with. Moreover, even the strongest of his characters seem dwarfed by the great apparatus of learning that he brings to bear on them. They are almost like atoms being smashed by a 250-ton cyclotron.

These are some of the reasons why Joyce was not a writer of the same magnitude as Tolstoy or Stendhal or Dickens or any of the great men whose subject was human actions in their social background. In his own field, however, he was absolutely without an equal. There are very few serious novels of the last twenty years that do not show traces of his influence, even if only at third hand. The writers of the world owe him an enormous debt for making discoveries that have opened new horizons even to those who completely disagree with Joyce's idea of literature. They will miss him all the more because, in the hard years that lie ahead of us, it is doubtful whether any great scientist of letters will have the opportunity to carry on his work. Perhaps there will not even be neutral countries to which they can escape. . . .

329. Stephen Spender, *Listener*

23 January 1941, xxv, No. 628, 124-5

. . . He was not only the greatest literary stylist of his time. He was also the only living representative of the European tradition of the artist who carries on with his creative work unaffected by the storm which breaks around him in the world outside his study. His spirit is one with Goethe standing like a cliff above the sea of the French invasion of Germany; of Beethoven continuing to write his music all through the bombardment of Vienna, even when he had to take refuge in a cellar.

That tradition of the great and isolated artist has today been challenged: and James Joyce's work constitutes in itself one of the best reasons for the challenge. . . .

It is impossible at this stage to pass judgment on Joyce's work. Perhaps *Ulysses* and *Finnegans Wake* will be regarded as great masterpieces by future generations; perhaps as monstrous curiosities, enormous earthworks and tunnellings thrown up by a great and mole-like brain working deeper and deeper into the darkness and disintegration of its own and a universal dream world.

One can, however, attempt to indicate the lines of Joyce's development, and the gigantic nature of the task he set himself. His early volume of short stories, *Dubliners*, is beautifully written, but contains nothing, except the one masterpiece, *The Dead*, which might not be the product of one of several poetic and sensitively-minded young minor Irish writers. The two volumes of poetry, *Chamber Music* and *Pomes Penyeach*, would confirm this view; the poems are delicate, musical, and finely observed, but they have a curious sentimentality, which is interesting only as a clue to a side of Joyce which is carefully concealed in the monumental elaborations of the other works. Also, both the poems and the stories show signs of that strain of sexual ambivalence in Joyce's work which, like his sentimentality, is concealed by a tremendous emphasis on coarse normality.

The Portrait of the Artist as a Young Man is the first volume of a great self-absorbed autobiographic work, which is treated objectively in *Ulysses,* and which, finally, in *Finnegans Wake* transcends itself and passes into the universal, disintegrating in the process. This may sound high-flown but it describes, as literally as I can, Joyce's development. In the *Portrait* we have a sensitive, introspective study of Stephen Dedalus, who evidently corresponds to James Joyce. At times the introspective method foreshadows the famous monologues of *Ulysses*. In *Ulysses* we see Stephen from the outside, without the method of introspection being abandoned. Joyce does not objectify his world by seeing it from the outside, but by seeing several characters through each others' eyes, from the inside. *Ulysses* is a series of introspective studies of people who are outside each other, so they are externalised not in their own, but in each others' minds. We get Stephen's and Molly Bloom's and Leopold Bloom's thoughts; all of them 'interior monologues', but we also see each character through the other characters. And through them all we get the macabre, vast picture of Dublin.

This method of the 'interior monologue' (which has influenced modern literature enormously) is a form of realism pushed to an extreme at which it finally breaks down altogether. It is a stupendous attempt to present us with a truer picture of the human mind than has ever been achieved before, by creating the discontinuous stream of thoughts, habits of mind rising from the past, disturbances caused by environment, and even suggested by purely physical movements of the body, which pass through the fragmentary and interrupted consciousness of people at every moment.

The objection to this method is that it finally breaks down communication altogether. It is quite true; the mental life of individuals is more fragmentary, more universal, less conscious, than we care to admit. . . . Since consciousness and unconsciousness merge in his picture into other consciousness and unconsciousness, since the present merges into the past, and places and bodies into other places and bodies; then the languages of the world merge into one another. With enormous genius and erudition, he has actually invented a new language in *Finnegans Wake* which is the beginning of a universal language. The clue to his method is the pun, because in the pun one meaning coincides with another. His puns are composite words suggesting several meanings in several languages. Not only is the book written in a universal language, but it is a stupendous attempt to write a book about *everything*; in which the whole of history, geography, literature and the life of individuals are recollected in a narrative which is like a story told in one's sleep, which seems a story and yet has no coherence.

It may be that Joyce only succeeded in writing about his own subjective fantasies. If that is so, his work remains a monument of self-portraiture, like Rousseau's *Confessions*. It is self-portraiture pushed to the point where it becomes universal. The books may be largely incomprehensible; they may lie unread, except by scholars; but the method which turns our picture of life inside out is one of those revolutionary visions of profound truth about the nature of existence which are bound to leave their mark. His books may be the starting off of a new literature, they may be the beginnings of a universal world literature. In any case, they are a fact to be reckoned with. They undermine our picture of life by pointing out that our conception of individuals is only a tiny approximation of the truth that we have deduced in order to be able to form rough charts of living for ourselves. At the same time, his books enormously enhance the value of life by making us realise how every single individual is deeply connected with the whole of life and the whole of the past. . . .

330. Oliver Gogarty, *Saturday Review of Literature*

1941

Extract from 'The Joyce I Knew', *Saturday Review of Literature*, xxiii (25 January 1941), 15–16 [3–4, 15–16].

At the end of biographical material Gogarty makes several judgements on Joyce. See the reply by Padraic Colum (No. 333).

. . . The lovely, simple notes of pure lyricism which are to be found in *Chamber Music* (named in mockery after the sound he made by kicking accidentally a night jar) died away and maniacal rage against all things established took their place in a brothel in his lacerated heart. . . .

In *Anna Livia Plurabelle* his experiment is at its best. Here there is intelligible evidence of that for which he was striving and that was to make words in a surrealistic way show roots as well as blossoms. His stupendous erudition is evident in every word. I don't know exactly how many names of rivers are suggested in the description of the Liffey's woven waves that drown the reader until the sense is submerged only to give him a moment's breathing space and a glimpse of it again. The history of Dublin, that city which for all his travelling he never left, is in it too and his mockery when he makes the two washerwomen who later become, one a tree and the other a stone, wash the dirty linen of the Church. The oncoming of twilight is suggested by sentences that waver abruptly on the wing like bats. *Finnegans Wake* may mean amongst many other themes, the death of Finn, the central figure of Ireland's Heroic Age which Yeats revived. Joyce must have found satisfaction at the national disillusionment which followed the entry of the Republicans to power in the Irish Free State. Even so a page or two should have been enough. Joyce was a great repudiator: he repudiated Ireland, he repudiated the Church, he repudiated the Classics and his more intelligible self.

When all is said, the choice between the Logos, the Divine Word, 'this godlike Reason,' and the large discourse and senseless mutterings of the subliminal mind's low delirium, yet remains to be taken.

There is room in this world of ours for every form of literature. But those whose gaze is clear and undimmed and steadfastly fixed on the Vision Beautiful as Yeats's was, must see what a waste of ingenuity and what nonsense this vast concordance represents.

To me it is like a shattered cathedral though the ruins of which, buried deep and muted under the debris, the organ still sounds with all its stops pulled out at once. . . .

331. Unsigned notice, *Times Literary Supplement*

25 January 1941

. . . Certainly James Joyce presents criticism with a problem. If *Finnegans Wake* was his sole work it would be easy to dismiss it as the vapouring humbug of a man who could not write and so pretended to be doing something better by using a language of his own making, a language of larger range and subtlety than that which was enough for all Shakespeare's purpose. But it was not his only contribution. His early poetry and prose may not be on the high level claimed for them, but they have distinction, dignity, strong individuality and clarity; his poetry, particularly, written within the tradition of English verse, has charm and an unexpected sweetness; *Ulysses* may not be—we think it is not—the marvellous manifestation of genius acclaimed by the devotees, for occasional flashes of lightning, even such strange new flashes, are not sufficient reward for the weary reader's plod through acres of boredom and brain-sick words.

But one thing these works established was that Joyce knew all about the art of writing. If one clear impression comes from the mass of obscurities in *Ulysses* it is that its author had read vastly and forgotten nothing. . . .

Joyce knew many languages. His world is a polyglot world where words, all words as well as the Joycean, have no objects but themselves. The word is not the flesh, but a substitute for the flesh. The soul of every man knows its own purgatory. Joyce's might have sojourned in a Tower of Babel, where his too sensitive ear apprehended with exquisite intensity the words of many tongues, his retentive memory storing them as a gramophone record stores sounds. So for him to write was just to put the records on the machine. But he alone knows what the sounds mean, he alone has the secret. For if it be true that he had in mind Vico's theory that the history of one nation is the history of all nations, and that *Finnegans Wake* purports to be a 'timeless, ideal history,' a composite mythology embracing all the ages and attributes of mankind, it can only be answered that Joyce alone can decide whether he succeeded. The work progressed into realms where it cannot be followed by others.

Baffled readers can sense, however, some hint of failure in working on Vico's theory. All the attributes of mankind? Here as in his other writings, in *Ulysses* and as far back as *Dubliners*, Joyce's people are all 'dead end' people, he sees men and women only on the seamy or the ridiculous side, people who are beyond the possibilities of a finer life. He observes them clearly and with an animation of interest that often breaks through the barriers of speech, but he observes them only as a spectacle of fun or of disgust. There is no tragic vision of their fate, no sentiment, no background of a sense of good or evil. Stephen Dedalus said in *Ulysses*. 'I will try to express myself in some mode of life or art as freely as I can and as wholly as I can.' Joyce confessed himself through Dedalus in *The Portrait of an Artist as a Young Man* as well as in *Ulysses*. And what is the final confession in *Finnegans Wake*? 'To see life foully' is a pointed expression used there. And that is not to see life whole.

If it is impossible, as has been said, to follow Joyce in the mysteries of his last work, then *Ulysses*, difficult as most of it is, is the work on which he must be judged. It is the book which is most acclaimed as marking a boundary line in English fiction. As to that, it need merely be said that only Joyce could write *Ulysses*, and any writer who attempted to follow him would make a colossal failure where he himself made a splendid one in an attempt almost heroic. It is a strange feast *Ulysses* invites us to, abundantly, brilliantly, boringly, obscenely, intellectually, bewilderingly mixed, a phantasmal expedition into the conscious and the sub-conscious. There are hypnotic qualities, scenes of genius in it—and long stretches of dullness and pretence. The reproductions made by his uncanny gift of visualizing are sometimes perfect, but often they are too trivial to be worth the effort. There are things beyond praise, uproarious Rabelaisian patches, and things beyond damnation. There are enticing pages of prose with the effect of music, and pages that are not prose nor anything recognizable as literature. One word-thought suggests another. Bloom walking the Dublin streets reflects that 'you never know whose thoughts you're chewing.' He chews thoughts of the beginning and the end of creation. . . .

332. J. Donald Adams, New York Times

26 January 1941, 2

It was a strange genius that died with James Joyce—one of the strangest in the history of literature. Whatever his ultimate position in that history may be, whatever value future generations may put upon his work, he is certain to be remembered as the author of two of the most singular books ever written. There is nothing in all literature really comparable to *Ulysses* and certainly nothing—if it too may be placed in that category—comparable to *Finnegans Wake*.

One other thing is certain—that along the lines of experimentation which Joyce followed it is impossible to carry further. One cannot conceive of the subjective method in fiction being pushed beyond the point to which he carried it in *Ulysses*; one cannot imagine greater liberties taken with language than those with which Joyce occupied himself in *Finnegans Wake*.

In his early work, in *Dubliners* and *A Portrait of the Artist as a Young Man*, Joyce made no extraordinary demands upon his readers; in *Ulysses* they are heavy; in *Finnegans Wake* they pass beyond all reasonable bounds. It was natural that his contemporaries should make the effort to determine what Joyce was about; one wonders how many, in the years to come, other than literary historians and writers absorbed in the technique of their craft, will find that necessary effort sufficiently rewarding. In the case of *Ulysses* there is little doubt that readers of sufficient tenacity and knowledge will be numerous, for in spite of its frequent obscurity and its occasional dullness there is an abundance of life between its covers, revealed in a manner not paralleled in any other writer. But *Finnegans Wake* seems destined to be one of the dipped-into but unread curiosities of literature.

Extravagant claims were made regarding the influence which *Ulysses* was likely to have upon the art of fiction. That influence is less evident today than it was in the years immediately following the book's publication. A convincing presentation of the stream of consciousness is difficult to achieve and difficult to read. It never can be completely convincing, simply for the reason that one knows one cannot penetrate into another's subconscious. It is not generally known that Tolstoy employed the method once, in a work not yet translated into English, but in that greatest of all novels, *War and Peace*, he managed very well without it. . . .

333. Padraic Colum, reply to Oliver Gogarty

1941

'The Joyce I Knew', *Saturday Review of Literature*, xxiii (22 February 1941), 11. See No. 330.

. . . But Oliver Gogarty fails completely in his approach to James Joyce the writer [*SRL*, Jan. 25]. He never understood any of the tragedy and compassion that James Joyce got into *Ulysses* and, I think, into *Finnegans Wake*; to him these books are all confusion and pedantry. He refers to William Butler Yeats in his article as the type of great artist who could be central, clear, and intelligible. I wonder whether Oliver Gogarty ever discussed Joyce's work with Yeats? If he did he must have discovered that Yeats had a high admiration for *Ulysses*—he spoke to me of its 'lonely intensity'; he read thoughtfully *Finnegans Wake* as it appeared as *Work in Progress*. If *Ulysses* and *Finnegans Wake* are confusion and pedantry to Oliver Gogarty it was something very different to the great artist whom he appeals to. . . .

334. Frank Budgen, *Horizon*

1941

'James Joyce', *Horizon*, iv (February 1941), 104–8. Also appeared in *James Joyce: Two Decades of Criticism* (1948, 1963), ed. Seon Givens, pp. 19–26 (from which the present text is extracted).

These reminiscences are full of short, critical comments which it has been necessary to extract from the larger bulk of remembrances.

. . . He put himself in all his books. He is the unnamed boy in *Dubliners*, Stephen Dedalus in *A Portrait of the Artist as a Young Man* and *Ulysses*, Richard in *Exiles*, and Shem the Penman in *Finnegans Wake*, and, if Joyce painted them himself, who shall say that any of them is a bad likeness? . . .

. . . It is worth noting that in all Joyce's work the relations between man and woman are of a monumental simplicity, and that complications and the subtler shades arise only in the relations between man and man. . . .

. . . Now we know that *Ulysses* was a best seller; but all the years of its composition Joyce labored on it, reckless of time, not knowing how or by whom it would be published, aware that he was writing a masterpiece, and just as aware that masterpieces may be the death of their creators. . . .

. . . In my hearing he answered (perhaps for the hundredth time) the question: 'Aren't there enough words for you in the five hundred thousand of the English language?' 'Yes, there are enough of them, but they are not the right ones.' Rebutting the charge of vulgarity against the use of the pun, he said: 'The Holy Roman Catholic Apostolic Church was built on a pun. It ought to be good enough for me.' And a studied riposte: 'Yes. Some of the means I use are trivial—and some are quadrivial.' August Suter, the Swiss sculptor, met Joyce as he was beginning to write *Finnegans Wake*, and Joyce's description of his enterprise was: 'I am boring through a mountain from two sides. The question is, how to meet in the middle.' There spoke the 'great artificer'. . . .

335. T. S. Eliot, *Horizon*

1941

'A Message to the Fish', in *James Joyce: Two Decades of Criticism* (1948, 1963), ed. Seon Givens, pp. 468–71. The same article appeared earlier in *Horizon*, iii (March 1941), 173–5.

On January 14, having read the obituary notice of James Joyce which had appeared in *The Times* of that morning, I addressed to the Editor of that paper the following letter:

Sir,

I hope that you will permit me to submit one or two cautious qualifications to your interesting obituary notice of my friend Mr. James Joyce. That Joyce failed to appreciate 'the eternal and serene beauty of nature' can, I think, be disputed by reference to several passages in *A Portrait of the Artist as a Young Man*, *Ulysses* and *Finnegans Wake*; but being separated from my books, I cannot quote chapter and verse. As for his inability to appreciate 'the higher sides of human character,' this stricture would, perhaps, be more applicable to Jonathan Swift, and I should ask the reader, before accepting such a judgment, to consider 'The Dead,' in *Dubliners*—one of the finest short stories in the language.

What I chiefly question, however, is the importance at this date of the opinions of men older than Joyce, holding the views of an older literary generation, such as Edmund Gosse, Arnold Bennett, or Æ. To some of Joyce's younger contemporaries, like myself, *Ulysses* still seems the most considerable work of imagination in English in our time, comparable in importance (though in little else) with the work of Marcel Proust. I do not believe that posterity will be able to controvert this judgment, though it may be able to demonstrate the relative insignificance of the literary achievement of the whole period.

Your obedient servant, etc.

As this letter was not published, I wrote a fortnight later to say that I presumed myself free to publish it elsewhere, and received a polite note from the Obituaries Department returning the letter, and expressing regret that restrictions of space had made publication impossible.

It was not a well-written letter, partly because I was ill with influenza when I wrote it. But its oddity is rather more due to the fact that I wished to write something that *The Times* would print, and I entertained the hope that it might get by as an 'Appreciation.' Had I not been hampered by illness and a sense (however imperfect) of the possible, I might have written in somewhat the following vein:

Sir,

I have read with stupefaction your obituary notice on the greatest man of letters of my generation. It is usual, I believe, for editors of newspapers to have ready obituary notices of all notable men and women. This practice is wholly to be commended; but the notices should be written by the right persons in the beginning, and should then be kept up to date. The impression given by your notice of Mr. Joyce is that it was written by someone considerably older than he—someone who by now must be well over fifty-nine. That it was in some sense brought up to date I must believe, since, being an obituary, it mentions the date and place of Joyce's death; but this does not cover the requirements. I am not alluding to oversights such as the failure to mention that *Work in Progress* was eventually completed and published under the title of *Finnegans Wake*; I refer to the inclusion of trivialities about the man, and the failure to show any understanding of the significance of his work in its time.

I am quite aware that at the present time considerations of space are of first importance. For this reason I venture to point out how you might have saved space. Whatever the various distinction of Sir Edmund Gosse, Arnold Bennett and Æ in other fields, none of them could lay claim to any authority as a critic; and phrases taken from what they said about Joyce many years ago could well have been spared. So could the estimate of your obituary writer. The first business of an obituary writer is to give the important facts about the life of the deceased, and to give some notion of the position which he enjoyed. He is not called upon to pronounce summary judgment (especially when his notice is unsigned), though it is part of his proper function, when his subject is a writer, to give some notion of what was thought of him by the best qualified critics of his time. I suggest also, in view of your limitations of space, that to mention that Joyce was one of a 'large and poor family' was unnecessary; and that a silly remark of his when he was a young man may give the reader the mistaken impression that vanity was the most conspicuous trait of his character, and the equally mistaken impression that we have the authority of Yeats for permission to ignore Joyce's work. And, as you did not have space to mention that *Ulysses* was eventually published in both England and America, it would perhaps have been better to omit mention of its previous suppression.

I must try to make quite clear that the issue which I raise has nothing to do with the difference between my valuation of Joyce's work and that of your writer. I am not concerned with matters of opinion, but with matters of fact; and were my opinion of Joyce still lower than that of your biographer, my condemnation of your notice would be the same. My motives in writing this letter extend much further than loyalty to a friend or desire to see justice done to a particular author. The name and fame of Joyce were known throughout the world: *The Times* has an equally wide reputation. I do not believe that your notice will much affect the world's opinion of Joyce; but I fear lest it may be used as evidence by those who choose to believe that England has lost respect for that one of the arts for which it has been chiefly renowned.

I am, yours, etc.,

T. S. Eliot.

336. Paul Léon remembers

1942

'In Memory of Joyce', *Poésie*, No. v (1942), 35. Also appeared in *James Joyce Yearbook* (1949), ed. Maria Jolas, pp. 117–18, 122–3 [116–25].

Meanwhile, however, the student of the human soul should read attentively Joyce's writings in which it is mirrored, for Joyce made no distinction between actual life and literary creation. His work is one long self-confession, and in this respect he is akin to the greatest of the romantics. . . . Joyce, however, seeks to attain to absolute sincerity, to all that is most human within us; he seeks to do away with writing that merely aims at covering the blank page, to do away with conventional self-expression, to do away with the very body which intervenes between the most secret 'I', Pascal's 'I beyond the soul', and the exterior world. He also seeks to do away with the writing hand, the listening ear, the seeing eye . . . and on this last point a pitiless fate met him more than half-way . . . But should one then accept to be silent? Joyce's work offers brilliant proof of the contrary, but it serves also as proof that he had the necessary courage, perseverance, inner strength and energy of mind—any one of which might easily have been insufficient—to overcome all obstacles, all suffering, and to attain perfection. When his work comes to be judged according to its true value, as posterity will judge it, it will appear overwhelming, if only because of the crushing labour that it obviously represents, and one man's life will seem to have been conceived on too small a scale in comparison with the immensity of the effort involved.

There exists yet another aspect of the intimate and indissoluble tie between Joyce's life and work, which it is perhaps even more important to mention here, since it will necessarily be something of a closed book to posterity, and that is the influence of his work on his life. Continuous self-confession, for Joyce, meant continuous creation; it was he who created the atmosphere and general conditions that surrounded him, and he never stopped creating them. . . .

The mystery of this attraction towards water has been revealed to us by Joyce himself in his revolutionary, astonishing, Pantagruelian, romantic *Finnegans Wake*, especially in the last dozen or so pages, which are composed of short, choppy, restless, rippling, flowing sentences that follow each other in rapid, turbulent succession. . . .

Among the innumerable critical reviews that I have gone through, I recall no mention of a point which, it seems to me, should strike us immediately: and that is the fact that the amazing postscript which concludes the work ends on an unfinished sentence, with the article 'the'; and the noun that follows this article is the first word of the book, that is to say, 'riverrun'. It is not for me to spell out all the meanings of what people are inclined to consider as a cryptogram; this task belongs to future generations of critics and literary historians. All I should like to do here is to introduce the testimony of one who witnessed the growth of this work. This postscript had probably been carried in its completed form for many years in the prodigious brain that engendered it. The first version, which was only about two and a half pages long, was written in one afternoon, in December 1938. It was a veritable deliverance. Joyce brought it with him when we met that evening for our usual half-past eight *rendez-vous* in Madame Lapeyre's pleasant *bistrot*, on the corner of the Rue de Grenelle and the Rue de Bourgogne. . . .

337. James Stephens remembers

1946

'The James Joyce I Knew', *The Listener* (24 October 1946), 565.
Condensed in the *Irish Digest*, xxviii (July 1947), 38–41, and later
appeared in *James, Seumas & Jacques: Unpublished Writings of
James Stephens* (1964), ed. Lloyd Frankenberg, pp. 147–55.

To end on the difficulty that is Joyce. All writers who are hatcheting out
a route for themselves in a wilderness are bent on avoiding the tradition
and the tone that is their inherited art and their language. . . .

So it is with the Joyce of *Finnegans Wake*. You need all the rest of
your life to read it, if you are going to read it, and you will then need a
life after that again to understand it. . . .

In *Finnegans Wake* Joyce was trying to write pure prose. When we
have said all that we can say about this book we will make two statements only: we shall say, 'It is unreadable,' and we shall add, 'It is
wonderful.' Upon these two conflictions James Joyce may sleep in
peace until his second of February comes round again.

Here is the end of the episode called *Anna Livia Plurabelle*.' Night
is falling, the river and the landscape is obscuring, and the words that
describe it are obscuring also; the river, and the landscape, and the
words have almost gone to sleep. You can't see and you can't hear, and
you can't bother. A stone is muttering drowsily to an elm tree:

[quotes from *Finnegans Wake*, pp. 215–16]

I'll just say that it's wonderful, and there is an endless much more of
it, in every mood that can be imagined.

338. Oliver Gogarty comments

1950

From *Rolling Down the Lea* (1950), pp. 116–17.

Now both smoothness and sequence are gone from the novel. The Subjective or Stream of Consciousness has been substituted. And the Subjective covers a multitude of sins. The so-called 'modern' novel appears to me to be a garbage-pail or ash-can which contains any or every cast-off remnant of living: old cloths, broken crockery, back numbers, stale food and decaying fish. I might has guessed that there was Chaos coming, for Joyce had his aileron out and caught rumblings from Rimbaud, rumours of a revolt that cast its shadow before the revolution, and was destined to turn things topsy-turvy until hideousness took the place of beauty, and slavery the place of liberty, and discord the place of harmony, disruption the place of unity—unless the cohesion that the galvanised garbage-pail gives to its contents be considered an unity: the bucket in this instance being the Subconscious. Naturally, these 'moderns' in their obscurity were left to talk to themselves for the want of an audience. Joyce went one further, and talked to himself in his sleep: hence *Finnegans Wake*.

339. Oliver Gogarty corrects memories

1950

'They Think they Know Joyce', *Saturday Review of Literature*, xxxiii (18 March 1950), 8, 9, 36, 37. Condensed in *Irish Digest*, xxxvii (August 1950), 19–23.

. . . In the Dublin use of the word 'artist' lies the key to James Joyce: the explanation of how this contradictory character, who in his early days knew beauty so well, became chief of the apostles of confusion and ugliness, the leader of the decadents.

In Dublin, 'artist' does not denote one who is devoted to painting or any of the arts. In Dublin an 'artist' is a merry droll, a player of hoaxes. . . .

I wonder what all the worshippers of Joyce would say if they realized that they had become the victims of a gigantic hoax, of one of the most enormous leg-pulls in history. . . . Rimbaud, disgusted with mankind, had withdrawn from the world. The logical end was for him to withdraw from all authorship because his kind of private writing would lead only to talking to himself. Joyce did not withdraw, so he ended by listening to himself talking in his sleep—*Finnegans Wake*. The Greeks have a name for such private persons—*idiotes*. . . . Above all, he would record the boredom of life in the cracked mirror of *Ulysses* with its preposterous and factitious parallel to Homer's fairy tales. He would depict a world open at both ends wherein nothing happened, though everything was just about to happen, and all would hurry on in a senseless, chaotic cataract. He would hold up a mirror to a Dublin that had come to nothing.

In future he would give the world the obverse side of the medal, the gargoyle and the grotesque, instead of anything that might exalt and beautify life. He would write so that all who run might read all that Dublin offered to him. On the backside of beauty he would inscribe his name. If the writing proved to be indelible, all the better. . . .

Suddenly Joyce found that his leg-pull had acquired an international audience. Suddenly he discovered that to write his name on the backside of beauty was the most significant action of his life. He dared not retract; money and fame were at stake. He dared not let anyone into a joke that had gone too far and had been taken too seriously. I wonder what he thought when he found himself taken seriously so far from the only place where he could count on understanding. He could not let down his followers nor his fans. . . .

Joyce's power of construction was weak, hence the obscene conjunction of *Ulysses* with the Homeric poem. As in the case of the so-called modern poets, Joyce's inheritors, a dislocated world demands a dislocated poetry to describe it. . . .

How does it happen that America should have become the chief infirmary for Joyceans? The answer is because America is the country *par excellence* of the detective story, the crossword puzzle, and the smoke signal. All these are supplied by *Ulysses*. Here, too, where mental homes are numerous, are to be found that unique class who think that the unravelling of an enigma or a puzzle is the height of poetry. The snake pits have become vocal. . . .

340. Mary Colum corrects Gogarty

1950

'A Little Knowledge of Joyce', *Saturday Review of Literature*, xxxiii (29 April 1950), 10–12 [condensed in *Irish Digest*, xxxvii (September, 1950), 39–41].

. . . he had no means of knowing the mature Joyce. Not only was the man who wrote *Ulysses*, *Finnegans Wake*, and *Portrait of the Artist*, unknown to him, but he had at no time any conception of the creator who was James Joyce. The man Oliver Gogarty did know was the youthful author of a book of poems, *Chamber Music*, and something of the man who wrote *Dubliners*. On the assumption on the part of his readers that Oliver Gogarty knew far more than this, he has succeeded in placing all over the country in strategic positions attacks and mis-informations about Joyce, his family, his friends, his readers, and his work. Whereas some of the misinformation in 'They Think They Know Joyce'—such as the reference to Mrs. Carola Gideon Welcker as Mr. Giedion-Welcker and the turning of the verb in Joyce's well-known line about himself 'Steeled in the school of old Aquinas' into the inept 'trained'—may be of no particular consequence yet these in-accuracies indicate the confusion and misinformation that permeate the article. It is true, of course, as Oliver Gogarty says, that floods of non-sense have been poured out about James Joyce, but the greatest compiler of nonsense has been Oliver Gogarty himself. I shall take this op-portunity of correcting some of it.

In his article Oliver Gogarty undertakes to explain what caused Joyce to produce *Ulysses*, attributing it all to Joyce's frustration over the cancelled publication of *Dubliners*. Thus he places on a Dublin firm, Messrs. Maunsell; but the publisher who originally refused publication after giving a contract was Grant Richards, who after years of postpone-ment from 1906 on finally published the book in 1914. . . . There is some Rimbaud influence in Joyce but not nearly as much as there is of other French writers—Flaubert in *Dubliners*, Mallarmé in *Finnegans Wake*, and, in general, the influence of the Polish-French critic and editor Wyzewa. Oliver Gogarty seems to have no knowledge of Rimbaud at all: . . . And as for the suggestion that Gertrude Stein imitated *Ulysses*, this is sheer nonsense; her writing comes out of a different conception altogether. Gertrude Stein not only did not imitate *Ulysses* but she did not care about Joyce's work; in fact, her opinion of it was not so remote from Oliver Gogarty's own. Joyce's work was dis-tinctively Irish: the remolding of language which he practises in *Finnegans Wake* has its correspondences with the designs in the *Book of Kells*, reproductions of whose pages Joyce had always before him. . . .

The trouble with the author of 'They Think They Know Joyce' is that he seems to have read nothing of Joyce except *Chamber Music*. He confuses *Ulysses* and *Finnegans Wake*; he has no sense of the structure of *Ulysses* nor of the design of *Finnegans Wake*. Some of the most beautiful and moving writing in modern literature is in these works. . . . How-ever, without taking too seriously the excursions into literary criticism of Dr. Jung or any other doctor, I should like to say that there is in the New York Public Library a copy of a very complimentary letter by

Dr. Jung to Joyce about *Ulysses*, in which he speaks about its wonderful psychological effects, particularly those in Mrs. Bloom's monologue: 'I think the devil's grandmother knows as much about the psychology of a woman; I don't. It is a string of psychological peaches.' Very Teutonic English but the meaning is clear. There are other statements in Oliver Gogarty's article that could be traversed but I think enough has been said to show how misleading the article is. . . .

341. Stanislaus Joyce corrects Gogarty

1953

Extract from *An Open Letter to Dr. Oliver Gogarty* (1953). Appeared in *Interim*, iv (1954), 49–56 (from which the present text is taken).

Corrections of Gogarty's errors in 'They Think they Know Joyce' (No. 339).

. . . You entitled your article 'They think they know Joyce'. As you are so sure you did, it would be advisable to try in any future article on him to be right at least occasionally about ascertainable facts. . . .

It is equally false to insinuate that my brother was influenced in writing *Ulysses* and *Finnegans Wake* by a precarious allowance from a rich lady which made it possible for him to live in comfort for the first time, and that it was, therefore, impossible for him to stop clowning since he had begun so successfully. . . .

All his long struggle proves beyond dispute that the motives you allege are not such as would have influence with my brother; but I fear that in Paris he guarded his heart less vigilantly against more subtle temptations—an overweening contempt for his readers and his critics, the bitter fruit of his triumph, and an overstrained application of a perfectly valid theory of dream language. He would not be the first innovator to fall a victim to his own spirit of innovation. . . . To come to the main point of your article, who do you think will believe that *Ulysses* is a 'leg-pull'? That my brother worked on it for seven years in ill-health and poverty, refusing invitations to write short stories for magazines, on the verge of blindness, unperturbed by the din of war, fighting relentlessly with censors and the truculent leaders of massed prejudice, to perpetrate a 'leg-pull'? Give your readers credit for a little horse-sense. . . .

You are an untrustworthy guide to my brother's life and character, but criticism of his work cannot be so easily answered, all criticism being so largely subjective. My brother's *Ulysses*, I see, is out of your reach, but his earlier work should be within it. . . . I will say, however, in passing, that there is no need for one to be a Sibyl in order to interpret *Ulysses*. It is admittedly a book with a key, but in many chapters the key is in the lock. . . .

My brother, for his part, was not so easily stirred by common or garden manifestations of beauty. He left its trappings and chocolate box ideals to you and 'poets of your ilk', as you phrase it. While still a student he had defined his object in an article on Mangan. He wrote:

'Beauty, the splendour of truth, is a gracious presence when the imagination contemplates intensely the truth of its own being or the visible world, and the spirit which proceeds out of truth and beauty is the holy spirit of joy. These are realities and these alone give and sustain life.'

In spite of the youthful sententiousness (he was twenty then), he was endeavouring to define a position from which he never receded. But put to the test, do these words mean anything? I think they do. . . .

My brother's self-appointed task was to rescue literature from the hands of those who had made it a parody of life, from the 'mummers', as he called them, and amongst the minor mummers you were one. . . .

342. Malcolm Cowley recalls Joyce and Sylvia Beach

1963

'When a Young American. . .' *Mercure de France*, cccxlvii (August-September 1963), 58 [57–59].

For me the truly fascinating chapters of *Shakespeare and Company* are those in which this publisher describes her most unbusinesslike relations with her author and divinity. Joyce accepted favors and demanded services as if he were not a person but a sanctified cause. It was, he seemed to be saying, a privilege to devote one's life to the cause, and those who paid his debts for him were sure to be rewarded in heaven. Miss Beach agreed with him. Admiring and almost worshipping his work, she invested all the profits of her bookshop, begged all the money she could from relatives, and mortgaged all her credit in publishing *Ulysses*. Joyce kept pushing her closer to bankruptcy by making more and more corrections in proof. When the book finally appeared on his fortieth birthday—February 2, 1922—it was a monument to the genius and patience of the author, but also to the self-sacrificing devotion of its publisher. . . .

343. Janet Flanner recalls Joyce and Sylvia Beach
1963

'The Great Amateur Publisher', *Mercure de France*, cccxlvii (August–September 1963), 46 [46–51].
Part of the tribute volume to Sylvia Beach.

. . . She became famous for having published only this one enormous magna opus of James Joyce, so difficult to read and fathom that readers and many critics had at first to take their time about it to appreciate it. At the beginning she was mostly thanked merely by the very commotion it increasingly provoked in the whole western literary world of the opening Ninteteen Twenties. . . . Where she did not escape the publisher's fate was as the beast of burden struggling beneath the crushing load of a singular author's genius and egotisms, heavy as stones or marble in the case of the Dubliner Joyce. There is no record of any other great writer of English prose in our time inhabited by so monumental a personality as he possessed or with a character so deeply inscribed and carved by his own ego. He was like a thin dapper granite column set up in his own honor.

A part of her fame came from her being an amateur woman publisher with the courage to publish so daring a modern masculine classic as *Ulysses*. All of Joyce's gratitude, largely unexpressed, should have been addressed to her as a woman. . . . That *Ulysses* became the sort of book it is is largely due to her, for it was she in this, her one publishing venture, who decided to allow Joyce an indefinite right to correct his proofs. It was in the exercise of this right that the peculiarities of Joyce's prose reached their novel flowering. . . .

344. An Irish last word

1964

Patrick Byrne, 'Joyce's Dream Book Took Seventeen Years To Write', *Irish Digest*, lxxxi (July 1964), 76, [73–76].

. . . When Joyce was asked for a guide to *Finnegans Wake* he referred the questioner to Sir Edward Sullivan's *The Book of Kells* which he said he had beside him while he was writing the work. He said the prose style of the *Wake* was like the delicate and intricate designs of *The Book of Kells*.

I managed to read *Finnegans Wake* once by devoting a couple of hours a day to it, over a period of about three months. Then I met American writer Thornton Wilder, himself a *Finnegans Wake* addict.

'My boy,' he said, 'take my advice. Don't ever try to read that book again. I have spent so much time reading and re-reading it that I have been unable to write many plays and novels that I wanted to write.'

I took his advice and beyond dipping now and again into the *Wake* to read a section here and there, Joyce's novel, parody, leg-pull or whatever you like to call it remains on my shelves as a reminder of a Herculean reading task I once endured, but which I will not say was unenjoyable. . . .

APPENDIX A: EARLY EDITIONS OF THE WRITINGS OF JAMES JOYCE

The Critical Writings of James Joyce: ed. Ellsworth Mason and Richard Ellmann, New York: The Viking Press, 1959. Includes the early essays and reviews, later political articles and the broadsides *The Holy Office* (1904 or 1905) and *Gas From a Burner* (September 1912); for a comprehensive list of Joyce's critical writings see John J. Slocum and Herbert Cahoon, *A Bibliography of James Joyce* (1953), New Haven: Yale University Press, London: Rupert Hart-Davis.

Chamber Music: 1907, London: Elkin Mathews.

Dubliners: 1914, London: Grant Richards Ltd.; three of the stories had appeared in the *Irish Homestead* in 1904; *Gens de Dublin*, 1926, Paris: Plon-Nourrit et Cie., French translation by Yva Fernandez, Hélène du Pasquier, Jacques-Paul Reynaud.

A Portrait of the Artist as a Young Man: 1916, New York: B. W. Huebsch; serially published in the *Egoist* (London), i, No. 3 (2 February 1914) to ii, No. 9 (1 September 1915); *Dédalus:* 1925, Paris: Editions de la Sirène, French translation by Ludmila Savitzky.

Exiles: 1918, London: Grant Richards Ltd.; *Esuli*, a translation by Carlo Linati in *Il Convegno* (Milan), i, No. 3 (April 1920), 27–52.

Ulysses: 1922, Paris: Shakespeare and Company, serially published in the *Little Review* (New York), in twenty-three installments, iv, No. 11 (March 1918), to vii, No. 3 (September-December 1920); five installments serially published in the *Egoist*, vi, No. 1 (January-February 1919), to vi, No. 5 (December 1919); *Ulysse:* 1929, Paris: Adrienne Monnier, French translation by Auguste Morel assisted by Stuart Gilbert, reviewed by Valéry Larbaud with the collaboration of the author; *Ulysses:* 1934, New York: Random House, first American edition; 1936, London: John Lane, The Bodley Head, first English edition.

Pomes Penyeach: 1927, Paris: Shakespeare and Company.

Work in Progress, for a complete publishing history see Richard Ellmann, *James Joyce*, 1959, New York: Oxford University Press, pp. 801–3, from a compilation by A. Walton Litz.
　　Anna Livia Plurabelle (FW 196–216): 1928, New York: Crosby Gaige; 1930, London: Faber & Faber.

Tales Told of Shem and Shaun (FW 152–9, 282–304, 414–19): 1929, Paris: The Black Sun Press; 1932, London: Faber & Faber.

Haveth Childers Everywhere (FW 532–54): 1930, Paris: Henry Babou and Jack Kahane; New York: The Fountain Press: 1931, London: Faber & Faber.

The Mime of Mick, Nick and the Maggies (FW 219–59): 1934, The Hague: The Servire Press.

Collected Poems: 1936, New York: The Black Sun Press, contains *Chamber Music, Pomes Penyeach* and 'Ecce Puer'.

Storiella As She is Syung (FW 260–75, 304–8): 1937, London: Corvinus Press.

Finnegans Wake: 1939, London: Faber & Faber; New York: The Viking Press.

Stephen Hero: 1944, ed. Theodore Spencer, London: Jonathan Cape; New York: New Directions.

The Early Joyce: The Book Reviews, 1902–1903: 1955, ed. Stanislaus Joyce and Ellsworth Mason, Colorado Springs: Mamalujo Press.

Epiphanies: 1956, ed. O. A. Silverman, Buffalo: The Lockwood Memorial Library.

APPENDIX B: BIBLIOGRAPHY

ADAMS, ROBERT M., *Surface and Symbol: The Consistency of James Joyce's Ulysses* (1962): New York: Oxford University Press.

BUDGEN, FRANK, *James Joyce and the Making of Ulysses* (1934): London: Grayson, new edition 1960: Bloomington, Indiana: Indiana University Press.

CAMPBELL, JOSEPH, and HENRY MORTON ROBINSON, *A Skeleton Key to Finnegans Wake* (1944): New York: Harcourt, Brace & Co.

DEMING, ROBERT H., *A Bibliography of James Joyce Studies* (1964): Lawrence, Kansas: University of Kansas Libraries.

ELLMANN, RICHARD, *James Joyce* (1959): New York: Oxford University Press.

GOLDBERG, S. L., *The Classical Temper* (1961): London: Chatto & Windus.

HART, CLIVE, *Structure and Motif in Finnegans Wake* (1962): London: Faber & Faber.

James Joyce Quarterly, annual bibliography by Alan M. Cohn.

JOYCE, STANISLAUS, *My Brother's Keeper* (1958): New York: The Viking Press.

——, *The Dublin Diary of Stanislaus Joyce* (1962): ed. George H. Healey: Ithaca, New York: Cornell University Press.

LEVIN, HARRY, *James Joyce: A Critical Introduction* (1941): Norfolk: New Directions; revised edition, Norfolk: New Directions, 1960.

LITZ, A. WALTON, *The Art of James Joyce: Method and Design in Ulysses and Finnegans Wake* (1961): London: Oxford University Press; revised edition, 1964.

MAGALANER, MARVIN, *Time of Apprenticeship: The Fiction of Young James Joyce* (1959): New York: Abelard-Schuman.

MAGALANER, MARVIN, and RICHARD M. KAIN, *Joyce: The Man, The Work, The Reputation* (1956): New York: New York University Press.

PARKER, ALAN, *James Joyce: A Bibliography of his Writings, Critical Material and Miscellanea* (1948): Boston: F. W. Faxon Co.

SLOCUM, JOHN J., and HERBERT CAHOON, *A Bibliography of James Joyce, 1882–1941* (1953): New Haven: Yale University Press; London: Rupert Hart-Davis.

SULLIVAN, KEVIN, *Joyce Among the Jesuits* (1958): New York: Columbia University Press.

SULTAN, STANLEY, *The Argument of Ulysses* (1964): Columbus, Ohio: Ohio State University Press.

TINDALL, WILLIAM YORK, *A Reader's Guide to James Joyce* (1959): New York: Noonday Press.

WILSON, EDMUND, 'James Joyce' in *Axel's Castle* (1931): New York: Charles Scribner's Sons.

774

APPENDIX C

Critical studies of such length that extracting or excerpting would limit their usefulness in this volume; critical studies which have been collected or reprinted in such form that duplication in this volume is unnecessary, the collections being readily accessible to the general reader.

BEACH, JOSEPH WARREN, 'The Novel from James to Joyce', *Nation*, cxxxii (10 June 1931), 634–6; revised and enlarged as 'Post-Impressionism: Joyce' in his *Twentieth Century Novel* (1932): New York, London: Appleton-Century Crofts Inc., pp. 403–24.

BEACH, SYLVIA, *Shakespeare and Company* (1956): New York: Harcourt, Brace, 1956; the first chapter appeared in *Mercure de France*, cccix (May 1950), 12–29; *Ulysses in Paris*, published by Harcourt, Brace in 1956, was for Miss Beach's friends, and represents pages 34–47 of the complete book.

BECKETT, SAMUEL, *et al*, *Our Exagmination Round His Factification for Incamination of Work in Progress* (1929): Paris: Shakespeare and Company, reprinted by New Directions, 1962; the articles in this collection originally appeared in *transition*, edited by Eugène Jolas and Elliot Paul.

BROCH, HERMANN, *James Joyce und die Gegenwart* (1936): Wien: Reichner; translated by Eugène and Maria Jolas as 'Joyce and the Present Age' in *The James Joyce Yearbook* (1949): Paris: Transition Press, pp. 68–108; translated as 'Joyce et son temps' by H. Hildenbrand and A. Lindenberg for *Lettres Nouvelles*, n.s. No. 13 (April 1961), 65–93.

BUDGEN, FRANK, *James Joyce and the Making of Ulysses* (1934): London: Grayson; reprinted by the Indiana University Press, 1960.

BURGUM, EDWIN B., 'Ulysses and the Impasse of Individualism', *Virginia Quarterly Review*, xvii (Autumn 1941), 561–73; also appeared in his *The Novel and the World's Dilemma* (1947): New York: Oxford University Press, pp. 95–108.

CANBY, HENRY SEIDEL, *Seven Years' Harvest* (1936): New York: Farrar & Rinehart, pp. 106–7, 128–9, 300.

COLLINS, JOSEPH, 'Ireland's Latest Literary Antinomian: James Joyce', in his *The Doctor Looks at Literature* (1923): New York: George H. Doran, pp. 35–60.

COLLINS, NORMAN, *The Facts of Fiction* (1932): London: Victor Gollancz, pp. 277–84.

DAICHES, DAVID, 'The Importance of *Ulysses*', in his *New Literary Values* (1936): Edinburgh: Oliver & Boyd, pp. 69–82.

——, *The Novel and the Modern World* (1939): Chicago: University of Chicago Press, pp. 80–147; revised edition, 1960, pp. 63–137; the first chapter, 'Dubliners', was reprinted in *Modern British Fiction* (1961): ed. Mark Shorer New York: Oxford University Press, pp. 308–21. Of the four chapters, the second ('*Ulysses* and *Finnegans Wake*: The Aesthetic Problem') and the fourth ('*Ulysses* as Comedy') were revised; the first ('Dubliners') and the third ('*Ulysses:* The Technical Problem') are substantially the same.

DUFF, CHARLES C., *James Joyce and the Plain Reader* (1932): London: Harmsworth.

DUJARDIN, EDOUARD, *Le Monologue intérieure: son Apparition, ses Origines, sa Place dans l'Oeuvre de James Joyce* (1931): Paris: Messein.

FEHR, BERNHARD, 'Bewusstseinsstrom und Konstruksion: James Joyce', in his *Die englische Literatur der Gegenwart und die Kulturfragen unserer Zeit* (1930): Leipzig: Tauchnitz, pp. 56–68.

FEIBLEMAN, JAMES K., 'The Comedy of Myth: James Joyce' in *In Praise of Comedy* (1939): London: Allen & Unwin, pp. 230–6.

FORD, FORD MADOX, *It Was the Nightingale* (1933): Philadelphia: Lippincott, pp. 290–4.

——, *The March of Literature* (1938): New York: Dial Press, pp. 323–4.

FORSTER, E. M., *Aspects of the Novel* (1927): New York: Harcourt, Brace, pp. 177–80.

GILBERT, STUART, *James Joyce's Ulysses, A Study* (1930): London: Faber & Faber; New York: Alfred A. Knopf, 1931; chapters of this work have appeared separately: 'Irish Ulysses: Hades Episode', *Fortnightly Review*, cxxxii (July 1929), 46–58 (Chapter VI); 'The Aeolus Episode of *Ulysses*', *transition*, No. 18 (November 1929), 129–46 (Chapter VII); 'Prote: *Ulysse*', *Echanges*, No. 2 (March 1930), 118–34 (Chapter III).

GILLET, LOUIS, *Stèle pour James Joyce* (1941): Grenoble: Presses des Grands Etablissements de l'Imprimerie Générale; second edition, Paris: Editions du Sagittaire, 1946; translated as *Claybook for James Joyce* by Georges Markow-Totevy, with an 'Introduction' by Markow-Totevy (which appeared originally as 'James Joyce and Louis Gillet', *James Joyce Miscellany* (1957): ed. Marvin Magalaner, New York: James Joyce Society, pp. 49–61), and a 'Preface', 'James Joyce and the Academician', by Leon Edel (which appeared originally in *James Joyce Miscellany*, 1957, pp. 44–8), and an article 'Desperate Words Call for Desperate Little Remedies', by André Gide (which appeared originally in *Le Figaro* [30–31 Mai 1942]): (1958), London, New York: Abelard-Schuman; contains translations of the following articles: 'Du Côté de Chez Joyce', *Revue des Deux Mondes*, xviii (August 1925), 686–97; 'Mr. James Joyce et son nouveau Roman "Work in Progress"', *Revue des Deux Mondes*, lxxxiv (August 1931), 928–39, translated by Ronald Symond in *transition*, No. 21 (March 1932), 263–72; 'Finnegans Wake', *Revue des Deux Mondes*, lx (December 1940), 502–13; 'Recuerdos de James Joyce', *Sur* (December 1941), 28–42; (January 1942), 53–65.

GOLDING, LOUIS, *James Joyce* (1933): London: Thornton Butterworth.

GORMAN, HERBERT, *James Joyce, His First Forty Years* (1924): New York: B. W. Huebsch.

——, *James Joyce* (1940): New York: Rinehart; revised edition 1948.

JALOUX, EDMOND, *Au Pays du Roman* (1931): Paris: Editions R.-A. Corrêa, pp. 97–109, 111–22.

KNIGHT, GRANT C., *The Novel in English* (1931): London: R. R. Smith, pp. 354–9.

LARBAUD, VALÉRY, *Ce Vice Impani, La Lecture: Domaine Anglais* (1936): Paris: Gallimard, pp. 230–52.

LEVIN, HARRY, *James Joyce: A Critical Introduction* (1941): Norfolk: New Directions, revised edition, 1960.

LOVETT, ROBERT M., 'Post-Realistic Novel', in his *Preface to Fiction* (1931): Chicago: Rockwell, pp. 113–27.

MARBLE, ANNIE R., *A Study of the Modern Novel* (1928): New York: Appleton, pp. 44–6.

MORE, PAUL ELMER, 'James Joyce', *American Review*, v (May 1935), 129–57; also in his *On Being Human* (1936): Princeton: Princeton University Press, pp. 69–96.

MUIR, EDWIN, *The Present Age, from 1914* (1939): London: Cresset Press, pp. 134–9.

MULLER, HERBERT J., *Modern Fiction: A Study of Values* (1937): New York: Funk & Wagnalls, pp. 288–316.

MYERS, WALTER L., *The Later Realism* (1927): Chicago: University of Chicago Press, pp. 70–3, 81.

POWYS, JOHN COWPER, *The Enjoyment of Literature* (1938): New York: Simon & Schuster, pp. 498ff.

SMITH, BERNARD, *Forces in American Criticism* (1939): New York: Harcourt, pp. 272–3.

SMITH, PAUL JORDAN, *A Key to the Ulysses of James Joyce* (1927): Chicago: Covici.

WALDOCK, A. J. A., 'Experiment in the Novel', in his *Some Recent Developments in English Literature: A Series of Sydney University Extension Lectures* (1935): Sydney: Printed for the University Extension Board by Australasian Medical Publishing Company, pp. 8–17; also appeared, as *James Joyce and Others* (1937): London: Williams & Norgate, pp. 30–52.

WILSON, EDMUND, 'Ulysses', *New Republic*, xxxi (5 July 1922), 164–6, and 'James Joyce', *New Republic*, lxi (18 December 1929), 84–93, appeared in *Axel's Castle* (1931): New York: Charles Scribner's Sons, pp. 191–236.

——, 'H. C. Earwicker and Family', *New Republic*, xci (28 June 1939), 203–6, and 'The Dream of H. C. Earwicker', *New Republic*, xci (12 July 1939), 270–4, appeared in *The Wound and the Bow* (1947): New York: Oxford University Press, pp. 243–71; later appeared in *James Joyce: Two Decades of Criticism* (1948, 1962), ed. Seon Givens: New York: Vanguard Press, pp. 319–42.

APPENDIX D: SELECT LIST OF EXCLUDED REVIEWS AND CRITICAL ARTICLES, IN CHRONOLOGICAL ORDER

CHAMBER MUSIC

William York Tindall, 'Joyce's Chambermade Music', *Poetry*, lxxx (May 1952), 105–16.

Anthony Kerrigan, 'News of Molly Bloom', *Poetry*, lxxxv (November 1954), 109–12.

DUBLINERS

Eugenio Montale, 'Cronache delle Letterature Straniere: *Dubliners* di James Joyce', *Fiera Letteraria*, ii, No. 38 (19 September 1926), 5.

A PORTRAIT OF THE ARTIST

Harriet Shaw Weaver, 'Views and Comments', *Egoist*, No. 3 (1 March 1916), 35.

James Huneker, 'James Joyce', in his *Unicorns* (1917): New York: Scribner's, pp. 187–94; originally appeared in the *New York Sun*, extensively quoted by William Carlos Williams, 'Advent in America of a New Irish Realist', *Current Opinion*, lxii (April 1917), 275.

Unsigned review, 'Queer, but Honest', *Brooklyn Daily Eagle* (3 March 1917), 6.

Unsigned review, *Bellman*, xxii (3 March 1917), 245, 250.

Unsigned review, *Glasgow Herald* (8 March 1917), n.p.

Unsigned review, *Cambridge Magazine* (10 March 1917), 425–6.

Unsigned review, *English Review*, xxiv (May 1917), 478.

Unsigned notice, *Continent* (Chicago) (3 May 1917), 548.

Unsigned review, *Nation*, civ (17 May 1917), 600, 602.

C.H.S.M., 'The Birth of an Artist's Soul', *Challenge* (London), vii, No. 161 (25 May 1917), 54.

Unsigned review, *Future* (June 1917), 237.

Unsigned review, *Catholic World*, cv (June 1917), 395–6.

Ezra Pound, 'James Joyce's Novel', *Little Review*, iv, No. 4 (August 1917), 7–8.

C. C. Martindale, 'Some Recent Books', *Dublin Review*, clxvi (January–February–March 1920), 135–8.

EXILES

Unsigned review, 'A Subtle Play', *Literary World* (3 October 1918), 150.

W. P. Eaton, 'Some Plays in Print', *Bookman*, xlvii (August 1918), 638.

Unsigned review, *Catholic World*, cviii (December 1918), 404–5.

Unsigned review, *Bellman*, xxv (7 December 1918), 637.

Joseph Wood Krutch, 'Figures of the Dawn', *Nation*, cxx (March 1925), 272.

Robert Benchley, 'Back to Form', *Life*, lxxxv (12 March 1925), 20.

St. John Ervine, 'At the Play', *Observer* (12 July 1936), n.p.

ULYSSES

T. S. Eliot, 'Contemporanea', *Egoist*, v, No. 6 (June–July 1918), 84–5.

Margaret Anderson, 'An Obvious Statement', *Little Review*, vii, No. 3 (September–December 1920), 8–16.

Jane Heap, 'Art and the Law', *Little Review*, vii, No. 3 (September–December 1920), 5–7.

Unsigned article, 'James Joyce and his Chef d'Oeuvre', *Observer* (11 December 1921), n.p.

George Rehm, '*Ulysses*', *Paris Review* (1 April 1922), 19.

Unsigned Review, 'Could the Irish Writers Help?' *Manchester Guardian* (2 May 1922), 5.

Matthew Josephson, '1001 Nights in a Bar-Room, or the Irish Odysseus', *Broom*, iii (September 1922), 146–50.

Edmund Wilson, 'Rag-Bag of the Soul', *Literary Review*, iii, No. 12 (25 November 1922), 237–8.

Babette Deutsch, 'On *Ulysses*', *Literary Review* (2 December 1922), 281.

Silvio Benco, 'l'*Ulisse* du James Joyce', *La Nazione*, v, no. 78 (1922), 1.

Clifton Fadiman, 'American Debut of *Ulysses*', *New Yorker*, ix (27 January 1934), 61.

N. P. Dawson, 'The Cuttlefish School of Writers,' *Forum*, lxix (January 1923), 1174–84.

Mary Colum, 'Modernists', *Literary Review*, iii, No. 18 (6 January 1923), 361–2.

David Garnett, 'Jacob's Room', *Dial*, lxxv (July 1923), 83–6.

Gerald Gould, 'On D. H. Lawrence and James Joyce', *Observer* (6 April 1924), n.p.

Malcolm Cowley 'James Joyce', *Bookman* (New York), lix (July 1924), 518–21.

Valéry Larbaud, 'A Propos de James Joyce et de *Ulysses*', *Nouvelle Revue Française*, xxiv (January 1925), 5–17.

Ernest Boyd, 'A Propos de *Ulysses*', *Nouvelle Revue Française*, xxiv (March 1925), 309–13.

Paul Rosenfeld, 'James Joyce', in *Men Seen* (1925): New York: Dial Press, pp. 23–42.

Bernard Gilbert, 'The Tragedy of James Joyce', *G.K.'s Weekly* (4 April 1925), 36–8.

John Palmer, 'Antic Literature', *Nineteenth Century and After* (October 1925), 614–26.

Carlo Linati, 'Joyce', *Corriere della Sera* (20 August 1925), n.p.

Sean O'Faolain, 'Almost Music', *Hound and Horn*, ii(January–March 1929), 178–80.

Francis de Miomandre, 'Vulgarisation', *Les Nouvelles littéraires* (6 April 1929), n.p.

Sinclair Lewis, 'Self-Conscious America', *American Mercury*, vi (October 1929), 129–39.

Montgomery Beligion, 'Mr. Joyce and Mr. Gilbert', *This Quarter*, iii (July–August-September 1930), 122–8.

E. M. Forster, 'The Censor Again', *The Author*, xliv (Spring 1934), 78–9.

John Pollock, '*Ulysses* and the Censorship', *The Author,* xliv (Summer 1934), 115–17.

ANNA LIVIA PLURABELLE

Oliver Scribe, 'The Modern Rabelais', *T.P. and Cassell's Weekly* (13 February 1926), 580.

Robert Sage, 'Footnotes', *Chicago Tribune* (Paris edition) (15 April 1928), 5.

Lester Scharaf, 'James Joyce the Unbounded', *The Adolescent* (Baltimore), i, No. 1 (Summer 1928), 17–18.

Robert Sage, 'Etc.,' *transition*, No. 14 (Fall 1928), 171–4.

Unsigned review, 'Joyce's New Book', *New York Herald* (Paris edition) (1 October 1928).

Gerald Heard, 'The Language of James Joyce', *The Week-end* (14 June 1930), 492–3.

C. H. Hodgson, 'Clarity or Incomprehensibility?' *Notts. Journal* (Nottingham), (2 July 1930), n.p.

Geoffrey Grigson, 'James Joyce Again', *Saturday Review*, cl (29 November 1930), 718.

Norah Meade, 'Nonsense of New Art', *New York Herald Tribune Books* (13 September 1931), 1, 5, 6.

Edward W. Titus, 'Mr. Joyce Explains', *This Quarter*, iv (December 1931), 371–2.

HAVETH CHILDERS EVERYWHERE

F. B. Cargeege, 'The Mystery of James Joyce', *Everyman* (11 June 1931), n.p.

Jennifer Courtenay, 'The Approach to James Joyce', *Everyman* (9 July 1931), 765.

G. Wynne Ruston, 'The Case Against James Joyce', *Everyman* (9 July 1931), 765–6.

Stuart Gilbert, 'The Joycean Protagonist', *Echanges*, No. 5 (December 1931), 154–7.

TALES TOLD OF SHEM AND SHAUN

C. K. Ogden, 'Current Literature', *Psyche*, xi (July 1930), 95–6.

E. C. Chilton, 'Twas Brilig', *English Review*, lvi (January 1933), 107–8.

FINNEGANS WAKE

Jacques Mercanton, '*Finnegans Wake*', *Nouvelle Revue Francaise*, xxvii (1 May 1939), 858–64.

William McFee, 'James Joyce's New York and a Key to its Significance', *New York Sun* (4 May 1939), n.p.

Ralph Thompson, 'Books of the Times', *New York Times* (4 May 1939), 21.

Harold Nicolson, 'The Indecipherable Mystery of Mr. Joyce's Allegory', *Daily Telegraph* (London) (5 May 1939), n.p.

Unsigned editorial, 'Ancient and Modern', *Irish Times* (5 May 1939), n.p.

Unsigned review, 'Mr. Joyce Expresses Himself', *Times Literary Supplement* (6 May 1939), 266.

Unsigned review, 'Two New Books', *Evening Post* (New York) (9 May (1939), n.p.

Unsigned review, 'Successor to *Ulysses*', *Edinburgh Scotsman* (11 May 1939), n.p.

Derek Verschoyle, 'A Private Document', *Spectator*, clxii (12 May 1939), 820.

Anthony Bertram, 'Views on Mr. Joyce', *Spectator*, clxii (19 May 1939), 858–9.

Robert Lynd, 'Why Authors Write', *John O' London's Weekly* (19 May 1939), 236.

L. J. Feeney, 'James Joyce', *America*, lxi (20 May 1939), 139.

Burton Rascoe, '*Finnegans Wake*', *Newsweek* (8 May 1939), 36.

(Whitaker Chambers), 'Night Thoughts', *Time* xxxiii (8 May 1939), 78, 80–2, 84.

Jack Conroy, 'Mr. Finnegan, Weird Hero of Joyce's Dublin Nightmare', *New York Daily Worker* (28 May 1939), n.p.

Ford Madox Ford ('Faugh an-Ballagh Faugh'), '*Finnegans Wake*', *Saturday Review of Literature*, xx (3 June 1939), 9; later appeared in *The Letters of Ford Madox Ford* (1965): ed. Richard M. Ludwig. Princeton: Princeton University Press, pp. 320–3.

Paul Rosenfeld, '*Finnegans Wake*', *Saturday Review of Literature*, xx (10 June 1939), 9, 20.

Earle Birney, 'Foolosall Choredom', *Canadian Forum*, xix (July 1939), 125.

Bonamy Dobree, 'Work Concluded', *New English Weekly* (6 July 1939), 189.

Barry Byrne, '*Finnegans Wake*', *Commonweal*, xxx (7 July 1939), 279.

Elizabeth Bowen, 'Reviews, Fiction', *Purpose*, xi, No. 3 (July–September 1939), 177–9.

Lynette Roberts, '*Finnegans Wake*', *La Nacion* (Buenos Aires) (27 August 1939), 1.

Archibald Hill, 'A Philologist Looks at *Finnegans Wake*', *Virginia Quarterly Review*, xv (October 1939), 650–6.

Salvatore Rosati, 'Inghilterra', *Almanacco Letterario Bompiano* (1940), 168–71.

Padraic Colum, 'Notes on *Finnegans Wake*', *Yale Review*, xxx (March 1941), 640–5.

YEAR-BY-YEAR CHRONOLOGY

Unsigned articles, '*Ulysses*', and 'James Joyce', *Almanach des Lettres Francaises et Etrangèrès* (Paris) (15 March 1924), 300; (28 February 1924), 233; (22 March 1924), 326.

G. B. Shaw and Archibald Henderson, 'Literature and Science', *Fortnightly Review*, n.s., cxvi (October 1924), 518–21.

Edmund Wilson, 'An Introduction to Joyce', *Dial*, lxxvii (November 1924), 430–5.

Simone Tery, 'Rencontre avec James Joyce, Irlandais', *Les Nouvelles litteraires*, iv, No. 126 (14 March 1925), 6.

Unsigned editorial, 'Enter the Super-Realists,' *New York Times* (3 November 1925), 24.

James P. O'Reilly, 'Joyce and Beyond Joyce', *Irish Statesman*, v (12 September 1925), 17–18.

Padraic Colum, 'Dublin in Literature', *Bookman* (New York), lxii (July 1926), 555–61.

Bertram Higgins, 'Notes and Reviews', *Calendar*, iii (January 1927), 340–2.

Stephen Low, 'Current Literature', *London Weekly* (5 March 1927), 300–1.

Unsigned, '*Ulysses* Protest', *Humanist*, iv, No. 4 (April 1927), 173.

Marjorie Peters, *New York World* (14 August 1927), n.p.

Samuel Roth, 'An Offer to James Joyce', *Two World's Monthly*, iii (September 1927), 181–2.

Unsigned article, 'Magazines', *Irish Statesman* (10 September 1927), 21.

Simeon Strunsky, 'About Books, More or Less', *New York Times Book Review* (16 October 1927), 4.

George R. Scott, 'Senescent British Fiction', *New Age* (10 November 1927), 18.

Karl Tuchoisky, '*Ulysses*', *Die Weltbühne*, xxiii (1927), 788.

John Rodker (trans. Ludmila Savitsky), 'Proteus, de James Joyce', *La Revue Européenne*, n.s., No. 1–2 (January–February 1928), 164–9.

Harold J. Salemson, 'James Joyce and the New World', *Modern Quarterly* (Baltimore), v, No. 3 (Fall 1929), 294–312.

Rebecca West, 'Letter from Europe', *Bookman* (New York), lxx (September 1929), 664–8.

Jonathan Curling, 'Obscurity in Modern Art', *Spectator*, cxliii (24 August 1929), 241.

Maurice Murphy, 'James Joyce and Ireland', *Nation*, cxxix (16 October 1929), 426.

Benjamin Crémieux, 'Le Règne des Mots', *Candide* (Paris) (14 November 1929), 3.

Edgar Calmer, 'A New Issue of *transition*', *Chicago Sunday Tribune* (Paris edition) (17 November 1929), n.p.

Richard Aldington, 'A Critical Attitude', *Referee* (24 November 1929), 265.

Peter M. Jack, 'Some Contemporaries: James Joyce', *Manuscripts*, i (1929), 24–7, 102–8.

Unsigned interview with Paul Souday, *Chicago Sunday Tribune* (Paris edition) (5 January 1930), n.p.

J. A. Hammerton, 'The Literary Show: What I think of James Joyce', *The Bystander* (23 April 1930), 194, 197.

Dudley Fitts, 'Two Aspects of Telemachus', *Hound and Horn*, iii (April–June 1930), 445–50.

A. Killen, '*Ulysses*', *Revue de Litterature Comparee*, x (April–June 1930), 323–7.

Arnold Bennett, 'Back to Riceyman Steps', *Evening Standard* (12 June 1930), n.p.

Edward W. Titus, 'Sartor Resartus', *This Quarter*, iii (July–September 1930), 130–41.

Michael Lennon, 'James Joyce', *Catholic World*, cxxxii (March 1931), 641–52.

Rene Lalou, 'Le Théatre', *Les Nouvelles littéraires* (11 April 1931), n.p.

Frederick LeFevre, 'l'Erreur de James Joyce', *La République* (5 May 1931), n.p.

Adelchi Barantono, 'Il Fenomeno Joyce', *Civilia Moderna* (December 1931), 1159–77.

P. E., 'Joyce oder die Höllenmaschine', *Prager Presse* (Prague) (3 March 1932), n.p.

Thomas McGreevy, 'Homage to James Joyce', *transition*, No. 21 (March 1932), 254–5.

Clifford Bower-Shore, 'Modern Authors', *Bookfinder Illustrated* (June 1932), 5.

William Carlos Williams, 'Readers & Writers', *New English Weekly* (10 November 1932), 90–1.

Carola Giedion-Welcker, 'Dazu Besprechung', *Mannheimer Tageblatt*, No. 5 (1932), n.p.

Carola Giedion-Welcker, 'James Joyce', *Frankfurter Zeitung*, No. 3 (1932), n.p.

Harald Theile, 'Credo der Ausgestossenheit zu James Joyces *Ulysses*', *Edart*, ix (February 1933), 70–8.

Unsigned article, 'M. James Joyce et son *Ouvrage en Train*', *Le Mois, synthèse de l'activité mondiale*, No. 26 (February–March 1933), 185–90.

Yvonne ffrench, 'Poetry', *London Mercury*, xxviii (May 1933), 69–70.

Francis Watson, 'Portrait of the Artist in Maturity', *Bookman* (London), lxxxv (November 1933), 102–5.

Unsigned editorial, 'What is Poetry?' *New Britain* (8 November 1933), 784.

Unsigned article, 'Another Repeal', *Nation*, cxxxvii (20 December 1933), 693.

Wieland Herzfelde, 'Geist und Machet', *Neue deutsche Blätter*, i, No. 12 (September 1934), 713–52.

Armand Petitjean, 'James Joyce et l'Absorption de Monde par le Language', *Cahiers du Sud* (Marseilles), xxi, No. 165 (October 1934), 607–23.

Robert Lynd, 'James Joyce and the New Kind of Fiction', *John O' London's Weekly* (25 May 1935), 245–6; also appeared in *Books and Writers* (1952): London: J. M. Dent & Son, pp. 147–51.

Alfred Kerr, 'Joyce en Angleterre', *Les Nouvelles littéraires*, No. 691 (11 January 1936), 6–12; translated by Joseph Prescott as 'James Joyce in England' in *James Joyce Miscellany* (1957), ed. Marvin Magalaner: New York: James Joyce Society, pp. 37–43; reprinted in *Diliman Review*, vii (October 1959), 386–92.

Unsigned editorial, 'Literature at the Cross-Roads', *Irish Times* (24 January 1936), 8.

Armand Petitjean, 'Signification de Joyce', *Etudes Anglaises*, i (1937), 405–17.

D. G. Van der Vat, 'Paternity in *Ulysses*', *English Studies*, xix (August 1937), 145–58.

Oliver St. John Gogarty, *As I Was Going Down Sackville Street* (1937): New York: Reynal & Hitchcock, pp. 83, 293–9.

Wyndham Lewis, 'Standing By One Thing and Another', *Bystander*, cxliii (30 August 1939), 316, 318.

Frank O'Connor, 'Æ', *Bell*, i, No. 2 (November 1940), 49–57.

David Daiches, 'James Joyce: The Artist as Exile', *College English*, ii (1940), 197–206; reprinted in *Forms of Modern Fiction* (1948): ed. William Van O'Connor. Minneapolis: University of Minnesota Press, pp. 61–71.

Neil Tomkinson, 'James Joyce', *Adelphi*, n.s., 3, vii, No. 5 (February 1941), 175–7.

K. R. Srinivasa-Iyengar, 'James Joyce', *New Review* (London), xiii (1941), 249–60.

Dwight MacDonald, 'Kulturbolschewismus is Here', *Partisan Review*, viii (November–December 1941), 442–51.

ACKNOWLEDGMENTS

I would like to thank the following for their considerable assistance and advice in the preparation of this book: Anna A. Russell and David Posner at the Lockwood Memorial Library of the University of Buffalo; Alexandra Mason and Terence Williams at the University of Kansas Library; Leland S. Dutton and Laura Fritz of the Miami University Library; Lawrence Houtchens and the Faculty Research Committee of Miami University; James Spoerri, Herbert Cahoon, Alan Cohn, Richard Ellmann and Harry Levin, all of whom were generous with encouragement; Gordon Wilson and Bonnie MacDonald of my own Department for their patience and help; Garth Pitman, Odette Scott and Annagret Ralston, who did the translations; Linda Cooper, Madelynne Diness and Janice Mosbach, who assisted with the manuscript; and finally I wish to thank my wife Anne, who did all things and a great deal more. The responsibility for any error, inaccuracy or faulty judgement is mine, however, and I absolve all of the above from any part in that responsibility.

I have attempted to secure permission to reprint from all publishers and individuals. Some have not answered my three letters of inquiry, nor have they replied to the inquiries of Mrs. Joan St. George Saunders of the Writer's and Speaker's Research Agency. I am extremely grateful to the following for granting permission to reprint the materials in this volume:

Franklin P. Adams, *The Diary of Our Own Samuel Pepys*, Volume I; © 1935; reprinted by permission of Simon & Schuster Inc. Reprinted from *Letters From Æ*, Alan Denson; © 1961 Alan Denson; by permission of Abelard-Schuman Ltd.; all rights reserved, 1961. Richard Aldington, 'The Influence of Mr. James Joyce', *English Review*, April 1921; 'Farewell to Europe', copyright © 1939, by the *Atlantic Monthly*, Boston, Mass. 02116; reprinted with permission. Karl Beckson and John M. Munro, 'Letters from Arthur Symons to James Joyce: 1904–1932', *James Joyce Quarterly*, Winter 1967; reprinted by permission of Karl Beckson and the Editor of the *James Joyce Quarterly*. Arnold Bennett, 'Books and Persons', August 1929; 'Books and Persons', 19 September 1929, *London Evening Standard*; reprinted by permission of the Editor. From *Things that have Interested Me*, by Arnold Bennett; copyright 1936 by George H. Doran & Company; reprinted by permission of Doubleday & Company, A. P. Watt & Son, and Mrs. Dorothy Cheston Bennett. Arnold Bennett, 'The Progress of the Novel', *Realist*, April 1929; reprinted by permission of Mrs. Dorothy Cheston Bennett and Macmillan & Co. Ltd., J. C., 'Experimentalists', *Birmingham Post*, 4 March 1930; reprinted by permission of the Editor. From John Peale Bishop, '*Finnegans Wake*', *Southern Review*, Winter 1940; reprinted by permission

ACKNOWLEDGMENTS

of the Louisiana State University Press. From *Selected Criticism* by Louise Bogan; copyright © 1955 by Louise Bogan; reprinted by permission of the Author. Georges Bourget, *Les Cahiers du Sud* (Marseille), November 1926; reprinted by permission of the Editor, Jean Ballard. From Ernest Boyd, *Ireland's Literary Renaissance*; copyright 1923, Grant Richards; reprinted by permission of John Baker Publishers Ltd. and The Richards Press. D. G. Bridson, 'Views and Reviews', *New English Weekly*, 5 January 1933; reprinted by permission of the Author. Marcel Brion, 'l'Actualité littéraire à l'Etranger', *Les Nouvelles littéraires*, 15 October 1927; 'Les Grandes figures européennes: James Joyce, romancier', *La Gazette des Nations*, 3 March 1928; '*Ulysse*', *La Revue Hebdomadaire*, 20 April 1929; reprinted by permission of the Author. From the book, *The Opinions of Oliver Allston*, by Van Wyck Brooks; copyright 1941 by Van Wyck Brooks; reprinted by permission of E. P. Dutton & Co. Inc. and J. M. Dent & Sons Ltd. Frank Budgen, 'James Joyce', *Horizon*, February 1941, reprinted by permission of the Author; 'Further Recollections of James Joyce', *Partisan Review*, Autumn 1956; © copyright 1956; reprinted by permission of the *Partisan Review* and the Author. Morley Callaghan, 'Into the Dream World', *Saturday Night*, 1939; © Saturday Night Publications Ltd., Toronto 1, Canada. Henry Seidel Canby, 'Gyring and Gimbling', *Saturday Review of Literature*, 30 April 1927; and *American Estimates*; © 1939 Harcourt, Brace; reprinted by permission of the Editor of *Saturday Review of Literature* and Harcourt, Brace & World Inc. Robert Cantwell, 'The Influence of James Joyce', *New Republic*, December 1933; 'Outlook Book Choice', *New Outlook*, March 1934; reprinted by permission of the Author. Jean Cassou, 'James Joyce, Poète Epique', *Les Nouvelles littéraires*, 9 March 1929; reprinted by permission of the Author. From Marc Chadourne, 'Un Evènement: *Ulysse*', *La Revue Européene*, May 1929; reprinted by permission of the Author. Jacques Chenévière, 'James Joyce: *Gens de Dublin*', *Bibliothèque universelle et Revue de Genève*, August 1926; reprinted by permission of the Author. G. K. Chesterton, 'On Phases of Eccentricity', in his *All I Survey*, 1933; reprinted by permission of Miss D. E. Collins and Methuen & Co. Ltd. George Rehm, 13 February 1922; B. J. Kosposth, 'All James Joyce Says Has Been Said Many Times in French', 5 May 1929, *Chicago Tribune* (Paris Edition); reprinted by permission of the Chicago Tribune. Austin Clarke, 'James Joyce', *Everyman*, 15 May 1930; reprinted by permission of the Author. The following items by Mary Colum are reprinted by kind permission of her husband, Padraic Colum: 'The Confessions of James Joyce', *Freeman*, July 1922; *New York Herald Tribune*, 24 April 1927; from *From These Roots*, copyright 1937, Scribner's Sons; 'The Old and the New', *Forum and Century*, October 1939; 'A Little Knowledge of Joyce', *Saturday Review of Literature*, April 1950, by *Saturday Review of Literature*. The following items by Padraic Colum are reprinted by the kind permission of the Author: 'James Joyce', *Pearson's Magazine*, May 1918; 'With James Joyce in Ireland', *New York Times Book Review*, June 1922; '*Pomes Penyeach*', *New York World*, January 1928; 'River Episode from James Joyce's Uncompleted Work', *Dial*, April 1928 and Doubleday & Co.; 'From a "Work

ACKNOWLEDGMENTS

in Progress"'. *New Republic*, September 1930; 'A New Work by James Joyce', *New York Times Book Review*, May 1939; 'The Joyce I Knew', *Saturday Review of Literature*, February 1941; 'Working with Joyce', *Irish Times*, October 1956. Cyril Connolly, 'A Note on James Joyce', from his *Previous Convictions*; copyright 1963 published by Harper & Row, Publishers; reprinted by permission. From *Exile's Return* by Malcolm Cowley; copyright 1934; © 1962 by Malcolm Cowley; reprinted by permission of the Viking Press Inc., The Bodley Head Ltd., and the Author. Malcolm Cowley, 'When a Young American . . .,' *Mercure de France*, August–September 1963; reprinted by permission of the Author. From *The Complete Poems and Selected Prose of Hart Crane*, edited by Brom Weber, 1966; reprinted by permission of Liveright Publishers, New York, N.Y. Hamish Miles, '*Tales Told of Shem and Shaun*', October 1930; Valéry Larbaud, 'The *Ulysses* of James Joyce', *Criterion*, October 1922; reprinted by permission of Faber & Faber Ltd. Henry Daniel-Rops, 'Une Technique nouvelle', *Le Correspondant*, January 1932; reprinted by permission of Madeleine Daniel-Rops. Alec Brown, 'Joyce's *Ulysses* and the Novel', January–March 1934; A.C., '*Finnegans Wake*', July–September 1939, *Dublin Magazine*; reprinted by the kind permission of Mrs. E. F. Starkey. Domini Canis, '*Ulysses*', 1922; C. C. Martindale, '*Ulysses*', 1922, *Dublin Review*; reprinted by permission of the Editor. Max Eastman, 'The Cult of Unintelligibility', copyright © 1929 by Harper's Magazine Inc., reprinted from the April 1929 issue of *Harper's Magazine* by permission of the Author; 'Poets Talking to Themselves', copyright © 1931 by Harper's Magazine, Inc., reprinted from the October 1931 issue of *Harper's Magazine* by permission of the Author. Léon Edel, 'James Joyce and His New Work', *University of Toronto Quarterly*, 1939; copyright © by University of Toronto Press; reprinted by permission of University of Toronto Press and the Author. Léon Edel, 'New Writers', *Canadian Forum*, June 1930; reprinted by permission of the Editor of *Canadian Forum*, Toronto, Ontario, Canada. Reprinted from *The Egoist*, June–July 1918; Ezra Pound, 'At Last the Novel Appears', February 1917; Diego Angeli, 'Extract from "Il Marzocco"', February 1918; reprinted by permission of the Executors of the Estate of Harriet Shaw Weaver, Monro, Pennefather & Co., London. T. S. Eliot, '*Ulysses*, Order and Myth', *Dial*, November 1923; 'A Message to the Fish', *Horizon*, March 1941; reprinted by permission of Mrs. Eliot and Faber & Faber Ltd. From *James Joyce* by Richard Ellmann; copyright © 1959 by Richard Ellmann; reprinted by permission of the Author and the Oxford University Press Inc. L. K. Emery, 'The *Ulysses* of Mr. James Joyce', *Klaxon*, Winter 1923–4; reprinted by permission of The Brunswick Press Ltd., Dublin, Ireland. Unsigned review, 8 April 1922, *London Evening News*; reprinted by permission of Epoque Ltd., London. Unsigned review, 3 July 1914; 'A Study in Garbage', 23 February 1917; 'Mr. Eliot and Mr. Joyce', 28 January 1933; Michael Petch, 'The Approach to James Joyce', 25 June 1931, *Everyman*; reprinted by permission of J. M. Dent & Sons. Reprinted by permission of the publishers, The Vanguard Press, from 'A Note on Literary Criticism', by James T. Farrell; copyright 1936, 1963 by

ACKNOWLEDGMENTS

James T. Farrell. Janet Flanner, 'The Great Amateur Publisher', *Mercure de France*, August–September 1963; reprinted by permission of the Author. Henri Fluchère, '*Ulysse*', *Le Foyer Universitaire*, May 1931; reprinted by permission of the Author. From the *Letters of Ford Madox Ford*, edited by Richard M. Ludwig; copyright 1965; reprinted by permission of the Princeton University Press. Ford Madox Ford, 'A Haughty and Proud Generation', *Yale Review*, July 1922; '*Ulysses* and the Handling of Indecencies', *English Review*, December 1922; 'Literary Causeries: VIII: So She Went into the Garden', *Chicago Tribune Sunday Magazine*, 6 April 1925; reprinted by permission of William A. Bradley on behalf of Mrs. Ford Madox Ford. Thomas Kettle, 1 June 1907, 'A Dyspeptic Portrait', 7 April 1917; 'Ibsen in Ireland', *Freeman's Journal*, 15 June 1918; reprinted by permission of the Editor, Independent Newspapers Ltd., Dublin 1, Ireland. Florent Fels, 'Revues', *Action*, December 1920; Julien Green, '*Ulysses* par James Joyce', *Philosophies*, May 1924; Georges Duplaix, 'Joyce à la "Revue des Deux Mondes"', *La Revue Nouvelle*, September–October 1925; Michael Stuart, 'Joyce After *Ulysses*', *This Quarter*, October–December 1929; reprinted by permission of Horace Marston and French Reproduction Rights Inc. Edward Garnett, reader's report for Duckworth & Co.; reprinted by permission of David Garnett. Carola Giedion-Welcker, 'A Linguistic Experiment by James Joyce', *transition*, 19–20, June 1930; 'On *Ulysses* by James Joyce', *Neue Schweizer Rundschau*, 1928; reprinted by permission of the Author. Stuart Gilbert, 'Growth of a Titan', *Saturday Review of Literature*, August 1930, by permission of the Editor of *Saturday Review of Literature* and the Author; 'A Footnote to "Work in Progress"', *Experiment*, Spring 1931; reprinted by permission of the Author. Louis Gillet, 'Joyce's Testament', *Quarterly Review of Literature*, Winter 1944; reprinted by permission of the Editor. Permission to reprint the following items by Oliver St. John Gogarty has been kindly granted by Oliver D. Gogarty as Executor of the Estate of Oliver St. John Gogarty: a comment on *Ulysses* quoted in Ulick O'Connor, 'James Joyce and Oliver St. John Gogarty', *Texas Quarterly*, Summer 1960, by permission of Ulick O'Connor and the Editor of the *Texas Quarterly*; *Rolling Down the Lea*, Constable Publishers, London, 1950; 'Roots in Resentment', *Observer*, 7 May 1939, by the Editor, Observer Foreign News Serice; 'The Joyce I Knew', 25 January 1941, 'They Think They Know Joyce', *Saturday Review of Literature*, 18 March 1950, by the Editor. Yvan Goll, 'The Homer of Our Time', *Living Age*, 1927; '*Ulysses* Sub Specie Aeternitatis', *Die Weltbuhne*, December 1927; reprinted by permission of Claire Goll. Stephen Gywnn, 'Modern Irish Literature', *Manchester Guardian*, 15 March 1923, and *Irish Literature and Drama in the English Language*, 1936, Thomas Nelson & Sons Ltd.; reprinted by permission of the *Manchester Guardian* and Thomas Nelson & Sons Ltd. Robert Hillyer, 'Recent Poetry', *New Adelphi*, March 1928; reprinted by permission of Mrs. Robert S. Hillyer. From *Paris Salons, Cafés, Studios* by Sisley Huddleston; copyright 1928; J. B. Lippincott Company; copyright renewed 1956 by Mrs. Sisley Huddleston as widow of the Author; published by J. B. Lippincott

ACKNOWLEDGMENTS

Company; from *Back to Montparnasse* by Sisley Huddleston; copyright 1931 by
Sisley Huddleston; copyright renewed by Mrs. Sisley Huddleston as widow of
the author; published by J. B. Lippincott Company. From *Confessions of Another
Young Man*, by Bravig Imbs; New York, Henkle-Yewdale, 1936; used by
permission of Crown Publishers Inc. Unsigned review, November 1914; unsigned review, *Irish Book Lover*, April-May 1917; reprinted by permission of
The Three Candles Ltd., Dublin, Ireland. 'The Modern Novel', 9 November
1923; 'Sixteen Years Work by James Joyce', 3 June 1939; Padraic Colum,
'Working with Joyce', *Irish Times*, 5 October 1956; reprinted by permission of
the Editor. Edmond Jaloux, 'Review', *Les Nouvelles littéraires*, 29 May 1926;
'Notes sur le Roman anglais', *Echanges*, December 1929; reprinted by permission of Mme Edmond Jaloux. From *Letters of James Joyce*, edited by Stuart
Gilbert; copyright © 1957, 1966, by The Viking Press Inc.; all rights reserved;
reprinted by permission of the Viking Press Inc. and Faber & Faber Ltd. From
Letters of James Joyce, Volumes II and III, edited by Richard Ellmann; copyright
© 1966 by F. Lionel Monro, as Administrator of the Estate of James Joyce; all
rights reserved; reprinted by permission of the Viking Press Inc. and Faber &
Faber Ltd. P. Beaumont Wadsworth, 'Visits with James Joyce', 1964; John
Kuehl, 'à la Joyce', 1964; Arthur Power, 'Conversations with Joyce', *James
Joyce Quarterly*, 1965, reprinted by permission of the Editor. Stanislaus Joyce,
'An Open Letter to Dr. Oliver Gogarty', *Interim*, 1954; reprinted by permission
of A. Wilber Stevens. Extracts from *The Dublin Diary of Stanislaus Joyce*, ©
1962 by Cornell University and George Harris Healey; used by permission of
Cornell University Press. From *The Collected Works of C. G. Jung*, Volume 15:
The Spirit in Man, Art and Literature, translated by R. F. C. Hull; 'Ulysses', pp.
109-10; Bollingen Series XX.15; copyright 1966 by Bollingen Foundation,
New York; distributed by Princeton University Press; permission also granted
by Routledge & Kegan Paul Ltd. Jack Kahane, *Memoirs of a Booklegger*, 1939;
reprinted by permission of Michael Joseph Ltd., London, and Curtis Brown Ltd.
René Lalou, *Panorama de la littérature anglaise Contemporaine*, 1926; reprinted by
permission of Mme Chr. Lalou. Lucie Léon-Noel, *James Joyce and Paul L.
Léon: The Story of a Friendship*, 1950, Gotham Book Mart; reprinted by per-
mission of Lucie Léon-Noel. Paul Léon, 'In Memory of Joyce', *Poésie 1942* and
James Joyce Yearbook, edited by Maria Jolas, 1949; reprinted by permission of
Pierre Seghers, Editor and Publisher of *Poésie 42*, Mrs. Maria Jolas and Lucie
Léon-Noel. Shane Leslie, 'Ulysses', *Quarterly Review*, October 1922; reprinted
by permission of Sir Shane Leslie. Harry Levin, 'On First Looking into *Finnegans
Wake*', first appeared in *New Directions in Prose and Poetry 1939*, and later
published in revised and longer form in *James Joyce: A Critical Introduction*, New
Directions, 1941, revised 1960; reprinted by permission of New Directions
Publishing Corporation and the Author. *Time and Western Man*, by Wyndham
Lewis, published by Chatto & Windus, 1927; reprinted by permission of Mrs.
Wyndham Lewis. From *Rude Assignment*, by Wyndham Lewis; Hutchinson
Publishing Group Ltd., 1950; reprinted by permission. Wyndham Lewis

ACKNOWLEDGMENTS

letter from *The Letters of Wyndham Lewis*, edited by W. K. Rose, 1963; reprinted by permission of the New Directions Publishing Corporation and Associated Book Publishers Ltd. Wyndham Lewis, *Blasting and Bombardiering*; © copyright 1967; reprinted by permission of Calder & Boyars Ltd. and the University of California Press. Jack Lindsay, 'The Modern Consciousness', *London Aphrodite*, August 1928; Brian Penton, 'Notes on the Form of the Novel', *London Aphrodite*, July 1929; reprinted by permission of Jack Lindsay. From Robert McAlmon, *Being Geniuses Together: An Autobiography*, London, Secker & Warburg, 1938; reprinted by permission of Robert R. Davis (nephew) for the Estate of Robert McAlmon. Desmond MacCarthy, '*Exiles*', *New Statesman*, 21 September 1918, and in his *Humanities*, published by MacGibbon & Kee, 1953, reprinted by permission of Michael MacCarthy Esq.; 'Le roman anglais d'après-guerre', *Revue de Paris*, May 1932; reprinted by permission of Michael MacCarthy, Esq. and the *Revue de Paris*. A. M., 'A Sensitivist', 2 March 1917; B. Ifor Evans, 'In Lieu of Review', *Manchester Guardian*, 12 May 1939; reprinted from the *Manchester Guardian* by permission of the *Guardian*, London. Adrienne Monnier, 'Lectures chez Sylvia', August-September 1963; Henry Davray, 'Lettres anglaises', *Mercure de France*, February 1919; reprinted by permission of the *Mercure de France*. Philippe Soupault, *Profils Perdus*, *Mercure de France*, 1963; reprinted by permission of the *Mercure de France* and the Author. Denis Marion, 'James Joyce', *transition*, Autumn 1928; reprinted by permission of the Author. 'James Joyce et le Snobisme', *Le Monde*, 2 May 1931; © copyright 1931 by Le Monde-Opera Mundi Paris; reprinted with permission. Adrienne Monnier, '*Ulysses* and the French Public', translated by Sylvia Beach for the *Kenyon Review*, Summer 1946; reprinted by permission of M. Maurice Saillet and Mme Marie Monnier-Bécat (Executors of the Estate of Adrienne Monnier), Mrs. Frederick J. Dennis (Holly Beach), and the *Kenyon Review*. George Moore letter to Edward March, 3 August 1916; letter to Louis Gillet, 20 August 1931; reprinted by permission of J. C. Medley and R. G. Medley. Louise Morgan, 'Wyndham Lewis: The Great Satirist of Our Day', *Everyman*, 19 March 1931, and in *Writers at Work*; copyright 1931, Chatto & Windus Ltd.; reprinted by permission of Chatto & Windus Ltd. Malcolm Muggeridge, 'Men and Books', *Time and Tide*, 20 May 1939; reprinted by permission of the Editor. From *transition*, by Edwin Muir. Copyright 1926 by the Viking Press Inc.; 1954 by Edwin Muir; reprinted by permission of the Viking Press Inc. Edwin Muir, 'James Joyce's New Novel', *Listener*, 11 May 1939; reprinted by permission of Mrs. Willa Muir. 'Scientist of Letters', *New Republic*, 20 January 1941; reprinted by permission of *The New Republic*; © 1941, Harrison-Blaine of New Jersey, Inc. The following articles are reprinted by permission of the Editor of the *New Statesman*: Arthur Symons, 'A Book of Songs', *Nation*, 22 June 1907; unsigned review, *Athenaeum*, 20 June 1914; John Middleton Murry, 'Mr. Joyce's *Ulysses*', *Nation and Athenaeum*, 22 April 1922: Gerald Gould, *New Statesman*, 27 June 1914; J. C. Squire, 'Mr. James Joyce', *New Statesman and Nation*, 14 April 1917; 'Affable Hawk', 'Current Literature', *New Statesman*, 14 May 1927; G. W.

ACKNOWLEDGMENTS

Stonier, 'Mr. James Joyce in Progress', 28 June 1930; G. W. Stonier, 'Joyce Without End', 22 September 1934; G. W. Stonier, 'Leviathan', 10 October 1936; G. W. Stonier, 'Joyce's Airy Plumeflights', 20 May 1939; Cyril Connolly, 'A Note on James Joyce', *New Statesman*, 18 January 1941. Permission has been granted for the following items: From the *New York World*: Ernest Boyd, 'Concerning James Joyce', 25 January 1925; Padraic Colum, '*Pomes Penyeach*', 15 January 1928; from the *New York Evening Journal*: Gilbert Seldes, 'Joyce and Lewis Share Honors of the Week', 27 January 1934; from the *New York Herald Tribune*: Mary Colum, 24 April 1927; Ellen Glasgow, 'Impressions of the Novel', 20 May 1928; Rebecca West, 'Joyce and His Followers', 12 January 1930; Horace Gregory, 21 January 1934; Horace Gregory, 'Fifty Lyrics by the Author of *Ulysses*', 13 December 1936; Alfred Kazin, 'The Strange Dream World of James Joyce', 21 May 1939; permission to reprint granted by Herbert Kamm, Executive Editor, *World-Journal-Tribune*, New York, N.Y. 10015. For articles in the *New York Times*: © 1929 by the New York Times Company; reprinted by permission. For articles in the *New York Times Book Review*: © 1922, 1937, 1939, 1941, by the New York Times Company; reprinted by permission. Harold Nicolson, 'The Significance of James Joyce', *Listener*, 16 December 1931; 'The Modernist Point of View', *Listener*, 23 December 1931; reprinted by permission of Sir Harold Nicolson. Louis Golding, 'A Sidelight on James Joyce', April 1933; Alex Glendinning, 'Commentary: *Finnegans Wake*', *Nineteenth Century and After*, July 1939; reprinted by permission of Twentieth Century Magazine Ltd. From *Les Nouvelles littéraires*: Frederick LeFevre, 'Une heure avec M. Valéry Larbaud', 6 October 1923; Edmond Jaloux, 29 May 1926; Marcel Brion, 'l'Actualité littéraire à l'Etranger', 15 October 1927; Jean Cassou, 'James Joyce, Poète Epique', 9 March 1929; by permission of Mme Edmond Jaloux, M. Marcel Brion, M. Jean Cassou, and the Director of *Les Nouvelles littéraires*. Alfred Noyes, 'Rottenness in Literature', *Sunday Chronicle* (Manchester), 29 October 1922; reprinted by permission of News of the World Ltd. Salvatore Rosati, '*Finnegans Wake*', *Nuova Antologia*, 1 November 1939; reprinted by permission of the Editor. Sisley Huddleston, '*Ulysses*', 5 March 1922; Gerald Gould, 'Mr. Joyce and Others', 9 December 1928; Oliver St. John Gogarty, 'Roots in Resentment', *The Observer*, 7 May 1939; reprinted by permission of the Observer Foreign News Service, London. Frank O'Connor, 'Joyce—The Third Period', *Irish Statesman*, 12 April 1930; © copyright by Frank O'Connor; reprinted by permission of Cyrilly Abels, agent for Mrs. O'Connor and A. D. Peters & Co. Sean O'Faolain, 'The Cruelty and Beauty of Words', *Virginia Quarterly Review*, April 1928; reprinted by permission of the *Virginia Quarterly Review* and the Author; 'Almost Music', *Hound and Horn*, January-March 1929; reprinted by permission of A. P. Watt & Son and the Author; 'Correspondence: *Anna Livia Plurabelle*', *Irish Statesman*, January 1929; 'Letter to the Editor', *Irish Statesman*, March 1929; 'Letter to the Editor', *Criterion*, October 1930; reprinted by permission of the Author. E. Oldmeadow, 'Rot', *Tablet*, 14 January 1933; reprinted by permission of the Tablet Publishing

ACKNOWLEDGMENTS

Co. Ltd. Morton D. Zabel, 'The Lyrics of James Joyce', *Poetry*, 1930; reprinted by permission of the Editor and Otto W. Barnes. Thornton Wilder, 'James Joyce, 1882–1941', *Poetry*, 1940–1; reprinted by permission of the Editor and the Author. From *The Letters of Ezra Pound 1909–1941*, edited by D. D. Paige, copyright 1950, by Harcourt, Brace & World Inc. and reprinted with their permission; copyright 1950 by Faber & Faber Ltd., reprinted with permission. Ezra Pound, '*Dubliners* and Mr. James Joyce', *Egoist*, July 1914; 'Joyce', *The Future*, May 1918 by Ezra Pound; *Literary Essays*, all rights reserved, reprinted by permission of New Directions Publishing Corporation and Faber & Faber Ltd.; 'Past History', by Ezra Pound, *English Journal*, xxii, May 1931, reprinted by permission of New Directions Publishing Corporation, New York, agents for the Committee for Ezra Pound; 'James Joyce et Pécuchet', by Ezra Pound, translated by Fred Bornhauser, *Shenandoah*, iii, Autumn 1952; Ezra Pound, *Polite Essays*, all rights reserved, reprinted by permission of New Directions Publishing Corporation and Faber & Faber Ltd. Samuel Putnam, *Paris Was Our Mistress*, 1947; reprinted by permission of The Viking Press, Inc. Reprinted by permission of International Publishers Co. Inc.; copyright © 1935; Karl Radek, 'James Joyce or Socialist Realism?' in *Problems of Soviet Literature*. Herbert Read, 'The High Priest of Modern Literature', *Listener*, 20 August 1930; reprinted by permission of the Author. Herbert Read, 'James Joyce: Romantic or Classic', *Cambridge Review*, 13 June 1930; later appeared in *A Coat of Many Colors*; copyright 1945; reprinted by permission of Mr. Reuben Heffer and Routledge & Kegan Paul Ltd. Marcel Thiebaut, '*Ulysse* et James Joyce', 15 June 1929; Desmond MacCarthy, 'Le roman anglais d'après-guerre', May 1932; Georges Pelorson, '*Finnegans Wake* de James Joyce', September 1939; reprinted from the *Revue de Paris* by permission of the Secrétaire Général. Dorothy M. Richardson, 'Adventures for Readers', *Life and Letters Today*, July 1939; 'A Few Facts for You. . .', *Mercure de France*, August-September 1963; reprinted by permission of Rose I. Odle, Literary Executor of the late Dorothy M. Richardson. Y.O. (George Russell), review in the *Irish Statesman*, 23 July 1927, 29 December 1928; W. F. Trench, 'Correspondence: Dr. Yeats and Mr. Joyce', *Irish Statesman*, 30 August 1924; reprinted by permission of Mr. Diarmuid Russell. Paul Rosenfeld, 'James Joyce's Jabberwocky', *Saturday Review of Literature*, 1939; reprinted by permission of the Editor. William White, 'Irish Antitheses: Shaw and Joyce', *The Shavian*, February 1961; reprinted by permission of the Editor and the Author. Letter from George Bernard Shaw to Sylvia Beach, 11 June 1921; reprinted by permission of the Public Trustee and the Society of Authors. Extract from Edith Sitwell's *Aspects of Modern Poetry*, 1934; reprinted by permission of Gerald Duckworth & Co. Ltd. George Slocombe, 'The Week in Paris', *Daily Herald*, 17 March 1922; 'On the Left Bank', 14 July 1927; reprinted by permission of Odhams Press Ltd. Philippe Soupault, 'Autour de James Joyce', *Bravo*, September 1930; from *James Joyce Yearbook* (pp. 126–9), by permission of Maria Jolas, 1949; *Profils Perdus* 1963; reprinted by permission of the *Mercure de France* and the Author. Stephen

ACKNOWLEDGMENTS

Spender, 'James Joyce', *Listener*, 23 January 1941; reprinted by permission of A. D. Peters & Co. J. C. Squire, 'The Critic at Large', *Outlook*, 16 July 1921; reprinted by permission of Raglan Squire. James Stephens, 'The James Joyce I Knew', *Listener*, 24 October 1946; permission to reprint granted by the Society of Authors as the literary representative of the Estate of the late James Stephens. L. A. G. Strong, 'Unsigned review', *Spectator*, December 1932; 'The Novel: Assurances and Perplexities', *The Author*, Summer 1935; 'James Joyce's Dream World', *John O'London's Weekly*, May 1939; reprinted by permission of A. D. Peters & Co.; 'James Joyce and the New Fiction', *American Mercury*, August 1935, reprinted by permission of the *American Mercury*, Torrance, California. Signora Letizia Fonda Savio, permission to reprint a letter from Italo Svevo to Joyce, 8 February 1909. Italo Svevo (Ettore Schmitz), *James Joyce*; copyright 1950, New Directions Publishing Corporation; copyright 1967 by City Lights Books; reprinted by permission of City Lights Books. Permission has been granted by Times Newspapers Ltd. to reprint the following items from the *Times Literary Supplement*: unsigned review, 18 June 1914; Virginia Woolf, 'Modern Novels', 10 April 1919; A. Clutton-Brock, 'Wild Youth', 1 March 1917; A. Clutton-Brock, 'The Mind to Suffer', 25 July 1918; 'Interpretations of *Ulysses*', 23 January 1937; 'The Progress of Mr. Joyce', 6 May 1939; unsigned article, 14 October 1944; 'Mr. Joyce's Experiment', 20 December 1928; 'Mr. Joyce's Experiment', 17 July 1930; 'The Significance of James Joyce', 25 January 1941. William Troy, 'Notes on *Finnegans Wake*', *Partisan Review*, Summer 1939; © by *Partisan Review*, reprinted by permission of the *Partisan Review* and Rutgers University Press on behalf of the Estate of William E. Troy. Alec Waugh, 'The Neo-Georgians', *Fortnightly Review*, January 1924; reprinted by permission of the *Contemporary Review*. Letter from H. G. Wells, reprinted by permission of Collins-Knowlton-Wing, Inc., A. P. Watt & Son, and the Estate of H. G. Wells; copyright © 1957 by George Philip Wells and Frank Richard Wells. William White, 'G.B.S. on Joyce's *Exiles*', *Times Literary Supplement*, 4 December 1959; reprinted by permission of the Author. 'A Note on the Recent Work of James Joyce', from William Carlos Williams, *Selected Essays*; copyright 1931, 1954 by William Carlos Williams; reprinted by permission of New Directions Publishing Corporation. Letter by William Carlos Williams to Sylvia Beach, 24 June 1928. All rights reserved; reprinted by permission of New Directions Publishing Corporation, New York, agents for Mrs. William Carlos Williams. Stephen Winsten, 'G.B.S. on Joyce's *Exiles*', *Times Literary Supplement*, 18 December 1959; reprinted by permission of the Author. Reprinted with the permission of Charles Scribner's Sons from *The Letters of Thomas Wolfe*, pp. 321-2 and 585-6, edited by Elizabeth Nowell; copyright © 1956; Edward C. Aswell, Administrator C.T.A. of the Estate of Thomas Wolfe and by William Heinemann, Ltd. From *The Senate Speeches of W. B. Yeats*, edited by Donald R. Pearce; © copyright 1960; reprinted by permission of Indiana University Press and Faber & Faber Ltd. S. P. B. Mais, 'An Irish Revel and Some Flappers', *Daily Express*, 25 March 1922; reprinted by permission of the London Express

ACKNOWLEDGMENTS

News and Feature Services. Extract from Marcel Thiebaut, '*Ulysse* et James Joyce', *Revue de Paris*, June 1929; reprinted by permission of the Editor of the *Revue de Paris*, Mme Jacqueline Lefeu-Raphel, and the Société des Gens de Lettres. From *The Strange Necessity*, by Rebecca West; copyright 1928 by The Bookman Publishing Company Inc.; 1956 by Rebecca West; reprinted by permission of The Viking Press, Inc. From *The Letters of W. B. Yeats*, edited by Allan Wade; reprinted by permission of Rupert Hart-Davis. From Patrick Byrne 'Joyce's Dream Book Took Seventeen Years to Make', *Irish Digest*, lxxxi (July 1964); reprinted by permission of the *Sunday Independent*. Stefan Zweig, 'Anmerkung zum *Ulysses*', *Die Neue Rundschau*, xxxix (1928); reprinted in *Der goldene Schnitt* (1960), edited by Christoph Schwerin; reprinted by permission of the Atrium Press Limited. C. G. Jung, letter to Joyce (? August 1932), in *Letters*, Vol III, edited by R. Ellman, and in Ellman, *James Joyce*; reprinted by permission of Dr. Hans Karrer, for the heirs of C. G. Jung. From Frank Swinnerton, *The Georgian Literary Scene*; reprinted by permission of Hope Leresche & Steele.

Permission to reprint the following items by Eugène and Maria Jolas, and from *transition*, has been given by Mrs. Maria Jolas: Eugène Jolas, 'My Friend James Joyce', *Partisan Review*, March–April 1941, © 1941 by *Partisan Review*, reprinted by permission of the *Partisan Review*; 'The New Vocabulary', *transition*, February 1929; Harry Crosby, 'Observation Post', *transition*, June 1929; Michael Stuart, 'The Dubliner and His Dowdili', *transition*, November 1929; 'A Fellow Dubliner,' 'The Veritable James Joyce According to Stuart Gilbert and Oliver St. John Gogarty', *transition*, March 1932; Eugene Jolas, 'Homage to James Joyce', *transition*, March 1932; 'Marginalia to James Joyce's "Work in Progress",' *transition*, February 1933; 'Homage to the Mythmaker', *transition*, May 1939.

Index

The works of James Joyce (*in chronological order*)

344, 345, 348, 357, 422, 423,
463, 464, 472, 485, 517, 554,
562, 580-1, 583, 591-2, 593-5,
621, 638, 643, 652, 657, 725,
745
its influence on other writers,
580, 749
praised by Dr Jung, 767
Jewishness of Bloom, 262, 288,
300, 311, 312, 345, 361-3
passim, 370, 432, 440, 527, 575,
655
Joyce's own plan for the book, 19,
22
Jungian interpretation, 583-5
reflection of life, *Ulysses* as a,
196-7, 298, 356, 463, 472-3,
480, 603, 742
Russian reaction, 591, 643-5, 654-8
stream of consciousness, 466-7,
527, 552, 558, 562, 575, 592,
650, 702, 741, 754, 755, 763
unfavourable reactions, 19, 20, 22,
191, 192-4, 206-11, 219-22,
242-4, 271-2, 274-5, 280-1,
313, 433-4, 435, 462-5, 477,
481, 557-9, 584-5, 591, 596-7,
626-9
Pomes Penyeach (1927), 4, 6, 9, 26,
34, 45, 46-52 *passim*, 56, 248,
286, 347-53, 420, 430, 434,
519, 522, 647, 650, 748
American reaction, 353
emotional content, 48
favourable reception, 347, 350
lyrical element, 47, 48, 351, 650
musical content, 649, 651
relation to other works of Joyce,
651, 652
sentimental element, 348, 431, 748
tastelessness of poems, 51, 430-1
individual poems
'Alliteration', 47
'Alone', 47, 49, 50, 349, 430
'Bahnhofstrasse', 47, 353
'Flood', 52
'Flower given to my Daughter,
A', 49, 50, 650

'Memory of the Players, A', 48,
349, 651
'Night piece', 52, 647, 650
'On the Beach at Fontana', 47,
349, 650
'O World, O Life, O Time',
351
'Prayer, A', 48, 348, 647
'She weeps over Rahoon', 47,
347, 348, 349, 351, 352
'Simples', 48, 649
'Tilly', 34, 45, 352, 650
'Tutto a sciolto', 47
'Watching the Needleboats', 47,
351
Work in Progress, 2, 6, 11, 12, 23, 24,
26-8 *passim*, 45, 48, 49, 51,
249, 251, 255, 286, 346, 347,
350, 373-419, 422, 427-9
passim, 452-8, 474, 479, 487-
514, 516-18 *passim*, 531-41,
542, 545-7 *passim*, 550, 564-9,
570-3 *passim*, 581, 591, 600,
601, 603-10, 621, 622, 630-1,
632, 636-7, 638, 651, 652, 655,
657, 658-60, 674, 678-91, 731
adverse comment, 375-6, 382,
515-16, 453, 458-9, 493-5,
503-4, 511-13
Agenbite of Inwit, 467, 504, 635,
746
American criticism, 373-5
boredom of, 455
comparison with T. S. Eliot, 513-
14
Ulysses, 494, 496, 507, 538, 539,
601
dream element, 498, 500, 536, 539,
564, 568, 606, 637, 651
favourable criticism, 385, 490-2,
508-11, 513-14, 545-7, 582,
632
French reaction, 385, 409, 414-16
French translation, 324, 414-15
Freudian and Jungian elements,
535-6
German reaction, 495-9
Irish reaction, 385, 537

Aspects of James Joyce and his work

formlessness in the author's work,
92, 204, 211, 220, 366, 575, 634,
635, 648, 691
frankness of the author, 104, 198,
200, 223, 224, 257, 303, 483,
485, 500, 527, 560, 623
French period in author's life, 15, 18,
52, 166, 195, 235, 352, 430, 492,
525, 767
French, relations with, 18, 20, 21, 27,
69
genius of the author, 8, 10, 34, 35,
62, 64, 75, 92, 97, 104, 176, 197,
199, 214, 225, 276, 287-8, 295,
307, 322, 324, 336, 424, 428,
429, 432, 446, 454, 455, 468,
523, 534, 535, 563, 578, 586, 754
history, attitude towards, 28, 384,
411, 429, 496-7, 501, 516, 539,
551, 557, 604, 659, 664, 706,
733, 737, 738
humour and wit in Joyce's work, 20,
59, 61, 63, 65, 179, 188, 210,
221, 237, 240, 250, 273, 316,
328, 329, 332-3, 340, 342, 363,
417, 455, 472, 490, 498, 500,
514, 517, 539, 541, 544, 550,
564, 573, 579, 607, 689, 696,
732
impressionism, 175
Index Expurgatorius, 201
influence on other writers, 1, 16,
186, 188, 196, 238, 245, 269,
296, 397, 426, 473, 493, 494,
571, 574, 597-601, 622-3, 638,
644, 653, 656, 714, 747, 754
influence on the public, 17, 24,
426, 520-2, 524, 721
Ireland and the Irish, attitude towards
and insight into, 7, 11, 36, 38,
59-61 *passim*, 64, 65, 67, 94,
117, 175, 181, 253, 255, 298,
299, 314, 320, 355, 459, 517,
561
Irish nationalism, author's
antagonism towards, 644
jazz prose, Joyce's as an example of,
183

languages, Joyce's knowledge of
foreign, 384, 407, 445, 456-7,
489, 546, 609, 660, 674, 675,
687, 692, 711, 714, 751, 752
linguistic experimentation, puns
puzzles, etc., 6, 24, 27, 28, 51,
87, 180, 197, 199, 200, 203, 204,
222-3, 250, 256, 294, 298, 333,
358, 367, 368-9, 371, 375, 381,
402, 403, 406-7, 409, 411, 414-
15, 425, 428, 434, 442, 454, 457,
489, 490, 492-3, 494, 495, 497-9,
500, 503-4, 507, 509, 514, 520,
522, 527, 529, 534-7, 540, 546,
550, 555, 564, 567, 569, 573,
576, 587-9, 601, 605-8, 610,
627, 638, 640, 641, 655, 657,
659, 663, 674, 692, 729, 756
with children's talk, 604
meticulousness of the work, 424-5,
619, 638
morality of the author, 19, 196, 198,
206, 513
musical elements, 506, 508, 510, 517,
521, 540, 546, 564, 587-9, 590,
652, 665, 666, 669, 670, 705,
719, 729, 732
mythological element, 497, 536,
542, 543, 551, 603, 604, 632,
654, 655, 657, 659, 664, 670,
676, 681, 711, 741, 752
Naturaliste, Joyce as a, 187, 255, 256,
289, 302, 305, 360, 362-3, 592,
623
neologisms, 384, 394, 492, 493, 663
novel, Joyce's contribution to,
620-1, 636-9, 744, 753
novel of the mind, 287-8
obscenity and pornography, 6, 7, 11,
22, 63, 68-9, 86, 167, 170, 179,
189, 191, 192, 194, 201, 213,
214, 216, 218, 221, 234, 243,
245-7 *passim*, 261-2, 272-8, 281,
282, 292, 295, 296, 306, 307,
310, 313, 321, 328, 330, 360-1,
422, 423, 424, 431, 449, 453,
472, 483, 493, 533, 548, 575,
576, 635

Characters, etc., from the works mentioned in the text

Note: Stephen Dedalus and Leopold Bloom are mentioned on approximately 150 pages each; references to them, and to the City of Dublin, to which the same applies, have therefore been omitted.

Authors of works quoted in the text and authors with whom Joyce's work has been likened or compared

Miscellaneous references in the text

Newspapers and periodicals mentioned and quoted in the text

Articles and other works quoted from or mentioned in the text

For Product Safety Concerns and Information please contact our EU
representative GPSR@taylorandfrancis.com
Taylor & Francis Verlag GmbH, Kaufingerstraße 24, 80331 München, Germany

www.ingramcontent.com/pod-product-compliance
Lightning Source LLC
Chambersburg PA
CBHW070930100726
47908CB00001B/164

*9 7 8 0 4 1 5 4 8 7 5 1 1 *